THUNDER MOON
RISING

NOVELS IN THE DEADLANDS SERIES

Deadlands: Ghostwalkers

Deadlands: Thunder Moon Rising

DEADLANDS

THUNDER
MOON RISING

JEFFREY J. MARIOTTE

TOR

A Tom Doherty Associates Book
New York

DEADLANDS: THUNDER MOON RISING

Copyright © 2016 by Pinnacle Entertainment Group, LLC

Deadlands created by Shane Lacy Hensley

Cover art by Aaron J. Riley

Interior art by Steve Ellis

A Tor Book
Published by Tom Doherty Associates, LLC
175 Fifth Avenue
New York, NY 10010

www.tor-forge.com

The Library of Congress Cataloging-in-Publication Data is available upon request.

ISBN 978-0-7653-7528-5 (trade paperback)
ISBN 978-1-4668-4637-1 (e-book)

Our books may be purchased in bulk for promotional, educational, or business use. Please contact your local bookseller or the Macmillan Corporate and Premium Sales Department at 1-800-221-7945, extension 5442, or by e-mail at Macmillan SpecialMarkets@macmillan.com.

First Edition: September 2016

Printed in the United States of America

0 9 8 7 6 5 4 3 2 1

This book is dedicated, with the greatest appreciation and respect, to Gordon D. Shirreffs, who never knew the numerous ways his novel *Mystery of the Haunted Mine* affected my life, and to Sidney Offit, who does have a sense of *The Adventures of Homer Fink*'s impact on me. Anybody who says a single book can't change one's life doesn't know how to read a book.

Also, to Marcy, with love.

Acknowledgments

Inspiration is a funny thing, often coming around only when you've stopped looking for it. And anything as complex as a novel is born of dozens of inspirations, large and small. Some inform the whole work, others just a piece here, a character there.

Inspirations for this work include—but are by no means limited to—songs recorded and/or composed by Jimi Hendrix and Derek and the Dominos, Brian Wilson and The Beach Boys, The Rolling Stones, and Mark Lindsay. The work of the veterans' service organizations The Mission Continues and Team Rubicon played a vital role, too. Also inspiring and important were the works of dear writer friends James Lee Burke and Marsheila Rockwell, who also assisted with research.

Various reference books and museums were consulted for the historical aspects, including the Fort Huachuca Historical Museum at Fort Huachuca, Arizona, and the Tucson Rodeo Parade Museum and the Museum of the Horse Soldier in Tucson, Arizona. Any mistakes or reinterpretations of history (particularly crucial in this work, since Deadlands is not history as we know it but as it might have been) are my own.

The Deadlands publishing program would not

exist without Shane Hensley, Matt Cutter, and the gang at Pinnacle Entertainment; C. Edward Sellner, Charlie Hall, and the Visionary Comics crew; Tom Doherty, Greg Cox, Stacy Hill, Diana Pho, Patty Garcia, and the amazing team at Tor; Jim Frenkel; and Howard Morhaim; and they all have my deepest appreciation. Thanks are also due to pals Jonathan Maberry and Seanan McGuire for joining me in this incredibly rich sandbox to play with the toys.

THUNDER MOON
RISING

It is, alas, chiefly the evil emotions that are able to leave their photographs on surrounding scenes and objects and whoever heard of a place haunted by a noble deed, or of beautiful and lovely ghosts revisiting the glimpses of the moon?

—ALGERNON BLACKWOOD

PART ONE
Cutting Sign

Chapter One

Tucker Bringloe remembered his mother as a grim-faced woman with thin lips. Small black eyes floated on her graceless visage like bloated deer ticks that had landed there accidentally. She almost never smiled, in his memory, though there had been one occasion, when she'd been passing a kidney stone, that he had mistaken a spasm of pain for an expression of delight. His father said that when she was a young girl, she had shot her older brother to death with their father's rifle, in the false belief that he was a savage Indian. Tuck knew his father doubted her version of that story, since, as he'd said, "They lived in downtown Rensselaer, New York, at the time. Probably weren't no savages within twenty mile, and not any reason for one to bother her if they was."

A couple of years after that, Tuck's father had come home drunk from a barn dance, and had made suggestions to his wife that she had forcefully declined. When Tuck woke the next morning, she was sitting on their bed, using a needle and heavy black thread to try to stitch up a gaping hole in the man's throat. His body was limp and gray, and bed, father, and mother were all soaked in blood. One of his mother's carving knives was on the floor beside her feet.

"He was ornery," she explained. "Ill-mannered and grabby. But never you mind, he'll be fixed up directly." And so saying, she had met his gaze with those black buttons of hers, and her face had split into what he guessed had to be the first smile it had ever tried on.

It was ghastly, and he never forgot it.

But that wasn't what drove him to drink. Instead, it was a memory that mostly came back to him when he had been drinking and drove him to drink still more.

He had reached that stage. He slouched in front of the polished wooden bar in a saloon called Soto's, fingering his empty glass. Jack O'Beirne, the barkeep, glanced his way, and Tuck tapped the rim.

"Got to see some coin," Jack said.

Tuck swore and dug into the pockets of his tattered Union army coat. In the right one he found lint and some kind of sandy grit and an old piece of blue glass polished by weather that he had found once and thought pretty enough to keep. One day there would be a child, or a woman, someone he'd want to give something to.

He held out empty hands and caught a glimpse of himself in the mirror behind the bar: dark hair matted and askew, eyes so bloodshot he could see red from here. Pathetic. He looked away. "One for the road?"

Jack's thick black brush of a mustache twitched. "Got a dime?"

"No."

"Half-dime gets you a beer."

Tuck's hands clenched into fists. "I don't have it!"

"You're done, mister." The barkeep jerked his head toward the door.

His dismissive tone riled Tuck, but there was nothing to be done. Maybe he'd be able to scrounge up a coin or two somewhere. Sometimes one fell onto the floor around the poker tables, or he could snatch one from the piano player's cup when no one was looking.

Tuck swiveled away from the bar, stumbled, and caught his balance by grabbing the back of a chair. A cowhand was sitting there with a big redhead on his lap, and when Tuck's hand fell on the chair, the man shot him an angry scowl. The redhead was whispering something in his ear and grinding on him, though, and he didn't say anything.

For an instant, Tuck wondered if he should start something. The man was wearing a pistol. If he would draw it and plant a couple of slugs in Tuck, it would free him of his mother and the war and all the other things that haunted his every hour, asleep or not, except when drink stilled those ghosts for a few hours.

The man turned his attention back to the whore on his lap. Tuck wasn't even worth five seconds of his time. The worst part was, he couldn't argue with the cowboy's assessment. To shoot him would be to waste a bullet, because everything inside him that had ever been any good had died long ago. He would figure it out and fall down, one of these days, and that would be best for everyone.

He took a last look at the saloon. Above the piano was a bad painting of a nude woman who would have needed her backbone removed to pose the way she was. Senora Soto, who owned the place, sat at her usual spot in the corner, a drink in front of her and a revolver next to it, in case anybody tried anything funny with one of her girls. Two tables were crowded with poker players, and others with men there for the drink or the women or both. Some men sat alone or in quiet pairs, brooding and glum, but at most tables, people laughed and carried on as if they were having a good time. Maybe it was a good time lubricated by alcohol and maybe not, but everybody looked happier than he did.

Probably this wasn't the right place for him, after all.

Probably no place was right for him.

He breathed in the sweat and smoke and spilled beer and damp clothes, and walked outside into a downpour.

The drinks and now the rain conspired to remind him that his bladder needed emptying. He followed the boardwalk to the end of the block and stepped off into the muddy road. He had been in Carmichael for three weeks now, and Maiden Lane had been soup the entire time. He'd heard that the Arizona Territory was hot and dry, but was coming to think there must be two Arizonas. This one was hot, but the rains came almost every afternoon, drenching the town. By the time he had staggered back to the alley behind the saloon, he was soaked to the skin.

Between the clouds and the rain and the unpainted staircase to the floor above the saloon where Senora Soto's girls had their cribs, no moonlight leaked through. Tuck could have pissed in the street, and maybe found himself a warm, dry bed in one of the marshal's cells. But there were women in town. Kids, too, though not many. And as low as he had sunk (and that was very low indeed; Tucker Bringloe could have slid under a rattlesnake's belly without scraping), he hadn't lost every last ounce of the part of himself that had once been a Union officer. A warm bed was one thing, but was it worth the degradation of his last shreds of decency?

He put out one hand and gripped the back of a stair tread, to stay more or less upright while he relieved himself. When he was nearly done, a peal of thunder echoed off the walls and lightning lit the world with the sudden brightness of a thousand lanterns all uncovered at once, then closed again before the reality of it had set in. Tuck lost his grip on the stair, but caught it again before he fell into the mud that sucked at his boots.

As he put himself away and righted himself, he heard a footfall on the staircase above, and he realized that at the moment the thunder clapped and the lightning released its blinding glare, someone must have come out the door and started down. Tuck had faced Confederate soldiers with bayonets, had led his men into cannon fire, had taken a minié ball in his left arm and watched an untrained medic dig it out with a rusty blade. And he had seen much, much worse, sights he didn't like to admit were taken in by his eyes rather than constructs of the part of his mind that spawned nightmares.

But at this moment, swaying, barely able to remain upright, absolute terror gripped him. The man descended at a steady pace, neither fast nor slow. With every soft rasp of those boots against the stairs, an icy grip tightened around Tuck's heart. When the man's feet were even with his head, an odor like nothing Tuck had ever experienced enveloped him, soaking through his clothing like the rain. He worried, for a moment, that it was the last thing he would ever smell; that even if he lived through the next two minutes, the stink would never release him.

Then the man was off the stairs. He swung around and walked past Tuck, his steps as easy as if the alley floor had been bone-dry. Tuck tried to look away, but the man's eyes trapped his gaze; they seemed to glow with their own yellow light. Then lightning flashed again, brighter than before. In that instant, Tuck had a clear view of the man's face. He had sharp-edged features, a prominent nose, a heavy brow, a solid jaw. A wide-brimmed hat kept the rain from his face, though Tuck had the idea that rain might stay away from him anyway, just on general principle.

And even in the light, those eyes were hot and yellow as flame.

Tuck grabbed the stair again. His legs had started to tremble, his knees nearly giving way. The man strode quickly to the end of the building. When Tuck's legs felt sturdy enough to carry him, he followed. Reaching the corner, he saw the man again, mounted on a black mare with a white blaze on her snout and eyes almost as yellow as her rider's. Only this time—and Tuck was happy to blame it on the darkness and shadows—the rider's face had changed, and his hands, too. He had appeared human, on the stairs. But now his features seemed to have disappeared, so that his face was an indistinguishable dark mass, and his skin was black. Not dark brown, like the free men he had known, and those who had not yet been free who he'd fought to liberate in the war, before the Confederacy had taken that step and the war had turned on other issues, but black like ink, like jet, like the darkest hour of a moonless night. The man tore past Tuck without sparing him another glance. Lightning flared once more, revealing horse and rider galloping past the Methodist church, which perched just outside of town, as if afraid of contamination had it dared venture nearer. Then the light was gone, and so was the man.

When he was gone, Tuck felt the rain pummeling him again,

as if it had paused while the man was in sight but now returned with redoubled force. Wind-driven drops pelted him, stinging. He hurried for the protection of the overhang above the saloon's doorway, where the upstairs balconies faced onto the street, where Senora Soto's girls sometimes came out to call to the town's menfolk. He would not be welcome inside, but at least he could shelter under the overhang for a few minutes. Maybe the rain would end as suddenly as it had begun.

He had barely made it out of the weather when he heard screams from upstairs.

Chapter Two

Instinct took over and he pushed through the door. The odor made him crave a drink, but he had no more money than before, and now he was tracking mud and dripping rainwater on the plank floor. People were moving toward the staircase— Senora Soto, for one, clutching her revolver, her dark face tight with worry. At the top of the stairs, one of her crib girls stood with both hands on the banister, wearing only ruffled bloomers. Tears glistened on her cheeks and her mouth hung open. Screams issued from behind her.

The scene was chaos, barely controlled. Tuck couldn't make out any words in the overall din, until someone upstairs shouted, "Somebody cut Daisie!"

At that, there came a moment's stillness in the saloon, an unnatural silence. It just lasted for a second, then broke all at once. Men rushed the stairs, some drawing guns. Tuck started checking the tables and floors for stray coins, but then a terrible thought struck him and he wove through the crowd, shoving some men aside in his hurry to reach the stairs. The storm, the strange man on the stairs, and the palpable fear in the air had all conspired to sober him. He forced his way through the clot at the top of the stairs, past the half-naked woman. Others filled the upstairs hallway, and Tuck wove through them.

Senora Soto stared into one of the cribs. The revolver looked enormous in her small fist.

"Who did this?" Senora Soto demanded. "Who?"

"I don't know," one of the women said. "I never saw him."

Senora Soto asked the question again, and each woman responded in kind. Nobody knew, nobody saw a thing.

"I want that calico dress of hers," one said. "I always thought it'd fit me better than it did her."

"Oh, you hush up," another replied.

"Well, it would."

Tuck couldn't hold himself back any longer. He feared what he might see, but was more afraid, for reasons he could not elaborate and didn't care to try, of not seeing it. Senora Soto had abandoned her place at the door, so Tuck peered inside.

A woman lay on her back, her head and shoulders and arms hanging off the bed, on the side facing the doorway. Blood covered her neck and face, dripping from her chin and forehead onto a braided rug on the floor. Pink and gray and brown blobs—organs, Tuck guessed—dangled from her middle.

Her sternum had been slashed open, almost to her throat.

The odors of blood and bodily fluids and urine assaulted his nose, and Tuck's stomach heaved. He gripped both sides of the jamb to steady himself. He had seen that one, Daisie, in the saloon. She had always been pleasant enough, not dismissing him because of his drunkenness, his filth, his poverty. She had been decent, and now she was dead.

A chill caught him and he shuddered. He was soaked to the bone, so that was no surprise, but this came from a deeper place than that, as if freezing him from the inside out. Underneath the other smells in the room he noticed a stink, sour and rotten, that he had encountered before. Just minutes earlier, by the stairs.

"I know who did this," he said. No one heard. One man nearly knocked him down, angling for a better view of the poor woman's corpse.

"Ohh," the man said. "If that don't beat . . ."

He didn't finish his sentence, or Tuck didn't hear the end of it. He released the doorjamb and said it again, louder. "I know who did this!"

Finally, his words broke through the din. Senora Soto halted her interrogations and faced him.

"Who?"

"I don't know who he was," Tuck said. He could tell he was slurring his words, but not as much as he might have ten minutes earlier. "I saw a man go down the back stairs, couple minutes ago. Something about him that didn't set right with me."

"Where is he, then?"

"He took off on a big black horse. White streak on the muzzle."

"How do we know *he* ain't done it?" one of the men asked. "He's wet. He coulda gone out and downstairs and come back around, just to throw us off."

"Anybody know him?" another one asked. Tuck realized it was the cowhand from downstairs, the one who'd had a redhead on his lap. "Can anyone speak for this drunkard?"

"I seen him around," someone said.

"How would he get the money to go with Daisie?" one of the women put in. "He has to beg for drinks."

"Look at him," another said. "Daisie would never have gone upstairs with such as him. She has standards."

"I saw this one in the saloon earlier," Senora Soto said. "After Daisie went upstairs. He is not the one."

"That's what I've been saying. The guy rode south, out of town."

"We should get a posse together," the big cowboy said.

Murmurs of agreement turned into shouts as men spurred one another into enthusiasm. Tuck thought they sounded more like a lynch mob than a posse, but that was none of his concern.

"All I'm saying is you better hightail it if you mean to catch him," Tuck said. "He was riding fast, and in that storm he'll be hard to track."

"Clear the way," a new voice boomed from the staircase. "Something's happened to Daisie?" Carmichael's marshal came into the hallway. People parted before him, and he followed the open path to Daisie's door. He went inside. Tuck heard him choke, and when he emerged again he had gone pale.

"I've never..." he began. He wiped his face with his hands. He was a tall man, lean and broad-shouldered, and his hands were huge. "How could anyone..."

"We were thinkin' on puttin' together a posse, Hank," the cowboy said. "This rummy here seen the killer."

"You did?" the marshal asked Tuck.

"I think. I saw somebody, anyway. He went down the back stairs while I was in the alley. Got on a black horse and headed south."

"Storm's not showin' any sign of breakin'," the marshal said. "Be nigh impossible to track someone in that."

"You cannot let him get away with such a thing," another man said. Tuck had seen him before, though it took a moment to remember where. The man was stout but sturdy, bespectacled, with thinning hair and a ruddy complexion, as if he had just run several miles. His vest was open and his shirt half-unbuttoned, so Tuck figured any exercise he'd enjoyed was of a more indoors nature. After studying him, Tuck pictured him in a shopkeeper's apron and recalled that he ran a grocery a few doors down from the saloon.

"Look, Daisie was a nice girl," the marshal said. "But we got plenty of whores in this town. Might be these others wouldn't mind one less."

"Marshal Turville!" one of the girls snapped.

Senora Soto walked up close and laid a hand gently on his arm. She barely came up to mid-chest on the marshal, but she spoke with quiet authority. "Hank," she said. "My ladies are human beings, same as anyone else. I seem to recall that you enjoyed Daisie's company more than a few times, and I never charged you a cent. Now, I can't let someone come in and murder her—that would be very bad for business. And I liked Daisie. My heart is breaking."

"I understand all that, Senora Soto. But—"

"*Tch!* I am not finished, Hank. I would like you to organize a posse, or do whatever it is that you have to do. I would like you to find the man who killed Daisie, and make him pay for what he did. If you refuse ... well, I'm sure your wife would like to know about some of the more *special* activities you enjoy here, that she never does for you. Don't you think she would?"

Those big hands went to the marshal's face again, and this time Tuck wasn't certain he would ever lower them. "All right, Senora," he said after a long while. "Gentlemen, let's us form up a posse. Who's in?"

Some of the men, including the beefy cowboy and the grocer, stepped forward. Others made their way uneasily toward the stairs, happy to voice support for a posse when it didn't exist, but not wanting to put themselves on the line when it did.

Tuck hadn't spoken up in favor of it in the first place, except to point out that if they were planning to do it, they ought to be quick about it. He had sold his horse and the last of his guns long ago, and used the money for drink. He had seen for himself what guns could do, and he hadn't regretted losing those, though he occasionally missed the mare. He didn't even own a hat to keep the rain from his face. He had his old army coat, so ragged it barely cut the wind, and the clothes he wore underneath. He didn't want to go chasing after that strange man with the yellow eyes and the cloying stink. He wanted a glass of whiskey or whatever else he could get his hands on, and then another, and then some more. Now he had two more sights to forget—that man, and the sight of Daisie with her torso cut open and her innards hanging out.

He tried to join those who were taking themselves out of the running, but the marshal's voice barked out. "You! Rummy! Sounds like you're the only one who's seen him. You're comin' with us."

There was no question about to whom Turville was talking. Tuck wanted to slip downstairs with the other men, maybe see if there had been a glass or two abandoned on a tabletop with a little something still in it.

But he heard urgency in Turville's voice—urgency planted

there by Senora Soto's blackmail, but present just the same. He let the others flow around him like river water around a boulder. "Marshal," he said, "I don't have a gun or a horse or a hat. I might have been good at that sort of thing once, but now about the only skills I have left are cadging drinks and sleeping outdoors."

"You saw the man and his horse."

"I can tell you what he looked like." Even as the words spilled from his mouth, Tuck realized that was a lie. He would never forget the glimpse he'd had, but he could barely convince himself that he had seen it the way he remembered, and he could never accurately describe the man. Particularly since his appearance had seemed to change in the space of a minute.

"This man butchered that girl," Turville said. "I don't want to hang the wrong feller. This has got to be done right, pard'. That means you're joinin' us. I'll loan you a horse and some irons. You refuse, I'll string you up as an accomplice."

He was trapped. Anyway, he had abandoned his post before; how hard would it be to steal away from a posse? "Reckon I'm going, then," Tuck said.

Someone grabbed his arm, surprising him. It was one of Senora Soto's girls, a beauty with sparkling green eyes a man could sink right into. The color of her hair made Tuck think of sunshine through flowing honey. "Thank you for helping," she said. "Daisie was my best friend here. I know you have to be on your way, but if you get the man, when you get back, I'll buy you a hat. Does that sound fair?"

"More than, ma'am," Tuck said.

"I'm Missy Haynes," she said with a friendly smile. "You just ask for me downstairs."

"Tucker Bringloe."

"Well, Mr. Bringloe. Good luck on your hunt."

He appreciated the offer of the hat, but he thought he appreciated the wish for luck more.

He had a feeling he would need plenty of that.

Chapter Three

Y ou hear something, Pinky?"

Solomon Pincus hated that name, which all the hands called him by. But in the litany of things he hated on this particular night, that one ranked fairly low. It was late July, but he was freezing. Hail was still melting outside the small circle of the fire's warmth. The canvas lean-to had been ripped when hailstones had punched through it, and he felt like he'd been beaten with sticks. No part of him was dry, or likely would be any time soon. He could have gone to college like his brother, but the cowboy life had promised adventure and the freedom to be his own man, and until recently the reality of it had been everything he'd hoped for.

"Maybe," he said. "Hush a minute."

Picking out one particular sound from the midst of a herd of cattle was always a challenge. It was worse tonight. The rain had stopped, for the moment, but thunder still rattled in the Huachuca Mountains—which appropriately enough meant "Thunder Mountains" in Apache, Sol had been told—and the wind would not let up for an instant. But he had thought, right before Tom Hopkin spoke, that maybe he'd heard a high-pitched cry.

Then he heard it again, distinctly: a pained squeal that pierced the darkness. "Let's ride," Sol said.

They had set up camp on a rocky rise, out of the path of any flash floods. Their horses were picketed halfway down the slope, in the shelter of a couple of large pines. He and Hopkin had made torches from green branches, bark, and pine sap, and set them aside in case they needed them. They had one oil lantern between them. Sol grabbed the lantern, while Hopkin held one of the torches in the guttering fire until it flared to life.

The horses shied away from the flame, but the men mounted up and rode into the grass-floored valley. There they split up, guiding their mounts uneasily through already skittish stock, searching for the source of the cries while trying not to spook the big animals more than they already were. Cattle were ordinarily anxious in the dark, and with one of their own in obvious distress they were more so than usual, shifting about and lowing nervously. The smell of fresh excrement hung in the air, as fear tended to loosen their bowels.

Before Sol located the injured animal, it went silent. Cattle nearby pressed away from it, making him feel like he was urging his horse upstream, except instead of water this river was made of hide, horns, and hooves, and could easily gouge a man or knock him off his mount and trample him to death. Sol kept the horse under control, though it whickered with evident uncertainty, and he soon found what he was looking for.

The animal had been a big bull called Ol' Jim, one of Mr. Tibbetts's favorites. Now it was a ruined mass of torn hide and organs spilling into the blood-soaked mud. A few ribbons of flesh barely joined its head to the rest of it. Sol raised his head to the heavens, cupped a hand beside his mouth, and shouted out, "Tom!"

He waited several seconds and did it again. "Tom!"

With the wind and the thunder and the racket of the herd, he couldn't tell if Hopkin was within earshot. Hopkin would hear a gun, though. Tibbetts had a pair of hands on another range, not too far away, and they might hear that, too. Sol tugged his from its leather and fired twice into the air. A minute later came Hopkin's answering shot, then Sol saw a sputtering torch headed in his direction. He raised the lantern and waved it back and forth to give Hopkin a target.

"Tibbetts cain't hardly afford no more of this," Hopkin said when he had seen the dead bull. He held the torch high, its light falling on the remains. "Tibbetts cain't afford *us*. Herd split up into chunks, two men with each one? He's barely scrapin' by as is."

"He's a good man. He's straight with us."

"I didn't say he weren't," Hopkin countered. "Just he cain't afford to keep payin' us."

Sol ached for the rancher. Tibbetts had kept him on the payroll through lean times. Now he was losing cattle—seven, so far, mutilated like this one, sliced up and worthless, and no hint as to who had done it or why. "I'd work for him for nothing if I had to."

"I'm gonna go see Mr. Montclair," Hopkin said. "He always pays his hands, and better than Tibbetts does. I'll go tomorrow. You want to come with me?"

"No!" Sol snapped. "I just said I'd stay with Mr. Tibbetts."

"Ain't much to stay for, you ask me."

"I didn't."

"Let's get out from under these beeves," Hopkin said. "It starts rainin' again, I don't want to be down here with 'em."

Sol glanced at the pile of wasted animal on the ground, and his stomach gave a lurch. He felt the tension of the herd running through him, like he was a string on a fiddle and someone was plucking it. "Yeah," he said. "Let's go."

On the way back, Sol noticed that the tempo of the cattle's motion had picked up. They walked faster, breathed heavier, and when they lowed the sounds were higher pitched and more urgent. "I got a bad feeling about this, Tom," he said.

"Same here," Hopkin replied. "These critters is like to get boogered easy. Let's get a move on."

"No," Sol said, fighting to keep his tone even. It wouldn't do to lose control now.

"Hell with that!" Hopkin said. He jabbed his boot heels into his horse's ribs and shouted, "Giddyap, you son of a bitch!"

The horse bolted. As it did, it swiped against the side of a cow. Hopkin cried out in pain, and the cow gave a terrified bleat and lurched to its left, running into the nearest animal on that side.

With that, chaos descended.

One animal slammed into another, that one into yet more, and panic gripped the herd. Sol was in a dangerous spot. His horse was weaving and prancing, trying to stay clear of the cattle. Sol was trying to head it out of the herd's midst, to save his own skin, but he also understood the financial risk of a full-blown stampede. The cattle would take off at a sprint, running until they exhausted themselves. In the dark, in this high desert valley, some would be injured, breaking legs or worse, and have to be put down. Mr. Tibbetts's already precarious situation would get even worse.

Sol couldn't see Hopkin anywhere. The torch was out, probably dropped and extinguished in the mud. He might have reached safety, or he might be down somewhere in that churning sea of livestock. Quelling a stampede alone, in the dark of night, was no easy task, but Sol had to try. He knew what to do, but before he could do it he had to get out of the middle of the herd.

The earth rumbled and shook under the weight and motion of the herd. The air was thick with sound, and if the ground hadn't been soaked, the dust would have been choking. Sol's horse was almost panicked from the noise and the constant collisions with cattle, but she kept her head and allowed Sol to coax her, little by little, to the far right edge of the hurtling mass.

Once he had made it out of the river of beef, he breathed a little easier. He didn't allow himself to celebrate, though. Hopkin was still missing, there was a dead, carved-up bull behind him, and that herd was going to do itself serious damage if he didn't take action.

A little moonlight would have helped. His eyes had adjusted to the darkness as well as they could when he was still carrying around a lantern. He stopped the horse, extinguished the flame, then dashed the thing against the ground. That helped a little, but not a lot.

He couldn't see enough of the landscape ahead to form a decent plan. He was plenty familiar with the grassy valley, but there were dips and outcroppings of rock, big mesquites he didn't want to run into headlong, and other obstacles.

He would just have to hope for the best.

He gigged his horse and she took off at a gallop. They outpaced the cattle, the horse racing with utter disregard for the night and the dangers hidden in the moonless dark. Sol figured either he'd succeed or he'd die in the trying, and either outcome was equally acceptable at this point. When he reached the front of the racing pack, he rode as close alongside them as he dared, drew his pistol, and fired a shot into the ground. At the same time, he screamed with everything he had, meaningless sounds meant to cut through the hammering of hooves and the terrified bleats of the herd.

He fired twice more, holding the gun as close as he could to the leaders of the herd. He had one more bullet in the gun, then he'd have to reload—tricky at a full gallop, even if there weren't the risk of falling off his mount and into the stampeding cattle. He thought he heard gunshots from behind him, but over his own noise and the pounding of his heart in his ears and the racket of the stampede, he couldn't be sure.

His effort seemed to be working. The noise and Sol's proximity were forcing the leaders to curve around to their left. He stayed with them, edging his horse ever nearer. The cattle turned more. Sol kept at it, and the cattle kept turning, until finally the leaders were dashing headlong into their own followers.

At that point, faced with the wall of cowhide they had been leading, they gave up. The cattle coming up behind them had no choice but to slow, and with their momentum broken, although there were collisions and complaints, the herd settled into a restless stillness.

Sol halted his horse, reloaded his Colt, and headed back to look for Hopkin. He hollered out the hand's name, his voice seeming loud in the aftermath of the stampede.

Hearing no answer, Sol rode his back trail, peering through the night. Finally, he spotted Hopkin's horse, standing near a mesquite bush. He dismounted, looped a rein around one of the thorny branches, and did the same with Hopkin's horse. "Tom? You here, Tom?"

The horse whickered softly. Sol walked around it. The cattle had churned up the muddy earth as thoroughly as a plow, and his boots sank in with every step. A horrid stink reached his nose, reminding him that the cattle had raced across this ground in a panic. But this smell was worse than that. And he remembered smelling it before, near the dead bull. "Tom!" he called, suddenly more anxious.

Then he saw a dark mound in the mud. Hopkin. He rushed to the man's side, but the stink choked him and he backed away. In the dark, he couldn't make out much detail, but he saw enough to know that Hopkin had been torn apart. His left leg was more than a foot away from his body. His face had been mostly ripped free of its moorings and the bone of his jaws and cheeks were shockingly white. His throat was slashed, his chest split wide.

Sol took one more look, afraid his imagination had run away with him. As he did, a cloud drifted from in front of the moon, and he could see the carnage more clearly. He fell to hands and knees and puked up the beans and biscuits he'd had for supper.

When his gut was empty, he wiped his mouth on his dirty sleeve. He was trying to rise, unsteady on his feet, when that same sharp, awful smell came back, a wave of it. He heard something, which he realized after a moment was the squish of mud under someone's weight.

Sol made a dash for his horse, but the mud was too soft to get any speed. He grabbed for his gun, but his quaking, mud-slick hands couldn't get a grip on it. The stink intensified. Whatever the source was, it was closing in.

Knowing he wouldn't reach the horse, or be able to draw his piece, he turned to face it, and he was engulfed by the darkness and the odor and pain like he had never imagined.

Chapter Four

When they heard distant gunfire, Cale Ceniceros and Nate McHale mounted up and rode. They didn't like leaving the herd unguarded, particularly with the mutilations that had been happening. But Jed Tibbetts had made clear that his first concern was for the men, his second for the livestock. If the men on the other range were shooting at something, they might need help.

Even if they weren't in immediate danger, they might have encountered whatever was attacking the cattle. Either way, Cale and Nate needed to get there in a hurry. As he rode, Cale heard another sound, one he couldn't identify right off, but that sounded like grounded thunder. The way was dark and treacherous with the rain and the mud, but they got there and found the herd, then the horses, and finally the two cowboys.

Cale had never seen anything like it, and hoped he never would again.

"Someone's got to tell Mr. Tibbetts," he said.

"Yup." Nate had never been one to use a lot of words where one would suffice.

"And someone should ought to stay with the herd."

"Yup."

"Draw straws?"

"Sure." Nate tore a couple of leaves off the nearby mesquite and palmed them, the tips sticking out. "Long straw picks."

Cale drew one. Nate opened his hand. His was half as long as Cale's.

There were no good choices. Getting to the ranch house would mean a fast, hard ride through the dark of night, with the possibility that the rain could fall again at any time. But staying here, smelling those bodies, as the sun rose—Cale thought that would be even worse. "I reckon I'm riding," Cale said.

"Looks like."

"You be careful out here."

Nate nodded his head. Cale mounted up again, thinking that as much as he dreaded the thought of telling Mr. Tibbetts what had happened, he had got the easier end of the deal.

He wouldn't have wanted to stay with those torn-apart bodies for anything.

Rank has its privileges, people said. And it was true enough, to a point. Colonel Delbert Cuttrell, officer of the Confederate Army and garrison commander of Fort Huachuca, occupied the nicest house on the post, and he and his wife, Sadie, would keep it unless or until General Slaughter or Colonel Smyth returned from Richmond. Both men had been gone for months, summoned for high-level talks that seemed as endless as the war itself. The first few weeks they had sent back regular communiqués, but lately even those had dwindled. Cuttrell had begun to think they'd lost interest in this remote outpost, or the Confederacy had given up on it. When Union President Grant declared the Confederate States of America a free and independent nation, just weeks ago, Cuttrell had expected he would get more attention from Richmond, not less. So far, that had not happened.

Not that he minded, not a bit. He liked the house and the other perquisites of power, and he liked power for its own sake.

He was not, however, so fond of having his sleep interrupted before the sun had even come up by someone hammering on the front door and shouting his name. He rolled out of bed and started for the stairs.

"Just ignore it, Del," Sadie said, her voice thick with sleep.

"I can't, dear."

"Why ever not?"

"I'm an officer in the army, Sadie. My first duty is to my country."

"Your country's broken. Your men are largely degenerates, thieves, drunks, and scoundrels. Come back to bed."

Arguing was pointless. Conversation of any kind with her was more often frustrating than pleasant or useful. He loved her, but she drove him mad. He supposed she drove him mad because he loved her, because he couldn't bring himself not to care when she said things like that.

He walked down the stairs, listening to the rasping, nasal sounds that told him Sadie had already gone back to sleep.

Jimmy McKenna was outside, banging his fist on the door. Cuttrell opened it cautiously, afraid that McKenna had been pounding on it so long that he would keep pounding even without a door in the way. McKenna was broad-shouldered and strong and Cuttrell didn't want to start his day by being beaten half to death. "What is it, Lieutenant?"

"I'm sorry to bother you so early, sir," McKenna said. "I hope I didn't disturb your wife."

"I don't imagine you would have knocked if it hadn't been important. Come in."

McKenna looked at his boots. "That's not necessary, sir."

"Something the matter, Lieutenant McKenna?"

"No, sir. I mean, yes, there is. I just don't need to come in to tell you."

The man had looked uncomfortable at the suggestion, but Cuttrell didn't pursue it. Obviously McKenna had something on his mind. "Well, spit it out, son."

"It's—there's this mule train. And, well . . . sir, they're all dead."

"Who's all dead?"

"Everybody. In the train, that is."

"Start from the beginning, Jimmy."

McKenna took a deep breath, swallowed twice. He was some twenty years younger than Cuttrell. The colonel's beard showed some gray these days, and he had found a few silvery threads on his scalp, while McKenna had a thick dark thatch of hair, a sturdy build, and a face unlined by worry or age. Sometimes Cuttrell caught glimpses that reminded him of the man he had been as a young officer, during the early days of the never-ending war. Other times, he thought McKenna was hopelessly naïve and would never amount to much. "Some troopers came back early from patrol," McKenna said. "They found a mule train, on the old Ghost Trail."

"Not many mule trains out there anymore," Cuttrell interrupted. "Not since the Bayou Vermilion railroad went in."

"No, sir. Just every once in a while. Anyway, the troopers saw this one, but it wasn't moving. Everybody's dead."

"Dead how? Who do they think killed everyone?"

"Apaches, maybe. That was their guess, anyhow."

"And there's no one left? No rescue possible?"

"According to the troopers, no. But they don't know how many was on the train to start, so might could be there's some prisoners."

"I reckon we ought to go take a look," Cuttrell said. "Even if there's no way to save any lives, those who perpetrated the atrocity ought to be punished."

"That's just what I was thinkin', sir."

"Have the bugler call boots and saddles, son."

"Should I rouse the Buffalo Soldiers?"

McKenna commanded the Buffalo Soldier squad, and was always looking for an opportunity to put them to use. "That won't be necessary. We'll just use regular troopers for this one."

"Yes, sir."

McKenna stood in the doorway, as if waiting for some further instruction. "Is there anything else, Lieutenant? Something you still need to convey?"

"No, sir," McKenna said. A few seconds passed, and he seemed to catch on. "I'm going, sir. Boots and saddles."

"Good man," Cuttrell said. "I'll dress and be out momentarily."

"Yes, sir." McKenna snapped off a crisp salute, turned on his heel, and started toward the barracks. In the east, across the parade field, the sun was just beginning to gray out the horizon. Cuttrell was glad he had a reason to put on a uniform and ride out into the field. He had been spending too much time at the fort recently, too much time home with Sadie.

He loved the woman, but as with his other vices, he loved her most in moderation.

Sadie Cuttrell watched her husband ride out through the fort's front gate at the head of a procession of soldiers. He was a fine-looking man, his back straight, his still mostly golden hair catching the morning sun and gleaming in it. She was proud of him, proud to be married to him. She stood there, ever the dutiful wife, until the men were out of sight, dropping down toward the valley below the fort.

When they were gone, she went back into the house and closed the door. It was a big house, a little drafty, and when she was alone in it she felt like a ghost, not fully present, as if doors were merely conveniences and she could, should she choose to, simply drift through the walls. These days that feeling came more and more, sometimes when Delbert was in the house with her, sometimes even when they were giving a dinner party for the officers. If more of the officers had wives, that might help. A woman needed some other women around. There were women in town, of course, but she had left that life and those women behind. What she had left them for was, she hoped, something better. She thought it was. Some days, however, she had to wonder.

Sadie crossed to the kitchen and went into the pantry. From a low shelf, behind some spices, she took a small brown glass bottle. Carrying it back into the kitchen, she dribbled some of the liquid, the color of old rust, into a glass. She eyed it, then added a little more. The taste would be bitter, so she added a dash of Colonel Cuttrell's choicest brandy to mask it. If much brandy disappeared, he would notice, but he would never miss a tiny bit here and there.

She left the glass on the kitchen table and carried the laudanum back into the pantry. Delbert never cooked, never prepared anything for himself except the occasional drink, so he would be unlikely to find it there. Just the same, she hid the bottle well; behind the spices, it blended in and one had to know what to look for.

Back in the kitchen, Sadie swirled the liquid around in the glass, mixing it, then took the slightest sip. Even with the brandy, the flavor was unpleasant. The burning sensation on her lips was, too, but just for a moment. Then the heat began. She took another drink, a longer one this time, a good hearty swallow. With one more, she drained the glass. Almost immediately, she warmed from the inside, a glow like a tiny furnace in her belly spreading its comforting fire throughout her body. As the sensation filled her, she felt more real, more substantial. She could no longer pass through walls; in fact, she stumbled walking through the kitchen doorway, barking her shoulder against the jamb. She laughed once, a full-throated roar that Delbert considered most unfeminine, and found her way upstairs. There she sat in a seat by a window, watching the fort wake up without its commander or a large contingent of its troopers.

After a while, the laudanum had evened out her mood, and the business of the fort had settled into a routine. Sadie made her way back downstairs, almost floating from one step to the next, and out the front door. She knew where she was headed, but the time it took to walk to his house seemed to vanish, as if it had taken no time at all, as though she had merely blinked and she was there.

She didn't knock, because she didn't want to risk being seen. She believed—though she couldn't swear to it, because the passage from there to here had gone by with very little observation on her part—that no one had seen her come, and that was the way she liked it. But standing around waiting to be let in was asking for trouble. She just pushed the door open, closed it behind her, and called, "Jimmy! It's me."

He came into the room shirtless. His chest was deep, his arms sculpted like a Greek god's. His smile took her breath away, as it always did: somehow rakish and sincere at the same time, as if he truly believed all the lies he would tell her over the next hour. Perhaps he did; after all, what was an army officer but a politician in a uniform, and what politician had not mastered the art of self-deception?

"In broad daylight, Sadie?"

"He's gone. I couldn't wait."

"Come here, then." Jimmy held out his arms, stepping toward her as she wafted into them. He closed them around her, his grip crushing, the way she liked it.

He might have hurt her ribs, had the laudanum not been working its magic and keeping all pain and sorrow and shame at bay. He kissed her, hard, not the way Delbert did, but smashing his lips against hers and forcing his tongue into her mouth, where she took it willingly even when she pretended to be shocked. His right hand closed on her breast, as brutal as his embrace and his kiss. She responded to it as they both knew she would, as she would have even if she hadn't had professional training; she let her mouth fall open and her breath come more heavily, arching her back to press her breast more firmly into his grasping hand.

He was leaning in to kiss her again when they heard a knock on his door. "Damn it," Jimmy said.

"Last time that happened to me, it was you, and I was trying to sleep."

"Sorry. I couldn't wait on that."

"So I gathered, when Del came back in making a huge fuss about some mule train."

The knock came again, more insistent this time. "Sounds like you," Sadie said.

"I'll be back," Jimmy said. "Don't go anywhere."

"Where would I go?" she asked, mostly to herself.

Jimmy vanished. After a moment, she heard the door open. "Clinton," Jimmy said. "What is it?"

"Sorry to bust in on you like this, Loot," another voice said. She could tell it was one of his Buffalo Soldiers, and since she'd heard the name Clinton, figured it must be Clinton Delahunt. He was the best blacksmith on the post. His shoulders and arms dwarfed even Jimmy's, the contrast between them as pronounced as that between Jimmy and her husband. She wasn't trying to listen, and had lost the thread of the conversation anyway, immersed in her own thoughts. Laudanum did that. So did the fact that Jimmy rarely had anything worthwhile to say, so she only paid attention to the extent necessary to keep him interested.

He and Delahunt were going on and on about something, some project they were working on, it sounded like. Sadie bit back a yawn, then let the next one come, and wandered into Jimmy's bedroom. She sat on the bed and pulled off her shoes, then started in on the rest of her clothes. If he didn't return by the time she was naked, she would just start without him.

She didn't think he would mind a bit.

Chapter Five

Though he rode hell-bent for leather toward the J Cross T ranch headquarters, Cale Ceniceros couldn't help but be struck by the beauty laid out for him along the way. The rising sun brought a rosy, gold-tinged glow to the peaks of the Huachuca Mountains to the west, where remnant clouds from last night's storms were snagged like cotton fluff on the stem. As it climbed higher, the glow slid down the mountains' faces, then found the valley floor, bringing each blade of green, tufted grass, each creosote bush and mesquite and upthrust yucca stalk into crystalline relief. The sky turned from a deep, almost violet blue to a paler one with hints of salmon, before finally settling on the brilliant, vivid blue of an Arizona summer day. On the ride he saw jackrabbits and hog-like javelina, three kinds of snakes, the retreating form of a bobcat, and six or seven coyotes out on morning maneuvers.

When he thought he could ride no longer, that his rump had been flattened and his spine jarred so much he might never walk straight again, he came over the last rise. In the depression below stood the ranch house, the bunkhouse, a barn, and off to the side a corral and tack house. His back might be permanently out of whack, but he would make it. He urged his horse down the incline at full gallop, and reined her in as he entered the dusty yard. Cale leaped off her back as she skidded to a stop, and took a few lurching, unsteady steps toward the house.

Jed Tibbetts appeared in the doorway before Cale even

reached it. "Looks like you're in an all-fired hurry there, Cale. What's so important?"

Cale had been rehearsing his explanation for hours, but now that the time had come to give it, he became tongue-tied, his English fleeing him and leaving only Spanish behind. Mr. Tibbetts spoke a little Spanish, as most borderland ranchers did, but Cale knew he wouldn't understand the words that came to mind. He struggled to find the English ones. "It's . . . sorry. Mr. Tibbetts."

"Take a deep breath, boy. Couple of 'em. It'll come."

Tibbetts was a lean man, wiry and strong. His face was tanned and leathered by the elements, and deep grooves ran from high on his cheeks down to his jaw. His lips were always chapped and bloody, but his blue eyes were as clear as the Arizona sky and when he smiled, which he did less often lately than he once had, the effect was like a match struck in a dark room, at once illuminating and comforting. He smiled now, while Cale breathed and collected his thoughts.

"It's Hopkin and Pinky," he said at last. "They're dead."

The smile vanished from the rancher's face. "How?"

"Kind of like the cattle, I guess. There was a big bull close by, that had been cut up like the others. Same thing for the men. It was . . . it was awful, Mr. Tibbetts."

"You see who done it?"

"No, sir. We was over on our range, and heard gunshots from theirs. When we went over, we found both men dead. Nate stayed with them while I came to get you."

"Which means the stock in your range has been unprotected for hours."

"That's right. Sorry, boss, but we thought it was the best thing. To make sure the men weren't attacked more. Keep them safe for burial."

Tibbetts put a hand on Cale's shoulder and gave it a squeeze. "You did the right thing, son. I'll send a couple of men out to your range to check on the beeves there. Meanwhile, you and me and some others can go fetch those bodies. You up to another ride?"

Somewhere in the back of his mind, Cale had understood that

he would have to take Mr. Tibbetts back to Nate and the corpses. During the latter part of his headlong sprint to the ranch, though, he had pushed that out of his thoughts, focused only on getting there. It couldn't be helped, though. "Yes," he said. "Sure, of course."

Tibbetts cast an appraising eye at Cale's mount. "We'll get you a fresh horse. Looks like that one's plumb tuckered out. Go on inside, now, and Mrs. Tibbetts can get you some coffee and eggs while I get things movin'."

Tibbetts was as good as his word, and his wife's eggs and coffee, plus a biscuit and a little ham were even better. With Cale's stomach full and a lively Appaloosa under him, he felt halfway alive again. He led Mr. Tibbetts and two other hands, Marlon and Reisen, back out to the rangelands where he'd left Nate. All the way, he worried about what they'd find there. What if whatever or whoever had attacked the others had come back for Nate? If there were three human bodies on the ground instead of two, he would feel responsible. He had drawn the long straw, after all. He could have chosen to stay.

Cale's father had been a vaquero down in Sonora, his mother a white woman who had chanced to meet Enrique Ceniceros when the train she had been taking to Mexico City had broken down, and he had been nearby. He had offered the stranded passengers food and water and a pale-skinned woman with copper hair and freckles had caught his eye.

Enrique had been a natural horseman, a master horse trainer who used a *jáquima*—what Americans called a hackamore—to break wild horses so they had a soft mouth and responded to a rider like an extension of his legs. Cale had adopted American styles of dress, used short-roweled, blunted spurs, and even rode with an American saddle instead of a Mexican one covered with a *mochila*, but he had learned horsemanship at his father's side.

Cale's father had been shot through the ribs during an argument at an Hermosillo cantina, and shot again, in the hip, during a running fight with cattle rustlers. But it had been another man's sloppy rope work that had finally killed him, when a cow had broken free, mid-branding, and kicked Enrique in the face.

Cale's mother had died two years later, during an influenza epidemic. Unknown to him, his mother and Edith Tibbetts had been friends, and after her funeral, Mrs. Tibbetts had written to Cale, offering employment. The couple had practically adopted him, and he loved the ranch family like they were flesh and blood. Anything that hurt the ranch hurt them, and anything that hurt them hurt him.

As they neared the spot, his stomach roiled with tension. For most of an hour he hadn't been able to talk, but now he couldn't even spit. When he saw three horses standing together near the big mesquite that marked the place of the dead, tears rushed into his eyes. He wiped at them with the back of one gloved hand and fought back more. Bad enough that if Nate had died, that would be on him, but he didn't want to humiliate himself further by weeping in front of the men.

It wasn't until Nate started waving and calling out that Cale's stomach unclenched and he allowed himself a moment's relaxation. He was happy that Nate lived, but it was relief tempered by the knowledge that two men were still dead.

Mr. Tibbetts urged his horse on faster when he saw Nate. By the time Cale got there, the rancher had dismounted and Nate was showing him the bodies. Tears glistened on the rancher's weathered cheeks. He pawed at his right eye. He tried to say something, but the words caught in his throat.

Cale brought his mount to a stop. "Everything all right, Nate?" he asked as he stepped to the ground.

"Good enough," Nate said. "Considerin'."

"Yeah." Cale glanced at the bodies, and at Nate and Mr. Tibbetts, then studied the distant horizon as if something of great import were written there.

"Get those spades," Tibbetts said. "We got us some holes to dig."

When the bodies were in the ground and Tibbetts had said a few words over them, the rancher beckoned to Cale. "Marlon, ride up to Tombstone and tell Sheriff Behan what's happened. You other men, stay with the beeves. Cale, you come with me."

"Where to?" Cale asked.

"Town," Tibbetts said. "We got to get some more guns. If it takes every dollar I have, we got to keep the stock safe, and our men, both. We can't get those animals to market, we're done."

"Makes sense to me."

Tibbetts shot him an open-mouthed scowl. Cale didn't think it was directed at him, but at the circumstances surrounding them, and he tried not to take it to heart. He was only so successful. The man's pain was evident, and Cale felt it, too. The loss of his fellow hands was his loss, and so was Mr. Tibbetts's loss. He didn't pretend to think that he grieved more strongly than the rancher did. But maybe because the man was older, he had known more pain and knew better how to bottle it up, or swallow it down. He had shed some tears, but the sole emotion Cale could read in his eyes now was a grim determination to put things right. Tibbetts's eyes were a pale blue that edged toward gray sometimes, depending on the light. Just now, they reminded Cale of polished steel.

Chapter Six

Jasper Montclair came from someplace back east, and he came from money. Tibbetts didn't know where he hailed from, precisely, or what exactly the source of the money was. It was family money, he'd heard, but beyond that there were more rumors than known facts. Asking was out of the question—you didn't ask a rancher how many head of cattle he had, because that was like asking him what was in his pockets. His vast Broken M, which lay between Tibbetts's J Cross T and the mountains was, by all accounts, a successful ranch, and beyond that Tibbetts didn't know much.

But those things about Montclair were common knowledge around town. And they were apparent in the man's voice, his patterns of speech, and the words he chose. There was also something about the way he dressed. He wore more or less the same style of clothing as any other rancher, but he didn't wear it quite the same way. He had on boots and dungarees and a shirt and a kerchief around his neck, nothing fancy, not a silk wild rag like some of the boys wore on a night out. He had a leather vest that had probably cost more than all the clothes in Mrs. Tibbetts's wardrobe. His hat was black and dusty, but not too dusty, and there was no visible sweatband ringing it like on most working men's hats. He wore his brown hair long in back, where it fell limply past his collar.

That was the thing about Montclair's clothes, Tibbetts decided. They were too clean, too new. No wear on the knees of his pants or the cuffs of his shirt. Tibbetts owned three shirts at any given time, including the bib-fronted one he wore today. When he had worn one too long and hard to be patched anymore, he broke down and got a new one. His Sunday church shirt had lasted him for eleven years now, and had a good while to go yet.

Tibbetts and Cale had ridden straight into town and tied their horses near the bank. Montclair had stepped out through the bank's door at just that moment, and greeted Tibbetts, and Tibbetts decided to take a chance. "Montclair, you havin' any troubles with beeves gettin' all cut up?"

"I have no earthly idea what you mean, sir," Montclair said. His voice was a deep baritone, with just a hint of gravel in it. "Cut up in what manner?"

"In the manner that leaves 'em dead on the ground," Tibbetts replied. He had thought it was a pretty straightforward question. "Lookin' like somebody with a bad grudge took an ax to 'em."

Montclair's thin lips pursed like he was offended by the description. "I'm sure I would have been notified, if that had been the case. I haven't heard of any such thing."

The rumors around town were that Montclair's men didn't tell him much about what happened on his own land. Montclair, folks said, was only a rancher in the sense that he owned a lot of property and ran livestock on it. But he didn't seem to know what to do with it beyond that, and his hired men had to make all the decisions. "Well, you might want to keep an eye out. It's been happenin' to me, and last night I lost a couple hands, too."

"And you haven't a clue who's behind it?" Montclair asked.

"No idea. Not even if it's man or beast. I thought Apaches at first, but it don't seem like them, really."

"Hardly."

Tibbetts was already tired of the conversation, and he could see Montclair was, too. The man's gaze wouldn't settle on anything. His deep-set eyes were an odd color, somewhere between green and brown, and his right one shifted around in his head like it had lost its moorings, never looking at the same thing as his left. Above them, bushy eyebrows reached out in every direction, as if desperately clinging to the bony ridge that shadowed those eyes. "Listen, I gotta get to the—" Tibbetts began.

"Is there anything I might do to help?" Montclair asked him.

"Such as?"

"It sounds as if you're down a couple of men. I could loan you some of mine."

"Loan?"

"I would keep them on my payroll, of course. But I could spare some, if it would be of any assistance."

Tibbetts considered the offer briefly. He didn't want to feel beholden to Jasper Montclair. And the offer struck him like an insult, or a slap in the face. Montclair would pay men who were doing him no service at all, so that Tibbetts could put them to work. In three sentences Montclair had made the points that he was far wealthier than Tibbetts—as if the fact that he was working hard at buying up every ranch in the area didn't make that clear enough—that Tibbetts was struggling, and that whatever ill fate had struck the J Cross T had singled that ranch out and was not widespread. His cheeks burned, as if the slap had been real.

"Must be nice to have everything you'll ever need," he said.

"Excuse me, sir?" Montclair said.

"Forget it." Tibbetts took his leave of the man. Cale had been standing nearby, utterly ignored by Montclair, and probably, Tibbetts thought, the better off for it. As he reached the bank door, he turned and said, "Stay here, Cale. Mind the horses. I'll be back pretty quick."

"Yes, sir," Cale said. He was a good boy. Good young man, more accurately. He was seventeen now, full-grown and on his own.

Stepping inside, Tibbetts realized he was still fuming. Montclair had land and wealth, and in Carmichael, those things gave him power. But none of that made him a better man. His offer seemed generous on the surface, but Tibbetts thought the intent had been to belittle him. By emphasizing Montclair's generosity, he was drawing attention to the fact that even if Tibbetts had been similarly inclined, he couldn't afford to make the offer.

He had never accepted charity before, and he didn't intend to start now.

Inside, a handful of folks were lined up at the teller window. Tibbetts had lived close by long enough that he knew just about everyone in Carmichael, so he greeted them by name as he walked to the ornate desk belonging to Wilson Harrell.

Harrell rose at Tibbetts's approach. He was a stout man with a ruddy face that seemed out of place between his shock of white hair and small white goatee. His expensive suit had been custom-tailored, but fifteen or twenty pounds ago, so it clung here and there, emphasizing the added weight instead of hiding it. Tibbetts had never been to a big-city brothel, but he suspected that if he ever did, he would encounter curtains or wallpaper that reminded him of the pattern on the suit's fabric.

"Mr. Tibbetts," Harrell said with a grin exactly as sincere as his handshake. He gripped Tibbetts's right hand, gave it a hurried squeeze, and then released it as if afraid of catching some fatal disease. "What brings you in today?" He nodded toward a straight-backed chair next to the desk. "Please, take a load off."

"Thanks, Mr. Harrell," Tibbetts said. He didn't figure there was anything to gain from dodging the question. "I could use a loan."

"A loan?" Harrell looked away from him, pawed around his desk until he found his spectacles, then put them on. They perched near the bulbous tip of his nose, and he tilted his head back to regard Tibbetts through the lenses. "For what purpose, might I ask?"

"On account of something's been killin' my cattle. And now some of my men. I need to add on some hands, gunnies, mebbe. To find out who or what it is and stop it."

"Because if you can't, your stock will lose its value."

"Seein' as how these animals're bleedin' themselves dry out

on the range, what's left of 'em, yeah. I'm losin' value all over the place."

Harrell opened a ledger book on his desk, licked his thumb, and rifled through the pages. He stopped on one and ran his fingers along a few of the lines. "Hmmm," he said as he perused the book. After another moment, he closed it. "You're already quite extended, Mr. Tibbetts."

"I reckon I owe some. But if I lose many more beeves I'll never be able to pay it back. You know I'm good for it, if I can keep enough alive to sell."

"That is, of course, one consideration," Harrell said. "I would be remiss, however, if I didn't point out that the total of your current debt is more than you've ever cleared from the sale of your livestock, even in your best years. If your stock is already depleted by this . . . this attrition you've described, then I don't see that there's any chance you could pay back the current debt this year, much less any new debt you might take on."

"This year, next, one after that. You know I'll pay it, Wilson. Always have before, haven't I?"

Harrell studied him through those spectacles, like he was a scientist examining a new type of insect. "You've made regular payments, that much is true. But if you had actually paid it down, then it wouldn't be so high, would it?"

There was a tone of finality in his statement that Tibbetts didn't like. He felt the flush coming back, same as when he'd been jawing with Montclair. "What are you saying, exactly, Mr. Harrell?"

The banker took off the spectacles, setting them gingerly on the desktop. His expression was neutral, eyes blank. "I'm saying, sir, that I cannot loan you another nickel until I see some significant reduction in your principal. And if you don't make some serious headway, I'm afraid you'll lose your ranch."

"So no? Nothing at all?"

"Nothing at all, sir."

The fact that Harrell had started calling him "sir" was all

Tibbetts needed to hear. "Good to know where I stand, I reckon. After all these years."

"It's nothing personal, I assure you."

"To you, mebbe. To me, it's personal as all hell." Tibbetts stood up so fast the chair rocked back, and he barely caught it before it crashed to the floor.

"Mr. Tibbetts!" Harrell called. But Tibbetts was already stalking toward the door, aware that everyone in the bank was watching him. His boots were loud on the tiles, like handclaps in an empty church.

He and Cale went into Soto's. At midday, the place was reasonably crowded, but nothing like it would be come nightfall. Tibbetts snatched up an empty glass from an unoccupied table and rapped it on the tabletop three times. The room quieted.

"Most of you know me," he said. "I'm Jed Tibbetts of the J Cross T. I need a few men. Ones who aren't easily scared. If you got your own rifle, so much the better."

"What're ya payin'?" someone shouted from the back.

"A fair wage," Tibbetts answered. "But I'll be straight, it'll mebbe take a while before you get paid. In the meantime you'll get grub and a bed and a roof over you."

He heard laughter that made his cheeks burn with shame. A couple of men sitting together at a table stood up. They didn't look like they'd had a decent meal in a long time, or a bath, either. They were so dirty it was hard to tell where their clothes ended and they began. "We could work," one said. He was young, but when he opened his mouth it was nearly toothless. The other man was older, scrawny, with greasy gray hair plastered to his head. A patchwork of scars on that cheek offered mute testimony to some past catastrophe. Neither man looked like they were good for much, and Tibbetts wondered how they came up with the price of a drink between them.

But beggars couldn't be choosers—if they could, these two

would have clothes that fit and boots that didn't show their feet through the gaps—and nobody else was volunteering to work for the promise of some unspecified payment at some uncertain future time. "All right, you're hired," Tibbetts said. "Anybody else?"

He was met by silence. Somebody scooted a chair on the plank floor. Someone else coughed twice. Behind him, he heard the scuff of boots, followed by the clearing of a throat. He turned and saw Jasper Montclair in the doorway. "Mr. Tibbetts," he said. "A word?"

Shame and humiliation started to rise again in Tibbetts's throat, but he was running out of places to turn. "Sure," he said. Montclair ticked his eyes toward the door, and Tibbetts left Cale to talk to the pair of volunteers while he went outside with the other rancher.

"We had some miscommunication earlier. I am sorry if I offended you in any way. I noticed you weren't having a great deal of success in there," Montclair said.

"Not so much, no."

"I wanted to reiterate my offer, then. I'll need my whole crew soon enough, to round up my stock and get them to market. But until then, I can let you have four men, with horses. There would be no cost to you, beyond food and shelter. Please don't think of it as charity, sir. If there is someone preying on your herd, they might come for mine next. Even if not, sometime when I need extra hands for a limited time, you can repay the favor."

Tibbetts appreciated the effort Montclair had gone to, trying to make him feel better about accepting the handout. He still hated to do it. But four seasoned hands would do him more good than twenty of the kind he had found inside. You couldn't always judge a man by how he looked, but there were instances where that was a decent indicator. He needed men who could keep their heads, and shoot straight if it came to that. Those two inside appeared as likely to shoot each other as anything else.

"Fair enough," he said after considering for a few moments. He forced himself to add, "Thank you, Mr. Montclair."

"Think nothing of it," Montclair said, with a dismissive tone that made the rest of his comments into a lie. "I'll send them over directly." He turned and walked away without another word.

Tibbetts watched him go, then stuck his head back into the saloon. "Cale," he said. "Bring them two fellers and let's light a shuck out of here."

Chapter Seven

Sadie Cuttrell waited on the wagon seat for Jimmy McKenna to get down, walk around to her side, and offer his gauntleted hand. She took it, and he helped her down. She gathered up her skirts so they wouldn't brush against the packed dirt of Main Street, releasing them only when she was on the boardwalk. She had not been born into her current station in life, and there were times she thought her grip on it was tenuous at best. As a result, she clung to the physical trappings of it—the clothing, the fine things she was able to afford—and the mannerisms she had adopted, and was determined never to let those things slip away.

Appearances mattered. Jimmy was her husband's aide-de-camp, but because he was also the commanding officer to the Buffalo Soldiers, if they were left behind, he stayed back, too. The arrangement was convenient for her. And because his position with Delbert was well known, it was perfectly legitimate for him to bring her into town on a shopping expedition. She wanted to prepare a fine meal to mark her husband's return, so she needed provisions. But when she reached the door of Maier's, the town's sole grocer, there was a CLOSED sign hanging in the window.

"Damn!" she said, more loudly than she had intended.

"I heard something about a posse formed during the night," Jimmy said. "Maybe Alf was in on that."

"A posse? For what?"

"One of Senora Soto's girls was murdered."

She tried not to betray her interest, but Jimmy knew her background, so there was little reason to hide it from him. "Do you know who?"

"Daisie, I heard."

Sadie stood before the locked door. At the name, her spine stiffened, and she pictured, just for an instant, the bottle of laudanum in the pantry. "That's a shame," she said. She had never liked Daisie, not for an instant. She hadn't wished her ill, certainly not dead. But they had never been friends, or anything close to it.

"Anyplace else you'd like to shop, ma'am?" Jimmy asked.

"Perhaps the general store will have some of what I need."

"Worth a try," he said. Greavey's general store was on the other side of the street, so she had to scoop up her skirts again. Jimmy offered his hand to help her off the boardwalk. They had to wait for a couple of mounted men to ride down the street, then for a wagon drawn by two weary-looking mules. Its wheels threw mud clots behind it, but at least the usual clouds of dust didn't rise up.

Greavey's was open, and Jimmy held the door wide for her. As she stepped through the doorway, she met Alexandra Harrell, the banker's wife, coming the other way. "Good day, Mrs. Harrell," Sadie said brightly. "How are you?"

"Well enough," Mrs. Harrell said. Her voice was tight, the words clipped. She pushed through the door without a second glance at Sadie, or any thanks for Jimmy.

"Pleasant woman," Jimmy said when she was gone. "Real friendly type, isn't she?"

"Her husband owns the bank, so she thinks she's the Queen of England."

The shopkeeper came around the counter toward her, all smiles. His name was Will, she remembered, Will Greavey. "Mrs. Cuttrell," he said. "What a pleasure! What can I do for you today?"

"I wanted some food, Will, but the grocery's closed."

"Well, let me see your list, if you have one. I don't keep as much on hand as Alf does, but I've got my sources."

She did have a list, and she handed it to him, first clutching his arm for several long moments and holding his gaze with her own. "See what you can do, please. I'd be happy to bring more of my business here, if I can. Mr. Maier is not the most pleasant individual. And not nearly so handsome."

"Give me a few minutes, ma'am," Will said. "I think I can make some headway on this."

"Very well," Sadie said. "That's all right, isn't it, Lieutenant McKenna?"

"I'm at your disposal, Mrs. Cuttrell," Jimmy said.

Ascertaining that Will wasn't looking, she grabbed Jimmy's behind and squeezed tight. "You certainly are," she said softly.

She and Jimmy went outside to wait in the gentle breeze blowing out of the southeast. While they stood there, sheltered from the sun by an overhang, one of Senora Soto's former girls walked past. Cassandra was a big woman, as tall as most men and twice Sadie's weight. Some men liked that, Sadie knew. She couldn't for the life of her understand why. To her, Cassandra just seemed sloppy, but she was popular and had earned more than many in the Soto stable, before moving on to another house.

She showed Sadie a wide, toothy grin and ran her fingers through her curly red hair. "Why, Sadie! I haven't seen you in an age. How're things?"

"Cassandra," Sadie said without enthusiasm. "I hope you're well."

"You know me, Sadie. Nothing slows me down."

Jimmy eyed Cassandra, and Sadie caught him looking. "Goodbye, Cassandra," Sadie said, turning back toward the store. "Do you suppose Will is finished with that list yet?"

Cassandra took the hint. She kept going toward whatever her destination was. Jimmy opened the door again, and ushered Sadie through. "Like that, do you?" she asked over her shoulder.

"Not as much as I like you."

"Don't ever forget it, then."

"Not a chance."

"Will," Sadie called. "How's that list coming?"

Jasper Montclair stood in the shade of a covered walkway and looked out across the street. He saw a boy, perhaps eight or nine years old, wander out into the middle of the road, and he saw a horse coming, and for an instant wondered if he should do something. When he had been about that age, he'd seen a fast-moving coach strike an occasional playmate of his. It had knocked the boy into the corner of a building. The impact had opened the boy's skull and he had fallen like a bag of sand, if sand could leak blood and gore all over a city street. Since then, he had always been nervous about boys in proximity to wagons or vehicles of any kind.

But the boy made it across safely, so Montclair went back to watching the big one, the redhead who worked out of a saloon rather grandly called the Palladium, half a block down Maiden Lane. She strutted across the road and stepped up onto the boardwalk and then stopped and chatted with Mrs. Cuttrell. She moved with an energy and grace that Montclair found intriguing. She carried the weight well, and every time he had seen her, she appeared to be enjoying life. She laughed a lot, and heartily. But she reeked of cheap perfume and smoke, from living and working in and above a saloon.

But the other one, the colonel's wife—there was a woman to be reckoned with. The redhead was a soiled dove, and destined to remain one. Sadie Cuttrell had remade herself, through nothing but determination and sheer force of will. She had left one life behind and created another that she liked better. She was formidable in spirit, too stubborn to accept anything less than perfect victory, bright and willful and so very lovely.

He would need a woman like that on his arm, once he had seized everything else he had his eye on. Sadie Cuttrell was the most beautiful woman in the county, by far. In the entire territory, perhaps. When people saw Jasper Montclair with her, they would know they had met their betters.

Her past didn't bother him, and if it troubled her, he could always make her forget it. Such a thing was simple to do, a child's trick.

He watched her dismiss the whore and sweep back inside the general store. The fawning lieutenant held the door for her, then followed her in. He was like a lost puppy, determined not to lose sight of whoever had last given him a morsel. Montclair caught the scent of Sadie's sex on him, and his dried sweat on her. That was an interesting bit of information, one he might be able to use. Passing through the doorway, she looked back at the lieutenant and spoke a few words. Montclair waited until her breath wafted across the street and inhaled deeply. Laudanum. Also good to know.

Montclair climbed into the seat of his buckboard. The lieutenant would not be a problem. The colonel, perhaps slightly stickier, but not a real worry.

He cast one more look at the redhead as she sashayed down the boardwalk, caught a last glimpse of Sadie Cuttrell through the store's window, and urged his draft horses on. He had much to do, and ever less time to get it done.

Chapter Eight

None of the men had anticipated a midnight ride out of town, so by daylight they were all weary, soaked to the bone, chafed and uncomfortable. It had been slow going at first, trying to cut sign in the darkness and the downpour, with lanterns and torches, which the rain often doused, their only sources of illumination. Marshal Turville and Tucker Bringloe took turns dismounting to study the ground every time the trail became obscured, which was often.

An hour or so before the sun's first glimmer in the east, Tuck's hands started to shake. He was cold, but it was more than that. His throat was dry and he knew what he needed to calm the shakes. Most nights, he would be sleeping off a drunk at this time, and the sound sleep prompted by drink would get him through until morning's light, or someone kicking him out of a doorway or an alley, woke him. Upon awakening, his first thought would be the next drink.

But on this predawn morning, on horseback and surrounded by men he didn't know, one of whom was the town marshal, he had no idea where that next drink might come from. The fact that he hadn't been allowed to sleep meant his usual craving had taken on new urgency, and the shakes that might have been disguised by unconsciousness were growing progressively worse. When he got off the horse, it was harder and harder to climb back into the saddle. His foot slipped from the stirrup, and one time he threw his leg atop the animal only to pitch over backward into the mud.

The other men roared laughter, and Tuck managed to force out a few halfhearted chuckles. Being the object of laughter was nothing new. He made another attempt and this time got into the saddle, shaking more than ever, his clothing weighted down by water and mud until it felt like he carried another man on his back.

He tried to stay on the horse and let the marshal do the tracking after that.

As the day stretched on, the July sun hammered down on them. Already hot, it would be hotter still in the afternoon unless the clouds returned to block its rays. And if they did, then the rain might come back, too. July, Tuck reflected, was no time to be out of doors in the Arizona territory. Especially without a hat.

The main advantage of the sun, as Tuck saw it, was that as it baked the earth, the hoofprints of their quarry's mount were sealed as if intentionally imprinted. What had made tracking almost impossible now made it easy. Having made better progress for a while, when the men complained of bone-weariness and hunger, Marshal Turville called for a short break to stretch, rest, and eat.

Tuck's guts went into spasms. His head throbbed with every pulse of his heart, and he was soaked in sweat that chilled him from the inside, even as his clothes dried and stiffened in the sun. Alf Maier, the grocer, passed him a biscuit he had brought, cold and dry, and he tried to eat it, but gave up after two bites. For a few minutes, he was sure he would vomit, and he started to leave the circle of men to find a private place. But then he saw Ralph Hendershott tip a flask to his mouth.

At once, the rest of it was forgotten—the nausea, the cramps, the urge to lose what little food he had consumed over the past hours. That dull silver flask promised deliverance. Tuck stepped up to where Hendershott sat, back against a boulder, a spreading mesquite offering some modicum of shade. "Share a little of that?"

"Precious little to begin with," Hendershott said. He owned the livery stable in Carmichael, along with a partner named Charlie Darlington. Both had been in the saloon, or upstairs from it, when Daisie had been killed, and both had been roped into joining the posse. "I need to share what I got with Charlie."

Tuck's hand dropped to the gun Turville had provided him, ensconced in a similarly acquired holster. Would he really shoot a man for a drink? He wasn't sure what the answer to that question might be. If he did, in front of these men, including Hendershott's business partner, he'd never live to reach the flask. Still, that wasn't an altogether unpleasant proposition.

The marshal took the matter out of his hands. "Pour that out, Ralph," he said. "Now. Anybody else carryin' liquor, dump it into the dirt. We won't have any drinkin' on his posse, nor fightin'. Is that clear?"

"Hank, you can't make a man give up his liquor," Hendershott said.

Turville slid his rifle from its scabbard on his saddle. "Watch me."

"Ach," Maier said. His German accent was as thick as if he had just stepped off the boat, and Tuck sometimes could barely understand him. He wore thick glasses, and walked like the ground was burning his feet. "The girl was only a whore. Once the word spreads, there will be five more just like her on the next stage."

"She was a whore that you were particularly fond of, as I recall," Turville said. "And she spent money in your store. She lived in our town. If'n we don't go after her killer, who will? Who'll he kill next?"

"He rode out of town straightaway. Whoever he kills next is not your concern."

"We let it go this time, what's to say he won't come back? Figger our women are easy pickin's."

"Hank's right, Alf," Darlington said. He was a wiry, bandy-legged guy who Tuck thought was wound too tight for this. Whenever guns started going off, he didn't want Darlington behind him. "We got to do this, whore or no."

"Bringloe didn't even know her, and he's here," Turville said.

"He is not losing business every hour he is away from town. He is a drunkard who goes where he's told. Especially if there is a chance of a dollar in it. Or a drink."

"Neither one for him this time," Turville replied. "Ralph, pour that stuff onto the ground. You, too, Alf, I know you got a flask on you. In five seconds I'm comin' to take 'em away myself."

Hendershott gave an exaggerated sigh, took a final swig, and upended his flask. With fierce longing, Tuck watched the liquid soak into the dirt. Maier tugged his from a saddlebag and poured it out. Even Piet Vander Tuig, the cowhand Tuck had first seen with the big redhead in his lap, had a little bottle on him. The other men in the posse, Winston and Nickles, stood quietly and watched without letting on whether they had any to dump. Tuck smelled all the liquor as it splashed against the earth and ran off in little rivulets. He breathed deeply and took his hand off the gun and turned away from the sight, feeling like his legs would give out at any moment. He couldn't remember ever wanting a drink so much.

No, that wasn't true. He could hardly remember ever *not* wanting a drink, even though booze had not ruled him until these last several years. Since he had left behind the war that still raged. And even then, it had taken time to really catch hold of his innards. Now it refused to let go. He was shaking again, sweating, red-faced. He stepped away from the circle of men, put some dense mesquite and creosote bushes between them and him, and dropped to his knees, then lower, to hands and knees. A tear leaked from his right eye, cut a track down his dust-covered cheek, and dropped to the ground. If it had been booze, he would have put his face in the dirt and licked it up. Knowing that about himself filled him with sorrow and rage and shame, and made him wonder again if drawing on Hendershott might not have led to the best outcome.

"It's bad, isn't it?"

Tuck started at the sudden voice, then lowered his bottom to the ground and slowly turned. Hank Turville stood there, limned by the sun, his shadow falling over Tuck. He knew he cut a pathetic figure, sitting in the dirt with tear tracks on his face. "Guess I might not be everything you hoped, huh?"

"I did that for you, Bringloe. Making those men dump out the sauce. I know what you are, and what you're goin' through."

"You do?"

"Not the way you do, mebbe. I got my own problems, I reckon, but that's never been one of 'em. I've seen it, plenty, though. You arrest enough drunks, in time you see everything. I ain't judgin' you, mister. I know you got a problem. I know you might could *be* a problem. But I also know you got a hell of an eye. If you hadn't been half-drunk, I wouldn't'a had to get off my horse all night, 'cause you woulda spotted every sign there was to see."

"I've always been a decent tracker," Tuck admitted. That was an understatement. Hunting or at war, others had always looked to him when a trail went cold, and more times than not he'd been able to find it again. But that had been a long time ago, on the other side of the bottle. That had been a different Tucker Bringloe, one who had deserved to wear the uniform of the Union Army.

"That's why I want you sharp. We don't know how hard the trail's gonna be, or how long we'll be at it, or what we'll find at its end. You might hate me by the time we're done, Bringloe. All I know, you might hate me already."

"You wouldn't be far wrong, Marshal."

"I don't care if you do. I got a feelin' about you. I think you're mebbe a better man than you do. Figger you can't see much beyond your own reflection in a bottle. I see a little deeper'n that."

"There anything there to be seen?"

"An army officer. Wrong army, but still. And I reckon you were worth somethin' before that, too. Can be again, most like."

Tuck didn't feel like that, now. He felt like all he was doing was sucking up air that somebody more useful could have been breathing. "That's open to debate."

"One thing I can't stand is anyone feelin' sorry for himself, Bringloe. I don't want to see any of that. I want you sober and paying attention, because if we're gonna find this killer, I reckon it'll be you that makes it happen."

"Don't see that I have much choice, about the sober."

"You could always ride back to Carmichael."

"And you wouldn't shoot me in the back before I got five steps away? Or hang me when you got back?"

"I didn't say that, did I?"

"Don't think you have to."

Turville extended a hand toward him. Tuck took it and let the marshal help him to his feet. "We've wasted enough time," Turville said. He lowered his voice a notch. "I'm puttin' a lot of faith in you, mister. Don't let me down."

Tuck almost tossed off some smart remark, but he held his tongue. Walking with the marshal back to join the others, he tried to remember the last time anyone had counted on him for anything. During the war, he guessed. Had to be. After that he had been alone, riding ever westward, keeping his own company. Starting to drink to chase away the memories and the nightmares, and finding, almost to his horror, that it worked. Finding that it took more drink, always more, to keep them at bay. Anybody who had bet on him during those years would have been sorely disappointed.

Chances were, Hank Turville would be, too.

The clouds came, scudding in from the southeast and blanketing the sky, but the rain didn't. In the mountains, thunder boomed, and lightning flashed in the distance, in every direction, sometimes stabbing the earth for what seemed like seconds at a time. The killer's trail led east, then cut northeast for a while, crossing the river and gradually drifting southeast. They might be in Mexico by now, Tuck thought, though he hadn't seen any markers. They had made up some ground on the killer, which they could tell by the freshness of his tracks, but he was still well ahead.

The Huachucas were well behind them, but in this country, there were always more mountains ahead. The landscape rose in a jagged line, then dropped away to a broad, flat valley, on the far side of which were more mountains, with another valley waiting beyond.

The sun lowered beneath the clouds but above the distant peaks, and its light angled across the valley floor. The shadows of the posse members stretched out ahead of them, like giants walking the earth.

Men were starting to grumble again, first Maier, then Darlington joined in. "We been at this for nearly twenty hours, Hank. How much longer we got to do it? We lost the guy."

"We ain't lost him yet," Turville said. "We're catchin' up."

"If you and the rummy are right about whose tracks you're following. You ask me, we lost him that first night, in the rain. We're probably trailing some prospector or cowboy."

"We keep followin' him. When we know we're wrong, then we'll worry about it."

"I am so hungry," Maier said. "My business is suffering. My behind suffers more."

"We're dogging the right trail," Tuck said. "No reason to give up now."

"The reason is I'm plumb wore out," Darlington said. "And like Alf said, we got things waiting for us back in Carmichael. Ralph and I are both here, so who knows what's going on at our livery?"

"There's hours of daylight left," Turville said, scanning the sky. "We'll stop for the night, once it's full dark. How's that? I'll tell you now, though, *he* ain't likely to stop for the night. Just means tomorrow we'll have to ride harder to make up lost ground."

Darlington slowed his horse a little, letting Tuck catch up to him. As Tuck came alongside, Darlington shot him a scowl. "You're liking this, aren't you, rummy?"

"Liking what? Riding my ass raw chasing a guy who killed a woman I don't even know? It's not my favorite thing."

"You and the marshal seem like old pals."

"Never met him before last night."

"You say so." Darlington gigged his mount and sped up to a canter, slowing only when he drew up beside Hendershott.

More than ever, Tuck didn't want Charlie Darlington behind him with a gun.

Chapter Nine

When Kuruk, the Apache scout, returned to the company with word that he had located the mule train, Colonel Cuttrell ordered the men to a fast trot. He would rather have called for a full gallop, but Kuruk said they were getting close, and they had to pass through a narrow canyon to get there. The sun was already beginning to lower toward the mountains.

Kuruk led the way between steep, rocky walls that reduced the sky to a thin blue river overhead. Perfect spot for an ambush, Cuttrell thought. Chiricahua Apaches loved to roll heavy rocks down on their enemies, and this place was ideal for such an attack. But Kuruk assured him that he had scoured the upper reaches carefully, and they were safe.

Cuttrell hated to trust an Apache's word for that. Any one of them would sell the whole army to his brothers for whatever the Indian equivalent of a double eagle was. Those doubts were compounded by the fact that Kuruk was, himself, a Chiricahua, working for the army against his own kind.

But Kuruk had proved himself loyal so far, and Cuttrell thought the best way to destroy that trust was to reveal his doubts. Instead he kept a close eye on the man, directed his senior officers to do the same, and listened when Kuruk spoke, because he had always provided solid information. He was, Cuttrell had to admit, a brilliant scout. On a major operation, Cuttrell took along ten or twelve Apache scouts, who ran ahead of the troopers. They were tireless. If there was no enemy activity to report, by the time the column halted for the night, the scouts would have set up camp, brought down some deer or antelope or rabbits or turkey, and started cooking.

On a smaller sortie, like this one, he tried to always take Kuruk. The man's English was excellent. He was blessed with good cheer, strong legs and shoulders, a deep chest, and a handsome countenance. He kept his black hair tied down with a scarlet band, and regardless of whether he wore trousers or only a breechcloth, he was always dressed in a regulation gray CSA blouse, to which he had affixed buckskin fringe across breast, back, and sleeves, and decorated with feathers, bones, teeth, and other accoutrements he had collected. Despite those, when he moved, he was as silent as a shadow. At his waist he wore a cartridge belt, and he kept a canteen strapped across his chest and carried an old Spencer repeating rifle. On his feet were thigh-high moccasins with upturned toes, which he folded down to just below the knee. Other scouts had explained to him that the toe served as a kind of shield against sharp stones, or cactus thorns, and every Chiricahua of Cuttrell's acquaintance wore them that way.

Cuttrell didn't like the man, but he had little choice but to trust him, so he did. That practicality had served him well, as a soldier and an officer, so he saw no reason to change. As it happened, Kuruk was right about the canyon. They exited without incident and dropped into a depression that rose slightly on the far side and then sloped down toward the river. In the shallow bowl, Cuttrell saw the mule train. What was left of it, at any rate.

There wasn't much.

A bevy of vultures lifted off as the troopers bore down on them, an immense black cloud, the flapping of their wings like low thunder. They had been scavenging on a long line of mules and burros and some horses. The animals had been hacked to bits, and the carrion eaters had been at them, not just the vultures but coyotes, too, opportunists that they were. The ground beneath them was red from all the blood that had spilled. Guts had been yanked free of split-open carcasses, eyeballs eaten, in some cases brains strewn in the dirt.

The stink was sickening. To mask it, Cuttrell lifted a gloved hand to his mouth and sniffed the leather. All around him, troopers puked from their saddles or dropped to the ground to do it there, hunched over or on their knees.

Cuttrell estimated forty or so pack animals, most burdened with cargo, lay before him. Another fifteen horses, and a dozen burros. But among the animals were the people, maybe thirty of them. Civilians, it appeared, but there were plenty of weapons around, rifles and revolvers, swords and knives. They'd been outfitted like an army troop, even though they wore no uniforms.

"What do you make of it, sir?"

Cuttrell glanced at his second in command, Captain Hannigan. Ezra Hannigan was a burly, bearded brawler with short legs and an unexpectedly high, childlike voice. But his courage was unmatched, in Cuttrell's experience, and he was a dead aim with a rifle. "I think it's terrible," Cuttrell said.

"Yes, of course. I mean, why a mule train? If they're bringing in ghost rock from California, why not by rail? The Bayou Vermilion's faster and safer, I'd say."

"Maybe they were associated with one of the other rail companies. Dixie Rail has taken an interest in this region, I've heard. They might want to move quantities of ghost rock without letting Bayou Vermilion in on their plans. Even if not, Bayou might have refused them passage. Any number of reasons." Cuttrell looked at the corpses spread out below. "One thing's for certain, we'll not be asking them."

"No," Hannigan agreed. "We could ask, but they'll not be answering, will they?"

While his men dug a wide, shallow pit and laid the bodies into it, Cuttrell walked the line. The animals appeared to have been butchered where they stood, for the most part, although hoofprints in the soft earth indicated that some had either wandered off or been led away. Scattered here and there around the scene were foul-smelling, black, tarry puddles that no one had been able to explain.

What really made no sense, though—as if the entire scene weren't incomprehensible enough—was that the cargo had seemingly not been touched. Wagons mounded with ghost rock just sat there, the draft animals dead in their traces. Other beasts had cargo wrapped up and strapped to their backs, and the knots hadn't been undone, the wrappings were intact. Much of it was the standard stuff of any traveling caravan: cook pots, tools, food and water, rifles and shotguns and ammunition. But ghost rock was valuable stuff. Someone had gone to the trouble to mine it in the west and then transport it here, where someone else had attacked the mule train, then left with everybody dead but without the cargo.

Burning hotter and longer than coal and possessing other, less easily defined properties bordering on the preternatural—if not well across that line—ghost rock had become more valuable than gold in the years since its discovery after the Great Quake of '68. Ghost rock–powered weapons might yet turn the tide of the war for the Confederacy, and even now ships burning it steamed up and down rivers throughout the land. For anyone to have walked away from such a rich supply of it was staggering. Maybe they had taken all they could carry, but if they'd kept some of the draft animals alive, surely they could have left with more. Why kill all the people, then ignore the precious load they'd been hauling?

The reason for the attack appeared to be murder, and nothing more. Someone wanted to see blood spilled, to watch the vultures descend from the sky and bury their bald heads and scrawny necks in still-warm carcasses.

It was incomprehensible. Cuttrell had seen atrocities at the hands of Indians: white men trussed up like poultry and roasted over open flames. A man staked down, on his stomach, atop a colony of huge fire ants—they had eaten his eyes out first, then gone in through the openings they'd made and worked on the brain next. Women—he shuddered to think about the fates they had suffered.

But as much as he distrusted most red men, he was aware that each of those atrocities had been in response to something just as horrible done to them by whites. The roasted man had led a troop into an Indian encampment just before dawn one cold morning, and the soldiers had moved through the camp in an organized fashion, setting fire to each dwelling they came to and shooting everyone they found. A few braves had managed to get away, so the major who had led the assault had been identified and suffered accordingly. Indians could be vicious, but not senselessly so. If you followed the path of events back, in every case Cuttrell knew of, they were responding to cruelty, not initiating it.

This didn't seem like them. If they had attacked the train, they would have wanted the horses and mules. And they would have looted. They might not have been interested in the ghost rock—although that wasn't a given—but they would have taken guns and ammunition, some of the food, maybe clothing. Apaches loved to wear stolen hats, for one thing.

If it wasn't Apaches, who, then? Bayou Vermilion, taking revenge? But why? If they had turned down good money for hauling freight, that rejection would have sufficed. And if this had been payback of some sort, they would have wanted the ghost rock as well as the blood. No better fuel existed for powering a train.

He was left with one question on top of another, and he didn't like it. And he definitely didn't want to still be here when night enveloped the landscape. They could come back in the morning to recover as much of the ghost rock as they could.

"Get some earth over those bodies!" he shouted, clapping his hands twice for emphasis. "Let's go! Double time!"

The men were already moving as fast as they could. Nobody liked being here, breathing in the rank air, which seemed soupy with blood and death and whatever those viscous puddles were.

At Cuttrell's urging, some tried to work faster, with the result that they ran into one another, tripped, dropped mangled corpses on the ground. Cuttrell was about to call them away from the task, to put some distance between them and this place before full dark, when he heard Kuruk call out.

"This one's alive!" he cried. "It's a girl!"

"A girl?" Cuttrell echoed. He started toward where the scout was crouched, beside one of the few wagons that had fallen over and spilled its contents.

In a moment, Hannigan was beside him, legs scissoring quickly to keep up. "All the bodies I've seen have been men," he said. "No women or children. Just thirty-some well-armed men, and still, whatever got to them killed every mother's son of 'em. Without, as far as I can tell, firing a shot."

"No?"

"They've been . . . I don't know, torn apart. Knives, swords, something like that. No bullet holes, no arrows. It's the damnedest thing."

Cuttrell stopped in his tracks and clutched Hannigan's arm. "You're sure about this?"

"I haven't looked at every corpse," Hannigan said. "But the ones I've seen? Yes. I looked for bullet wounds. I looked for arrows, or parts of them, heads or shafts. Nothing."

"What the—" Cuttrell interrupted himself, remembering Kuruk and the girl. "Come on," he said, returning to his original course.

By the time he reached them, other troopers had gathered around. Kuruk was doing his best to keep the soldiers at arm's length from the girl. Cuttrell bulled through the pack. "How is she? Is she hurt?"

Kuruk was kneeling on the ground, holding a young woman's head and upper torso across his thighs. Her eyes were closed, her face badly bruised and cut in dozens of places. She didn't look to be more than eighteen or nineteen. Her hair was long and dark brown, matted and with twigs and dirt worked into it. She was a white girl, though, with fair skin and a scattering of freckles

across cheeks and nose. "She breathes," Kuruk said. "But she sleeps deep."

"Be careful with her, man," Cuttrell said. "Does she have any broken bones?"

"Don't think so. Anyhow, I haven't seen any."

"Where's Dr. Spring?" Cuttrell demanded. He had last seen the company surgeon examining corpses, to whom he could be no help. "Find him!"

A few minutes later, Hannigan returned with the surgeon. Spring was getting long in the tooth, and extended rides were hard on him. He looked pained when he crouched beside the girl, and one hand went to the small of his back, rubbing there momentarily before attending to her. He glanced at Cuttrell. "These men . . ." he said.

Cuttrell took his meaning. Checking her condition would require examining her entire body, since she was unconscious and couldn't tell them where she was hurt. It might have been awkward at any time, but worse with the troopers gathered around. "Don't you people have something better to do? Are all the bodies dealt with?"

Some of the men mumbled obedience and went to continue that unpleasant task, but others stayed to watch the inspection of the girl. Spring worked his hands up and down her limbs, coming at last to her torso. "I'm not finding anything, Colonel," he said. "She doesn't seem to be bleeding anywhere, either."

"Well, something happened to her. Look at her face. She looks like she fell out of a wagon and rolled. Where did you find her, Kuruk?"

"Behind this wagon, Colonel," the scout said. He glanced toward the sky. "There was shade, in the afternoon. But not the morning. Still, her skin is hardly burned."

"Perhaps she moved to stay in the shade," Spring said, prodding her torso.

"Unconscious?"

"Perhaps she passed out later."

"Maybe we can ask her, but not until she wakes up," Cuttrell said. He fixed his gaze on two of the privates who stood there watching. "Find a wagon that's upright and in good repair. Hitch a couple of our horses to it. We need to get this girl away from here."

"Yes, sir," the younger one said. He caught his companion's gaze, touched his arm, and they both raced away. Cuttrell watched them, hoping they had sense to actually pick a serviceable wagon.

"Sir," Spring said. Then, with more urgency, "Sir?"

"What is it?" Cuttrell demanded. He swung around toward Spring and the girl.

Her eyes were open. They were brown and wide, but for all they revealed, she might have been dead. "Can you see? Hello, miss. Can you hear me? Can you see?"

The girl's brutalized lips parted, but no sound escaped them. She stared past Cuttrell at nothing in particular.

"Her head, Kuruk," Cuttrell said. "Is it badly hurt?"

"Cut, bruised. Not bad."

"What's the matter with her, then?"

"We don't know what she's been through," Spring pointed out. "What she's seen. What happened to her."

"And we never will if we can't get her fixed up." He looked over his shoulder. "Where's my wagon?" he cried.

"Coming, sir!" someone answered.

"I want it now, damn it!"

"Yes, sir!"

He looked back at the girl. She hadn't budged. Her unseeing eyes remained open, her cracked, swollen lips slightly apart. "Who are you, girl?" he asked. "What are you doing here? Why are you the only female with this train?"

The thought briefly flitted through his mind that maybe there had been other women, but the Apaches had taken them. Then he remembered what Hannigan had said. No bullet holes, no arrows. "Kuruk, could Apaches have done this?"

"No," the scout answered. His response was immediate, without any consideration. Cuttrell didn't think he answered that way because he was trying to hide something—it was simply inconceivable to Kuruk that his people could have been involved. Cuttrell had reached the same conclusion, and Kuruk's certainty buttressed his belief.

"You're sure?"

"Sure," Kuruk said.

The scout was somewhere in his thirties, Cuttrell thought. But he looked ageless. He could have been fifty or seventeen. His hair was as black and shiny as a raven's wing, his dark skin almost unlined.

"I don't think so either," Cuttrell said. "But I would sure as hell like to know who did it."

They made camp a half mile away, on the other side of the narrow, rocky canyon. Colonel Cuttrell had considered posting guards to ward off any more animal predation and protect the ghost rock until it could be collected, but in the end had decided he didn't want to ask his men to do anything he wouldn't do, and he would never assign himself such a morbid duty. Kuruk was glad to be away from there. It was no good to spend a lot of time with the dead. He desperately hoped no troopers had taken any of the dead's possessions; if they had, those dead would be with them for a long time.

While the troopers set up camp, he watched over the girl. They had transported her here in the bed of the wagon, but then he had taken her out, wrapped her in blankets, and sat her up against a rock. When troopers came around to look at her, he warned them off with a fierce glare or a few well-chosen words. He knew he was pushing his luck—he was a scout, not a soldier, and any one of them had more authority than he did. A word to the colonel and he could be dismissed. But he felt protective of the girl, for reasons he couldn't explain, and the men seemed willing to let him deal with her. Perhaps, he thought, they were a little afraid of her—a young lady, by herself with the train, and alive when no one else had made it. There was something strange about her, and Kuruk could sense it. Probably the troopers could, too.

She hadn't spoken a word. She had blinked a few times, but if she was seeing anything at all, it wasn't in this world. She gave no indication that she understood anything that was said to her. Every soldier had come around at least once for a glimpse of her, but Cuttrell had them busy now, pitching tents, starting fires, cooking. Kuruk had a small fire going, Apache-style. Big fires were too hot to sit near, and too easy for enemies to see. This one would keep her warm, and he had done his best to make her comfortable. He spoke to her in his language, telling her tales of the old times, when White Painted Woman and Child-of-the-Water walked the earth.

The sun had nearly fled from the sky, but streaks of gold still sliced through the indigo onset of night. Kuruk watched the girl, wondering if she would fear the darkness, or embrace it, or even notice it. As he observed her, her eyes rolled up in her head, and then her head tilted and turned a little. Kuruk followed her gaze, which seemed to be focused on something for the first time. He caught a glimpse of a golden eagle, soaring overhead and disappearing behind the hills. After a moment, it swooped back out from another position, cut some arcs across the sky. Kuruk watched it, and watched the girl. Her head moved with the hawk—not, he thought, in response to it, but in time with it, in perfect harmony. She moved when it did. Then it vanished once again, and didn't return.

"You know him? Brother eagle?" he asked.

Her chin lowered and her head shifted back to its usual position, eyes looking straight ahead. Maybe she *did* see. Maybe there was more going on inside her than he could tell.

"What do they call you, girl?"

She gave the same answer she had all the other times he'd asked. Silence. A blank stare.

"Very well," Kuruk said. "Then I will call you Little Wing. She who speaks with the birds. Do you like that?"

Silence. The same blank stare.

"No argument. Good. Little Wing it is, then. Welcome to D Troop, Little Wing. Twelfth Cavalry, Army of the Confederate States of America, out of Fort Huachuca in the Arizona Territory. My name is Kuruk, Little Wing. And believe me, I know what it's like to be alone."

She didn't respond. They sat, Kuruk speaking softly in English and Apache. The last light fled as the eagle had, and darkness settled, broken only by Kuruk's fire and those, farther away, around which the soldiers sat.

With the dark, Little Wing became agitated. Kuruk noticed that if the firelight flagged, she tensed. At first it was barely noticeable, but it became more pronounced the more it happened. He fed more wood into the fire, and built it up again, and she visibly relaxed. After a while longer, her eyes closed. Kuruk kept talking for a while, until her deep, steady breathing told him that she had fallen asleep.

Almost at once, she started to twitch. Her fingers bunched toward her palms, then relaxed. Her shoulders bobbed up and down. Her lips parted, moved, as if she were trying to speak, but no sound came out. Her eyes moved behind her eyelids. He expected whimpers, perhaps even cries. She was dreaming, and the dream didn't strike him as a pleasant one. A nightmare. He stroked her cheek, her neck, her shoulder, whispered to her of fine things, of clear rushing streams and long fast rides on horseback and the glory of a spring morning in the desert, and he kept it up until she appeared to be at peace once more.

He didn't sleep all night, but sat up watching her to make sure it didn't happen again.

"Be at peace, Little Wing," he told her, over and over. "Nothing will hurt you now. Nothing will ever hurt you again."

Chapter Ten

Nate McHale wasn't anxious to spend another night out on that haunted range, watching over cattle but knowing all the while that something was stalking them—and possibly him. He had spent hours with the bodies of Pinky and Hopkin. He'd tried not to look, but every now and then curiosity got the better of him. It wasn't so bad in the darkness, but as the sun rose and the flies began to swarm them and the stench thickened, he allowed himself short glances, then longer ones. At one point he quit fighting the urge and walked in a slow circle around them, observing the vicious cuts that flayed away flesh and exposed white muscle and bone and pink organs. Blood had soaked into the ground, and the flies liked that too, they liked it just fine, as if it were a holiday spread and they the invited guests.

He didn't know what could have done that to two human beings, men who were armed and knew the country and, he had to assume, wouldn't have taken foolish chances. Whatever it had been, he had no interest in meeting it.

But his options were limited. He could quit Mr. Tibbetts's employ, and find himself on the trail, penniless and jobless, trying to find someplace else that would hire on a cowboy who had one leg shorter than the other, could barely write his own name, and had a newfound fear of the dark. Or he could stay and do what he was told. Anyway, the old-timers said Mr. Tibbetts tried to be generous to his hands, once he'd closed a deal and sold whatever stock he meant to for the year. Nate wanted to hang on until then, if he could.

At least he wasn't alone. He was with Gamewell Reisen, one of the men who'd been with the J Cross T the longest. Reisen had a full beard that was sprouting wiry white hairs along with the brown, small eyes hidden behind folds of flesh but that missed nothing, and the look of a man who had faced every kind of adversity at one time or another. Most of those challenges had left scars of some kind—the first time Nate had seen Reisen with his shirt off, he was astonished the man was still alive, given the patchwork of cuts and burns and bullets that had left their marks.

Joining them was a man from the Broken M, Montclair's outfit, a man who introduced himself only as Colby. He was a dark man with black hair and pale eyes and skin so deeply tanned he might have been an Indian. Even his clothes were black. It was, Nate thought, almost like he was his own shadow, or carried it close all the time. He wore a pair of revolvers (their grips black, not white—well, once white, anyway—like Nate's own), and there was a Winchester rifle in the scabbard on his big black mare that looked like it had seen plenty of use. Though Colby didn't say much, he carried himself with the air of a capable man, and Nate figured that capability extended to violence when it was called for.

Tomorrow, they would combine the divvied-up herd into one summer pasture. It would be crowded, but already the monsoon storms were greening the grass, so the hope was that the stock would have enough to eat through the summer months. Those who had night guard duty tonight could choose to be excluded from tomorrow's drive, but the work would go faster with every hand taking part. Nate figured he could survive tonight and tomorrow, then get some rest after that. The important thing was to make sure whatever had been preying on the herd was stopped, before they lost any more head.

Nate, Reisen, and Colby would stand watch on the west side of the herd, nearest the mountains. Three other cowboys had taken up positions on the east side, facing the valley. They had a couple of dogs with them. The men had arranged a signal: two shots fired in quick succession, then a pause, then a third shot, meant "come quick."

So far, the night had been a quiet one. The herd was settled, peaceable. Most of the time, clouds blotted out the moon, but once in a while it managed to peek through. When it did, Nate took advantage of the illumination to study the herd and the surrounding landscape, watching for anything that seemed out of place.

"Nate," Reisen said softly. The moon had shone briefly, and he was still standing up and surveying the distance as it slipped back under the blanket of clouds. His focus on the animals, he hadn't even heard Reisen walk up behind him.

"What?" he asked. The man's sudden appearance had startled him, and he snapped his response. "Sorry."

"Walk down here with me a minute."

"Down where?"

"Just over here." Reisen led him down a little footpath from the shelf they had settled on to watch over the herd. He was keeping his voice quiet, and Nate asked him why.

"It's Colby," Reisen said.

"What about him?"

"What about him? Haven't you smelt him?"

Nate tried to think if he had. "I guess, some."

"He smells like a javelina climbed inside his skin and died there."

"I ain't been able to draw a full breath through my nose since spring," Nate said. "So I can't hardly smell nothing." He glanced out toward the herd. "Cow shit, but that's about it."

"Have you noticed that if you stand near him, it's colder'n anywheres else?"

"It is?"

"Do you know when you step outside if it's rainin' or sunny? Do you know if it's day or night, right now?"

"Sure, it's night."

"Well, go over and talk to Colby a minute, and tell me if there isn't something off about him."

"What do you think it is?"

"I don't have any idea. Maybe a javelina really did die inside him. Maybe he rolls in their scat. He's just a mite odd, all I'm sayin'."

Nate couldn't think of anything to say to that. He looked at Reisen in the dim light for a few seconds, then walked back up onto the rocky shelf. Colby was sitting away from the fire, carving something out of the sole of his boot with the point of a knife. Nate went closer to him than he ordinarily would have. "Quiet night," he said.

"Seems like."

"Figger it'll stay that way?"

"Can't say."

"You from these parts, or what?"

Colby took the knife point out of his boot and sat holding it, point more or less directed toward Nate. "You always talk so much?"

"Reckon I'm just a little nervous." Nate took as deep a breath as he could through the plugged-up morass that was his nose. He caught a faint scent of something sour, and then he tasted it, and was glad he couldn't smell much of anything. "Is it true your boss has never been on the back of a horse? He rides everywheres in a wagon?"

"I look like I've known him his whole life?"

"I'm just sayin' what I heard." Nate took a step closer to Colby. Colby didn't lower the knife. "You need something?"

"No, sorry," Nate said. He had gone close enough to sense what Reisen had mentioned, the circle of frigid air that seemed to surround the man. The night was warm and so was the fire, but being near Colby was like standing too far from the stove on a winter's day. He could feel the heat from the fire on his back, but the side that faced Colby was chilled. He stepped away, quickly. "Didn't mean nothing."

"Keep your distance, then."

"Sorry," Nate said again.

"I got to work with you for a spell," Colby said. "Don't mean we're friends."

"It surely don't," Nate said. "Don't mean nothing like it."

He hurried back down to where Reisen waited. "You're right," he said. "Something about that man ain't right."

"I told you."

"What do you reckon it is?"

"You asked me that before. You think I figured it out standin' here?"

"It's just strange, is all."

"Hell yes, it's strange," Reisen said. "That's why I told you to smell him."

Nate was about to say something else when one of the beeves let out a terrified scream. Anyone who doesn't think cattle can scream, he thought, has never heard what he did in that moment. It lasted for almost a minute, and instantly the herd was on edge, lowing and shifting about. "What was that?" he asked.

"Let's find out!" Reisen said. "Colby! Grab a torch!"

The men ran to the horses. Colby came behind, with the torch, and the three of them mounted up and rode out into the restive herd. They couldn't find the cow that had cried out, though, or any that had been butchered. The hands from the other side had heard the commotion as well, and rode in. After a while, they gave up and went back to their separate sides. The cattle were still spooked, but gradually settling again.

"You reckon we scared it off?" Nate said when they were gathered around the diminished fire again.

"Doubt it," Colby said.

"Why?"

"Think about it. Something can kill a creature as big as a cow or a bull—not just kill them, but really tear 'em apart, like folks say. And then do the same to a man. You think you're gonna scare that?"

"What do you think it is?" Reisen asked.

Colby hadn't sat down. He reached for the buckle of his gun

belt, and undid it, stooping to lower the belt gently to the ground. "Well, I doubt that it's a man, precisely," he said.

"Some kind of animal, maybe?" Nate said. "A bear or a big lion or something?"

"I don't think so," Colby said. He took the knife from his sheath, balanced it by its point on the tip of his finger for a second, then put it down by the gun belt.

"Not a man or an animal?" Reisen asked. "What, then?"

Nate was getting anxious. Colby was a strange one, that was for certain. Nate didn't understand what he was doing, why he was putting down all his weapons, when whatever it was might still be out there. The odd behavior frightened him even more than the cow's screaming had. Sweat trickled down his ribs, and his knees started to quiver.

"Well," Colby said, gazing into the fire. "I reckon it'd be something you've never seen. And if you ever did . . ." He looked up, his gaze meeting Nate's, only his eyes weren't the same as they had been; no longer pale, they were as yellow as the flames. His face was changing, too, elongating, the features kind of melting in and becoming indistinct. When his mouth opened it showed rows of teeth that looked huge and razor-sharp. ". . . Well," he continued. "I don't guess you'd see it for very long, and you'd never get to tell anybody about it."

"What the hell—" Reisen started to say. At the same time, he pawed his gun free of its holster. Before he could pull the trigger, Colby had cleared the distance between them. His hands—but they weren't hands anymore, Nate realized, they were something else, something with ferocious claws—were outthrust, and he slashed at Reisen. He cut from the older man's collarbone down to his gut, spewing blood and snapping through bone and releasing organs from their inner cages, and Reisen didn't even have a chance to cry out.

Nate wanted to scream and he wanted to shoot the thing that had been Colby, but his guts turned to water and his knees wouldn't hold still, and when he managed to free his gun from his pants, his hands wouldn't grasp it and it fell into the fire.

He reached for it, knowing the flames would burn but that wouldn't be as bad as what had happened to Reisen. But he barely managed to touch it before the thing was on him, and its claws were just as sharp and wicked as they'd looked, and so were its teeth.

Chapter Eleven

The posse had been riding away from the Huachuca Mountains, but as they followed the killer's path, Tuck noticed that it was starting to turn back toward them. The sun had dropped below peaks that had become familiar, though seen from farther south than he had ever been. They were in Mexico for sure, and the Mexicans didn't always appreciate lawmen from north of the border. "He's circling around," he told the marshal. "Heading back toward the territory."

"Back toward the mountains, anyhow," Turville agreed. "Could be he thinks he lost us."

"Or he doesn't care," Tuck said. They were riding through a grassy meadow, dotted here and there by a yucca standing up as if to wave at passersby. "Maybe that's where home is, after all, and he's going there to make his stand."

"He's got some pardners there, mebbe."

"Hard to say."

"We're losin' the daylight," Turville said.

"You told the men they could rest at full dark."

"I know. Sorry now I did. We're gainin' on him, and I'd hate to lose him."

"We don't, you might lose the rest of your posse."

Turville spat into the grass. "I know it, Bringloe. Good thing about a posse is they're men who volunteered to ride for justice, with no promise of reward or anything but a long, hard haul and the chance of gettin' shot. Bad thing is they're amateurs who give up too easy. I could use a few more like you."

"I haven't done anything yet to help you."

"You were the only one who could follow those tracks the first night, in the rain. You helped me hold the men together earlier. I don't know if it's your officer trainin', or just your natural disposition, but when you ain't drinkin', you're a good man to have around."

Tuck just gave him a single nod. The mention of drink set his heart to racing and his thoughts to wandering. He remembered the pleasure of that warm sensation in the throat and gullet, like swallowing a lump of hot coal right out of the fire. He thought about the fogginess that came with three or four drinks—that had come, in earlier days, with one or two—the buzz that filled his mind, like there were bees under his hat, and that prevented other thoughts and memories from taking up space in his head.

He realized Turville was watching him. "Sorry," Tuck said. "Forgot myself for a minute."

"Reckon forgettin's the point of it, isn't it? The drinkin'?"

"That's a big part of it."

"What are you tryin' to disremember?"

"That's complicated, Marshal."

"The war? A woman?"

"Those are part of it."

"You don't want to talk about it?"

"Not hardly," Tuck replied. "I did, I more'n likely wouldn't drink to keep it all away."

"I won't ask, then. Again. You want to tell me, though, you can."

"Thanks," Tuck said. The last thing he wanted to do was to talk about things he was so desperate to forget. But the marshal was the first man in a long time who had offered anything other than scorn and perhaps a kick in the rear. He couldn't say the sensation it raised in him was unwelcome. Instead of saying anything more, he checked the trail to make sure they were still on the right path, then studied the valley ahead. "What's that?" he said after a couple of minutes.

Turville followed Tuck's pointing hand. "Looks like a horse. No saddle, no rider."

"Wild, you think?"

"Can't rightly say."

The animal was browsing a bushy mesquite, probably picking off beans that were beginning to swell with seeds. It didn't race off as they drew nearer, nor did there seem to be others with it. She was a skewbald mare, chestnut and white, and looked to be well cared for, her mane brushed and clipped, her coat smooth.

"No, she's not wild," Turville said when they were close enough to tell. "Not lookin' like that." He looked back over his shoulder. "Any of you men handy with a rope?" he asked. "Looks like somebody lost a horse."

"Perhaps it belongs to your killer?" Maier said. "Perhaps he hides in the tall grass?"

"She don't look rode too hard," the marshal answered. "And she's got no tack on her."

"I don't know as we have time to return a lost horse," Tuck said.

"We might could happen to pass someone who knows where she belongs," Turville said. "Hate to do that and not have tried to collect her."

"Not much light left."

The marshal pulled back on his reins and stopped his mount in front of Tuck's. Tuck had to rein in quickly. "You want to say somethin' to me, Bringloe?"

"I'm just saying, we're trying to track a killer. You want to spend time chasing after a horse when it's nearly dark, and you promised the men we'd take a break for the night when it was. Seems like you need to decide what you want to get done here, and do that thing."

Turville chewed on his lower lip. "I reckon you got a point," he said. "Might could be she'll follow us on her own, anyhow."

"She might," Tuck said, without conviction.

The trail they followed veered away from the horse, but she did follow, at a distance. The posse members' animals whickered to her, and she answered, holding some sort of equine conversation that humans could never understand. A short while later, with the men once again beginning to grouse about how late it was getting, how the sun was gone from the sky and dusk was making it hard to see, they rounded a low hill and saw a small rancho spread out before them. No pastures were fenced, but near the hacienda stood a corral and a barn and a couple of other outbuildings.

"You know whose place that is?" Tuck asked him.

"No. Don't typically find myself in Mexico."

The house was small, made of adobe bricks that had weathered in the harsh winters and wet summers of the high desert.

"You think that horse came from here?"

"Might could be. Nearest ranch we've seen."

"No horses in the corral," Tuck observed. "Nor any other stock I can see. No lamp burning inside the house, either."

"Trail's heading straight for it," the marshal pointed out. "I got a bad feelin' about this, Bringloe."

Tuck had the same feeling. "Let's go," he said. He urged his mount on. Turville shouted something to the others, and did the same. Riding at a full gallop, they reached the ranch house in just a few minutes. The corral gate stood open, as did the barn door. Tracks from multiple horses had crisscrossed the trail they were following, obscuring it at least partway. The horse they had seen was no doubt one of these, but there was no way to tell if the others had been taken, or just allowed to wander away.

Turville reined up in the yard. "Hello in the house!" he shouted. "This is Marshal Hank Turville, from the United States! We're on the trail of a killer! Anybody here?"

No one answered. Turville and Tuck exchanged worried looks, and Turville dropped to the ground. "Anybody home?" he called. "Hello!"

Still, the house was quiet. A gentle breeze fingered the leaves of a pair of sycamores that shaded the house's south side. Tuck could hear the rustle and jingle of his mounted companions, but that was all.

On the wind, he thought he smelled something.

He thought he smelled death.

"I'm goin' in," Turville declared.

"Not alone," Tuck said. He dismounted and drew his borrowed rifle from its saddle scabbard. "This isn't good," he said quietly.

"Folks who live here could be in town, mebbe. Or out on the range."

"Can't hurt to look."

"Careful, though. And with iron in your hand. You men wait here," Turville told the others. "Eyes wide. Shout or shoot if you see anything."

"Anything like what?" Darlington asked.

"Anything at all," the marshal answered. "We'll be back directly."

He and Tuck stepped lightly to the door. They had announced themselves, so if anybody was inside, lying in wait, there would be no surprising them. Just the same, neither man wanted to be the first to present a target.

The door was ajar. Turville went in first, a revolver in his fist. "Hello?" he said.

Tuck already knew what they would find inside. An empty house had a special kind of silence to it. This one held that silence inside, and something more, the odor he had tasted on the breeze. "They're dead," he said.

"Who?" Turville asked. Even as the word escaped his lips, he paused and his face wrinkled up. "Yeah, you're right, Bringloe." To the house's dim interior, he added, "Anyone here? We're comin' in."

No answer met them but the stench of death, thickening the farther they went into the house. They hurried through it, not talking now, looking for the dead.

They were in the bedroom. Three of them, all Mexicans. A man, a woman, and a boy of about ten. The man had no shirt on, and his body was thin, almost hairless. The woman wore a dress—or what was left of it—that had been patched so many times there were more patches than original fabric. They were both on the bed, though the woman's legs dangled over the side. The boy was on the floor at the foot of the bed, whatever clothes he had been wearing reduced to ribbons.

The position of the woman, halfway off the bed, wasn't the only thing about the tableau that reminded Tuck of Daisie's body, back at Senora Soto's.

All three of these people had been gutted the way Daisie had: gashes all over them, blood pooled around them, organs exposed to the air. The flies had already come and were crawling around, creating the impression of writhing patches of dark shadow. The reek made Tuck's gorge rise, and he fought to keep from vomiting.

"This was him," Turville said, his voice thick with anger. And something else. Disgust, and maybe fear, Tuck thought. He didn't blame the man a bit. Terror had snaked into his soul at the smell outside, and the closer they came to this room, the deeper it had burrowed. It owned him, now. The killer they were chasing was something more than just a man—or something less. He was someone so broken, so inhuman, that he not only could do these things to other people, but he wanted to. He liked doing them. Nobody could force himself against his own will to commit such evil acts.

"We've got to find this bastard," Tuck said. "Soon."

"Won't rest until we do, Bringloe."

"You promised the men they could take a break. We'll go faster in the morning if we all get some shut-eye."

Turville sighed. "Let's get out of here," he said. "I can't take this a second longer." He didn't wait for Tuck's answer, but stormed from the room, from the house. Outside, he took deep breaths. Tuck joined him. They were still too close to the house for the air to be pure; the reek of death hung heavy in the air, and that other scent lay underneath it, the sour stink that Tuck believed belonged to the killer. Still, it was better than the air inside.

"What'd you find, Hank?" Hendershott asked.

"Mexican couple and their boy. They're dead. Cut all up, like Daisie was."

"But he's not in there? The owl hoot we're after?"

"No sign of him. Same man, though, I'm sure."

"So what's next?"

"Next we get away from here and get some rest. Few hours. Then we get back on the trail, and we ride hard until we find him and put a rope around his neck. We got to assume he's got a fresh mount and a full belly."

"Finally," Maier said. "I think I am three inches shorter than when we started out."

"But just as ornery," Turville said. "Come on, let's find a place to camp where we can't smell the dead."

Chapter Twelve

They made camp on a ridge from which they could see the dim outline of the Huachucas against the marbled sky. Moonlight tinged the clouds with white, and lightning in the mountains lit them from within, like someone carrying a candle past the windows of a large house. Tuck felt exposed up on the crest of the hill, but during the summer monsoon, they didn't dare try to sleep in low-lying areas. A storm miles away could send floodwaters rushing down a wash or even across a flat plain, and anyone caught unawares when the flood hit might never be found again.

The men wasted no time dismounting, getting a fire going and some coffee, beans, and biscuits under way, and trying to relax. Tuck shared Turville's sense of urgency, but the men needed a break. And they really would make better time in the morning, when they could clearly follow the trail, than they would in the dark. Outside the firelight, what seemed like millions of crickets sent up a wall of noise that was almost a physical object, so pervasive was it.

Once coffee was brewed, Hendershott downed a cup in about thirty seconds and poured another one. Halfway through, he set his cup down, rose to his feet, scratched his belly, and announced his intention to piss like a tanked-up mule. He slipped from the circle of light, heading partway down the hill, and was soon lost to the darkness. Tuck could hear him, though, grumbling and scratching, and then heard his rushed stream striking the rocky slope.

When the stream ended, Tuck expected him to find his way back to the fire.

Instead, the man cried out in what sounded like pure terror.

Tuck jumped to his feet. He hadn't taken off his boots, and he had kept his rifle close at hand. "Fill your hands, boys!" he shouted, snatching up the weapon. He pointed to the west. "Hank, Alf, Darlington, Nickles, you go around that way, see if you can head off whoever it is. Vander Tuig, Winston, you come with me, and we'll try to flush him toward them."

Turville was ready in seconds, but Maier insisted on pulling his boots on. The desert was full of thorns and creatures that bit, so Tuck didn't blame him, but wished he hadn't doffed them to begin with. Vander Tuig and Darlington followed his orders without hesitation.

Before they had left the fire's glow, though, there was another pained cry from Hendershott, and then a sound like a sack of meat being dropped from a height, followed by silence. It was too late to help him, Tuck feared.

For a few seconds, he had wondered if Hendershott had really met the killer they were after, or had perhaps stepped on a rattlesnake or a Gila monster or something. But now he smelled a familiar stench, and knew the murderer was nearby.

"Don't shoot if you can't see who's behind him!" he called. "We don't want to plug each other! But if you get a clear shot, take it! We got to stop this hombre!"

He ran toward where Hendershott's last sounds had come from, wishing he hadn't been sitting so near to the fire. He didn't have his night vision yet, and doubted if the others did. If some posse member didn't put a round in another in the next few minutes, he'd be pleasantly surprised.

The racket of the men racing down the hill, stumbling, crashing into mesquite or yucca and yowling from the piercing of thorns and sharp-edged leaves like dagger blades, drowned out whatever sounds the killer might have made. A couple of shots were fired, but by wild, inexperienced men shooting out of fear. Then there were more screams, and a grim certainty filled Tuck. Someone else had met the killer, and had fallen, like Hendershott.

The crickets, Tuck noted, had gone silent. "Anybody see him now?" he shouted. "Anyone see the killer?"

His query was greeted by a chorus of negatives. Too many were dying; somehow the killer had an edge in the darkness. "Find the man nearest you, then, and get back to the fire!" he shouted. "If you see the killer, shoot, but don't go looking for him!"

He headed back up himself and watched the others return in pairs. Turville and Darlington, Maier and Vander Tuig. "Where's Winston?" Tuck asked. "And Nickles?"

"I heard at least one go down," Turville said.

"I thought it was two," Darlington added. "I thought sure I heard Winston start to scream. Then he choked off, like his throat was full of water."

Or blood, Tuck thought. He didn't say it. Instead, he walked to the fire's edge. "Winston!" he called. "Nickles! You men out there?"

No answer came back. A minute later, one cricket started its song again, then more joined in.

"You!" Tuck called. "We're close, now. You'd best make your peace with whoever you care to. Before another sun sets you'll be swinging from a gallows!"

It was hard to tell over the night music of insects, but there might have been something like low, quiet laughter mixed in with them.

Before Tuck returned to the firelight, Turville came up beside him. "You did good work there, Captain Bringloe," he said. "The men followed your orders like they had been drilled and trained."

"We lost three of 'em," Tuck said.

"Not your doing. I don't know what that thing is out there, man or beast or somethin' else. But like you said, we're close now.

Don't appear as if we can beat him in the dark, but come daylight we'll be on his trail."

"We got to finish him."

"We will," the marshal said. "I just wanted to tell you, I was impressed."

"Thanks."

Turville stepped away. Tuck stood a few moments longer at the edge of night, wishing his vision could cut through the darkness. He wanted a look at his quarry. He wanted to know if his enemy was human or something else.

He appreciated Hank Turville's words. His days of giving orders, much less expecting them to be obeyed, were long past. He had missed that, he realized. His plan had been thrown together on the spur of the moment, and it had failed, as those of men in battle often did. He would take more time to develop the next one, if it came to that.

Now he regarded the men sitting around the fire, nursing their wounds, thinking about fallen comrades. Their eyes were hollow, in the way of men who've been through battle and come out of it when others haven't. These men were merchants, cowboys, laborers, not soldiers. But they had come together for a common purpose, and there was a camaraderie born of that, of riding together and facing death, and living to see another hour or day or decade. They had a mission, and that mission joined them even when their separate lives would not have. That mission had become Tuck's, too. It was the first time in a very long while that he'd had a goal beyond finding the next drink or a hole to sleep in out of the weather. By bringing him on this quest, Hank Turville had rekindled a sense of duty in him, one that only came, in his experience, from trying to help others without regard for what it might do for himself.

That sense of duty, that camaraderie—these were things he had lost when he'd left the army behind.

And there was something else he'd been missing, but he recognized it when he walked back into the firelight and saw how the men looked at him.

He had almost forgotten it was possible, but here it was.

These men respected him.

That, he hadn't known for years. That had vanished from his life. Now it was back. Maybe it wouldn't last long, but he would hold on to it for as long as he could.

It was better, he told himself, than that first splash of whiskey across the tongue and into the throat.

He took his place beside the fire, and he felt a warm glow that came only from within, and he gave it back to these men who had carried guns on his say-so, and put themselves in harm's way, not for themselves but for a dead whore and a family they hadn't known.

He would have to thank the marshal, when he had a chance. For making him join the posse, for trusting him with weapons and a horse, and for giving him back something he had thought was lost forever.

That would wait until morning, though. For tonight, he needed some sleep. Tomorrow would be a hard day, and there would be more dying before it was done.

Chapter Thirteen

As a soldier, Delbert Cuttrell had slept on the hard ground, on cold nights and hot, in rain and snow, with dangers human and animal alike lurking about. Now that he was older, though, and in a command position, he greatly preferred sleeping in a bed. Even better, a bed with Sadie's lush, soft, warm body beside him. Tents and scorpions and snakes and unforgiving earth were suitable for enlisted men and junior officers, he had decided. It toughened them up. Creature comforts distracted the mind from the tasks necessary for survival. At his age, he was thoroughly educated about the threats a soldier might face, and no longer needed the reminders offered by uneasy rest and an aching back.

So when Hannigan came to his tent that night, clearing his throat in the absence of any solid door upon which to knock, Cuttrell was already awake. "Damn it, Ezra, spit if you need to, but don't stand there all night making those repulsive noises."

"Sorry, Colonel," Hannigan said. He ducked inside, carrying a lit candle. "One of the men on picket detail reported—well, he's not sure what he reported."

"What does that mean, Ezra? It's too late at night for riddles."

"He thought he heard a sound," Hannigan explained. "Footsteps, he thought. Not animal, he said, but human. He challenged, but got no response. He took another trooper and they went out with a lantern, but they found no one."

"Apaches," Cuttrell said. "They can be devilishly quiet when they want to."

"No, sir. At least, according to the guard."

"If he didn't see anything, how does he know?"

"He's . . . not quite sure, sir. He says the sound was there, and then it wasn't. It didn't fade away, or drift away. It was just that sudden. There, and not there."

"We can't have pickets who are inebriated on duty," Cuttrell said. "That's a good way to kill us all."

"I smelled his breath myself. It's Carlton. He's as sober a man as has ever worn a uniform."

"That's not saying much."

"Still," Hannigan went on. "He's sober, I'd swear to it."

"What do you think he heard, then?"

"I have no idea."

"And you'd like me to do what, exactly?"

"I . . . I'm not sure, Colonel."

"Do you think Carlton really heard something?"

"He says he did."

Cuttrell tilted his head and narrowed his eyes. Finally, Hannigan continued. "I believe him, sir. Or I believe that he thinks he did."

"My best guess is still Apaches," Cuttrell said. "Double the pickets. No, triple them. If they hear something else they can't identify, tell them to shoot. Better we wake up the men for no reason than let them sleep through an attack."

"Yes, sir," Hannigan said. "I'll take care of it."

"See that you do," Cuttrell said. When Hannigan was gone, he tried to settle in again, but there was no comfort to be found on the ground. He thought about Sadie, alone in their bed, and the pleasures offered by a mattress and a pillow, the soothing weight of a quilt, and he knew that he had slept his last for this night. Morning couldn't come soon enough.

Kuruk watched the increase in the number of posted guards with trepidation. He'd heard what sounded almost like the rasp of booted feet out in the darkness. He slept lightly at the best of times, and even more so when he was away from the fort. This night, he had not even tried, because he wanted to keep an eye on Little Wing. He had heard, too, the muffled conversation between the troopers, Carlton and Root, and though he couldn't catch every word, he got the gist of it.

Most of the soldiers would assume an Apache raid was imminent. Although he'd been a scout for years, their assumption would lead them to doubt his loyalty. He was barely trusted as it was; any time there was Apache trouble, that trust was stretched ever thinner. It hadn't sounded like Apache to him, though. If a raid were in the offing, a lone brave wouldn't venture so near the army camp. Even if one did, he wouldn't wear boots.

And though he had at first assumed he'd heard the scrape of a boot sole against a stone, when he listened to it again in his mind, it sounded more like a hoof than a boot.

At any rate, it wasn't what he had heard that disturbed him. It was what he sensed. A presence, in the darkness. Malevolent and strong. He was almost glad the troopers couldn't see it, because if they could, they would engage it. Who knew what harm might befall them if they did?

Little Wing was moving in her sleep. She lay on her left side. Her legs, bent at the knees, shifted as if she were walking up a steep staircase. Her hands reached, grasped, and released empty air. Her brow wrinkled, her nose twitched, her mouth opened and closed, releasing occasional mewling sounds. Kuruk moved to her side, stroked her shoulder, her soft cheek.

"Be still, little one," he told her. "No harm will come to you."

Her only response was a frightened whimper. That worried Kuruk more than the fears of the troopers. What was she seeing that scared her so?

He brushed her brow, which was damp with sweat. "Fear not," he whispered. "Kuruk watches over you."

After a few minutes, she relaxed again. Her hands opened, her lips parted, the twitches and tics of her face stilled.

He sat beside her and watched the soldiers, anxious for the dawn, peer into the impenetrable night.

She woke with the sun.

It had just edged from behind the far hills, painting the undersides of the clouds with shades of rose and salmon. Kuruk watched it, spoke a few words of thanks, and when he looked back at her, Little Wing was sitting up. She rubbed her eyes with her fists, and a smile broke across her face. The effect, Kuruk thought, was much like that of the sun on the eastern sky.

"How do you feel?" he asked, not expecting an answer.

"Re . . . redemp . . . tion," she said. Her voice was thick, raspy as a rusted hinge that hadn't been used in months. She had spoken the single word slowly, as if trying it out for the first time. Kuruk handed her a canteen and she drank deeply, then handed it back with an open-mouthed smile. Her eyes were wide and bright, her gaze level.

"Redemption, did you say?"

"Re . . . birth," she said haltingly. "Re . . . flection."

He understood the words, but not the meaning. Not the way she was using them. "I don't follow you."

"Sun."

"Yes, the sun is rising. Giving birth to a new day?"

"Each morning . . . births a new day . . . a new chance for re . . . demption."

"Yes," he said. "But—"

"Don't," she said.

"Don't what?"

"Comp . . . licate."

"Complicate how?" He wasn't sure he had ever been so lost in a conversation. White folks were always saying crazy things, but not like this.

She frowned then, and twisted her head and shoulders away from him, as if he had hurt her feelings in some way.

"What's wrong?" he asked.

She glanced his way, shook her head. She acted, Kuruk thought, like someone just learning to speak a new language, with complicated concepts in her head that she couldn't find the words for. He had been the same way as a young man, trying to learn the white man's tongue.

"I am Kuruk," he said. He patted his chest when he said it. "Kuruk. Who are you?"

She met his gaze. "Blessed," she said.

He touched his chest once more. "Kuruk. What is your name?"

"Call me . . ." she began. "Little Wing."

He was about to ask her more, though he doubted that she would provide any real answers. Still, he wanted to know if she had heard him call her that, or if it really was her name. He wanted to know where she had come from, why she was traveling with the mule train. He wanted to know what had happened to the train.

But before he could, Ezra Hannigan strode up to him. "Colonel Cuttrell wants her in that wagon," he said. "We're rolling out of here soon."

"Are you ready to travel?" Kuruk asked her.

"Blessed," she said again.

"When the wagon's ready," Kuruk said, "she will be, too."

Sadie opened her eyes and looked at the ceiling. It was unfamiliar, not the hammered tin ceiling of the bedroom she shared with Del. There were sheets twisted around her, and she was on her back, so in somebody's bed.

She shifted her head just enough to see a muscular arm and a hairy back. Jimmy, she remembered. Jimmy McKenna. "God," she said.

"Mmmh?" he answered. He turned toward her, blinking. "What?"

"I was just suffering a momentary bout of self-respect," Sadie said. "Don't worry about it; it'll pass soon enough." She sat up in the bed. Her head felt like someone had taken a hatchet to it. Unconcerned by her nakedness, she stood and walked to a table. "Where's that bottle?"

"Do you have to say things like that?" McKenna asked her. "That's cruel. Don't you know how that makes me feel?"

"I know I had a bottle here," she said.

"The laudanum again? You just woke up, darling. Do you really need it already?"

She found the bottle, underneath where her bloomers had been tossed. Not broken, thankfully. There was no spoon handy, or glass, so she unstoppered it and took a sip right from its mouth.

"'Darling?'" she repeated. "Jimmy, let's not pretend what we have here has anything to do with love."

"But, Sadie, I—"

She slammed the bottle down on the tabletop, hard. "Don't!" she said. "Don't you say that. Don't say anything to me that you wouldn't say to one of Senora Soto's girls. That's all this is, Jimmy. The only difference is that I'm not asking you for money."

"That isn't true, Sadie. It's not like—"

"It is for me," she said, cutting him off. She checked the bottle, to make sure she hadn't cracked the glass, then walked around to his side of the bed. He was sitting up now, his gaze fixed on the sway of her heavy breasts. She sat beside him, reached under the sheets. "In fact," she said, "that's exactly how I want you to treat me. Right now, Jimmy. If I were one of her girls, what would you do with me right now?"

She felt him stirring to life under her hand, and she smiled. The attack of self-respect had passed even quicker than she'd expected.

That was fine, though. For a woman in her position, self-respect was a luxury she could ill afford.

Chapter Fourteen

Cale had worked for Jed Tibbetts long enough to know the rancher was trying hard not to break down weeping at the sight of two more dead cowboys. He would later, Cale was certain. For the moment, though, he was trying hard to contain his emotions.

When they rode up, Montclair's man, Colby, was sitting on the ground near the bloodied corpses, rolling a smoke. He saw Tibbetts and Cale coming, put the cigarette in his mouth, struck a match and held it to the tip. When it glowed brightly, Colby shook out the match, tossed it aside. As Tibbetts dismounted, Colby eyed him through a long ribbon of smoke.

"What happened here, Colby?" Tibbetts demanded. "What happened to those men?"

"Got killed," Colby said. He was still sitting in the dirt. Cale wanted to kick him for his disrespectful tone.

"Killed, how? You were with them, weren't you?"

Colby shrugged. "Something bothered the stock," he said. "They didn't want to ride out to look, so I did. When I came back, they were here, like this."

Cale jumped down from his horse. "I don't believe it! Gamewell weren't afraid of nothing! He was as loyal as an old dog."

Tibbetts held up a hand toward Cale, silencing him. "What the boy says is true, Colby. I don't believe for a second these two men would sit here and let you go out by yourself. I told all of you to stay together."

"Reckon they didn't listen, then," Colby said. Finally, he stood. Kicked at the dirt. "You can believe me or don't. Makes no nevermind to me."

"Listen, Mr. Colby, as long as you're in my employ—"

"I ain't. Mr. Montclair pays me."

"Well, you're on my spread. I'd fire you if I could. I might just kick your ass if I have to look at you for another minute, so if I were you, I'd light the hell out of here."

Colby tossed his smoke on the ground. "Have it your way," he said. "Boss." He climbed onto his horse and rode away at a slow walk. Tibbetts watched him go, his hands shaking with anger.

When he was some distance away, Tibbetts turned back to Cale. "I don't like that man," he said. "I don't like his attitude. I don't like the way he smells. I see him again, I'm likely to shoot him."

"I wouldn't blame you, Mr. Tibbetts," Cale said.

"You see him around here again, Cale, you can shoot him, too."

"I'll keep that in mind."

"See you do."

Tibbetts looked at the bodies again. They had been hacked up, like the others. He started to say something more, but then the sorrow overtook him. A tear slipped from his left eye, and then he doubled over and dropped to his knees. Spasms rocked him, and he fell forward into the dirt.

Cale left him to his grief and fetched a shovel.

"Maybe it's time, Edith," Jed Tibbetts said. "Past time, more like. We've talked about it before."

She sat in the rocker he had made for her a dozen years earlier. Her feet were firmly planted, as always. Her hair hadn't been gray then, like it was now. Her face had been less lined. But her stubborn expression hadn't changed in any meaningful way. She knitted her brow and turned her mouth into a straight line and crossed her arms across her chest, and when she looked like that she didn't really have to speak, because her feelings were as plain as day. "That's nonsense, Jed, and you know it."

"You don't know what it's like," he said. "The way the men look. The brutality. It's sickening."

"I'm sure it is. But it can't last forever. The sheriff's got to do something, right?"

"Behan's got a whole county to look after, but he can hardly be dragged out of Tombstone. Marshal Turville's twice the man he is. Almost makes me wish we lived in Carmichael town limits. Now there's two more dead, I sent a man up to let Behan know it's gettin' worse, not that he'll do anything. Still, this isn't anything normal-like. There's no stock bein' rustled, nobody bein' robbed. Just cattle and men being chopped up and left there for no reason."

"Could there ever be a reason for that? One that made any sense?"

"I reckon not." Tibbetts looked out the window. The view outside was as it had always been. A dusty front yard, with the corral and barn off to the west and the bunkhouse the other way. The land sloping down toward the San Pedro River in the far distance, a line of cottonwood trees standing along its banks. On the horizon, the Mule Mountains glowed under the noontime sun.

There had always been dangers in that landscape, from weather, from snakes and bears and mountain lions and other creatures, from Apaches and whites alike. But he and Edith had carved out a life here, built a ranch that kept them fed and clothed, and neither had fallen victim to those constant threats.

Whatever was out there now, though, was something different. Something elemental, he thought, and steeped in evil. Something that killed, as his wife said, for no reason at all. No that wasn't quite true, there had to be a reason. It just wasn't one he could understand. It killed because it loved the act of killing, because it wanted to taste blood, to see bones and muscles and organs opened up to the air. It killed because killing was the only thing it knew how to do. He would never know the real reason until he learned what it was, and maybe not even then.

"I don't want to lose anything else," he said to the window. When Edith didn't reply, he continued. "No more people, no more stock. If we sold out now, before we lose any more head, we could maybe get somethin' for the land, somethin' for the beeves. Find us a place in town somewheres, Carmichael or Tombstone or even Tucson. Stop gettin' up before dawn every day of our lives."

He heard the chair squeaking, which meant she was rocking, which further meant she was getting angry. "Nonsense," she said. "Jed, you would hate that life. You'd sit in a chair and rot if you didn't have chores to do, animals to attend to. You wouldn't be happy for an instant of it."

He whirled away from the window. "You think I'm happy now, woman? Ridin' out every mornin' to see what's been slaughtered?"

"You talk to the sheriff," she said. "Don't send one of the men. Tell him he's got to stop it, or bring in the army and let them do it. You've got your hands full as it is."

"Reckon I could try that," Tibbetts said. "It's my ranch, so it's my problem. But Behan might could be useful if he's pushed hard enough."

"You've always been good at pushing, Jedediah Tibbetts. You weren't, we wouldn't be here now. Well, you might be, but not with me."

"No way I'd rather have it, Edith."

"So we're staying put, then." She didn't say it like it was a question, and she had stopped rocking. Her feet had never left the floor, and he expected it would take a cannonball to budge her.

"I reckon so."

"Good. I'd hate to have to put up with you moping around some house in town all day long, every day. You belong here."

"You're right, Edith." He didn't mind admitting it. He wouldn't tell her how relieved he was that she hadn't agreed to his suggestion. She was right; he hated the very idea of living in town, and he would hate the reality of it even more. But he'd wanted to make the offer anyway. Bad enough to be losing cattle and hands, but if whatever was doing that came closer to home—if Edith was threatened in any way—he wouldn't be able to live with it. If it could keep her from harm, he would live in a city a thousand miles from the Arizona territory. He wouldn't do it gladly. He loved everything about this place, despite the various hazards and the often harsh climate and the dry years when the grama grass didn't want to grow and the cattle went hungry.

But he would do it, and he wanted her to know that.

So he was glad she had refused his offer. It was a settled matter, now.

Unless it appeared that whatever it was, whatever evil force was out there, was coming close to her.

Then, he would either fight it and kill it, or walk away from the ranch and the livestock and everything else that made him want to get up in the morning, in order to keep her safe.

He walked over to the chair and gave her a kiss on the cheek. She twitched her head away from him, and wiped at it with her hand as soon as he was done.

But when he glanced back at her, he saw that she was beaming.

Cale had been in the kitchen of the little ranch house, finishing the lunch that Mrs. Tibbetts had made for him, when he over-heard some of their conversation from the other room. What he heard, he didn't like. Sell the ranch? They owned it, and could do what they liked with it. A cowboy was always aware that his employment could be cut short at any time, by money troubles or injury or illness, or simply because a ranch owner or foreman decided he didn't like your face.

But he couldn't imagine a place he could ever like working more than here, or an employer he would be more comfortable with. If they did sell, he would lose what few roots he had in the world.

He didn't know what he might be able to do against whoever was murdering on Tibbetts land. But if it would keep his only family here and safe, he would try to come up with something. He had to.

He didn't think he could take losing another home.

Chapter Fifteen

When the posse came upon the dusty little village, they weren't sure which side of the border it was on. There wasn't much to it: a few low buildings, including one that had obviously been a church, hunkered around a central plaza. Beyond the far side of the plaza was a big barn or livery stable. All the structures except the barn were built from adobe, from which any paint had long since faded, and sharp corners had been rounded by rain and sun and wind. Many of the walls were pockmarked, and Tuck realized what had happened—Apache depredation, no doubt. The pocks were bullet holes, and the townsfolk had either been slaughtered, or given up fighting and moved to someplace where the government could offer better protection. No sign announced the place, and none of the men had ever seen it before; they had simply come up out of a depression in a valley and there it was, baking in the midafternoon sun.

It was a forgotten hamlet. Weeds grew along what had once been roads. Windows were broken or missing altogether; doorways were gaping entries into shadow. No one had lived in this town for years, Tuck was sure.

But between the church and the little building beside it was a hitching rail with a horse tied to it. The animal had its head down, munching at the weeds, and barely bothered to look up when the posse stopped at the edge of the town.

"What do you figger, Bringloe?" Marshal Turville asked. "That his?"

"Only one set of tracks leads here," Tuck pointed out. "Pretty much has to be."

"He is tired of running," Maier suggested.

"Or he means to kill us all here," Tuck said.

"He can try," Turville said.

"So far he's been damn good at it."

"There's five of us and one of him," Darlington said.

"Hasn't bothered him so far," Tuck reminded him.

"If he's here, he's dead," Turville said. He dismounted, and bade the other men do the same. They looped their reins around a post at the town's edge.

"Spread out," Turville ordered, quickly gauging the width of the road. "Four feet between each man. He wants to shoot us, make him show what he's got."

The men did as the marshal said. Turville took the center position, Tuck to his right, Darlington right of him. Maier and Vander Tuig were on Turville's left. Each carried a rifle and wore a pistol. Turville wore two.

Tuck had his doubts about the whole idea. The killer hadn't shot anybody yet, to his knowledge. He couldn't swear the man he'd seen had a gun at all. But he'd attacked them in the dark, moving without being seen, and had killed multiple armed men. Maybe he had a reason for making a stand here, in daylight. If he did, Tuck didn't think he wanted to know what it was.

By now, the killer surely knew they were here. They hadn't taken any pains to hide their approach, and they'd been speaking in normal tones since then. The town was small and silent. He was inside one of those dozen or so buildings, watching from a window or doorway. Tuck tried to check each in turn, but there were too many, and the darkness inside them was impenetrable from this distance. As soon as he looked away from one, the guy might be there, or there might be a gun barrel poking through.

They were almost to the plaza when the first shot rang out. Piet Vander Tuig took a step back, as if he had been pushed in the chest. But when he took another halting half step, Tuck looked and saw blood running down his face from a hole in his forehead. "He's shot!" Tuck cried as the man sank to the ground. "Find cover!"

Darlington dropped to a crouch and raised his rifle. He fired two shots toward the stable at the end of the street. Tuck was racing for the shelter of a recessed doorway, but he saw Darlington jerk twice, and heard shots at the same moment. Darlington started to rise to his feet when he jerked again. This time his knees crumpled and he pitched forward, blood running into the road.

"The stable!" Turville shouted. "He's in the loft!"

The marshal and Maier had taken cover behind the corner of a building. As long as they stayed where they were, and Tuck remained in the doorway, the killer couldn't get to them.

But they couldn't get to him, either.

He did have a gun, after all, and he was pretty handy with it. All the horses, including his own, were in clear view, and in range if the man had a rifle. If he had another way out, maybe a horse hidden in the livery, or behind it, he could strand them here. Or he could wait until they showed themselves, and kill them one by one.

Or they could try to outwait him.

Tuck wasn't very confident of that option. They didn't know what he had in terms of supplies. They didn't know if there was another horse, though there had been no tracks visible from the other end of town. He might have met allies here who could, even now, be sneaking around the posse.

Eventually, the sun would set. The man was better in the dark than they were, by a clear margin. Even if it didn't rain—and clouds were building up in the south, headed their way—if they were still here when night fell, they were all dead. Tuck was as sure of that as he had ever been of anything.

"Hank!" he called. "We got to get in there! We let it wait till dark, we're goners!"

"I was just thinkin' that!" Turville replied. "Got any ideas?"

"I was hoping you did!" Tuck readied his Winchester and leaned out of the doorway. He saw movement in the loft, and fired a shot. It went high. He ducked back in as two return shots chipped the adobe beside him.

He'd only had a glimpse of the man in the loft, at a distance, and the man had been in shadow.

But it was the same one he had seen outside Senora Soto's that night, coming down the stairs. He was certain of it. He couldn't have said why—something about his presence, more than any specific visual similarity.

Didn't matter.

"That's him," he said.

"The feller you saw?" Turville asked.

"Yep. Same man."

"We got to go around," Turville said.

"Around, how?"

"We go up this main road, he'll kill us. But Alf and me can go around this building, up the back side of the next couple. He shouldn't be able to see us until we're almost there."

"Could be," Tuck said. Their presence wouldn't come as a surprise—he doubted if much could surprise the man in the loft—but they'd be closer, anyway.

He tried the door next to him, which was solid, and closed, unlike most he'd seen in this little town. Nothing barred it on the other side. He pushed it and looked in.

A few pieces of furniture had been left behind when the place had been abandoned. Sand and sticks and other desert detritus had blown in through a window, and spider webs were everywhere. If there was an opening on the other side, a window or another door, then he could loop around the church and come at the stable from the opposite angle as Turville and Maier.

He waved the rifle ahead of him to clear away the webbing. A spider bigger than his palm scurried onto a wall when its web was disturbed. A doorway, thickly webbed, led into a dark inner room. Tuck swept away as much of the webbing as he could and stepped through. Tendrils clung to his face and neck, and he tried to wipe them away, hoping there were no snakes or spiders bigger than the one he'd just seen, lurking inside.

Across the room a thin line of light indicated an opening of some kind. He made for it, found a shutter over a window, its hinges frozen by dirt or rust. He pounded at it with the flat of his hand, then the butt of his rifle, aware that the noise he was making could be heard throughout the town. That might, he decided, impact the effectiveness of their plan.

But it worked. The shutter opened enough for him to grab it and wrench it from the window—again, not soundlessly. Broken glass faced him. As long as he was making a racket anyway, he smashed out the rest of it with the rifle.

Then he hurried back through the house, ignoring the webbing that he picked up on the way. At the doorway again, he saw Turville staring his way. "You knockin' the place down?" the marshal asked.

"Just opening up a passageway. I can get out the far side, go around the church, and come up on the other side of the stable from you two."

"Sounds good," Turville said. "Let's go now. When we get there, we try to get inside. He'll have the high ground, but there's three of us."

"Leave Alf outside the back door," Tuck suggested. "If he tries to go out the back, from either level, someone's got to be there to shoot him."

"I will try," Maier said. "I have never shot someone before."

Tuck wished he had brought that fact up sooner, but this wasn't the time to discuss it. "Just point at his chest and pull the trigger. Don't stop until he's dead."

Maier looked uncertain. But there wasn't much choice. They were the only ones left. He knew Turville would fight on until he dropped. He had started the posse under duress, but now that so many of his own townsfolk had died, and done so because they rode with him, he was determined to put an end to it. And Tuck felt the same way. If Maier needed to shoot, he'd better be able to do it.

If he didn't, he would die, too.

"Let's move," Turville said. "We'll try to get to the front door unseen, and we'll go in once Alf is around the rear."

Tuck nodded his assent and went back into the darkened house once more. This time, he kept going, through the far window. Behind the house was what might once have been a garden patch, but the desert reclaimed all things, he was learning, and it was doing the same here.

He couldn't see the plaza or the livery, which meant the killer couldn't see him. He started toward that end of town, past a couple more small adobe structures. Then he had to dash across an open space to reach the cover of the church. As he rounded its bulk, he came into view of the stable. Once he moved again, depending on which way the killer was looking, he could easily be seen until he was hugging the stable's wall.

Easily seen, and easily shot.

Chapter Sixteen

Still, there was nothing else for it. He paused at the corner, eyed the loft. He saw no movement, no trace of the killer.

He bolted from cover and raced across the open stretch. As he ran, he spotted Turville and Maier doing the same. Tuck and the marshal both stopped on this side, pressing themselves flat against the wall. Maier kept going.

Turville gave Tuck a little nod. So far, so good, Tuck figured it meant. No shots had come from above, no sign indicated that they'd been spotted. The man hadn't fired a round in some time. There was a chance, however slight, that one of their bullets had found him, or that he had simply hightailed it out of there. Cautiously, they made their way toward each other, toward the stable door. Each watched the loft opening, his rifle pointed in that direction in case of any motion.

Soon they had reached the door, which stood partly open. To show themselves at that gap could mean catching a bullet, but it had to be done.

Turville took the chance. He peered in. No bullet came. After almost a minute, he waved, turned back to Tuck. "Maier's there," he whispered. "I'm goin' in."

"Watch yourself," Tuck replied. "I'm right behind."

Turville slipped inside. Tuck followed. Dust motes danced in the slivers of light falling through the open doors on either side. Here and there, hay spilled out of stalls that hadn't known horses in years. The place still smelled like the animals that had once inhabited it, but with an overlying stink of rodents, bats, and more.

And one more thing: the sickening, sour scent that Tuck had become all too familiar with. The stink of the killer.

He eyed the ladder up to the loft, and the opening there, and the gaps in the floor that would allow the killer to see them, though they couldn't see him. He would fire at the first hint of motion from up there. But he couldn't discount the possibility that the man had come down, either. There were too many places to watch; he couldn't possibly keep his eyes on them all at once. He and the marshal moved carefully, checking each stall they passed. They worked toward the ladder, knowing death could visit at any moment.

Even so, when it came, it was a shock.

Tuck's eyes were becoming accustomed to the dim light. He checked the stalls to the right of the central passage, while Turville watched the other side. He had just passed one, empty but for the wisps of straw and rat droppings left behind, when Turville cried out.

Tuck spun around, holding the Winchester at waist level and ready to shoot. Turville blocked his shot, though, and for a moment, his view. But the marshal dropped back a step, bringing up his own gun, and what Tuck saw then made no sense.

A plank was missing at the back of the stall, creating a space a few inches across and nearly two feet high.

Something squeezed through that space, like a rat slipping through an opening that seemed hardly large enough for a tiny mouse. This something was dark, like a shadow unmoored from its source. On this side of the gap, it was becoming solid again and taking on its full size.

Turville fired, levered, fired again. The bullets had little visible effect. The black shape drew back momentarily, but then kept coming, coalescing into something vaguely human-shaped. But not human. Its hiss was an awful noise, loud enough to hurt Tuck's ears. Details were hard to make out in the half dark, but it seemed to be all gnashing teeth and claws and burning yellow

eyes, and despite the marshal's rounds, it set upon him, slashing and tearing. Turville started screaming.

Tuck sidestepped to get a better angle and opened fire. He was screaming himself by then, from horror and rage. He put one bullet after another into the thing. Finally, it released Turville. The marshal dropped to the ground, limp, and the creature turned to Tuck.

Tuck kept firing. His bullets had an impact—he saw the thing jerk in evident pain when each one struck—but they didn't stop it altogether. When the rifle was empty, he whisked it around and swung it like a club. It smashed into the dark shape, and Tuck was relieved to feel the shock in his arms and shoulders, testifying to the thing's physical mass.

If it was alive, if it had shape and weight, it could be killed.

It charged at Tuck. When it came, cold air surrounded him, as if he had opened an icebox freshly filled. That horrific smell nearly made him gag. He reached for the knife he wore, and freed it from its scabbard as the creature got a claw into his left arm.

Tuck slashed out with the knife, felt it cut solid flesh. The creature's hiss changed to a cry of alarm. It kept coming, claws gripping Tuck's shoulders, tearing through clothes and skin, trying to get close enough to use those vicious teeth. He stabbed upward with the knife, catching the thing under the chin. He drove the point home and yanked it toward him.

The claws fell away. Tuck wrenched the knife free and stabbed again, in the middle of the dark mass. When he felt the resistance of solid flesh he pushed harder, breaking past it. Again and again, he pierced the thing's outer skin. It tried to come at him, but it was weakening. Tuck didn't stop. He raised the knife and drove it home over and over, until finally the thing lay lifeless on the stable floor.

When it did, he drew the knife from it again, tossed it aside, and went to Turville. "Hank," he said. "Are you—"

The marshal didn't let him finish the sentence. "I'm done, Bringloe," he said. His voice trembled, barely audible even in the fresh silence. "So cold."

Tuck was amazed Turville was speaking at all. His chest had been torn open. Blood slicked him and the ground and gushed from the wound like a creek through a ruptured dam. "Maier!" Tuck cried. "Get in here and help me with Hank!"

The back door opened with a squeal and Maier rushed in. "Is he hurt?"

"He's dying," Tuck said. His first words to Maier had been a lie—there was no helping Turville now, except to offer comfort until death took away his pain. "He beat the thing, most of the way, but it got him."

"Ach, Hank," Maier said. "You're . . ."

He didn't finish the thought. There was really nothing to say.

But Turville wasn't finished yet. His right hand flopped to his breast. Tuck thought at first he meant to close the wound, though it was too late for that. Instead, the marshal's hand closed around his badge and yanked it from his vest. "Your . . . hand, Bringloe," Turville said.

Tuck offered his right hand, not sure what the marshal wanted with it. Turville pressed the badge into it, the points of the star biting into Tuck's palm. "You got to be the . . . law, now, Tuck," he said. "Br . . . bravest man I ever knowed. Carmichael . . . needs your kind. Needs you."

"Hank, just rest," Tuck said. "You'll be—" He couldn't finish the lie, so he went quiet again, letting Turville speak. He could hardly hear the man now. The end was close.

"It . . . an honor," Turville managed. "Captain Bring—"

With that, the life rushed from him. Tuck held him for several minutes longer, Maier standing by and watching with a look of terror on his face.

"What . . . is that thing?" he asked finally.

"I don't know," Tuck admitted. "It's what killed Daisie and the others. But it's nothing I've ever seen before. Not human, but like no animal, either."

He released Turville, at last. He rose, unsteady, still clutching the badge in one fist. He put his other hand against the wall for balance. "We got to get them back to town," he said. "Tur-ville and that . . . that thing, both."

"I heard what he said," Maier told him. "When he gave you the badge. When we are back in town, I will tell the others, back you if you want to be the marshal."

"I got a choice?" Tuck asked.

"There is always a choice," Maier said. "You could ride out now, the other direction. You could leave me to find my way home by myself. But I do not think you will."

"No," Tuck said. He didn't have to reflect much to know the answer to that. "No, I'll go back with you. Got nowhere else to go, and being marshal can't be the worst job ever."

But his gaze landed again on the dark, motionless shape on the floor, and he wondered how much truth there was to that, after all.

PART TWO
Memento Mori

Chapter Seventeen

There was nothing quite like a victorious return to the fort, Cuttrell thought. Any return was, by definition, a victorious one, at least for those who made it. Survivors were greeted with smiles and celebration; the only exception being, in his experience, when those who returned were fewer than half of those who left.

This time, though, everyone who'd ridden out had come back, bringing one more besides, along with extra wagons loaded with ghost rock. Instead of skirting the edge of Carmichael he led the column down Main Street, across the hard-packed roadway that ran north and south, separating town and fort, and through the front gates, the ones that opened toward Main. The fort had been there first, and the town grew up just outside its walls, the nearest buildings less than a stone's throw from the ramparts. Behind the fort, the mountains shouldered up close, so all the building had been done in the valley before it. Cuttrell waved at those who came out to watch, even the whores on their balcony at Senora Soto's.

He could see by their expressions, and pointing fingers, that it was the girl—the one Kuruk called "Little Wing"—who attracted the most attention. People cheered on the soldiers, but their cheers faded and their smiles dimmed, replaced by curious looks and shouted questions when they saw her sitting up in the back of the buckboard with an army blanket over her shoulders.

As they passed through the doors to the fort, Jimmy McKenna

ran up and threw a crisp salute. Cuttrell beckoned him over and leaned out of the saddle. "Jimmy," he said, keeping his voice low. "We have no idea who the girl back there is. She was with the mule train—the only female on the whole train, as far as we could tell, and the only survivor. See if you can get a manifest for the train. I want to know everything. Who was behind it, where they were going, and most of all, who that young lady might be."

"Yes, sir," McKenna said. "Everything go well otherwise?"

"Well as can be expected," Cuttrell replied. "The slaughter was horrible. Just horrible."

"Indians?"

Cuttrell wasn't sure how to answer that. "It doesn't appear so, no," he said after several seconds.

"Who, then?"

"That, Mr. McKenna, is something else we'll have to find out. Get busy, now, and find out who our young passenger is. One mystery at a time."

He brought the column to a halt at the parade field. People from town and from the fort had followed them in and surrounded them, extending their welcomes and good wishes. Cuttrell dismounted and worked his way back to the wagon. He had assigned a sergeant to drive it, but Kuruk had stayed close any time he wasn't out ahead, performing his scouting duties. He had taken a special interest in the girl, for reasons Cuttrell didn't understand. She seemed to respond better to him than to anyone else, too, so he didn't discourage it. Some would no doubt object to an Indian being allowed in such proximity to a white girl, but he would address that when the time came. For now, Kuruk seemed a calming influence on her, and he protested any time she was out of his sight.

Kuruk rode beside her now as she sat in the wagon, clearly terrified by so much attention. "People, people, leave the young lady be!" Cuttrell called as he approached. "All your questions will be answered in due time. She's a stranger here, so let's show her some Fort Huachuca hospitality instead of trying to frighten her out of her wits."

He cut through the crowd, waving his hands, and most of the people gathered around dispersed. Others stayed close, curiosity overwhelming common sense, but they backed far enough away for him to approach the wagon. "Welcome to Fort Huachuca, young lady," Cuttrell said. She tried to smile, though panic was never far from her eyes. "This will be your home, at least until such time as we determine where you belong. I trust you'll find it to your liking. These folks"—he raised a hand at the gathered crowd—"will settle down, in time. Try to ignore them." He offered her a hand, to help her down from the wagon.

She took the hand in hers, and said, "No soul is lost, only mislaid."

"Excuse me?" Cuttrell asked. She gazed blankly at him, as if she hadn't spoken a word.

"She doesn't say much, Colonel," Kuruk said quietly. "And what she does say doesn't make a lick of sense."

Cuttrell didn't pursue the subject. He eased her down off the wagon, and as he did, he saw Sadie coming toward them. Her gaze took in the girl, and their joined hands, and he could see the moment it all sank in for her. Her smile vanished and her eyes turned glacial.

Everyone had questions about the girl, it seemed. But he had a feeling Sadie's would be more pointed than most.

Chapter Eighteen

If Maier had been mildly annoying when there were several men on the posse, he was worse on the way back to town, pelting Tuck with questions about his service in the war, where he'd been since, what he had done besides drinking himself unconscious most nights. That wasn't a question Tuck had much of an answer for. He had chased oblivion with the single-mindedness of a big-game hunter after a prize lion. The only difference was when the hunter bested the lion, he put its head on a wall. With oblivion, there was never any winning, just the constant pursuit.

He felt better than he had in months, or longer. But Maier's insistence on asking might, he reflected, be the one thing that could drive him back to the bottle.

He asked himself sometimes what he had been hiding from all those years. The answer to that wasn't simple. He had spent most of his life trying to escape childhood; his mother's madness, his father's violent end, and all the pain that those things had brought. He had, he thought, found a kind of peace in the army. He fought to preserve the Union, to free the slaves, to bring the rebel states back into the nation's fold. The cause was just, the pursuit noble.

But he had found out that, causes aside, men were still men and only as noble as their most base motivations. High-minded rhetoric and lofty ideals could not compensate for venality and the love of violence that prompted some to take up arms.

That lesson had come through a series of events, escalating one after the other with the inevitability of a natural force. As surely as rain soaked the ground and made the creeks rise, the occurrences of that autumn cascaded one after the other in a way that could not be resisted.

It had started as an expression of honest terror, an emotion with which no man who had been through combat was unfamiliar, or could deny in any other. Captain Bringloe's forces had vanquished a smaller cadre of Confederate troops, in Pennsylvania but near the Maryland line. After the battle, survivors among the enemy were being rounded up and taken to a central point to be questioned and sent to prison camps. A couple of Tuck's soldiers had been assigned to count the dead and to make sure that they truly were dead, not feigning death in hopes of escape once the combatants had left the field. For this task, they used bayonets, and sometimes the toes of their boots.

The fighting had been fierce, and there were plenty of dead on both sides. Tempers still ran high, and Tuck didn't doubt that his men were more adamant than absolutely necessary when they performed their verification. At one point, he had looked over and seen a private named Roberts kicking a body, hard and repeatedly. The sound carried across the quiet battlefield, like a butcher tenderizing meat. "Easy, Roberts!" Tuck had shouted. "The fighting's over for today!"

"Just making sure!" Roberts called back.

"Make sure more gently," Tuck said. "Or I'll assign someone else the chore."

"Sorry, Cap'n," Roberts said.

Tuck had thought that would be the end of it.

It wasn't.

Rather than using his feet, Roberts had switched to the bayonet test. One didn't have to stab hard or deep with a bayonet—if someone was pretending to death, the first touch would tell the tale.

As Roberts moved through the ranks of the dead, poking and prodding, he was finding only genuinely dead people, and one who was wounded badly, not pretending but unable to stand on his own. A couple of soldiers took a stretcher to that one and carried him to the field hospital, where, despite his Confederate leanings, he would be treated.

When he came to one body, Roberts poked it with the bayonet and watched for any telltale signs. Nothing happened, but Roberts, unsatisfied, reached down and rolled the body over so he could see the man's face. He poked again, harder this time. Apparently satisfied, he moved toward the next corpse.

But he had scarcely moved a foot away when the "dead" body sat straight up. Tuck had been looking elsewhere, but the shouts of several turned his attention to the field and he saw the rebel, sitting up, arms thrown out to his sides. His face had been largely obliterated, the skin flayed from it and burned around the edges, bone showing underneath.

Roberts, though, had been so startled by the rebel's sudden seeming rebirth that he stopped in his tracks and drove his bayonet through the back of the young man's skull, using all the force he could muster. The point of it burst through the ruined face. The man had been dead all along, animated by some bizarre function of nerves, Tuck had thought. But the Confederate prisoners had only seen Roberts spear an obviously wounded, helpless young man from behind.

Tuck didn't know how word spread from prisoners to enemy soldiers in the field, but spread it had. Word got around about Roberts in particular, but the whole company had developed, through that one fluke incident, a reputation for unnecessary brutality.

And every Confederate they engaged reminded them of it. When enemy troops realized they were up against "Bringloe's Bastards," they fought harder, showed no mercy, were resistant to surrender because word had spread that surrender meant death. Tuck didn't understand that part, since if he had actually killed his prisoners on that one occasion, there would be no such rumors to contend with.

The next escalation had come in North Carolina, after

another bloody battle in a thickly wooded area outside Durham. Casualties had been high on both sides, but the Rebs had bulwarks and cannon on their side, and Tuck's company had taken the brunt of it. During the fighting, Roberts had been captured. Tuck had been forced to retreat, leaving his dead where they'd fallen. But after they regrouped, they discovered that Roberts was missing. No one had seen him go down, although it was possible, they determined, that he had done so during the retreat, and nobody noticed.

The next morning, Tuck and some of his men returned to the site of the battle, to collect their dead and see if Roberts was among them. They found him right away. He had been stripped naked, lashed to a tree, and flogged until flesh hung from him in curled ribbons. His eyes had been put out, his tongue and the end of his nose cut off. They had taken his scalp, and stabbed him dozens of times. When Tuck saw him, he was still alive, but barely. He moaned piteously, obviously in more pain than any human ought to have to endure. Tuck put an end to his suffering with a shot to the brain. He hoped Roberts's torture and murder would put an end to the unreasoning animosity toward him and his company, which had gone far beyond the simple rivalries of war.

But he hadn't counted on the fury of his own men. Having seen Roberts's state, some were caught up in a ferocious bloodlust that could not be quelled. Tuck tried to rein them in, to remind them that they were at war, and their activities had to be guided by strategic planning and the rules of combat, not a reckless thirst for revenge.

He was overruled, and when he tried to physically prevent his men from acting, they threatened mutiny. In the end, his men did what they wanted. They found some of their enemies from the previous day's battle, seven junior officers and a handful of enlisted men, having supper at a large farmhouse set upon the banks of a river. They were in the company of a dozen women and nine or ten children from the nearest town. Tuck's soldiers stormed into the yard, between house and river, where supper was being served. They surrounded the officers and their civilian companions and shot them all. The women and children, they killed quickly, but they made the officers witness the atrocity before ending their lives.

Tuck witnessed it, too.

Then he tore off every patch and insignia that identified him as a soldier of the Union Army. He took his bedroll and canteen and haversack, his guns and his horse, and he abandoned his own company in the midst of enemy territory. Whether they ever made it to safety, he had never heard. Nor had he cared.

He had seen what hatred could do. He had watched what happened when men were filled to overflowing with it, and had guns with which to express it. He had decided, that day, that he hated, too—he hated war and he hated killing and he hated guns and he hated the compulsion to seek violent revenge for acts of violence. Hated it in large measure, he knew, because he shared it. There was only one direction such a chain of events could spiral in, and it led straight to hell.

Tuck had ridden toward the sunset, and he had not stopped in the four years since, except when the opportunity for obliteration presented itself. He had traded away the horse and the guns and eventually the haversack, bedroll, and canteen, all for liquor. He'd cowboyed when he could, begged when necessary, stolen when that was his last resort. He had run out of money and opportunity in Carmichael, on his way toward California, so he'd stayed put. And he had now awakened to find that he had become pathetic, a source of pity and amusement for people he once would have thought beneath him intellectually and morally, and he knew that he was everything they thought he was, a drunkard, an idiot, a punching bag, someone to look down upon when they needed to feel superior.

During those lost years, he had decided his mother had been right all along. He was no better than his father, a useless waste of skin. Becoming an army officer had been an accident, no doubt due to the long war and a certain fluency with killing that Tuck thought might have been the only trait his mother had passed on to him.

Hank Turville had changed all that. Turville had needed him, had trusted him, had counted on him. He had let Hank down, in the end, or he would be riding home with the man instead of leading a horse that carried his body. But still, he had been given back himself, the best gift anyone could receive. He had a long way yet to go, but he had tasted—after a long drought—respect and a sense of purpose that he had never thought he would again know.

So he put up with Maier's questions, though he offered little by way of response, and he rode toward Carmichael, bearing the marshal's badge and the determination to wear it himself, and to help keep the peace in that place that had given him so much.

"Bringloe?" Maier said, when they were less than a day's ride from town.

"What is it, Alf?" Tuck asked, expecting another question for which he had no answers.

"He's . . . leaking."

"Who's leaking?" Tuck asked.

"The . . . whatever it is that you killed. He . . . it . . . is *leaking*."

"Leaking, how?" Tuck turned his horse around. Maier was riding behind him, leading the horse on which they had lashed the killer's body, rolled up in a tattered blanket they'd found in one of the small hamlet's houses.

"Look," Maier said.

Tuck looked.

Maier was right.

A thick, oily black drop dangled from the bottom of the rolled blanket. Behind them, other drops had hit the ground, marking their trail for who knew how far. "You just now noticed this, Alf?"

"It's behind me," Maier said. "Why would I look at a dead man in a blanket?"

Maier had a point.

"What is it?" Maier asked. "Is it blood?"

"Doesn't look like any blood I've ever seen. You know anything that bleeds black?"

"No . . . but I have never seen the likes of that one before, either."

"Makes two of us," Tuck said. He dismounted, handed his reins to Maier, and went back for a closer look. The drop that had been dangling finally released, hitting the ground with a dull splatting sound. Another one had already started to form, and Tuck realized that each one carried the horrible stink of the killer. His stomach churned, and he found himself wishing for a bottle, to blot out the sight and sound and smell and memory. With difficulty, he pushed that thought aside.

"We gotta get him off there," he said.

"I do not want to touch that," Maier said.

"Fine," Tuck said. "Hold the horse steady and I'll do it."

He pulled his knife—the same one he had finally killed the dark thing with—and sliced through the ropes holding the blanket fast to the horse's back. When he cut the last one, the bundle started to slide. Tuck gave a gentle push, and it fell to the dirt with a liquid sound.

There, Tuck pulled on the blanket, unrolling it from around the dead creature.

Maier swore softly, in German, then started vomiting off the other side of his horse. Tuck was silent, stunned by what he saw.

The thing was considerably smaller than it had been, with no more form than a lump of dough. Whatever had once looked human, or nearly so, was gone. It was black and greasy and had stained the inside of the blanket, but there was no indication of anything that might have ever resembled a man. This blob could not have worn clothes or fired a gun or convinced Daisie to take him upstairs so he could slaughter her in her bed.

"We can't take this to Carmichael," Tuck said.

"It's terrible!" Maier said. "Let us leave it here, Bringloe. Please. I do not want to take another step with that thing."

"We can't just leave it," Tuck said. He wasn't sure why he felt that way, but it seemed to him that as evil as the thing had been, to abandon it for some other traveler to happen across might be too dangerous. Such evil could likely reach out from beyond death, he thought, and infect someone else.

"We must!" Maier argued.

"No," Tuck said, determination lending a commanding aspect to his voice. "We'll burn it."

"Must we?"

"Yes. Come on, Alf. Tie those horses up and let's get busy."

Chapter Nineteen

In the end, the thing burned as easily as lamp oil. Tuck had barely touched fire to the soiled blanket when it ignited in a huge *whoosh* that almost singed his eyebrows. Smoke coiled up from it, thick and black and stinking like the creature had. Tuck tried not to let it get into his clothes or his hair, afraid it would never wash away.

When the blanket and its contents were nothing but ashes scattered on the ground, Tuck was ready to ride again.

"We must never speak of this," Maier insisted. "To anybody. They would think we had lost our minds."

"Can't argue," Tuck said. "The *Tombstone Epitaph* might be interested in this sort of thing, but any sane person would have to doubt our sanity."

"Yet we both saw it," Maier said. "Smelled it. It was real, wasn't it? Now it's gone, I almost can't convince myself."

"It was real," Tuck said. "But it's not anymore. It's gone. You're right, Alf. Not a word. To anyone."

They shook on it, then mounted up and continued the trek toward Carmichael. The horse that had carried the bundle only made it another couple of miles before it went lame, and Tuck had to shoot it. Once again, he had used a gun to put a merciful end to a living creature's unspeakable agony.

He dearly hoped he would never have to do that again.

The mayor of Carmichael was a gaunt, sepulchral man named Oliver J. Chaffee, who Tuck would have assumed was suited only to the trade of undertaker. He was astonished to learn that the man owned shares of three mines around Tombstone, a piece of Senora Soto's, and a laundry in Carmichael that was run by a Chinese couple he employed. Most people assumed that because it was called Wu Fang's, it belonged to someone named Wu Fang. But Chaffee, it turned out, had made up the name from whole cloth.

He had an office in town hall, the most ornate building on Carmichael's main street, which wasn't saying much. He had decorated it with Chinese antiques, with lots of shiny black wood and finely detailed, lacquered surfaces. He, a rancher named Jasper Montclair, Alf Maier, and Wilson Harrell, the bank owner, comprised Carmichael's town council. An hour after they got back to town, having dropped off Hank Turville's body with the actual undertaker, Tuck was in that office with the town council members, and Maier was describing—leaving out certain crucial elements, like the nature of their foe and what had happened to it—how the marshal's death had come about, and how he had passed the badge on to Tucker Bringloe.

"He was adamant," Maier was saying. "He wanted Captain Bringloe to be our new marshal."

"Unless I misremember the town charter," Montclair said, "the outgoing marshal is not tasked with appointing his own replacement."

"You are correct," Maier said. "But in this particular case, I believe Marshal Turville's opinion should be considered."

"You're the only one who heard it, Alfred," Harrell put in. "Besides Mr. Bringloe, of course." When he spoke Tuck's name, he added an unmistakable note of acid. Tuck couldn't blame the banker overly much; certainly, he had not worried about creating a good impression among the townsfolk. And how could he argue that he was no longer the drunkard they had known? He didn't know that about his own self. For all he knew, the first time he'd walk into a saloon, he would forget everything the past several days had shown him, and drink his way back into the gutter. Seemed more likely than not, in fact.

"Have you anything to gain, Mr. Maier, from the appointment of Mr. Bringloe to that position?" Chaffee asked. "Has he, for instance, made any promises to you? Offered you any special treatment or compensation?"

"Of course not," Maier said. Violet coloration splotched his cheeks, and his voice had risen by a few octaves. "What could he offer me? I am an honest businessman!"

"A fact of which we are all well aware," Chaffee said. He let his gaze rest on Tuck for long enough to be uncomfortable, then continued. "We have no reason to doubt your description of Captain Bringloe's courage, or his skills. Given the fact that we're in need of a marshal, and the captain appears to have the necessary qualifications, I suggest we honor Marshal Turville's dying wish. Are there any objections?"

Harrell looked like he wanted to say something, but he swallowed it back. Montclair sat in a high-backed chair like some kind of royalty, looking down his nose at the peasants surrounding him. Only Maier spoke.

"Of course there are no objections. I tell you, Bringloe is the best man for the job."

"Shall we call it unanimous, then?" Chaffee asked.

"Aye," Montclair said, without emotion.

"I suppose so," Harrell agreed.

"There you are, Captain," Chaffee said. "The town of Carmichael would like to officially offer you the position of town marshal. The salary is one hundred dollars a month. The town also pays your deputy, currently Mr. Kanouse, so you needn't worry about paying him from your salary. In some jurisdictions, marshals can supplement their income by taking a percentage of taxes collected and fines levied, and such like. Here, I'm afraid that Sheriff Behan already owns that particular business, so you'd have to negotiate any cut with him."

Behan was the county sheriff, so had more power than any town's marshal. Tuck wasn't going to be able to slice into his action. "In that case," he said, "how about making it one-twenty-five?"

"Alf, have you discussed salaries with the captain?" Chaffee asked.

"Of course not," Maier said. "That is private town business."

"Gentlemen? Any objection?"

Harrell, Maier, and Montclair all kept quiet, so Chaffee nodded. "One hundred and twenty, Captain. And if there's any equipment you feel you need that is not already in the marshal's office, you buy it yourself. We'll supply a horse, but feeding it is up to you."

"Deal," Tuck said. He might have been able to hold out for a slightly better arrangement, but he'd been worried that if he pushed too hard, they would rescind the offer and give the job to Mo Kanouse, instead. The deputy had rousted him a few times, and had once beaten him badly with a club for the crime of being drunk in public. He'd heard about other beatings Kanouse had dished out, too. He considered the man cruel, lazy, and unprofessional. Once he'd gotten to know Hank Turville, he was surprised that Kanouse had kept the job as long as he had. If the deputy was hired and paid by the council, though, that could explain a lot.

They all shook on the agreement, and Mayor Chaffee made a big production out of pinning Turville's badge on a shirt that Tuck wanted to take off and burn at the earliest opportunity. Tuck accepted the badge, though, and asked for a week's pay in advance. Chaffee took it from a drawer in his desk and handed it over, and Tuck's first thought was how many drinks it would buy. But he touched the badge and pocketed the money and tried to put that idea out of his mind. He had responsibilities, now. People depended on him. He had fouled that up before, but he didn't want to repeat old mistakes.

There were too many new ones, after all, just waiting to be made.

————

Tuck was filthy, caked in mud and grime from the roots of his hair to the spaces between his toes. He literally couldn't remember the last bath he'd had. Years, he thought.

There was a bathhouse in town, so he stopped in there and got a bath and a shave and haircut. While he was in there, he sent a boy to Greavey's general store for a new set of clothing. Later he would visit the town's sole haberdasher for more, but a vest, a cheap shirt, trousers, and underclothes would do for the moment. He also summoned the town's doctor, who complained bitterly about the condition of Tuck's arm wound while he cleaned and dressed it. By the time Tuck came out, he felt about fifteen pounds lighter and several dollars poorer.

Newly presentable and smelling of bay rum rather than sweat and horse, he asked the bathhouse proprietor where Hank Turville's widow could be found. The man described a house on the north side of town, with a large veranda and a scrub oak in front. Tuck found the place, which looked cozy and comfortable. He should have found it sooner, he knew. He had spent a few hours on other tasks, but with every minute that went by, the chances increased that someone else had already told her about her husband's fate.

He wouldn't have minded that, but it was rightly his job to do. That had been true as an army officer, and it was true as a town marshal, as well. It was, he reflected, likely the worst part of either profession.

He steeled himself, strode up to the house, and knocked on the door.

It took a couple of minutes for anyone to answer, and when a woman finally opened the door, Tuck knew at once that she wasn't Turville's wife. Mother-in-law, maybe. She was about as tall as a ten-year-old boy. She had steel-gray hair and her face was deeply creased, with veins showing through flesh that looked paper-thin. She wore black, but then, she had the air of a woman who always wore black regardless of the occasion. Still, her presence, and the practiced frown she had locked in place, told him that Mrs. Turville had already heard.

That made no never-mind, though. He still had his task to perform. "Ma'am," he said. "Is Mrs. Turville available?"

The old woman fixed her gaze on his star. "You're the replacement."

"That's right, ma'am. I'm Marshal Bringloe. Tucker Bringloe."

"She's in the parlor, Mr. Bringloe. She's in a state."

"I'm sure she is, ma'am. I won't keep her long."

She stepped back from the doorway, giving him space to enter. He was suddenly more conscious than he had been in days of the fact that he didn't own a hat. If he had, he'd have pulled it off, and could fiddle with it while he spoke to the widow. Now that the thought had crossed his mind, he didn't know what he would do with his hands. "This way," she said.

She led him through the entryway and into a parlor stuffed with heavy furniture and thick draperies. The air was close, cloying, as if the funeral were already underway. On the wall above a fireplace was a framed photograph of a deceased infant in his casket; locks of hair were encased under glass with the image. Turville had never mentioned losing a son, but that's who Tuck guessed the child in the *memento mori* had to be.

Two women sat in separate chairs. One was at least as old as the woman who had answered the door. The other could only be Turville's wife. She was in her thirties, Tuck speculated, a pretty brunette with dark eyes and a sad mouth. Her eyes were red and her nose raw, and she clutched a damp handkerchief like she was drowning and it was her lifeline.

"Mrs. Turville," he said, "I'm Tucker Bringloe. I was with your husband. When he . . . when he was killed. I want you to know how sorry I am. But I also want to tell you how brave he was. Not that it matters much now, maybe, but right up to the end, he was as strong and filled with courage and heart as any man I ever met. He earned my admiration and respect and appreciation."

She tried on a smile, but it didn't take. "Thank you, sir," she said. Her voice caught on the last word, and her eyes glimmered as tears filled them.

"I couldn't ever explain to you how much he meant to me, ma'am. I didn't know him long, but it's safe to say that he changed my life. Saved it. I expect I'll always be grateful to him for that."

"Thank you," she said again. "I understand you brought him back home."

"Yes, ma'am. Me and Alf Maier."

"That was very kind," she said. With every word, she fought back tears, but Tuck could see she would lose that battle soon. "He loved it here. I would hate it if he hadn't been able to come back."

"Seemed like the right thing to do, Mrs. Turville." He wanted to get out before her tears infected him. "I'm powerful sorry, ma'am, about the way things worked out. Hank was a good man and I wish I could have known him longer."

She tried to respond, but then the tears sprang from her, bringing on sobs. She turned away, seemingly trying to wedge herself into the chair. The little gray-haired woman shot Tuck a look of distaste. "I believe you've done enough here, mister. Go on, now. Wreck somebody else's day."

"That wasn't my intent, ma'am," Tuck said.

"Intent or not, it's what you done. Go on, now. Get."

She made a shooing motion at Tuck. He decided getting out before the other old lady came out of her chair was a good idea. She had a mean look to her, like she might bite before she spoke a single word.

He didn't have a hat, so he inclined his head once toward the widow and hurried for the door.

Chapter Twenty

Tuck's next stop was Senora Soto's. Walking toward it, his stomach clenched. He felt like he could already smell the liquor, already feel it splash against the back of his throat and slide down like liquid fire. He almost turned back, worried about the temptation waiting inside.

Instead, he made himself go in. He could hardly be the town marshal if he couldn't enter a saloon. His knees turned wobbly and his hand was shaking by the time he reached the batwing doors, but he shoved them aside and walked in.

The saloon was quieter during the day, with no piano player banging at the keyboard and no card games in progress. A few people sat at scattered tables eating lunch, and Senora Soto held court in her usual corner, cards and pistol on the table in front of her. She had a glass of beer, which she had barely touched, and she was reading a book.

She looked up when Tuck came through the doors, and gave him a professional, welcoming smile. He could tell by the curious look in her eyes that she didn't recognize him at first. When she did, her mouth dropped open in surprise. "Oh," she said. "I didn't—"

"I know, ma'am," he said. "It's me, Tuck Bringloe."

"You're wearing a star."

"That's right. Marshal Turville didn't make it. The hombre that killed Daisie got him, and most of the rest of the posse."

"I'd heard about that. News travels fast around here, Mr. Bringloe. Especially if it's bad."

"I reckon it does. Anyway, I wanted to let you know that we got him. Alf Maier and me. We couldn't bring him in alive, but we killed him, and I thought you'd want to hear."

She had been holding her finger inside her book, but now she inserted a ribbon between the pages and set it on the table. "It doesn't bring Daisie back, does it?"

"No, ma'am. Can't do that. Hard for me to know the difference between justice and vengeance, sometimes. Mostly, I just wanted you to know he won't be killing anybody else."

"That's something, anyway. Thank you, Mr. Bringloe. I appreciate you stopping by."

"You're welcome, ma'am." He started back toward the door, but was stopped by a voice from the stairs.

"Is that really you, Mr. Bringloe?"

Several of Senora Soto's girls had gathered near the top of the staircase. Missy Haynes was in the front of the pack, and she was the one who had spoken. "Yes, ma'am," he said. "It surely is."

"Well, you look a powerful sight different than you did before," Missy said. "Doesn't he, ladies?"

"He looks positively delicious," another woman said.

"I had a bath and a shave. Got some new clothes."

"But still no hat," Missy said.

Tuck smiled. "No, ma'am. I think I'm owed one."

"Well, we'll have to take you out and get you one, Mr. Bringloe."

"You're not going to keep him all to yourself, are you, Missy?" another girl asked. She was dusky skinned, with thick black hair and sleepy eyes.

"I figure that's up to him."

"Congratulations on your new job, Mr. Bringloe," Missy added. "I hope we'll still see you in here from time to time."

"I'm sure you will," he said. "If you ladies will excuse me, I got to figure out where my office is."

"Thanks for gettin' the bastard that killed Daisie," the dark-haired one said. "I hope it hurt when he died."

"He didn't go easy, I can say that for certain."

"Good," she said.

Tuck faced Senora Soto, touched his forehead. "Ma'am," he said. Then he left the saloon quickly. The smell of the liquor was getting to him, washing away his resolve. Staying a minute longer would mean he would never leave.

Despite his comment, Tuck did know where the office was. The fact that he had never spent the night in one of the three cells visible from the doorway was a bit of a surprise, but he guessed that Marshal Turville had more important things to do than locking up drunks. Besides, his days of drinking and starting fights had ended long ago; lately, drinking left him without the motivation or energy to do anything but keep drinking. As a result, he was rarely in trouble with the law.

Deputy Mo Kanouse was a foul-tempered bull of a man who had taken an early dislike to him. Their encounters hadn't ended with Tuck's arrest, though; Kanouse seemed satisfied with the painful beating he had delivered. Tuck suspected that Kanouse probably didn't want to arrest anybody because there might be paperwork involved, and a prisoner might have to be held and fed until a circuit judge visited.

On the long ride back into town, during the times Maier had finally lapsed into silence, with Hank Turville's badge riding in his pocket like a burning coal, Tuck had thought many times that if he were actually offered the job, his first order of business would be to fire Kanouse and hire a new deputy.

Now that he had the position, though, he came to the opposite conclusion. He didn't like the man, but Kanouse knew the town, and the people in it, far better than Tuck did. Tuck didn't know the first thing about marshaling. He needed somebody with experience, at least until he got settled into the role and figured out where trouble might come from. He'd been an army captain; he had experience commanding people, even when they were difficult.

When he walked into the office for the first time wearing the star, he nearly changed his mind.

Kanouse was sitting behind the marshal's desk. He had his mud-caked boots on the desktop, his arms folded over his chest, and he was chewing on the remains of a fat cigar. Flecks of tobacco clung to his lips and his whiskered chin. He tilted his head back when Tuck entered, eyed him, and said, "First time you been in a lawman's office without chains on?"

"Get your feet off the desk, Mo," Tuck said. "Then clean the desk off. You got mud on it."

Kanouse glared at him, but he put his feet on the floor and wiped at the surface of the desk a couple of times with the palm of his hand, using exaggerated motions. "Better?"

"Look, I don't know how well you and Marshal Turville worked together, Mo, but there are bound to be some changes now. I'm not him. I know you think of me as the run-down, no-good drunk you slapped around a time or two. And I don't deny that was me. But this is me, too. I'm a soldier, an officer, and I don't take any guff from my men. I'm glad to keep you on as a deputy. You know the town better than I do, and you know who's likely to need watching. But you'll treat me with the appropriate respect, or we're like to have some serious problems."

Kanouse took the cigar from his lips. He was heavily muscled but with a gut that spilled over his belt. He had small eyes, a flat nose, and a cruel mouth, all set in a broad face and topped by curly dark hair. "Well, that's mighty generous of you, Marshal," he said. "What's your name again?"

"Bringloe. Tucker Bringloe."

The deputy gave a low chuckle.

"Something funny?" Tuck asked.

"Nah, not really."

"I mean it, Deputy Kanouse. We can get along and work together, or you can find a different place to work. I won't tolerate any disrespect."

Kanouse tongued a tobacco fleck off his lip and spat it onto the floor. "Mebbe we should have us a drink, you and me, and talk about how it's gonna work."

"There'll be none of that," Tuck declared. "No drinking on the job. Understand?"

"You sure you're the same walkin' whiskey vat that used to stink up Senora Soto's?"

"Get out of that chair, Mo," Tuck said.

The deputy hesitated long enough to make his statement, then rose.

"Come here."

The man slowly walked closer. "You gonna hit me?"

"Not yet," Tuck said. "But don't keep pushing me. When I do hit you, you'll know it."

Kanouse stopped, close enough for Tuck to have hit him if that had been his intent. He wore a defiant expression. Tuck was starting to think it was the only one he owned. "Do you want this job, Mo?"

"I like it good enough."

"Then don't give me any trouble. Next time you mouth off to me will be your last. Tell me you understand."

Kanouse nodded his head once.

"Say it."

"I understand, boss."

"That's better." Tuck looked out the open door. "I'm going to take a walk, introduce myself to some of the merchants. Mind the office. And keep your damn boots off my desk."

Chapter Twenty-one

In all the days of his life, Cale Ceniceros had never seen a prettier female.

He had driven a buckboard to Fort Huachuca to deliver a load of beef the army had contracted for. Waiting on the driver's bench outside the quartermaster's shop while soldiers unloaded the sides from the wagon's bed, he caught a glimpse of her. She wore a straight skirt that was too short, revealing her ankles and a little calf, and a blouse that was too large for her, and she had brown hair that fell to the middle of her back. Instead of walking flat-footed, she seemed to put a little bounce into every step, sliding her foot along the ground and springing off it. All the while, she held onto the skirt with both hands, as if afraid it would escape. She walked like a child, Cale thought, like a girl on a warm spring day, enjoying the out-of-doors after a winter spent inside. An Apache man walked beside her, staying close, keeping one eye on her and one on their surroundings at the same time.

As he watched, she stopped and slowly turned in his direction. He looked away, not wanting to be caught staring. But after a moment he glanced back. She was staring at him, now. He shifted his gaze away again, embarrassed, but he couldn't help risking another peek, and she still looked at him. The Apache tugged on her arm, but she pulled it free. Cale knew his cheeks were flushing. He met her gaze, and this time could not pull himself away.

"Son?"

From the impatient tone, Cale figured it was not the first time the man had tried to get his attention. He dragged his head around and saw Colonel Cuttrell standing there, hands on his hips and an impatient look on his face. "Huh? Sorry, Cutt—sorry, Colonel," he said.

"You here to deliver or gawk, boy?"

"I . . . deliver, sir."

"For the Tibbetts ranch?"

"That—that's right, sir." Cale was red-faced, aware that he was stammering but having a hard time catching his breath or controlling his words. "The—the J Cross T."

Cuttrell's right hand went to his mouth. He squeezed his lips toward each other, distorting them and reminding Cale of a fish he had caught once, then had a devil of a time working the hook free. "Yes, I thought so," the colonel said. "Thought I recognized you. I was hoping Tibbetts would come himself. Well, you'll have to deliver him a message for me. Can you do that?"

"Yes, sir. I can do that."

"Very well, boy. Tell Mr. Tibbetts that we have to cancel his contract."

"Cancel?" Cale echoed.

"For the beef. We'll take what you brought today, obviously. But Mr. Montclair's offered us a much better price, and we'll have to buy from him unless Tibbetts can beat it. And I already know he can't."

"Well, you gotta let him try, though, right?"

"Son, I represent the Army of the Confederate States of America. There isn't much I 'gotta' do, and not many who can make me do something I don't want to. In this case, I've already discussed pricing with your boss, and he told me the price I was getting was the lowest he could go. Any less, he said, would put him in the poorhouse."

"But then what's *not* selling to the army gonna do to him? That'd be worse, right?"

"According to him, no. He seemed to think selling to us at a loss would be worse than not at all. I've already told Montclair I've accepted his offer, and he starts delivery next week. Run along and tell Tibbetts what I said."

Cale swallowed hard, fighting back the tears he didn't want to shed in front of a military man. Or that girl. He risked a quick glance around to see if she was still in sight.

"Pretty, isn't she?" Cuttrell asked.

"Huh?" Cale's cheeks caught fire again. "Yes, sir, I reckon she is." He wanted to ask about her, who she was, why he'd never seen her before. And where she had gone, since she was no longer in sight. But he didn't dare question the colonel about that. When he was silent for a few moments, Cuttrell walked away.

Cale checked the wagon's bed. The sides of beef were gone. There were no soldiers lounging around, no one to ask.

And as curious as he was, he was more sad and scared for Mr. Tibbetts. Terrified, really. He couldn't begin to predict how his employer would react to the news. The army contract was the steadiest money he had coming in. It wasn't a lot, but he could count on it being regular. Especially with everything else that had been going on, this news would just about destroy the man, and Mrs. Tibbetts, too.

And *he* had to deliver it. He could hardly bear the thought.

What might Mr. Tibbetts do?

He only knew it wouldn't be good.

Cale was hiding something. The young man had been neck-deep in chores since his return from Fort Huachuca. He hadn't said two words in a row, and he couldn't meet Jed Tibbetts's eyes.

Finally, Tibbetts tired of waiting. He found Cale outside the henhouse, where he'd just spread twice as much feed as needed and was sitting with his back against a fence post and sorrow in his eyes, staring into the far distance.

"Cale," he said. "What is it?"

Cale blinked a couple of times, looked at him. The wide-eyed innocence was an act, easily seen through. "What's what, Mr. Tibbetts?"

"What's eatin' at you, son? You been down in the dumps since you come back from the fort."

As if something fascinating had just taken place near his feet, Cale wrenched his gaze away. "It's . . . nothin'."

"I think we both know it's somethin'," Tibbetts countered. "Out with it, boy."

When the young man lifted his head again, there were tears in his eyes. "It's the army, Mr. Tibbetts. I'm really sorry. They canceled your contract. I talked to that colonel, Cuttrell. He said Montclair give him a better deal."

Ordinarily, Tibbetts would have corrected his grammar. He felt a certain responsibility for Cale's upbringing, although the boy had only come to them a couple of years earlier. But the news hit him like he'd been gutshot. Montclair? That Easterner had already priced him out of the army's horse contract. Tibbetts had supplied the fort for years, and those times had been fine. Without that, the beef contract was the one sure thing he had going, the difference between barely hanging on and complete ruination. He had given the army the best price he could, just to keep selling to them.

After Cale filled him in, he left the young man sobbing quietly with just the hens for company, and walked toward the house. He'd have to tell Edith, to warn her that they were losing a meaningful piece of business. On the way, he imagined a picture of himself as if he had genuinely been gutshot, lying on his side in the dirt as the life bubbled out of him. The pain would be intense, but surely not more so than he already felt. He would grow gradually colder, would start to shiver as death neared. His feet would beat a rapid drumroll, his breathing would become shallow, but soon enough it would all be over. No more worries about the ranch, about money. No more feeling like he had disappointed Edith or let down the men who worked for him. No more concerns at all, at least in this life.

Tibbetts shook his head to clear it. The vision had been so true, so solid, that it had seemed momentarily real.

More frightening still, it had seemed appealing.

He found Edith in the kitchen, chopping vegetables for stew. She took one look at him and knew something was wrong, so she laid the knife on the carving board with the carrots. "What is it, Jed?"

He started to speak, but then words failed him. He pulled a chair out from under the table and sank heavily onto it. After a couple of minutes, he was able to repeat everything Cale had told him.

When he was done, he felt wrung out. His big hands hung loosely at his sides, and all the energy had left him. He had thought Edith would be crying, frantic, but she just stood by the counter, dry-eyed, her mouth a grim but determined line.

"So you're giving up?" she asked.

"What choice do I have? Without the army contract—"

"Take it to a judge. You have that man's signature on a piece of paper."

"Montclair owns every judge in the territory, Edith."

"Go talk to Cuttrell yourself, then," she said. "What he told the boy doesn't mean a thing. Unless he's talking to you, you ought to consider the contract still in force. See if he can tell you to your face that he'd prefer Jasper Montclair's business. If that doesn't work, talk to Mr. Harrell again. See if Senora Soto will increase her order for the saloon. Talk to Mr. Maier and see if he won't buy more for the grocery. You have to make them understand that Montclair means to be the only rancher in the territory, and if he is, he'll be able to charge whatever he wants. If they want competition, they've got to help others stay in business."

Tibbetts was dumbfounded. He hadn't thought of it like that. He had just assumed that without the army's trade, he was finished. But maybe there was a way to fight back. Maybe he could convince Cuttrell to change his mind, or drum up customers elsewhere. Or both.

Edith had always been the rock he relied on, the stronger of them by far. The smarter, too, it appeared. He was a lucky man, that was for certain.

It was far too late in the day to go into town for business discussions. After talking with Edith for a while, he went out and stood in the yard, peering off at the Huachucas. They were shrouded in shadow, the sun having already dropped beneath the peaks. Business could wait until tomorrow—it would have to. But that meant that tonight all he could do was fret and hope Edith was right, that there were other customers out there for his beef.

And with night coming on, he had one more thing to worry over ... what might happen out on the range. How many men might he lose tonight? How many head of cattle? And could the attacks be stopped before he was driven bankrupt, regardless of how many customers he had?

Once again, he thought about ending his troubles with a bullet. He couldn't do that to Edith, though. She was strong, but she still needed him.

Anyway, she would never forgive him, and he couldn't face an eternity of her disapproval. She was the one thing in life he had that was true and good and permanent.

He put those thoughts away, and went to wash for supper.

Chapter Twenty-two

I should like to see the girl."

The trooper on guard duty straightened his spine. "I was told no visitors, ma'am, except for the scout. Kuruk."

"You know who I am, don't you?"

"Yes, ma'am. You're Mrs. Cuttrell."

"That's correct. The wife of the commanding officer of this fort. There are precious few women here in the first place, and none as highly ranked as me. And that girl needs a woman's touch."

"She's being well cared for."

Sadie *hmmph*ed. "There are things about which you have no idea, soldier," she said. "At least, I hope you don't. Female things."

The private blushed, and his posture returned to its earlier slump. "I'm sure you're right, ma'am."

"Let me pass, then. And don't listen at the door, because you won't like what you hear."

He hesitated, but she had already won. The trooper lowered his weapon and stepped to the side.

There were few facilities for unmarried women on the fort, and those were fully occupied. But there were some vacant officer's quarters, so a small cottage had been provided for her use until it could be determined where she had come from and what to do with her. Del had mentioned letting her stay if she would become a laundress, but Sadie didn't know if anyone had discussed that with the girl. Most of the townsfolk assumed she wouldn't have been with the mule train unless she was a sporting lady, paid to be there to service all those men. Sadie had more than a little experience herself in that area, and she would never have gone alone on such a journey. The girl was younger than her, though; perhaps she was up to the challenge.

She found it strange that her husband had allowed the Apache to become the girl's ward and protector. A white girl, looked after by an Indian? It didn't make sense. She wondered if the girl had made some arrangement with him, had used her wiles to get herself the freedom that she wanted. After all, an Apache couldn't be counted on to provide any real care.

But another thought had occurred to her. From everything she'd heard, the girl was more than a little touched. Was insanity catching, like influenza? She wasn't sure. Others might not be, either. Maybe nobody wanted to be around the girl, in case her madness spread to them. Maybe the Indian was the only one willing to risk it, and then only on Del's orders.

Either way, Sadie wanted to see for herself what the girl was like. She tapped twice on the door, then opened it and stepped inside. "Hello, dear," she called as she did. "Little Wing, is that your name? It's certainly an odd one, for a white girl."

The cottage had been occupied previously by a young captain and his wife, but he had died from complications following the bite of a scorpion, and she had returned to South Carolina after his death. From what Sadie had heard, there she had gone quite mad, and had been sent to an asylum after peeling most of the flesh from her left arm and upper torso, complaining about bugs under her skin. She had left the cottage fully furnished, and since then it had been used as a bivouac for visiting officers. Perhaps it was the perfect place for a mad girl, after all.

Sadie closed the door and stood just inside. After a moment, the girl appeared at the opposite doorway. First it was just her fingers, gripping the jamb. Then she showed the top of her head, and her eyes, wide and questioning.

"It's all right," Sadie said. She spoke as she might to a frightened infant. "You can come out. Please."

The girl revealed more of her face. She had a nose that might have been cute, except for having been broken at some point, so that it sat crookedly on her face, out of alignment and pointing a little to her left. Her lips were parted. The effects of weather and her harsh journey were evident: lips raw, skin burned and scraped. Sadie felt momentarily sorry for the girl.

Little Wing didn't budge from the doorway. Sadie glanced around and spotted a chair that didn't look too dusty. "Do you mind if I sit?" she asked. "Generally when one has visitors, one invites them to sit."

The girl didn't speak. Sadie took that as license, and sat. "Tell me," Sadie said. "How did you come to be here? How are you finding it? I trust we've made you feel welcome."

"A baby laughing," the girl said. Speaking seemed to make her more comfortable, and she moved through the doorway. As Sadie had suspected from a distance, "girl" hardly defined her. She was a young woman, with a healthy figure that would have made her popular at Senora Soto's. She had thought as much, from the way her husband had eyed her.

She didn't believe that Del had accosted Little Wing in any way, or made any overtures to do so.

Yet.

But she didn't doubt that he would, in time. If she had faith in anything in this world, it was that betrayal was inevitable.

"I'm sorry?" Sadie asked.

"What makes you happy?"

"I don't see what that has to do with—"

"Happiness? That has to do with everything."

"Not with why I came to visit you."

"Yes."

"I'm sorry?" Sadie asked again.

"Not yet," Little Wing said.

Sadie was losing patience with her nonsense. "Excuse me?" she snapped. "I don't understand what on earth you're saying, young lady. Make yourself clear."

"He would not, you know."

"Who? Who wouldn't do what?"

"You met him because he did, but he would not. No more. No longer."

"I'm sure I don't know what you're talking about. I don't think you do, either."

"It will not be the death of you," Little Wing said.

Sadie bolted from the chair. "What won't?"

"Little bottle."

"Excuse me?"

The girl finally came fully into the room, and crossed the distance between them with a few quick strides. Sadie tried to back away but the chair blocked her path. Little Wing took her forearm, held it in a tight grip. "Your bottle. It will not kill you. You might wish it had."

The laudanum? But how could this child know about that?

She couldn't. That was impossible. She was guessing, that's all.

"I came here to be nice to you," Sadie said, though that wasn't quite true. She shook her arm free of the girl's grasp and spun away from her, making for the door. "I can see that was a mistake."

She yanked the door open and burst through, storming past the startled private. Outside on the parade ground, she nearly bowled over Mrs. Hannigan, the captain's wife, who was walking in the twilight with her young daughter. "I'm sorry," she said.

"Oh, Mrs. Cuttrell," the woman said. "Were you coming from that strange girl's house? The one with the Indian name?"

"She's as crazy as I don't know what," Sadie said. "Completely insane. You can't believe a word she says."

Mrs. Hannigan cast a worried eye toward her daughter. "Is it safe to have her here?"

"As long as they keep guards on her, I suppose," Sadie replied. "I'll see if my husband can do anything about her. Excuse me now, I've got to get home."

Had to get back to her bottle, she meant. She was so upset that it would take more than a few sips to calm her now. Mrs. Hannigan said something else, but Sadie was already stalking toward home, her mind fixed on that shelf in the pantry.

Kuruk had seen Mrs. Cuttrell leave Little Wing's quarters from across the parade field. He watched her have a brief, animated conversation with Captain Hannigan's wife, then bustle away toward her own house. An Apache learned as a young boy to cover ground with economy and grace, and the parade ground was considerably flatter and less full of dangerous creatures, thorny plants, and other threats than the mountains where he had grown up. He made it across to the house. Private Lamar saw him coming and stepped to the side.

"Was Mrs. Cuttrell just in here?" Kuruk asked.

"For a little while," Lamar said.

"Why?"

"I don't know. She wanted to see the girl."

"I mean, why did she get in? Aren't you supposed to be keeping people out?"

Lamar shuffled his feet nervously. "She's the colonel's wife."

"Is she the colonel?" Kuruk knew he was overstepping. Lamar was only a private, but he was a white man and a soldier. Kuruk was an Apache. If Lamar wanted to shoot him, he wouldn't have to explain his action in any more detail than to say he thought the Indian was threatening him or the girl.

"Of course she ain't."

"Then she doesn't get in, unless the colonel is with her. Understand? Nobody goes in there without my say-so. Is that clear? Nobody."

"Yeah," the private said. "Sorry."

Kuruk rapped on the door three times, then opened it. "Little Wing," he called. "It's me. Kuruk. Are you all right?"

There was no answer. The house was dark inside, except for a single lamp burning in the front room. Just that morning, seven members of the Ladies' Church Auxiliary had called on her. They were a group of women from town who had never met a sinner they couldn't despise or onto whom they couldn't slip a second helping of shame. They had come to warn Little Wing of the pernicious influences of the town's soiled doves, and of the soldiers who patronized them; or more likely, Kuruk thought, had come to express their disapproval of one they believed was already plenty soiled. They had clucked and complained, and Little Wing hadn't come out from under her bed for hours. "Little Wing!"

He hurried through the rooms, peering through the gathered darkness. In the room she had taken as her bedroom, he found her, crouching in the corner. Her eyes were wide, darting here and there, her mouth open, her breath coming in ragged gasps.

"Little Wing," he said. "It's me. Don't fret, little one. Nothing will hurt you here."

Her gaze fixed on him, but her expression didn't change. She reminded him of nothing so much as a cornered animal, desperate for a way out.

He lowered himself to a crouch, across the room from her so he wouldn't make her feel more trapped. He put a hand on the floor for balance, and to let her see that it held no weapons. "Little Wing," he said, his voice as soothing as he could make it. "There's nothing to fear. I don't know what that woman said to you, but don't let her upset you. She has no power over you, anyhow."

As he spoke, she relaxed, some of the tension visibly leaving her. She moved to a sitting position, her legs splayed out, hands between them, resting on her skirt. Her mouth closed and her eyes calmed. "Afraid," she said.

"I know. But you don't have to be."

"The night. The dark."

"You're safe here, Little Wing. Private Lamar is right outside your door, and—"

"No!" she said, nearly shouting it. "Let her in. That lady."

Sometimes she seemed like a lost, sorrowful six-year-old, but she could just as easily come across as wise beyond her years. There was a mystery about her, but Kuruk couldn't make out the shape of it. As if to prove his unspoken point, she said, "She is a bad woman. She is not good for the colonel or the lieutenant, or herself."

"Can you explain that?" Kuruk asked.

She looked down at her hands. "No."

"Cannot, or don't want to?"

Little Wing didn't answer. He crouched with her for a few more minutes. "Do you want to talk?" he asked.

"No."

"All right," he said. "I'll be outside your door all night. Not Private Lamar. Me. Will you feel safe, then?"

She hesitated before answering, but not for too long. "Yes."

"Sleep well, Little Wing. Soon, we must talk. Really talk."

"Yes," she said again. He wasn't sure if she was agreeing, or just reiterating her satisfaction with his offer.

He had been up with the sun, as usual. Now he would be up until it rose again, and after.

It was a sacrifice he would make, for Little Wing.

If he had been asked, though, he couldn't have explained why.

Chapter Twenty-three

Marshal Tucker Bringloe walked the streets of Carmichael, reflecting on change.

Just days ago, he had been a worthless drunk, someone the town's upright citizens would cross the street to avoid. Had he been on fire, most of them wouldn't have spared the liquid to spit on him, or taken the effort to kick him into the rain. Was he really different now? Or did the badge he wore just create the impression that he was different? Could a piece of tin make a man acceptable in the eyes of those who had previously despised him, if they thought of him at all?

And if it could, what did that say about the man? It was the tin that had changed their minds, if in fact they had changed. How long would that last? Would the effects wear off once they saw that he was the same man? Or was the badge so blinding that they would never realize it?

He had walked all the way to the edge of town and stood there, looking into the open high desert beyond. Scattered clouds blotted out the stars here and there, now and again showing the moon as it swelled toward full. He didn't think it would rain tonight. A brisk, warm wind blew out of the southeast, though. Tuck let it wash over him, almost as if it were the first time he had felt such a wind. Almost as if he really were a new man.

But as he considered it, he heard something underneath the gusts, a kind of scrabbling, scratching sound. Wind whipping tumbleweed across the desert floor? Some night creature, a javelina or a wolf or even a deer, making its way unseen in the dark? He thought he saw motion out there, but whether it was a windblown creosote bush or something else, he couldn't be sure.

Maybe it was nothing at all, a trick of the wind and the shifting moonlight through the clouds.

He wished he could convince himself of that. He lowered his hand to the Colt he had kept, the one Hank Turville had loaned him for the posse. It was town property, so his to use as long as he wore the star. But he didn't draw it, and he couldn't tell if the sound and motion had been anything or not. He watched and listened awhile longer, but they didn't recur.

The gun felt comfortable in his hand, he realized, and that disturbed him. It was as if his hand was made to hold a whiskey glass or a gun. He had seen what guns could do, and had foresworn them because of it. They were, in their own way, as compelling as whiskey, and at least as destructive, though a gun could more rapidly destroy others as well as the one who held it.

The two things in life his hand was made for, and he hated them both. Hated them, because of how much he loved them.

Disgusted with himself, he headed back to Main Street and the marshal's office.

His office.

As he was nearing Senora Soto's, he heard shouting and cursing, the crash of furniture and glassware breaking. A brawl. His first real task as marshal.

He started toward the door, but before he reached it, two men tumbled out. They were battered and bloody, their clothes torn, and they were hanging on to each other with murder in their eyes. Tuck didn't know either of them; if he had ever seen them, he had been too drunk to remember it.

On the boardwalk outside the door, one man clambered to his feet and launched a fierce kick at the one still on hands and knees. His boot caught the other man in the chin, whipping his head backward and dropping him back down again. "Hold up there!" Tuck called. He threw his arms around the standing man and wrenched him backward before he could throw another kick. The guy was short and stocky, with a barrel chest and dark hair and whiskers. He smelled like he'd bathed in a barrel of beer. "That's enough of that!"

"Let me go, you bastard," the man said. "I'll kill you once't I'm done with him!"

"I'm the law," Tuck said. "Marshal Bringloe. You don't want to spend the night in a cell, you won't talk like that."

The man on the ground rose to a shaky crouch, then held on to the saloon wall to draw himself up to a standing position. He glared at the man still struggling against Tuck's grip, and his hand pawed at an empty holster on his belt.

"No guns," Tuck said. "You gonna behave, now?"

The man in his arms nodded, and Tuck released him. "Let's all just cool down," Tuck said.

He started toward the second man, who had released the wall and was wobbling like he might fall down again. "You okay, partner?"

Tuck heard the motion from the first man more than he saw it, but he whirled around at the rustle of clothing and the stamp of a boot on the boardwalk, and he spotted the glint of steel in the man's hand. He caught the man's wrist just as the Bowie knife arced toward him. He stepped to the side and used the man's momentum to tug him forward, and threw his left fist into the man's chin.

The guy's head snapped back under the impact. At the same time, Tuck wrenched his knife arm. The weapon dropped from his hand and clattered to the boardwalk. Kicking it away, Tuck twisted the man's arm behind his back and bent him forward.

By this time, the doorway had filled with spectators from inside the saloon, and more had spilled out. "Anybody know which one started it?"

"It's hard to say, Marshal Bringloe," a woman answered. Tuck looked at the crowd and saw that the speaker was Missy Haynes. She pushed through to the front and pointed at the man Tuck was holding. "That one stumbled into him, and he pushed back, and then they were at it. They're both pretty drunk."

Tuck had already reached that conclusion, from the smell and the fact that he had overpowered the one so easily. "They do much damage?"

"Broke a table and about eleven glasses." This was Jack, the barkeep. "A dozen, might could be."

"You know 'em?" Tuck asked. "They local?"

"Yeah," Jack answered. He gestured to the one Tuck had doubled over. "That there's Ned Calhoun. He works for Alf Maier. T'other one's Billy Simpkins. You workin', Billy?"

Simpkins had given up trying to stand, and was leaning against the saloon wall. He was even struggling with that. He was in his early twenties, Tuck judged, lean and fair-skinned. "Naw," he said. "Not no more."

"Well, you're both coming with me," Tuck said. "You can spend the night in a nice, dry cell and see how you feel in the morning."

"I ain't done nothin' wrong," Calhoun said. He was having a hard time speaking clearly.

Tuck gave his arm an extra twist, earning a pained grunt. "You going to go along quietly? Or do I have to take you there like this?"

"I'll go," Calhoun managed.

"What about you, Simpkins?"

"Might have some trouble walkin'," he replied. "But I'll try."

"Anybody want to help Simpkins walk to my office?" Tuck asked.

Nobody answered for a bit, then Missy spoke up. "I will."

"Can you handle him?"

She threw her head back and laughed. "Marshal, I guess you never were in my line of work. We can't handle a man's got a few drinks in him, we don't last long in the trade."

The rest of the crowd chuckled at that. Tuck eased up on Calhoun's arm and let him resume a more or less upright posture, but kept a grip on him. "Let's go," he said. "Pretty sure you know the way."

They started toward the marshal's office. Missy came behind them, one arm looped around Simpkins's waist to keep him on an even keel. "How do you like the job so far, Marshal?" Missy asked.

"I don't hardly know yet, Missy," Tuck said. "And please, call me Tuck."

"I'll do that," she said.

"You two lovebirds gonna jaw all night?" Calhoun grumbled.

Tuck gave his arm another wrench. "You want to keep this in its socket, you'll keep your mouth shut."

Looking ahead, he saw Mo Kanouse standing outside the open door to his office. "That Ned Calhoun?" Mo asked. "Guess I shoulda told you to keep an eye out for him."

"You know him?" Tuck asked.

"He's kind of a regular guest."

When they reached Kanouse, Tuck shoved Calhoun into his arms. "Put him to bed," he said. He relieved Missy of the burden of Simpkins. "Come on, Billy. Time to turn in."

Simpkins felt like he weighed almost nothing. He gave Tuck a sleepy smile. If not for the fact that his clothes were torn and blood caked his mouth and chin, he hardly looked like someone who had just been brawling. Kanouse took Calhoun into the office, and Tuck followed with Simpkins. "Thanks, Missy," he said over his shoulder.

"I'll be getting back, then," she said. "I hope all your days on the job are this easy."

"First day in town and he's already got a whore girlfriend," Calhoun said as Kanouse shoved him in a cell. There were three of them lined up along the back wall. The one Calhoun occupied had a small barred window, too high for a man to reach on his own and too narrow to fit through. Two desks, a safe, a stove that was burning despite the season, and a rifle rack on the wall completed the furnishings. On the wall behind the marshal's desk, a map of the area had been tacked up, but what Tuck had at first taken as possibly significant markings had turned out to be swatted flies and other insects, along with a few bloodstains of uncertain origin. On the desk was a glass vase containing wildflowers of various colors that he was certain hadn't been there before. A gift from Kanouse? Seemed unlikely.

"Pretty sure he's never had any he ain't paid for," the deputy replied. "But he ain't new in town. He's that rummy used to sit in Soto's and beg free drinks."

Calhoun sat on the stiff bunk and eyed Tuck. "Cleaned up some, ain't he?"

"Figger it won't last," Kanouse said. "But while it does, he's got the star on."

"Mo, I'm warning you," Tuck said. "If I'd known you and Calhoun were pals, I'd have just shot him where he stood."

Kanouse chuckled. "Oh, me and Ned go way back."

Simpkins went into the second cell, next to the one Calhoun sat in. When Tuck released him, he nearly fell over, but he caught himself on the bars. Tuck clanged the door shut and turned the key in the lock, then dropped it in his pocket. "Easy, Billy," he said. "You might want to sit before you hurt yourself."

Simpkins eyed the bunk a couple of times, as if making a mental measurement of how many steps he would need to reach it. Finally he released the bar, took two stumbling strides, and made it to the bunk just as his knees gave way beneath him.

"You okay?" Tuck asked.

"Fine, Marshal."

"The marshal will take real good care of you men," Kanouse said. "On account of he's no doubt spent considerable time in cells his own self." He took a coffeepot from a stove, poured some into a mug that looked relatively clean. Handing it to Tuck, he said, "Reckon you got it covered, Marshal? Been a long day for me."

"Go on," Tuck said. He didn't have any other place to sleep, since he doubted it would look good for the town marshal to be caught curled up in an alley somewhere. He took a sip of the strong, hot coffee. "I'll be here."

"Calhoun, keep an eye on the marshal," Kanouse said. "He's new at this, probably got no idea what he's doin'."

Calhoun laughed. "I'll steer him straight, Mo," he said.

"Kanouse," Tuck said before the deputy reached the door. "Where'd those flowers come from?"

"Some feller brought 'em, said they were from the town council," Kanouse answered. "Kind of a gift, I reckon."

"What feller?"

"I disremember his name. He's a hand out at the Broken M."

"Montclair's ranch?"

"That's right."

"Thanks."

Kanouse gave a casual nod and went out the door. Tuck settled into the chair at his desk. He didn't like Kanouse, and he couldn't argue the fact that up until a few days earlier, he'd have been far more likely to be in the cell than wearing the star. But the man made a decent pot of coffee, he had to give him that.

Chapter Twenty-four

Tuck woke to screams.

He was sitting upright in his desk chair, where he must have been all night. His muscles were so stiff that when he craned his head toward the cells, he felt like Calhoun had spent the night working him over with that Bowie knife. Morning sunlight streamed in through the little window in Calhoun's cell. Tuck noted it, but turned his attention to Billy Simpkins, who was standing in his cell, fists clenched in front of him, shrieking.

"Simpkins, what the hell?" Tuck asked. He was just becoming aware, as his senses awoke, of a strange, sour smell in the room. His eyes were gummy, but he knuckled them open.

Simpkins didn't answer. He took a deep, wet breath, then kept screaming.

Tuck followed his horrified gaze.

Calhoun was in his cell, up against the back wall. His toes barely touched the floor. A noose encircled his throat, which looked like it had been stretched a couple of inches. The other end was tied to the bars of the small window. Calhoun's face was a dark purple color. His mouth was open, his tongue hanging out like a fat, dark worm.

As if that weren't enough, he'd been split open down the middle, from the center of his chest to his belt. His innards had either spilled out or dangled from the opening.

Simpkins kept screaming.

"Shut up, Billy!" Tuck ordered. "Can't hear myself think!"

Tuck's head ached something fierce. He tried to make sense of the scene, but nothing about it was right. He forced himself out of the chair, moved awkwardly to Calhoun's cell, and tugged on the door. Locked, as it had been last night. He felt his pocket and found the key.

Some of the stink came from Calhoun. But there was more to it than that, and as Tuck moved away from the cell, he realized what it was.

The smell of the killer he had killed in that ghost town, the one whose body had turned to liquid and dripped out of the blanket. He had smelled it in Daisie's room, and again in the ranch house where he and Turville had found dead bodies. It was familiar by now.

And it was here, in his office.

"Marshal?" Someone had burst through the front door, probably because of Simpkins's continued screaming. "What's goin' on?"

It was Will Greavey, who owned the general store, Tuck realized. He took a step toward the man, but his legs locked up. He staggered and almost fell to the floor, barely catching himself on his desk. When he looked again, two more people had joined Greavey in the doorway.

"There's a man dead," Greavey announced. "And that new marshal looks drunk."

"He *is* a drunk," someone else said. "I seen him over at Soto's, barely able to stand."

"Billy!" Greavey called. "Can you tell us what happened?"

Simpkins took a couple of hitching breaths, trying to bring himself under control. "I . . . I don't rightly know," he said. "Marshal arrested us last night, me and Calhoun, cause we was fighting. Calhoun's friends with Mo Kanouse, and he and Mo made some fun at the marshal. Next thing I know, I wake up and Calhoun's like . . . like that there."

"Now hold on," Tuck said. "That's not the way it went."

"I was at Soto's last night," the same person who had answered

Greavey before said. "I seen the fight, and this rummy marshal arrestin' them. Him and some whore brought 'em both down here."

"All right!" Tuck slammed his palms down on the desk. "Everybody out! I got a crime to figure out here!"

"Ask me, he's the one who done it!" somebody said.

Tuck spun to the rifle rack and snatched up a sawed-off shotgun. "Out!" he cried.

"Marshal's gone crazy!" Greavey shouted. "Clear out!"

The doorway emptied. Tuck swore softly, knowing his new job—his new life—was in jeopardy before it had really begun.

He couldn't understand how it had happened. How could somebody have got in and done that, with him sleeping right there at the desk?

A thought came to him. He grabbed up the half-empty coffee cup from the desk, sniffed it. It smelled like strong, stale coffee, but that was all. Still, he didn't trust Kanouse. Kanouse and Calhoun had been pals, but maybe not good friends. Kanouse had a key to the office, and one to the cells—he could have slipped in while Calhoun and Simpkins were sleeping off their drunk, and hanged the man in his cell. If he'd drugged the coffee somehow, Tuck might have slept through the whole thing. Then his gaze fell on the flowers. Or those? They looked innocent enough. The coffee seemed more likely.

Tuck opened the door. Clutches of people stood on the street, whispering to one another and looking his way. He tossed the coffee into the dirt, wishing there were some way he could know for sure if anything had been slipped into it.

He didn't think there was, but he knew who to ask.

He couldn't leave Simpkins in here with the corpse, so he unlocked the man's cell and told him to skedaddle. Once Simpkins was gone, Tuck drew the curtains over the big front window and left the office, locking the door behind him. He would have to come back and deal with the body, but not yet.

First, he wanted to talk to Mo Kanouse.

The deputy lived in a house at the north end of town. It wasn't much more than a shack, thrown together out of odds and ends of wood, with one adobe wall anchoring it. Tuck became more awake and angrier with every step. Already, word was spreading around town. People eyed him with suspicion, and some spoke to him with outright hostility. He ignored them, focused on finding Kanouse and shaking the truth out of him.

When he got to the house, he pounded on the door. Nobody answered, so he shoved the door open and went in. "Mo!" he shouted. "Kanouse! You in here?"

The place looked worse on the inside than it had out. Kanouse seemed to have held on to everything that his hands had ever lighted on, and it was all tossed haphazardly into the front room. Clothing, boots, old saddles, scraps of paper and cloth and leather, broken-down guns, children's toys, bones . . . Tuck could hardly think of a category of item that wasn't represented, except maybe books. He didn't see any animal corpses, but that didn't mean there weren't some under the top few layers. A narrow path threaded through the debris, leading to an open door. Tuck took the path, hoping he wouldn't have to stay here long. The smell was awful in a different way from that he'd left behind in the office; it was the aroma of failure, he thought, and poverty, and hopelessness, aged in this little shack along with sweat and piss and booze.

"Kanouse!" he shouted again.

"Huh?" a voice answered from the other side of the door. Tuck went to the doorway and stopped.

In the next room there were additional piles of random belongings, but in the middle of it, like an island in a sea of detritus, was a bed. Mo lay on top of it, on his side, naked. Beside him, face up, legs spread, was a dark-haired woman with pendulous breasts and a round belly. There were a couple of empty liquor jugs beside the bed, and from the smell of them, Kanouse and the woman had poured the contents over themselves. "Kanouse!"

Tuck said. "Put some clothes on. Ma'am, you'd best dress and get out of here."

She started to roll out of bed, but Kanouse reached over and slapped a big hand down on one breast. "You stay put, Joy," he said. "The marshal won't be here long."

"You don't make that call," Tuck said. "I'll stay till I get some answers. Ma'am, it's time to go."

"Answers to what?" Kanouse demanded, not releasing the woman.

"Where you were last night, for starters."

"I was right here. With Joy."

"All night?"

The woman laughed. It was the kind of laugh that could put ideas in a man's head. "Oh, we was here all night, that's for sure," she said.

"Ma'am, please put something on," Tuck said.

"Women make you nervous, boss?" Kanouse asked. He released her breast but clamped his hand between her legs. She squealed with pleasure. Tuck turned away.

"No, but I have some manners," he said. "Guess you don't."

"Should I tell him what you were doin' to me all night, Mo?" she asked. "How you rode me for hours?"

"I don't need to hear that, ma'am."

"You might like it, Marshal," Kanouse said, adding a raucous laugh. "You want to give her a try, mebbe? Joy ain't too particular once she gets goin'." He moved his hand on her, and the woman squealed again.

Tuck had heard enough. He wouldn't get anything out of the deputy, not today. He made his way down the narrow path and banged through the front door.

A boy of about thirteen was waiting outside the marshal's office when Tuck got back. Other folks had gathered around, peering through the window, trying to see the body. Tuck was glad he had drawn the curtain. There was a window set into the door, but it didn't offer a clear view of the cell in question. As Tuck approached, everybody cleared out, except the boy. "Mayor Chaffee wants to see you, Marshal," he said. "He gimme two bits to tell you."

"You did your piece, boy," Tuck said. "Run along."

The boy did as he was told. Tuck looked in through the window. As he'd thought, he couldn't see the corpse from there. He could see flies, though, buzzing in lazy circles. No doubt coming in through the barred window in back, the one Calhoun was hanging from.

He wanted to open the office and get the body out. But the mayor was waiting. If he fired Tuck now, dealing with Calhoun's remains would be somebody else's job. Tuck could go to Soto's and start drinking, and not come out again until he had burned through every penny of his advance pay.

He cursed and turned his back on the office. He had worn the star for less than twenty-four hours. Still, that was almost a day longer than he had ever expected to. He crossed the street and went into the town hall building. People looked away when they saw him coming. He made his way upstairs, tapped twice on the mayor's door, then opened it.

Mayor Chaffee was standing at the window, as long and lean as an afternoon shadow.

"I watched you crossing the road," he said, without turning around. "I watched people stepping aside to avoid you. Whispering behind your back. Marshal Bringloe, you have managed to find an inordinate amount of trouble for your first day on the job."

"You don't have to believe me, Mayor, but—"

Now the mayor did turn, his motions graceful and economical. "I don't want to hear excuses. Or justifications. You stepped in something, Bringloe. Something that reeks to high heaven."

"Yeah, only—"

Chaffee cut him off again. "Ahh! Alf Maier swore to me that you had sobered up, on the posse. I heard from several citizens that you were drunk this morning. Drunk, with a prisoner dead in your cell and another one screaming like a child. This was not what we had in mind when we appointed you marshal."

"I know that, Mayor Chaffee. I wasn't drunk. I fell asleep sitting up in my chair, and when I woke up, Calhoun had been butchered and Simpkins was screaming." He thought about adding his suspicion that he'd been drugged, but since he couldn't back that up, he kept quiet about it. "You can ask at Soto's, or ask Simpkins. Nobody saw me drinking, because I wasn't."

"You're a mighty sound sleeper, I suppose."

Tuck hesitated, but again decided to leave out his theory about Kanouse's coffee. "I don't know what happened, but I'll find out. Believe me, I want to get to the bottom of it more than anybody."

"I'm not sure about that," Chaffee said. "We on the town council appointed you. I think it's safe to say we're very invested in you finding out the truth. Or simply telling the truth, if it's what it appears to be from here."

"It's not," Tuck said.

"I certainly hope not, for all our sakes. You be careful, Mr. Bringloe. Either you're a falling-down drunk like people think, or you have made a very bad enemy of someone. The result is that the townsfolk are turning against their lawman. That's never a good sign. You need to wrap this up in a hurry, or resign and turn in your badge."

"I aim to," Tuck said. "Wrap it up, I mean."

"See that you do, then. And at the first hint of you drinking, you'll be fired, and you'll owe the town for every nickel we advanced you. You might want to keep that in mind before you go buying a lot of new clothes."

Chaffee faced the window again. "Thanks for the flowers," Tuck said to his back. "They were . . . unexpected."

"Flowers? I have no idea what you're talking about." He blew air from his nose in a snort.

Tuck knew he'd been dismissed. He hurried down the stairs and outside. His head was pounding. The sunlight on the street was like a lance driving through his eyes into his brain. He stood in the shade, leaning against a post, unwilling to risk the bright stretch of road he would have to cross back to his office.

While he stood there, a buckboard rolled past, a lean, older rancher at the reins and a younger man, barely more than a boy, beside him. Neither one looked happy. They didn't glance his way, just pulled to a stop outside the bank. The man got down and started for the door, and Tuck could see that he was nervous, jittery. His hands quaked and his knees looked like they wanted to fold up at any time.

The younger one waited on the buckboard's bench, less anxious than the man, Tuck thought, but more sad, like he might start crying at any moment, and never stop.

Tuck knew just how he felt.

Chapter Twenty-five

Sir," McKenna said. He was on his feet, and he had an urgent tone to his voice that drove Cuttrell mad. The lieutenant seemed to be perpetually courting favor from somebody, most often him. Cuttrell counted on McKenna, but that didn't mean he liked him or wanted him around. Mostly, he liked having a man he could assign a task to and know it would get done. But when he didn't have something specific for McKenna to do, he hated having the man buzzing around trying to impress. "Sir, I've been gathering information about some strange goings-on in the vicinity."

Cuttrell looked around the table. His entire command staff was gathered for this meeting, so Cuttrell couldn't just tell McKenna to shut up and go away. He had to at least pretend to be interested in the man's tales. "I hardly think that's the army's chief concern, Jimmy," he said.

"But sir, it has to be *a* concern. We're responsible for the safety of the citizenry, and that safety is in considerable jeopardy just now."

"Maybe Lieutenant McKenna can tell us what sorts of things he's talking about," Captain Hannigan suggested. "And then we can decide as a group what our response should be."

"If any," Cuttrell added.

"Indeed," Major Eccles said.

McKenna appeared slightly mollified. He took his seat again, and spread his hands on the tabletop. "There are so many things.

The slaughter of the mule train. Over on the J Cross T, cattle being slaughtered. Mutilated. Then cowboys, meeting the same fate. That prostitute murdered at Senora Soto's, then most of the posse dying in the effort to find the killer. Supposedly, the two remaining members did track him down and kill him, but they returned without a body to show. One of them has since become the town marshal, but today there have been reports that on his first night in the job, a prisoner in a cell was murdered—hanged from window bars, and mutilated there. This is, I think you'll all agree, a much more significant series of events than we usually see around here. Bad, bloody events. Colonel Cuttrell, this is not normal. This is beyond anything we've seen before, and I think we need to respond officially in some way."

"Jimmy," Cuttrell said. "I understand your point. I do. But all I see is a series of murders. Gruesome, ghastly ones, yes. The situation with the mule train, I agree, requires military action, if we had the first clue to what we were responding. But absent a trail we can follow, absent any information at all about who might have been responsible, I'm at a loss as to exactly what to do. The inescapable conclusion was that it was not Apache predation, and our primary purpose here—besides guarding what few mule trains still follow the old Ghost Trail, now that the railroad is in business—is protecting the town and the outlying ranches from Apaches. They've been quiet and well behaved lately—"

"Well behaved for Apaches, that is," Hannigan said, to a general round of laughter.

When it died down, Cuttrell continued. "So what is it exactly you propose we do? Someone was murdered, the killer was himself killed. Or perhaps not, since no body was presented. Cowboys died on a ranch that's failing anyway. If there had been similar killings on the Broken M, I would agree that a response was called for, since Montclair is the most prosperous rancher in the vicinity, and we have contracted with him to supply all the fort's beef. The new marshal has proven himself to be a poor host to his overnight guests. Do you, Lieutenant McKenna, have any specific plan of action? Do you know who the enemy is we might move against?"

"Who the enemy is? No, sir," McKenna replied. "Nor do I know if we're talking about one enemy, or many. If we can find out who we're after, I have—"

Cuttrell cut him off. "Until we know who we're dealing with, there's no point in discussing specifics." He let his gaze wander across the other officers at the table. "If there's nothing else, gentlemen, let's declare this meeting adjourned and get to work."

The other officers indicated their assent, and with much scraping of chairs and clomping of boots across the hardwood floors, they made their way back to their respective duties. Only McKenna remained behind when they were gone, standing near the door and eyeing Cuttrell.

"Yes, Jimmy? What is it?" Cuttrell asked.

"Sir, I've received a wire in response to mine. I don't have the full manifest yet; that's en route via the railroad. But I'm told positively that there were no girls or women traveling with that mule train. It was all men. Wherever that girl, the one Kuruk calls Little Wing, came from, she wasn't with the train when it left California."

"So they found her along the way?"

"I don't think there's anyone alive who can answer that, Colonel. Except perhaps the girl. Kuruk says she isn't talking much, and what she does say is most often nonsense. I think whatever happened probably made her lose her mind. If she wasn't already loopy to begin with."

Cuttrell considered the lieutenant's words. Perhaps the girl would be able to explain her origins at some point, and perhaps not. Either way, she couldn't remain the army's problem indefinitely. He would give her another week, he decided, and that only because he didn't need to assign troopers to watch over her. If she was up to it, she could work as a laundress and remain on the fort. If she hadn't regained her senses by then, he would turn her over to one of the churches in town, or perhaps to Senora

Soto or one of her competitors. "Very well, Jimmy," he said. "Let me know if you find out any more."

"Yes, sir."

McKenna remained standing by the door, where he had been. "Is there something else?" Cuttrell asked.

"No, sir."

"Then you're free to go, Lieutenant."

"Yes, sir." McKenna snapped off a crisp salute. "Thank you, sir."

He hurried from the room, leaving Cuttrell alone. He had dismissed Jimmy's concerns, in the meeting. But that didn't mean he didn't share them, to some extent. There was something going on. Whether it was centered on Carmichael or Fort Huachuca remained unclear. But it needed watching, just the same.

And watch, he would.

McKenna hustled toward the blacksmith's shop, past the barracks. Sergeant Delahunt had promised a status report on their project today, and McKenna meant to have it, whether Cuttrell cared or not. There was something about taking orders from the colonel that grated on him. It had done so, even before he'd started sleeping with Sadie, but it got worse after. The more she told him how much better he was in bed than her husband, the less respect he had for Cuttrell. If he were any kind of commander, he would be able to satisfy his wife, wouldn't he?

Lost in thought, he almost didn't see Kuruk and the girl. Little Wing, people were calling her. The Apache called his name, and McKenna blinked and stopped short. "Kuruk," he said, touching his hat's brim. "Ma'am. The fort treatin' you well?"

"Like spun sugar," she said. McKenna had no idea what she meant by that. But from what he understood, nothing she said made a lick of sense, so he didn't bother asking for an explanation.

"Glad to hear it." To Kuruk, he added, "I'm headin' over to Delahunt's. Want to tag along?" The Apache scout got along with the buffalo soldiers better than the white ones, most of the time. He supposed that wasn't surprising. White men had mistreated the blacks and the Indians pretty much forever.

"We're heading into town," Kuruk answered. "Little Wing needs some things from the store."

He didn't volunteer what sorts of things, and McKenna, figuring they were women's things, didn't ask. Kuruk had just about adopted the girl, and that was all right with him. He wasn't saddled with her, which was all he cared about. He excused himself, and hurried off to find Delahunt.

Chapter Twenty-six

Wilson Harrell barely looked up when Jed Tibbetts approached his desk. "I'm very busy, Mr. Tibbetts," he said. "Is there something you need?"

"Five minutes of your time," Tibbetts said. He doubted he would get that much, but if he didn't ask for it he would get even less.

Harrell stopped fiddling with papers and let his hands rest on the swell of his stomach. "As I said, I'm quite busy today. What is it?"

"I know you turned me down for a loan," Tibbetts said. "And I don't expect you to reconsider. But I just lost my contract with the army, so things are bound to be tight until I can figger something out. I wanted you to know that I'll pay what I owe. I'm a man of my word. But my payments might have to be smaller for a spell, and farther between."

Tibbetts wasn't sure what to expect. The banker had already indicated his utter lack of interest in the J Cross T's survival. Tibbetts believed, though, that he'd want to see the ranch last until the bank loan was repaid. He hoped that by coming clean with Harrell, they could work out some sort of arrangement.

So he was surprised when Harrell waved his hand to stop him from continuing. "I'm sorry, Mr. Tibbetts," he said. "I can't even have this conversation with you."

"What does that mean, Wilson? I'll pay it back, but I gotta—"

"Mr. Tibbetts!" Harrell said forcefully. "I can't talk to you about this. This bank no longer holds your note."

Tibbetts must not have heard him right. "I'm sorry?"

Harrell blew out a sigh. "I've sold your note, Mr. Tibbetts. You no longer owe a penny to this bank."

"Sold it? Without asking me?"

"It really is not within your purview. That note is a negotiable instrument, transferrable at will."

"First I've heard about that."

"Perhaps you didn't read the agreement thoroughly."

"Sold it to who?"

Harrell picked up a stack of papers from his desk and straightened out the edges, tapping them on the desktop until they were neatly aligned. "To Jasper Montclair," he said, his voice barely a whisper.

Again, Tibbetts thought he had misheard. "To who?"

"Montclair," Harrell said, louder this time. "I sold your note to Jasper Montclair. He made a generous offer, and frankly, I had to doubt your ability ever to repay it."

Tibbetts felt the world drop out from under him. He was dizzy, his head spinning in fast, tight circles. "You did what? To Montclair? How could you do that?"

"I assure you, it's perfectly legal. It's all spelled out in the contract you signed."

"Wilson, I didn't read that. You're a man of honor. I take you at your word. You told me that was a deal between me and your bank—you didn't say anything about turnin' it over to somebody else. Least of all someone like Montclair. You understand he's my competitor, right?"

"I'm sorry, Mr. Tibbetts. What's done is done. You have no further business with this bank. You'll have to arrange a payment plan with Mr. Montclair."

Tibbetts made his way to the door. He was half-blind with panic, and the world spun crazily beneath his feet. With every step he thought he might fall down and never hit bottom. *Jasper Montclair?* He might as well have put a bullet in his own gut after all.

He was done. Montclair would make repayment of the loan impossible. He didn't want the money. He wanted the J Cross T. He always had. It abutted his ranch, blocking it from spreading all the way across the valley floor to the river. He'd made several offers, and Tibbetts had always turned him down, refused to entertain the possibility of selling. In hard times, he had occasionally wished he'd made a different decision, but that never lasted for more than a day or two. He and Edith had scraped by, with the help of good grazing land and hands he could rely on.

But he'd always counted on the bank to carry him through the leanest times. Now he didn't even have that. Instead, he owed money to Jasper Montclair; money that, given present circumstances, he couldn't begin to repay.

He'd have to let Edith know to start thinking about where she wanted to go next. Now that Montclair owned his note, the J Cross T's days were numbered.

Mr. Tibbetts had told Cale to stay with the wagon. Cale could tell the rancher was despondent, and had been since he had delivered the colonel's news yesterday. Tibbetts had hardly said two words on the way into town. But his first stop had been the bank, and Cale hoped that meant he had a plan of some kind. He'd overheard Mr. and Mrs. Tibbetts talking the other day, and he knew the ranch could be in trouble if something wasn't done. Still, he couldn't quite conceive of anything truly disastrous occurring. Mr. Tibbetts had weathered some bad storms, but had always come out all right. He would this time, too.

He just *had* to.

Cale was trying to keep his mind off his boss's troubles by watching the townsfolk go about their business. He had never lived in a town, and couldn't quite imagine what everybody did all day. It looked as if they bustled around without purpose, in one door and out another, sometimes shopping for things nobody really needed, occasionally climbing on board a train or a stagecoach for a journey to some distant locale.

Then he saw that girl, the one he'd noticed at the fort. She was walking with the same Indian, and he was carrying a package all wrapped up in paper. Cale didn't know if that meant he had bought something, or she had and he was just toting it for her. They were the object of considerable attention from the townsfolk; people stopped in their tracks and stared, then spoke in hushed tones to one another. Cale figured she wouldn't even notice him, with all those folks making such a fuss. But she saw him looking, and this time he didn't turn away, although he felt his cheeks flushing under her gaze.

She didn't turn away, either. Instead, she smiled.

He took that as an invitation. He'd never talked to girls much, but he'd daydreamed about them plenty. And in those imaginings, the girls had never smiled at him the way this one did. Her whole face got involved, mouth and eyes and cheeks.

He hopped down from the wagon and walked up to her. Or near her, anyhow. He stopped about three feet away and glanced at the Indian. The Indian gave a quick nod and stepped back a pace.

"Howdy," Cale said. "My name's Cale. Cale Ceniceros. That's a Mexican name, on account of how I'm half Mexican and half white, on my momma's side."

"Sunshine," she said. "Birdsong."

"That's your name?" Cale asked. "Sunshine Birdsong?"

"Happy-making," she said. The smile hadn't left her face.

"Those things make you happy? Sunshine and birdsong?"

"Yes," she said.

"What's your name? If you don't mind me askin'."

She touched her breast. "Little Wing."

"That sounds like an Indian name. You're not Indian, are you?"

She looked over her shoulder at the Apache. "She don't know her name," the man said. "We call her Little Wing. She likes it, anyhow."

"It's pretty," Cale said. He had already run out of conversation.

"Pretty," he said again. He was not just referring to her name, but couldn't bring himself to elaborate.

"The sky in the morning," she said. "A flower as it opens. The first snow on a meadow."

Cale couldn't follow her train of thought at first. Then he realized what she meant, or hoped he did. "Things that are pretty?"

"Yes."

"You're pretty."

She raised a hand to her face, felt the line of her cheekbone with the backs of her fingers, then ran them down her jaw and neck. He couldn't help wishing that was his hand. "Pretty," she said.

"Yep," Cale said. Again, he felt like the conversation had run out of steam, and he wasn't sure where to go with it. And Mr. Tibbetts could be coming out of the bank at any moment. He needed to say something, anything, that would allow for a continuance at some future time. He didn't understand much of what she said, but he loved watching her say it. The way her face moved as she spoke, her expressions pure and unguarded, her smile so genuine it was like brightest daylight; these were things he had never seen or expected to see, but having seen them he didn't want to stop. The sound of her voice *was* like birdsong, or the trickle of a cool mountain stream on a hot, thirsty day, and he didn't want to stop hearing it. He had never felt this way before, about anything or anybody. But he didn't want it to end.

"Do you reckon I could call on you sometime?" he asked. That was a crazy question. He didn't own his own horse, didn't have but a few nickels to his name at any given time. And with the ranch problems, he doubted Mr. Tibbetts would be able to pay him, much less provide the extra it would take to buy some decent clothes and pay a visit like a real gentleman would. He would never be anything but a poor, dumb cowboy, nobody a beautiful girl like her would look at twice.

"Yes," she said.

"Yes?" Cale echoed. "You mean it?"

"Yes."

"I can call on you?"

She grinned, then tapped her teeth with her fingertips. When she did, she wore a curious expression. That and the way she had touched her face made Cale think maybe she didn't even know what she looked like; she was exploring herself with her hands, trying to cement her own image in her mind. Maybe she didn't have a mirror. "Yes," she said at last.

He wasn't entirely sure she had understood the question. But then, he hadn't understood much of what she'd said, and that didn't bother him one bit.

"At the fort?" he asked.

"She'll be there," the Indian said. "We got to go, now."

"My name's Cale," he said. "So she doesn't forget."

"We'll remember," the Indian said.

"Bye, Little Wing," Cale said.

"A lion's teeth," she said as the Apache led her away. "Ice on the river. Fire through the trees."

She was still muttering as she walked back toward the fort, but Cale couldn't hear her anymore. "Things that are pretty," he said to himself. But as he climbed back up onto the buckboard, another thought came to him. "No," he corrected himself. "Things that are dangerous."

Chapter Twenty-seven

Waiting for the undertaker to collect Calhoun's body, Tuck studied the scene in a way he hadn't before. What he couldn't figure out was how it had been done. The cell door had been locked, and remained so. The key was in his pocket, though it was possible that Kanouse had one. The cell was eight feet deep, so nobody outside it could have strung Calhoun up from there, much less gutted him. Whoever had done it had to have been inside the cell. Which meant Tuck had been sleeping far more soundly than he ever had when sober.

He unlocked the cell door and went in, shooing away flies as he did. He couldn't tell much of anything from the wound. The edges looked fairly clean, which implied a sharp blade of some kind. But the body had been there for hours, drying out, and the wound's sides were kind of curling up, which made even that guess suspect.

The rope around Calhoun's neck was thin, braided. The flesh of his neck had folded over it, or it had sliced deeply enough into the skin that Tuck couldn't see much of it. Between there and the window was a length of about two and a half feet. It was tied to two of the bars, wrapped first around one and then the other, then knotted between them. The whole thing couldn't have been more than about four feet long.

And the end of the knot was on the inside of the cell, so again, it looked like it had been done from this side. That was almost a given, though—Tuck didn't see how anybody would have been able to loop it around Calhoun's neck from outside. They'd have to have been standing on a twelve-foot ladder, for one thing.

All of which led to one conclusion. Somebody—probably Mo Kanouse—had slipped him something to knock him out. Probably in the coffee, he figured. Kanouse pouring him a cup should have been his first clue. The deputy would be more likely to throw a cup of scalding coffee on him than to serve him one.

At a knock on the door, Tuck turned away from the corpse. He looked through the door glass and saw the undertaker, Hubert Chalmers, standing outside with a couple of assistants. He couldn't remember when he'd last been so glad to see somebody. The sour stink that had filled the office had dissipated, but that only allowed the overripe, meaty smell of the corpse to fill the space.

"I'll wait outside," he said as he opened the door. "Do whatever you need to do."

Chalmers and his men went inside, and Tuck stepped out, sucking in fresh air as he did.

While he stood in the street, a man rode up on a fine brown horse, tricked out in a saddle and bridle that together looked more expensive than all the horses and tack Tuck had ever owned put together. He dismounted and tied the animal to a hitching post, then started in Tuck's direction. He was a slender man, wearing a white shirt under a paisley vest, a little derby hat, and black pants. On the vest was a round badge with a star in the middle. He smoothed down his mustache as he approached.

"You must be Bringloe," the man said. He was a bit of a dandy, with a high voice.

"That's right."

He put a hand out as he approached, and Tuck took it, gave it a shake. "I'm Sheriff Behan. John Behan."

Johnny Behan. That explained the pricey clothing and gear. Behan collected ten percent of all county taxes, plus the same slice of all Tombstone's prostitution, liquor, gambling, and theater businesses. "Pleased to meet you, Sheriff."

"Likewise."

"What brings you to Carmichael?"

"You do." Behan took a step back and scrutinized Tuck. "You don't look as bad off as I'd heard."

"Had me a shave, a bath, got some new clothes. Guess I can't complain."

"The way they tell it in Tombstone, you're barely able to stand on your own two legs."

"Appears they exaggerate." Tuck hadn't known anyone in Tombstone was aware of his existence, much less talked about him.

"Probably they do, yes," Behan said. "Still, I know you're new in the job. I know you've had a rough start. That was an undertaker I saw going into your office, right?"

"It was."

"Then that part's true, anyway. About the murder last night, in a cell."

"That's true."

"And it's also true that until a few days ago, you were a rummy. No job, cadging drinks wherever you could."

"I'm not proud of it, but yep. That's true, too."

"And now, suddenly, you're reformed. Sober. A man to be relied upon."

"I don't know as I'd go that far. How about trying to be?"

"It might look easy, Mr. Bringloe. This law dog business. But it's not. I guess you got a taste of that already."

"More than a taste, I'd say."

"Fair enough."

"I'm sorry, Sheriff Behan," Tuck said. "I appreciate you coming down here to say howdy, but you're the sheriff of all of Cochise County. I can't help feeling like you must have better things to do with your time."

"Might could have," Behan answered. "I like to introduce myself to new lawmen whenever they show up. Some of them, they show up and are gone about as quick, so I don't like to waste time."

"That's mighty neighborly, Sheriff."

"I figure we got to work together to keep things peaceable. Also, I want to remind you of something."

"What's that?"

"Something you can't forget. But seeing as you're new in these parts, you might not know it going in, so I thought I might just mention it. You're a town marshal, and that gives you a badge and a gun and a little bit of power over folks."

"I understand that. I was an army captain once, Sheriff. I know about power, and its limits."

"That's something," Behan said. "But it's a little different here. You've got power, yes. But you also have people who have power over you."

"Like you?"

"Yes, but that's not what I'm getting at. I'm saying you need to understand who wields power locally. Me, yes. But here, where you are? There's the town council. They appointed you and they can cut you down just as quick. Mayor Chaffee is a big man around here, elected with more than seventy percent of the vote. Jasper Montclair is the wealthiest rancher in the county, bar none. Colonel Cuttrell is—"

Tuck interrupted him. "The fort and Montclair's ranch aren't even in my jurisdiction."

"That's my point, Bringloe. The people who have power over you aren't necessarily people you have any sway over. I'm not in your jurisdiction, either. You can't say boo to us, but we can yank your strings any time we need to. I'm including myself in that, even though I don't have any intentions in that regard. I can't speak for Montclair or Cuttrell or them. I'm only saying to keep that in mind. They run you, you don't run them. That clear enough?"

"Crystal," Tuck said.

"I wish you luck here, Marshal. You're not off to a good start. Maybe you can turn that around."

"I'll give it my best shot."

"All a man can ask for." Behan made an abrupt swivel and went back to his horse. He climbed into the saddle, touched the brim of his derby, and rode away. Tuck thought he might stop somewhere on the street, but he kept going, out of town and back toward Tombstone.

So he had only come to deliver that message? What did that mean? What had he gotten into here?

Chalmers and his men were hauling something out of the office, covered in a blanket. Tuck knew what it had to be, but he didn't want to think about that right now. He wanted to try to figure out what the hell Behan had been yammering about.

All he knew was, the combination of the undertaker and his guys carrying a body out in pieces and Behan's warning, if that's what it was, gave the day a decidedly sinister cast.

"If you think it is bad now," a female voice said behind him. Startled, Tuck spun around, his hand dropping to the grip of his revolver. He didn't draw it, because when he turned he saw a chestnut-haired young woman wearing clothing that didn't quite fit and a smile he could only describe as beatific. Her hair was worn loose, and reached well past her breasts. "Just wait."

"Excuse me?" Tuck said. "I don't think I caught that, miss."

"I will help if I can," she said. "But I do not know . . . I do not know if that will be enough."

"Enough? Enough for what?"

The smile didn't dim, but her eyes took on a momentary glimmer of disquiet. She moved her shoulders a little, but didn't answer.

"Miss?" Tuck said. "I didn't quite catch what you said."

"I . . . I cannot say," the girl said. "I . . ."

An Apache man walked up behind her. He bore a paper-wrapped bundle and had on a CSA blouse decorated with fringe, feathers, bones, and other objects. "I'm sorry, Marshal," the man said. "She don't always know what she's saying. She didn't mean nothing by it."

"For a second there, she was the only thing that made sense all day," Tuck said. "Maybe that says more about me than her."

"Might be," the Apache said.

"What's your name, miss?" Tuck asked.

She kept smiling, and wiggled her shoulders again.

"We call her Little Wing," the Apache said. "She's been through a lot."

"You're with the army?" Tuck asked him.

"I'm a scout, yes. I'm called Kuruk. That means bear, to you."

"Apaches like bears?"

"Apaches *hate* bears," the man corrected. "Bears, snakes, and owls. They're creatures of the darkness. They called me that because I was a big pain in the rear."

"They knew when you were born that you were a pain?"

"No. When I was about nine or ten, I guess. Before that my name was Brings the Sun."

"Because you were the light of your momma's life?"

"Because I screamed so loud, I woke the sun up. Believe me, being named after a beast everybody hated was kind of an improvement."

"Well, Kuruk," Tuck said. "I'm Tucker Bringloe. Folks call me Tuck."

"Or Marshal."

"Just lately. Not sure how long that'll last, either. Figure people might just as well call me Tuck, cause that's more likely to stick."

"Anyhow," Kuruk said, "I hope Little Wing didn't disturb you. She don't mean any harm."

"Not a bit," Tuck said. "It's a pleasure to meet you both."

"I will help," Little Wing said.

Kuruk smiled patiently and led her away by the arm. Tuck watched them go, a little saddened by their absence. The Apache was nice enough, but the girl had a warmth about her that he had rarely seen. She might have been a little touched, as the Indian had suggested. But she seemed real, at the same time. Real, and honest. She might be crazy, but he was starting to think that term applied universally, so what was the difference?

Chapter Twenty-eight

His office still stank like death.

Chalmers and his assistants had cleared out the body, but there remained a sticky puddle of blood and other fluids, black in the middle and pink around the edges. The flies were thick on it. Tuck would have to get some lye and water and wash it down. Until he did, he couldn't work in there, and he certainly couldn't lock anyone up. He stepped outside again, in quest of fresh air.

Hearing footsteps on the boardwalk, he looked to his left to see Missy Haynes approaching, wearing a black dress with red trim and bearing a hatbox.

"You didn't," Tuck said.

"I *did*. I told you I would."

"You never even measured my head."

"I guessed. I'm pretty good at that."

She handed him the box. He had some trepidation about opening it. He had never been given a hat, at least not since he'd been a young boy. And, he supposed, the hats furnished by the Union Army weren't exactly gifts, but he hadn't been able to choose them. Other than those, he had picked out every hat he'd worn, and he considered it as personal a selection as a pair of boots.

But Missy stood there with an expectant smile on her face, so he pulled off the lid. Inside was a fine, black, beaver hat, more luxurious than any he'd owned. "It's beautiful," he said. "Thank you."

"Put it on, silly," Missy said.

He tilted his head toward his office door. "We can't go inside. It's kind of a mess."

"I heard. That's all right. I have a pocket mirror if you want to see."

He removed the hat and set the box down on the walkway. He liked the shape of it, and the way it felt in his hands. With a grin he was sure looked as awkward as it felt, he put it on.

The fit was perfect. It was snug across the brow and temples, but not too tight. It would stay on in a stiff breeze without giving him a headache. "That's just right," he told her.

Missy held out a mirror, but Tuck shook his head. "I don't need to look at myself. Seen enough horror already today. I can tell it's just right. Missy, you're one hell of a judge of heads."

She snorted a laugh at that, but Tuck didn't ask her to elaborate. Given her profession, he was sure there was much he didn't want to know. "I'm glad you like it," she said once she'd regained her composure.

"I do. Thank you."

"Thank *you*," she said. "You found Daisie's killer. I know you've had a rough start to this marshal job, but at least you're willing to try." She studied on him for a moment, then added, "And you know, you're not all that hard to look at, once you're cleaned up."

"Well, thank you again," he said. He knew he was blushing. "You might want to see a doctor about your eyesight, but I'll take the compliment. You're quite a lovely woman yourself."

"I know what my flaws are, and I try to work around them," she replied. "But I'll allow as how some men don't seem to notice them."

Tuck was hard-pressed to see any at the moment, but again, he felt like saying that out loud would lead into a conversation that he wasn't ready to have. Instead, he touched the brim of the hat. "If I'd known this was the reward, I'd have started chasing down killers long ago." He shot a glance back toward his office. "I expect I'll have plenty more opportunity, though."

"I won't promise a hat every time, Tucker," she said. "And I won't say your job will be easy. But there's folks around here who'll be glad to have an honest lawman in town."

"Turville wasn't honest?"

"I don't know as I'd go that far. But he knew who he worked for, and the interests of a few men in town were always put above those of everybody else."

Which had more or less been the message Johnny Behan had tried to get across. Tuck was beginning to calculate that this job might be far more complicated than he had at first assumed.

"Well, I don't reckon I owe anybody too much of anything, excepting maybe Hank Turville," he said. "And he's not here to collect."

Missy put a hand on his arm. He liked the way it felt there. "I have a feeling about you, Tucker. I think underneath it all, you're a good man. They're hard to come by in these parts."

"I can't vouch for that, Missy. I haven't known myself very well, these last few years, but I haven't much liked what I saw. Not sure what you'd find if you scratched the surface."

Missy was about to say something more, but her gaze lit on Jasper Montclair stalking up the far side of the street. In profile, he looked like a raptor on the hunt: sharp-beaked, his eyes alert for prey. "Speak of the devil," she said.

"Montclair? You don't like him?"

"I don't have an opinion one way or the other. I'd as soon keep it that way."

Tuck thought he saw Montclair's target, a pretty, slim blond woman in what looked like an expensive dress. "Who's the lady?" he asked.

Missy had to turn to see. "That's Sadie Cuttrell."

"Cuttrell, like the colonel?"

"His wife," she said.

As they watched, Montclair said something to Mrs. Cuttrell. The woman stopped and listened. From the look on her face, whatever Montclair said might have been offensive. Still, she answered him, and the two engaged in a conversation that appeared to grow ever more intense.

"She can take care of herself," Missy said. "She used to work in the crib next to mine, before she married the colonel."

"She was a—" Tuck broke off his own sentence. Montclair had grabbed Mrs. Cuttrell's arm, hard. From her expression, it looked like it hurt. "Excuse me," he said.

He stormed across the street. Montclair might have been a prominent man in these parts, and on his own ranch he was outside Tuck's jurisdiction. But here in Carmichael, he would treat women with respect.

"Montclair!" he said as he got close. "Leave go of her!"

Montclair released the woman's arm and swung around to face Tuck. "This is none of your concern, Marshal," he said.

"You're manhandling a soldier's wife on the streets of my town," Tuck replied. "That makes it my concern."

"A *colonel's* wife!" Sadie Cuttrell snapped. "And maybe you should keep out of affairs that aren't your business, Marshal. Like Mr. Montclair said, this doesn't involve you."

Tuck was astonished. He'd thought he was rescuing her, but she didn't seem to want any help.

"You need to keep in mind who put you where you are, Mr. Bringloe," Montclair said. Tuck noted the absence of the word "marshal" in that sentence.

"You need to keep your hands to yourself while you're in town," Tuck said. "I don't care who put me here, there's things I won't stand for."

"Are you arresting me, Bringloe?"

"He wouldn't dare!" Mrs. Cuttrell said.

"You haven't broken any law that I'm aware of," Tuck said. "See you keep it that way." He turned to Sadie. "You sure you're all right, ma'am?"

"Just leave us the hell alone," she said. The bitterness in her tone saddened Tuck. He wondered what a woman had to go through to sound like that.

"We'll talk again," Montclair said to her. He walked away briskly and disappeared into the bank. Sadie Cuttrell showed Tuck her back and headed toward the fort, sitting at the far western end of the street. Tuck crossed back to where Missy waited.

"Everything all right?" she asked when he joined her.

"Far as I can tell. Mrs. Cuttrell told me to mind my own business. Montclair agreed with her."

"Like I said, she can take care of herself. She also knows how to latch on to powerful men. From here, I'd say it looks like she might be trying to trade in an army colonel for the richest rancher in the county."

"I really don't understand that kind of thing," Tuck said. "All I know is marshaling is tougher than it looks."

"Some women are drawn to power or wealth, or both," Missy explained. "Even when I was working with her, Sadie obviously was. She was the prettiest of us, and you could see how she'd light up when an important or influential man came into the place. Soon enough she had 'em all eating out of her hand. When she landed the colonel, she thought she had struck gold. She pretty much had, I guess."

"What's Montclair's story?"

Missy took a deep breath. Tuck watched the way it swelled her bosom, and admired the fit of her dress. Sadie Cuttrell was a looker, all right, but in his mind she didn't hold a candle to Missy Haynes. "I don't know that much about him," she said. "I don't guess anybody does. His daddy owns a company back east. Montclair Arms?"

"Sure," Tuck said. "I never made the connection. I've carried a couple of their guns, and fired plenty of their ammunition. Union Army had a contract with them for years."

"That's them. Anyway, Jasper came from money. He showed up here one day, a few years ago, and just started buying up ranches. First it was spreads adjoining one another, but then he got so he'd buy them even if they didn't, and he'd squeeze out whoever was in the middle. It got so ranchers would start packing when they saw him coming, because he was paying so much more than they could ever hope to make on their land."

"There are still a few smaller ranchers around, right?" he asked.

"A handful, but fewer all the time. Jed Tibbetts's land adjoins Montclair's. He had one of the bigger outfits until Montclair came in. He's always refused to sell."

"Is Montclair a good rancher, or just a rich one?"

"His place is successful, partly just because it's so big and he's got so many head. I never got the impression he was really interested in ranching, though, so much as in owning land and livestock. It's like a game for him, something fun to do with his daddy's money."

"Not the type of game I'd be familiar with, I reckon," Tuck said. "But it takes all kinds, doesn't it?"

Chapter Twenty-nine

Missy had enjoyed talking to Tucker Bringloe. He was a handsome man, once the stink of defeat had been washed off him. For a drunk he was still in good physical condition. His blue eyes were clear and his jaw was solid and he struck her as someone not to be taken lightly. Drink had damaged him, but it hadn't destroyed him yet, and if he could keep away from it maybe he would come back stronger than ever.

She was, she reflected, fairly expert in the ways a person could ruin herself. She was skilled, and she made decent money, but she was under no illusions that hers was the kind of life her late mother had wanted for her, back in Missouri. Or that she had dreamed of for herself.

Before she reached Senora Soto's, the young woman Missy had seen talking to Tuck earlier came out of a shop. The Apache man trailed behind her, burdened with more packages than before. "You're having a little shopping spree," Missy said. "Are you enjoying our town?"

"Lovely," the young lady said.

"It's not bad. I like the mountains."

"*You* are lovely."

"Well, thank you. I'm Missy. Missy Haynes."

"Little Wing."

"Delighted to meet you, Little Wing," Missy said.

"She would be happy," Little Wing said. "You are lovely and

healthy and you do not let the men harm you." She touched her own forehead, then put her hand over her heart. "Here or here."

"She who?" Missy asked. "Who would be happy?"

Little Wing didn't answer.

"Who?" Missy asked again. Then it struck her. "My mother?"

Little Wing's smile never faltered. She nodded once. "You do what you must. You make the best of it. You stay strong."

"Who are you?" Missy demanded.

"Little Wing."

"Well, Little Wing, stay . . ." She had been about to tell Little Wing to stay out of her head. The idea that this total stranger could have known she was thinking about her mother—and *what* exactly she was thinking—was disturbing. But the young woman was right. She hadn't sought out the life she had now, but once she had realized it was the only course open to her— short of returning to Missouri and telling her mother she'd been right all along, that she couldn't find her own way in the world— she had been determined to make the best of it. She watched her money carefully, she was careful with the clients, and all things considered, she was doing better than she'd ever expected.

How Little Wing could have known any of that, she couldn't say.

But she had almost forgotten it herself. Little Wing's unexpected reminder was welcome. "You're quite remarkable, Little Wing," Missy said. Then, to the Apache, she added, "Is she always like this?"

"More and more," he said. "I don't understand it, either. But it's fun to watch."

"She might want to be careful. Not everybody wants to know everything about themselves."

"I think she knows," the man said. "She knows who's ready to listen."

"You're probably right," Missy said. "It's good to meet you, Little Wing. I hope we can talk again sometime."

Little Wing smiled and nodded her head so briskly that her long dark hair bounced around. "We will," she said. "We will."

Somehow, Missy couldn't bring herself to doubt the truth of that.

Montclair always felt better when he was back on his own land. He had amassed more than six thousand acres so far. That wasn't enough, but it was a start. And as the valley floor rose and became mountain, nobody had staked any claim to the land. It was thickly wooded at the lower elevations, with oak and maple predominant. Higher still, evergreens clung to the slopes until the bare rock of the craggy peaks resisted even their hardy roots. It was no one's land, useless for ranching, so Montclair counted it as his own.

As he rode toward his ranch headquarters, he admired the changes being wrought around him. A rider crossing onto his spread for the first time wouldn't notice anything at the perimeter of the property. The high desert landscape of wild grass spotted with skyward-reaching yuccas and erupting mesquites and round clumps of creosote bush seemed to last almost forever.

But that rider would soon learn otherwise. As the valley dipped toward its center, where the San Pedro River bisected it, subtle changes would begin to be evident. Different varieties of cactus, sparse in the valley's rich grasslands, grew bigger and closer together, creating nearly impenetrable walls of thorn that could shred the unwary traveler. If he were paying close enough attention, he might even see that the cacti edged together when some unwary soul tried to pass through.

Creosote bush typically grew in circles, each bush propagating a new one beside it and forming a green ring that blossomed with yellow in the spring. The rider might notice that the creosote bush deep in Montclair's property didn't quite grow in rings, but he would have had to have the vantage point of one of the buzzards that soared overhead constantly—because there was always *something* dying on his land—to have seen the shapes they formed instead: symbols from ancient books never meant for human tongues to read aloud, from forbidden rites, from scratchings found inside unholy mausoleums and charnel houses. From that same vantage point, he might have seen that a deep-cut, sandy wash outside the property was transformed on the inside by red rocks and soil, until it looked like a vein carving its bloody way across the earth.

On the Broken M, the creatures that died were predated by buzzards, coyotes, wolves, and more, but their bones were never carried away. Some parts of the property resembled ossuaries, their contents spilled across the landscape.

Montclair rode over the land, admiring the changes that had been wrought, and were still happening—the leaves on that agave, its tip spearing the sky, for instance, had always been bladelike, sharp and serrated, but before the edges hadn't been crimson, as if running with fresh blood.

It was a work in progress, but that progress pleased Montclair. There was more to do, much more. But things were changing faster than they ever had, as if having reached a certain point, the changes themselves generated more. Montclair didn't know precisely how the land would look when the process was finished—if it ever would be—but he took pride in what had been accomplished to date.

All of it was leading toward a certain moment, and that moment came nearer every day. If he didn't own the Tibbetts spread in time, he would have to wait another year.

He didn't think that would happen, though. Every portent was favorable, every indication suggested that things were falling into place.

He was, after all, only fulfilling the role he had been born to play. By manufacturing weapons and ammunition, his father had spread death—bringing fire into the world, in a manner of speaking. Now the son was the new Prometheus, bringing light instead of heat. His gift would be knowledge, and once given the world would never be the same.

There still might be obstacles: that new marshal, for one. He wasn't sure how to read the man, and that rarely happened. Turville could be used, and that was often helpful. Montclair had thought Bringloe would be the same; perhaps more so, given his usual state of inebriation.

But there was a core to the man that had started to present itself. Any trouble he created could be overcome; however, the idea that he *could* make trouble was itself disturbing.

Montclair had already taken some steps to control Bringloe, but if the man got in the way, he would have to be dealt with in a more comprehensive fashion.

Maybe his bones would join those already littering the desert floor.

That thought made Montclair smile. So did the sight of his ranch house, up on the next ridge.

Chapter Thirty

Tired of losing hands, Jed Tibbetts had pulled in all his cowboys from the range and told them to stay together in the bunkhouse for the night. Whatever happened to the livestock would happen, but at least Tibbetts would not be responsible for more dead men.

Cale supported the rancher's decision. There weren't that many hands left to begin with: himself, Marlon, Biggs, Stratford, and the two men Tibbetts had hired in town the other day, Keller and Rose, neither of whom were much good in the saddle. A few hands had up and quit over the past few days, and Tibbetts had sent the men borrowed from the Broken M back to Montclair. Cale had seen the anguish in the rancher's face as he considered what he was doing. Tibbetts understood that the ranch was teetering on the edge of failure, but decided to place the lives of human beings above the potential profit he could make on his beeves.

Ordinarily when there were that many men in the bunkhouse there would have been laughter, games, music. Arguments or fistfights might break out. Tonight, there was none of that. The men were quiet, still, paying one another no mind but each alone with his own thoughts and fears. The smells of tobacco and sweat filled the air. Cale was trying to read a book Mrs. Tibbetts had loaned him. It was called *Roughing It,* and it was by a writer named Mark Twain, who described the west that Cale knew with great humor and insight. Most times Cale had a chance to read it, he was immediately drawn into the words, but on this night he had difficulty concentrating, and found himself reading the same passage over and over without really taking it in. Finally, he closed the book and put it under his bunk. He slipped on his boots and tugged on a jacket that had become tight in the arms and shoulders and short in the sleeves over the past year or so.

"You goin' somewheres?" Bill Marlon asked.

"Just over to look in on the Tibbettses," Cale said.

"Jed tole us to stay indoors."

"It ain't but a few steps to the house, Bill."

Marlon shrugged. "Your neck, not mine."

A couple of brief downpours had slammed the ranch that afternoon, and the ground between the bunkhouse and the main house was muddy and slick. Cale slipped once, catching himself on his hands and one knee. Half covered in mud, he considered going back to the bunkhouse after all.

Instead, he wiped the mud from his hands on trousers that were already coated with it and continued to the house. He would just stand outside the door and make sure they were safe.

When he rapped on the door, Mr. Tibbetts opened it, looked out at him, and said, "Come on in here, boy. You're a right mess. Edith, get Cale a towel or some such!"

"I shouldn't," Cale said.

"Nonsense," Tibbetts said. "Scrape some of that mud off your boots and get inside."

Cale obeyed the man's instructions. Soon, he'd wiped off most of the mud and was sitting at the kitchen table with a cup of hot coffee. "The men gettin' by all right?" Tibbetts asked him.

"They're pretty quiet," Cale reported. "But I think they're glad to be inside. They all seen what can happen out on the range."

"I've seen too much of it," Tibbetts said. "I won't see any more. I'll let this ranch fall apart around my ears before I'll let another man die for it."

"I hope it don't come to that, Mr. Tibbetts. Working here is about the best life I can imagine."

Mrs. Tibbetts laughed. She was standing at a washbasin. Mr. Tibbetts sat across from Cale at the table. "You ought to imagine better than this, Cale," she said. "Let your mind wander. You can't do a thing in life without you can imagine it first."

"I reckon that's true," Cale said. He had been impressed, during the time he had known the Tibbettses, with how smart she was. He couldn't figure out how she knew so much. She'd told him it came from reading books and paying attention to the world around her, but some of it just seemed to come from her own thoughts.

Cale was sipping his coffee and trying to think of what to say next when he heard a strange noise outside, like the rush of feet across hard ground. Except there was no hard ground out there, just squishy mud. "What was that?" he asked, putting the cup down on the table so hard that some of the liquid splashed out.

"No tellin'," Mr. Tibbetts said.

"I'll take a look."

"No! Cale, you stay put."

"Jed's right, boy," Mrs. Tibbetts added. "It was probably just the wind blowing something around."

"Yeah," Cale said. "Probably." He didn't believe it, though. His heart was hammering, and when he reached for the cup again, his hands were shaking so much he didn't dare pick it up. Mr. Tibbetts went to the kitchen window and peered out into the darkness.

Before Cale's hands had stopped quivering, the night erupted with other sounds, these more easily identified. They were the terrified shrieks of grown men and the cracks of multiple gunshots.

Cale knew what Tibbetts would do before the rancher even made a move. He bolted from the chair and raced to the door, throwing himself in front of it. Tibbetts spun away from the window and started for the door, but Mrs. Tibbetts threw her arms around him from behind and tried to hold him back. "No, Jed!" she cried.

"But . . . those boys!"

"They'll fend for themselves or they won't," Cale said. "You can't help 'em now!"

Jed Tibbetts kept edging toward the door, dragging his wife behind him. "I got to try."

The gunfire died out, as did the screams. The silence that followed was even worse. "It's too late," Cale said. "They probably saw a wolf or something, and shot it."

Tibbetts's shoulders slumped and his face seemed to break apart, the pieces losing all cohesion. "You know that ain't true," he said.

"I don't know a thing," Cale argued. "Neither do you. Except I know that you going out there won't help them, and Mrs. Tibbetts would just about die if she lost you."

"I would," she agreed.

"Anyhow, you'd have to go through me, and I ain't moving."

"All right, damn it!" Tibbetts said. He shook off his wife's arms and sat heavily at the table. "You're right, I'm too late. Whatever's done is done." He lowered his head, shaking it slowly, sadly. Cale didn't realize he was weeping until his shoulders began to hitch. "Those boys," he said between sobs. "Those damn old boys."

Jack O'Beirne carried a basin of dirty water into the alley behind Soto's to dump it. Senora Soto would only allow him to wash glasses in the same water for so long, then she insisted it had to be changed out or the glasses wouldn't really be clean. "Just because you can't see the dirt," she often said, "doesn't mean it's not there."

He liked his job and he liked his boss, so although hauling basins of water around was not a particularly pleasant task, he did his best to keep track of the water's condition and to be quick about it when he had to pour it out.

Anyway, it was kind of a relief to escape the noise of the saloon for a minute. He could faintly hear the roar of voices and the tinkle of the piano working through "Sweet Betsy from Pike."

Inside, the din could seem deafening. When he got home after a shift, his ears would keep ringing for hours.

He wasn't overly fond of the smell in the alley, primarily of urine and plugs of tobacco and other, less immediately recognizable sources. But he breathed through his mouth and took a moment, letting the tranquil night soothe his nerves.

He was just turning to go back inside when he saw them at the mouth of the alley: three men, coming his way. He didn't recognize them, but it was dark back there and he couldn't make out any detail beyond silhouettes. Even those seemed to change as he watched, as if the men's forms weren't fixed, and they were becoming heavier or taller or more broad-shouldered right in front of him. "E-evenin', gents," he croaked uneasily.

The men didn't answer. They didn't say a word, even to one another. But as if they'd all had the same thought at the same instant, they charged forward. Their speed was astonishing; they hurtled down the alley as fast as Jack could grasp what they were doing. He had time to take one step back and to raise the basin to chest level, as if it might shield him from the inevitable impact. In the final instant before they reached him, he realized that they weren't men at all, but figures as black as the deepest shadow on the darkest night, shapes with no distinguishing features. And as they reached him, he felt a chill, as if they carried the icy blast of winter with them, and he caught a foul scent that put him in mind, in the last moment of his life, of a shovelful of earth from a fresh, mass grave.

Chapter Thirty-one

Luke Falcone wanted another drink.

He had been in the mountains for nine days, and he had brought back a bear, four deer, and a jaguar, the carcasses strapped to the mules he'd taken with him. He had dropped them off with a man who would skin them and process the meat. A lot of people didn't like bear meat, but Frank had no problem with it. The bears in the Huachucas didn't eat a lot of fish, which could make the meat taste bad. He would sell the venison and keep the bear for himself. He would try to keep some of the jaguar, too—he had a fondness for big cat meat, preferring it over elk or deer—but if he got a decent price for it, he would have to let it go.

After delivering the carcasses, he had come straight to Soto's. Some people might complain about his aroma, but when a man came back to town after days and days alone, he needed to wash the dust off his insides first. Tomorrow would be soon enough to bathe. After that, he could come back here and have his way with one of the girls.

He'd had two drinks so far, and a third would be just enough. But Jack was gone from behind the bar, and had been for a while.

Falcone turned to the man nearest him. "Where the hell's that bar dog?"

His neighbor gave him a bleary-eyed grin. "The hell do I know?" He showed Falcone his back and raised his mug to his lips.

Falcone shook the guy on his other side. "You seen that bar-keep?"

This man was not as deep in his cups as the first one had been. "He went out back to dump some old water," he said. "Few minutes ago. Ain't seen him since."

"Out back?" Falcone echoed. He was probably out there piss-ing or smoking, when he should be inside pouring booze.

Well, he would fix that. He shouldered his way through the crowd and found the back door. The air outside stank something fierce—so bad, he could even smell it over himself.

He looked down and saw Jack. Or some of him, anyway. He lay in the shadows, but Falcone could see that his head was mostly severed, connected by only a few ribbons of flesh. A dark pool, which Falcone guessed was blood, surrounded him.

He whipped his knife from its sheath and took another step into the alley, checking it in both directions. It was empty to his left, although a coyote loped past that end, moonlight silvering the fur on its back. As he was turning to his right, recognizing that taking a second to eye the coyote was a mistake, he heard the rush of something tearing through the air toward him, so light on its feet that the liquid sound of the alley's mud barely registered.

He brought the knife around and dropped into a defensive crouch, but too late. Whatever was coming slammed into him with the force of a charging bull. Falcone went down across the bar dog's back, his head splashing into the pool of blood. He lashed out with the knife and felt it slice through something, but he couldn't tell what. Before he could bring it to bear again, though, whoever or whatever had knocked him down fell on him. A huge hand clamped across his nose and mouth, forcing his head back. Falcone strained to shake the attacker off, but he couldn't breathe and he felt the tendons in his neck start to tear, and then he didn't feel anything at all.

The piano was loud, and the laughter and general merriment inside Soto's was louder still, and that was the way Senora Soto liked it. When people couldn't hear themselves think, they were less likely to be sad, and if they weren't sad they were more likely to buy drinks and spend time with her girls. A sad drunk could sit in a corner for an hour, nursing a drink. She didn't want that kind taking up table space. If a drunk was going to be sad, she wanted him to be the kind who would down several drinks in a hurry, so at least he would have paid for the room he was taking up.

But it had been awhile since anyone had seen Jack, and people were starting to grumble. She enlisted one of the men drinking at a nearby table and sent him in search of her barkeep. When he came back into view a couple of minutes later, he was pale and quivering, and he looked like he'd been sick on himself.

Senora Soto instantly regretted having allowed anyone but herself to search for the missing barman. Jack was loyal and he took his work seriously; only something bad would have kept him out of the bar for so long. It was too late now, though. Already, word was spreading through the place. Conversations were dying out. Even Franklin, the piano player, dropped his hands from the keyboard and stared at the man.

"Out there . . ." the man said. "Jack. Some . . . other feller. In back."

Senora Soto was on her feet, skirts gathered in her hands, sweeping toward the back door. She meant to be the first one out, but others were nearer the door than she, and people were lurching to their feet, some barely able to stand, so her way was blocked time and again. When she finally shoved through into the alley, people were vomiting into the mud or standing around like idiots, unable to come to terms with the tableau at their feet.

Somebody held up a lantern, and in the swaying light, Senora Soto saw Jack and another man, one she didn't know well, though she'd noticed him inside a short while earlier. Both had been torn apart, as if by a pack of wild dogs or wolves. But that would have made noise, wouldn't it? Snarling and yapping. The saloon had been noisy, so maybe she would have missed that. But—

"What's that?" someone asked, interrupting her thoughts.

"What?"

"Right here." The man who'd seen it reached down and picked up two similar objects, each one dark and curved, thicker than Senora Soto's thumb at one end and tapering to a vicious point at the other. "The hell is this?"

"Looks like claws," someone answered.

"Claws? These're twice the size of the biggest bear's claws. More than."

"Just sayin' that's what they look like."

Senora Soto snatched them from the man's hand. "Give me those," she said, though she'd already helped herself. "Somebody get Mr. Chalmers over here to gather up these bodies. The least we can do is treat these men with some respect."

She tucked the claws, or whatever they were, into a pocket. The last thing she wanted was anyone showing those around inside the saloon. Bad enough this had happened right out back, and to Jack, of all people, who people associated with her business as much as they did her. Jack's name wasn't on the sign out front, but when people thought of Soto's he was who many thought of first.

Business was done for the night. Sure, a few people would order drinks, and those most disturbed might have more than usual. But what she feared had already started to happen by the time she went back inside. People were huddled quietly together. They looked afraid. Their safe world had been attacked, shown to be not so safe after all. There was no fun left in the room, only terror and a sense of loss.

She hoped her business would recover. But it would take days, or longer, before it did. Until then, Soto's would represent bodies in the alley, covered in blood, and the ungodly claws that had done the deed.

As she sat in her usual chair at the corner table, she struggled to keep her expression impassive, and she hoped the place would survive.

Chapter Thirty-two

Cuttrell admired patient men. He had read about the lives of the saints, those holy men who could accept whatever torments life threw their way and attribute their suffering to God's plan. Those were tests, perhaps, not to prove anything to their Lord but to themselves. They could, it was said, find good inside the most heinous evil, and know that God was with them, taking their suffering onto his own shoulders.

He wished he were that way. He wished he didn't hold his own suffering deep inside, dwelling on it in quiet moments, in wakeful times after midnight, knowing even as he did that it was eating him alive.

But he was not like the saints. He stored anger inside his heart until it bubbled out as rage.

Sadie sat on the edge of their bed. She had known him long enough to recognize the state he was in. Her arms were crossed over her chest, her legs crossed, even her ankles. When he spoke, she flinched, as if surely a blow must follow.

"Don't just tell me you talked to him," he said. He strived for patience, but he could feel it sliding from his grasp. "I already *know* you talked to him. Which is why I asked you about the *nature* of that conversation."

"It was . . . it was nothing. The weather. He admired the dress I was wearing, I think. He asked after you."

"Jasper Montclair asked after me? Was that before or after he tried to wrench your arm from its socket?"

"It was nothing of the sort," she said. "Whoever told you that is imagining things."

"Both of them? Imagining it the same way? I hardly think that's likely. Do you?" That was a lie. He had only heard it from one source, and that one barely trustworthy. But the man had sworn that he thought Montclair would have struck her if not for the intercession of that new marshal. "What did he say to you?"

"Nothing! I told you, he was just passing the time of day."

"And I'm supposed to believe that?"

"It's the truth."

"I'm sure it's not, Sadie. You can still tell me the truth, though, and save yourself some trouble."

"The kind of trouble you like to dish out? That, again? This has all been just an excuse, hasn't it?"

Her words stung, but only briefly. She was right, he did, he supposed, take a certain pleasure from administering the discipline she needed from time to time.

As he removed his belt, he watched her watching him, her eyes wide with fright, her lower lip quivering.

It was for her own good, he told himself. She wasn't that far removed from the upstairs at Senora Soto's. She was a wife now, a military wife, and that meant something.

But before that, she had been a whore. And sometimes, that taint still had to be knocked out of her.

This was one of those times.

At Little Wing's request, Kuruk had moved into the cottage she'd been provided. He slept in the front room, on the floor, or that's what he told her. The truth was, he didn't sleep much at all. He was worried about her. She was getting better, day by day. Her injuries were healing, and she was able to converse better, speaking in whole sentences and sometimes answering questions in ways that weren't completely unintelligible. Kuruk didn't think she was cut out to be a washerwoman, but it was better than some alternatives the colonel had proposed, so he had been trying to persuade her to give it a try.

But other times, she reverted to the confused and confusing creature she had been when they found her. And when she slept, she was haunted by something Kuruk couldn't identify. So most of the time she was sleeping, he stayed awake in case she needed him.

On this night, she was more troubled than usual. He had looked in on her several times. After the last one, he had retreated to the front room and sat on the floor, eyes closed, when he heard her cry out in alarm.

He bolted up and rushed back to her room. She was still in bed, thrashing around, kicking at the blanket covering her. She spoke rapidly, in an extended monologue of which he could only catch snippets. He thought he made out the words "mead," "Devil's" something—maybe deck, or dead—and then something that sounded like "Cemetery Ridge" or "Bridge."

She was delirious, muttering nonsense. He sat beside her for a while, brushing hair off her forehead and placing his cool hand over it, speaking gently to her. She calmed, after a while, and when her breathing was even again, her face serene, he once more left her room.

He had always thought better out of doors, so he left the house to walk on the parade field, to feel the earth beneath his feet and to see the starry sky above. Her presence here meant something, but he didn't know what. He couldn't wait for the army to figure it out, because they never would. White people had a very narrow approach to understanding anything, and white soldiers were even worse. The Apache people thought in broader strokes, making greater allowances for magic and mystery.

Before he had reached any conclusions, though, a figure emerged from the darkness. "Evening, Kuruk," Jimmy McKenna said.

"Howdy."

"Don't you ever sleep?"

"Sometimes. When I need to."

"And the rest of the time?"

"Don't need to."

"What about now?"

Kuruk shook his head. "I could, but I can't."

McKenna regarded him for long enough that Kuruk started to feel uncomfortable. "What's bothering you, Kuruk?"

"Did I say anything was—"

McKenna cut him off. "You just about did. Anyway, I can see it on your face. What is it?"

Kuruk trusted McKenna more than he did most whites, so he saw no reason not to tell the truth. "It's Little Wing," he admitted. "When she sleeps, she is troubled. She rolls around, she cries out, sometimes she appears terrified."

"What do you think that's all about?"

"Can't say. But sometimes when she is very agitated, bad things happen. Tonight, she is very very agitated."

"Bad things?"

Kuruk had expected McKenna to dismiss his concern immediately. In his experience, whites were not predisposed to accept such ideas. "Sometimes real bad."

"There's a lot of those around, these days."

"There are?" Kuruk asked.

"Sure. People getting killed. Hell, I didn't even see that mule train, but you did. Sounded horrible. You think animals did that? Or human beings?"

"Definitely not animals," Kuruk said. "People, maybe so."

"Not the way I heard it. No bullet holes. No arrows, or spears. You think somebody snuck up on forty armed men and slashed them all to death with a knife?"

"I suppose not."

"Damn right. I don't know what's going on, and I can't get Colonel Cuttrell to take it serious. But something is. And I'll tell you true, Kuruk, it's starting to scare me."

"You're not alone, Jimmy. Little Wing is afraid. If she's afraid, I am, too."

"Cuttrell won't listen." McKenna closed his mouth and

glanced in every direction, seeing whether anyone was close enough to hear. "But I'm not waiting on him."

"What do you mean?"

"Can you keep a secret?"

"Ever met an Apache who couldn't?"

Jimmy chuckled. "I've met a few Apaches, but I guess I never tested them before. Not that way, at least."

"Well. I keep secrets from white folks every day."

"Come with me, then."

"Where?"

McKenna stepped closer to him, and kept his voice low. "To the blacksmith shop," he said. "Delahunt and I have been working on something. Well, mostly he's been working on it. I've had some ideas, but he's the one who figures out how to do them, and then puts them together."

Kuruk nodded. "Delahunt, he's a pretty smart guy."

"He is that," McKenna said. "Some kind of mad genius."

Kuruk didn't know what to expect as he walked with McKenna toward Delahunt's shop. He looked forward to being surprised.

The real surprise was how surprised he turned out to be.

Chapter Thirty-three

Tuck didn't want to sleep.

He wasn't sure he ever wanted to sleep again, as long as he lived, though he doubted he would live very long without it. The last time he had slept, a man had been viciously murdered not ten feet away from him. That was the kind of thing that could put a man off his feed—or his sleep—for a good long while.

To stay awake, he walked through the town. Rain had fallen off and on during the late afternoon and evening, and now a massive cloud blotted out the stars and seemed intent on staying awhile. Deep, booming thunder sounded and lightning revealed the mountains that loomed over Carmichael in jagged flashes. Rain washed across the town like an upended ocean. Crossing the space between one building's covered walkway to another's, Tuck was drenched.

At least the chafing and rubbing of his wet clothes would keep him alert.

The streets were empty, which he attributed to the downpour. But it wasn't just that, he decided. Curtains were drawn over windows, doors were closed up tight. It was as if everybody in town had become afraid of the same thing, and he was the only one who hadn't yet heard what it was.

Even when the weather was bad, Soto's was usually lively. He was across the street, wondering why he didn't hear the usual music and rowdy laughter from there, when instead, he heard a gunshot. The sound was unmistakable, and it was followed, in this instance, by the thump of something heavy hitting the floor, and a few halfhearted screams.

Tuck jumped from the boardwalk into the street, and cursed as he tried to take another step and the muck threatened to yank his boot off. He freed it, and crossed as fast as he could under the circumstances. By the time he gained the walkway on the far side, his legs were coated in mud up to the knee. He clomped awkwardly through the batwing doors, drawing his Colt at the same time. "Nobody budge," he ordered. "Who fired a gun?"

The scene became clear immediately. A man lay on the ground, writhing in pain, blood spreading out from a hole in his belly. His hands were clasped over it, but the life was slipping through them. Another man stood by the bar, clutching a revolver with two fingers and a thumb on the grip, looking at the wounded man as if he'd never seen anything like him. The rest of the people in the room—a tiny crowd, for this time of night, as if something had emptied the place out early, leaving only those truly serious about their drinking—stared on in quiet shock. The acrid scent of gun smoke still hung in the air, reminding Tuck of Durham. He shoved his weapon back into its holster. It felt like a rattlesnake coiled around his leg.

"What happened?" Tuck asked.

The man with the gun cleared his throat a couple of times. His eyes were huge and liquid, his hands trembling. He was no killer, Tuck judged, just a man caught up in the circumstance of the moment. Put a gun in a frightened man's hands and he was only one mistake away from murder.

"I . . . I th-thought he was drawin' on me," the man said. "He b-bumped into me, and I said s-somethin'. Then he come around with his h-hand at his h-h-hip, and I . . . I thought there was iron in it."

Tuck crouched by the wounded man. "Anybody go for a doctor?"

"Not yet," Senora Soto said. She was behind the bar instead of at her usual table. "Franklin, fetch Doc Crabtree. And fast."

The piano player had been sitting at a table with a couple of empty glasses and half of a ham sandwich in front of him. Nobody was where they ordinarily would have been. He scraped back his chair and stood, then on unsteady legs he wove between tables toward the door.

Tuck knelt beside the wounded man and put a hand on his shoulder. "Help's on the way," he said.

The man tried to respond, but his voice was so feeble Tuck couldn't understand him. "Just hold on, pard'," he said. He checked the man's hands and the floor where he had fallen, but didn't see any guns. The man wasn't wearing a gun belt, either.

"Anybody pick up his gun?" Tuck asked.

"No, Marshal," Senora Soto said. "Nobody's gone near him."

He rose, turned back to the man with the gun, and held out his right hand. "Better give me that," he said. The man complied quickly, as if he couldn't wait to get rid of the thing.

Tuck stuck the revolver in his belt. "I'll have to take you in," he said.

The man's face turned three shades whiter. "Don't put me in that j-jail!" he said. "I ain't ready to die!"

Tuck was about to ask the man what he meant by that, when the answer came to him. "I know what you're thinking," he said. "But nobody else is going to be killed in my cells."

A burly man at a nearby table slammed his hands down on the tabletop and hoisted himself to his feet. He had a thick, dark beard and a bull neck and wide shoulders. His clothing looked as if he'd slept in it for a year before having it dragged through town behind a team of horses. "That a fact, Marshal?" he asked.

It wasn't a promise Tuck could keep, because if he could, Calhoun would still be alive. Now that he knew it might happen, though, he would take greater pains to make sure it didn't. He didn't want to explain all that; he just wanted to get this man behind bars until a circuit judge could decide his fate. "Count on it," he said.

"You say so," the big man said. He yanked a gun from its holster and squeezed off three quick shots before Tuck could even react. Two hit the first gunman in the chest and the third tore through his face, beside his nose, and blew out the back of his skull. The gunman dropped, not far from the man he'd gutshot. His feet tapped an uneven rhythm on the floor. No matter how soon the doctor arrived, it would be too late.

Tuck drew his Colt and leveled it at the burly man. "Drop that!" he ordered. The man obeyed, his piece hitting the table and bouncing to the floor. "What'd you do that for?"

The man grinned, showing a half-dozen teeth and more blank spaces. "Way I figger, your cell's probably the only place in town a feller *can't* get killed. Thought I'd make sure you had to park me there for a spell."

Tuck couldn't believe it. This man had shot another human being dead in cold blood, just to ensure that he would spend time behind bars. Now the fifteen or so people in the saloon were staring at him, waiting for him to do something about it. "What are you worried about?" he asked the man. "Who else got killed?"

"I guess you haven't heard, Marshal Bringloe," Senora Soto said. "Come with me."

"Where?"

"Just out back."

Tuck didn't want to leave the big man in the saloon, un-guarded, though it seemed a man who wanted to go to jail was unlikely to run. He navigated between the tables, picked the man's revolver up, jammed it into his belt with the other one, and looked the man in the eye. "We're not done," he said. To the room at large, he added, "Make sure he stays put."

Nobody answered him. Then it struck him: What he had taken as shock was really fear. Every person in the saloon was terrified. Of what, Tuck didn't know.

But he had a feeling Senora Soto was about to show him.

He stood in the rain and studied the corpses. Water ran off the brim of his new hat in rivulets. "How long they been here?" he asked.

"An hour, maybe," Senora Soto said. She stood in the doorway holding a lantern, out of the worst of the weather. "Little more."

"Why hasn't anyone carted them away?"

"We've told Chalmers. I think he doesn't want to come for them in this downpour."

"Can hardly blame him." The bodies were soaked, of course, but the weather had kept the worst of the flies away and diluted the blood. They didn't smell as bad as he had feared, though there was a rank, familiar scent to the air around them. They looked ghastly, and he shivered. "Know what happened?"

"Jack came out to dump some water. When he didn't come back, this other man wanted a drink, so he went looking for Jack. Then somebody else found them and told everybody. Since then, everybody who didn't take off right away has been just sitting around, quiet and scared."

"So nobody knows who did it?"

"Who or what," she corrected.

"I don't follow."

She reached into a pocket and pulled out two dark objects. He examined them in the lantern's glow. "They look like claws."

"I'm sure that's what they are."

"Big ones."

"Very."

Tuck shivered again, though this time it had nothing to do with his wet clothing. The way those bodies were torn apart reminded him of what he had seen before, with Daisie and Hank Turville and most recently Calhoun. That stink in the air, partly washed away by the rain, was a remnant of the same odor he'd encountered on those occasions. And these black claws could have been cut off of the creature that had gradually melted on the way to Carmichael. "I'll take those, if you don't mind," he said.

"You're welcome to them, Marshal. I don't want them anywhere near me."

He took them from her hand, wrapped them in a bandanna, and stuffed them in a pocket. They would probably vanish soon enough, but he wanted to hang on to them if he could.

With luck, he would be able to find whatever monster they had come from.

Back inside, Tuck went from table to table, asking everyone if they had seen anything in the alley. The responses weren't helpful—everyone had been inside, blissfully unaware until a man named Sherman Bostik had come in with the news. Bostik had left shortly thereafter, so when he was finished talking to the people still in the saloon, Tuck went to Bostik's home and woke the man from a liquor-induced sleep. Bostik couldn't add anything Tuck hadn't already heard, and he wasn't making much sense. Tuck thanked him and sent him back to bed.

The first gunman had died while Tuck and Senora Soto were out back, but Doc Crabtree had shown up and thought he might be able to save the wounded man. Tuck hadn't bothered arresting the burly fellow. Chances were he'd be too scared to leave town anyway. And if Tuck couldn't figure out what was behind the fear that had gripped the town—and what those mysterious, murderous creatures were—everybody would soon be shooting at everybody else. Having one man in a cell wouldn't make a lick of difference.

When he finally got to his office, the rain had moved on and the moon, inching ever closer to full, rode high in the sky. Mo Kanouse was in the office, making himself useful for a change, cleaning the shotguns on the gun rack.

"Thought you'd be asleep at this hour," Tuck said.

"I figgered *you* would be. I don't sleep so good, most nights. Unless I got a bottle or a woman, or both."

"I don't think many people in this town are sleeping tonight, Mo. Or are likely to soon."

"Why not?"

"Folks are scared. And fear spreads like wildfire in dry brush. It's not something that just happened, either. I don't know who or what is back of it, but I aim to find out."

"How you figure to do that?"

"I'll need your help," Tuck said. He leaned against a corner of his desk, folded his arms. "Ride up to Tombstone. You know where the office of the *Epitaph* is?"

"'Course I do," Kanouse said. He eyed his boss suspiciously. Tuck guessed it was because he could tell he was going to be made to do his job.

"Go up there and bring me back copies of the paper for . . . I reckon the last three years will do."

"You mean, one from this year, one from last, and one from the year before?"

"*All* of them," Tuck clarified. "Every paper they've put out in the last three years."

Kanouse shook his head. "I'd need a wagon for that."

"Then find one," Tuck said. "I need those as quick as they can get here."

"Bringloe," Kanouse said, "you're a real piece of work."

Chapter Thirty-four

The night seemed like the longest one ever. Mr. Tibbetts didn't sleep a wink of it, but sat in the kitchen, drinking coffee and looking at the door. Cale didn't, either, because he stayed up keeping an eye on Tibbetts. When morning finally lightened the sky, Tibbetts found his feet. "I'm goin' out there, Cale. I love you like my own son, but if you stand in my way, you'll regret it."

"I'll go with you," Cale said.

"No."

"How do you mean to stop me, once you're out there?"

"Reckon I can't," Tibbetts admitted.

"Then you might as well give your blessing."

Tibbetts sighed. Cale took no pleasure in the look of defeat he wore. "You'll do whatever you want, I suppose. Always have done."

When the rancher's hand was on the doorknob, Cale asked, "Should I fetch Mrs. Tibbetts?"

"Let her sleep." Tibbetts swung open the door and stepped outside. Cale waited only seconds before following. The air didn't have the fresh after-rain smell, tinged with the sweet scent of wet creosote bush, which typically blanketed the high desert the morning after an early-season monsoon storm. Instead, it had a coppery, metallic bite.

Tibbetts reached the bunkhouse first. "Wake up, boys!" he shouted. In the man's voice, Cale detected a quaver that worried him. "You're burnin' daylight!"

He threw the door open, started to step in, then stopped halfway. A choking sound escaped from his throat, followed by a plaintive "Oh, God."

Cale picked up his pace. When the rancher realized Cale was behind him, he spun around, his face a mask of grief. "No, boy! Don't look!"

But it was too late. Cale hadn't had a clear view, with Tibbetts standing in the doorway. He had seen enough, though.

The bunkhouse floor was awash in blood.

Almost at the door, as if someone had been trying to escape, Cale had seen a hand, fingers down and curled. He couldn't tell whose hand it was, because no arm joined it to a body; it ended at the wrist. On the floor a little farther back had been what looked almost like a sheet of torn, discolored paper attached to a thatch of fur. Just before Tibbetts turned on him, Cale was able to make the elements make sense in his head, and he saw that it was the upper half of somebody's face, with the scalp still attached. The empty eye holes looked like careful cutaways.

Cale hadn't eaten anything since dinner, but he'd had plenty of coffee. He whirled away from Mr. Tibbetts and the gaping doorway and dropped to hands and knees just before it all spewed up from his gut and out his mouth and nose. Retching, down in the mud like an animal, he burned with shame.

When he was done, or hoped he was, he wiped the back of his hand across his mouth and looked up. Tibbetts had left the bunkhouse door open and was walking, almost staggering, really, toward the nearby corral. When he got close, he cried out in anguish. "No! God, no, no!"

Cale forced himself to his feet and dashed after him. Tibbetts was clutching the corral fence, staring into the open space, tears rolling down his cheeks.

In the corral were the horses, slaughtered and savaged. Cale couldn't count how many; like the cowboys in the bunkhouse, there were more parts than whole animals. The ground was a churned-up mess of red-tinted muck. Cale's stomach was empty, but he spat bitter-tasting bile onto the earth. What kind of creature would do something like that? He had seen wolf predation, and had once run across a bear feasting on a dead deer. None of those scenes had resembled this one.

But if it hadn't been an animal, that only left people. Could human beings actually do such a thing?

Tibbetts climbed up on the corral fence. At first, Cale didn't understand why—a cowboy sometimes did that to rope one of the horses, or to watch someone else work in the corral. But there was no reason to rope butchered stock, and no one working. Then he realized that the rancher was trying to see into the nearest pasture, and he got a better view of it from that elevated position.

"Mr. Tibbetts," Cale said. "The beeves. Are they . . ."

Tibbetts turned toward him, his face a mask of agony. "Them, too," he said. "God bless it, them, too."

"I'm sorry," Cale said. "I don't know what coulda . . ." He let the sentence trail off. Tibbetts was already walking back toward the ranch house, shoulders slumped, his posture one of utter defeat. Cale started to follow, then changed course.

Things were the same in the chicken yard and the hog pen. Not a creature was intact. He should tell Mr. Tibbetts, he thought, but Tibbetts had probably already deduced how it would be.

There was nothing Cale could do here, nothing that would help. Mr. Tibbetts would tell his wife, and they would probably appreciate some privacy. Meanwhile, if whoever or whatever had committed these horrible deeds was not just targeting the J Cross T, people needed to be warned. Carmichael was a good distance away, and he'd have liked a horse, but that was obviously not to be. Instead, anxious to keep the images he'd seen from haunting his thoughts, he took off running.

He might be too late, but he had to try.

Kuruk wouldn't have summoned him without a reason, Jimmy McKenna knew. So when a trooper found him eating breakfast and delivered the Apache's message, he had downed his coffee quickly and abandoned the rest. He hurried to the cottage Little Wing was using, which was where he'd been told Kuruk would be waiting. When McKenna arrived, the scout was waiting at a window. He saw the lieutenant approach, and met him outside.

"Thank you for coming," Kuruk said.

"Of course. What is it?"

Kuruk tilted his head toward the door. "It's her. She had a bad night. She's awake now, but she's afraid."

"Afraid of what?"

"I don't know. She can't say, or else she won't. I think she doesn't know. But it's bad, anyhow. Whatever it is."

"How sure are you about this, Kuruk? What if she just had a nightmare? She's a little touched, right?"

"She might be," Kuruk replied. "Don't mean she's wrong."

"What do you want me to do about it?" McKenna asked. He liked Kuruk well enough, but he barely knew the girl, and from what Sadie had told him, she couldn't be trusted.

"Anything you can, Jimmy. Something bad is coming. Or could be it's already here. Little Wing can see it better than we can, and it's bad enough to scare her. Scares me, too. I don't know—what you're working on with Delahunt, could be that'll help. Or not. I just don't know enough."

"I'll talk to the colonel again, Kuruk," McKenna said. "It might not do any good, but I'll try."

"Can't hurt."

"I hope not."

"Depending on what it is, a whole army might not be enough to do any good."

"Depending on what it is," Kuruk said, "a whole world might not be enough. I don't know how bad it is, though. I only know that I've never seen her so scared."

"You haven't known her that long."

"Nope. Long enough, though."

"You sure about this, Kuruk?"

"Sure enough. She has some kind of sight, I know that. And

if she's afraid, so am I. You should be, too." The scout took a deep breath and let it out slowly, then said, "Everybody should be."

He stood on the crest of a hill, facing east, his naked form bathed by the red light of dawn. Other red painted his flesh, too: the blood of an innocent. The girl's parents would have worried about her, sought her out, had they lived. They would not be a problem, though, and her blood was pure and clean and rich.

He raised his arms over his head and chanted the ancient words, in a tongue that had died out before human beings had ever walked this land. At the right moment, he took a breath and turned to the north, then chanted a verse. Then to the west, and the south, and finally to the east again, where the sun had fully broken above the horizon and the light was more yellow than red.

His name was Jasper Montclair. He knew that, but he knew also that he was only a link in a chain, and that chain reached back to when the Earth had been young, and forward into the age when the sun would wink out and the planet would be a cold and lifeless orb, spinning through space.

He was only a link, for now.

Soon, though, he would be so much more.

Some links, it turned out, were more important than others. Some could break the chain, others strengthen it. Very few could determine its direction, shift one of its end points.

He would be one of those few. When Thunder Moon came, he would be ready. He would be present. Thunder Moon came soon, and it came for him, and he had to have all the pieces in place by then.

And he would. This ritual greeting of the sun was a small part of that. The sun, the earth, the seasons, all were part of what Thunder Moon would bring about.

Montclair stood, nude, sunlight catching the patterns he had painted in blood and limning them as if with fire.

When the ritual was done, he closed his eyes and felt the warmth of the sun on his skin. The new day had come.

Another new day was on the way, and when it dawned, nothing would ever be the way it had been. Not for him. Not for anyone.

Montclair smiled, and the dried blood on his cheeks cracked and flaked off and drifted, unnoticed, to the earth. And the earth, swimming in blood since before humans had walked upright, accepted it as an offering, and continued to turn.

Chapter Thirty-five

Tuck unwrapped the claws Senora Soto had given and showed them to Alf Maier. They were in the back of Maier's shop, in a storeroom full of high shelves. Most were empty, but others held merchandise, dry goods and the like.

"Recognize these?" Tuck asked.

"Should I?"

Tuck was surprised. "That thing we fought? The killer? It had claws like these."

Maier blinked behind his thick glasses. "No," he said.

"What do you mean, no?"

"You are wrong."

"Alf, you were there. You saw the guy. I don't even know if that's the right word. That *thing*, whatever it was. Black as a lump of coal. You've got to remember the stink of it, if nothing else."

"No," Maier said again. "That was a man. Just a man."

"Look, Maier," Tuck said, trying to rein in his anger. "You were there. I was there. There's nobody else here, just you and me, so I don't know why you're pretending."

Maier was shaking, his face turning violet. "Mr. Bringloe. He was a killer, a terrible person. But he was a person, that's all. I think you had better go now. And do not spread stories you cannot prove. Leave this alone. It is better that way, trust me."

"What do you know, Alf?"

Maier showed Tuck as phony a smile as he had ever seen in his life. "Me? I am a simple merchant. I know nothing. Nothing at all. Now please, Marshal. I am a busy man, as I am sure you must be."

Tuck wasn't getting anything more out of Maier. He didn't know what had changed the man's mind, but he obviously wasn't getting anywhere with him. At any rate, he knew what he had seen; he would have liked someone else's confirmation that the claws Senora Soto had given him were similar to the killer's, but Maier was the only other person who'd been there.

It didn't matter. Tuck knew what he knew.

Still, what he didn't know would fill a much deeper well.

Wilson Harrell was trying to pack up his desk when Alf Maier bustled into the bank looking like his pants were full of bees. Harrell's desk was right out on the floor, so customers could easily find him. Sometimes it was inconvenient, as when he had to turn down someone for a loan or tell them he was foreclosing on their property. People were ashamed when that happened, ashamed that their financial situations had become so dire, and often upset that they were, in their view, being denied the help they needed. For his part, it didn't bother Harrell. He thought it was good for the townsfolk to see one of their own go through tough times—it taught them to take better care with their own finances. Or so he liked to tell himself.

But because his desk was accessible, he didn't like leaving anything out on top of it. When it was covered with paperwork, he had to make sure it was put away before he left for the day. On most days it wasn't so bad, because he stayed until the bank closed, or a little later, and he opened the door in the morning, so he knew nobody would disturb his work. But today, he was leaving well before noon, which meant clearing everything off and finding places for all the paperwork.

The last thing he needed was an agitated grocer getting in his way.

As he feared, Maier made straight for him. Harrell shoved some papers into a leather case and put the last of them into a desk drawer, turned the key, and slipped it into the pocket of his vest. "Wilson," Maier said as he approached, his tone sharp with urgency.

"What is it, Alf?" Harrell asked. "I'm just about to leave for the day. I've got very important business out of town. You know what I mean."

"I will walk outside with you," Maier said. "Better we talk out there."

Harrell suppressed a sigh. A man couldn't always control who he went into business with—he had to deal with those who had something to offer in return. But that didn't mean he liked them all equally well. His patience for Alf Maier was limited at the best of times, and this moment was not that. "Fine," he said, snatching up the leather case. "But quickly."

"Yes, yes, I understand." Maier walked beside him to the door and out to where Harrell's wagon waited in the road. The grocer's odd, waddling gait was one of the things—one of many things, in point of fact—that Harrell most often mocked when he discussed Maier with others, and he noted it now, despite his impatience. It was as if the man walked around with pebbles of uneven size inside his shoes.

Harrell stopped beside the wagon, dismissing the clerk who had brought it around with a hasty nod. He wanted to get his business taken care of. Jed Tibbetts would make a fuss, but he was a law-abiding man, and he knew when he'd been beaten. He would sign the paperwork transferring the deed to his place over to Montclair, though he would act as if it was killing him to do it. Harrell didn't like emotional scenes, and he would as soon skip this one. But what had to be done had to be done, and this was the moment. As much as he dreaded the encounter, his deeper fear was what price might need to be paid if he failed to get that signature. "Out with it, Mr. Maier. My business can't wait."

"It is the new marshal, Bringloe. I know I supported him, at first. I wanted to keep him where we could watch him, and I believed he could be trusted."

"What about him, then?"

"I no longer think that. Now, I believe he is dangerous. He asks too many questions. He knows things he should not."

"What would you suggest, then?"

"He has to be fired."

Harrell climbed aboard and settled his bulk on the seat. "Fired? That's all?"

"At least," Maier said.

The banker took up the reins and the whip. "Alf, I'll back you up. I'm sure Montclair will, too. Talk to Chaffee, and make any arrangements that have to be made. I'm on your side, and you can tell Chaffee that. But I've got to get going. The hour's growing nigh."

"Yes, yes," Maier said, waving his hands. "Go on, Wilson. I will talk to Chaffee. We will work things out, do not worry."

Harrell applied the whip, delicately, and the two horses in the traces started forward. "I'm not worried," he said as Maier slipped past him. "I'm not worried at all."

Which was a lie. He was plenty worried. A man would be a fool not to be.

But he wasn't worried about Maier, or Chaffee, or even that Bringloe fellow. They were pawns, dispensable pieces whose absence from the board would hardly be felt.

No, the things that worried him were much, much more consequential. But he would do his part, and then he would have no worries at all.

Sadie moved through the house slowly. Her ribs felt like she'd been mule-kicked, and under her dress, her torso was already showing bruises that would be there for days, if not longer, turning colors as they aged. There were days—and this was one of them—when she hated her husband.

As she made her way down the stairs, every inch of her aching, she heard Del and Jimmy coming in the front door. She thought about turning around and going back up, but it was too late; they would see her anyway, and she didn't want to look like she was trying to escape.

"...going on," Jimmy was saying. "I can't explain them, and I doubt that anyone can. But we need to be aware of—" He cut himself off as he entered and saw Sadie on the staircase.

Del glanced up at her without giving any indication that he saw her. "And we are aware, Jimmy," he said, continuing the conversation as if her presence didn't matter at all. "Because you keep telling me."

"I keep telling you because I'm worried," Jimmy countered. "The men are—"

They swept into Del's office and shut the door with a bang. Neither man had greeted her or given the slightest indication that she was there, except for Jimmy's momentary hesitation. The business of men took precedence over everything else, she supposed. Even simple decency to one's wife.

With them hidden away behind closed doors, she continued down the stairs and into the kitchen. There was only one thing that could take the edge off her physical pain and the emotional anguish that went with it. The bottle behind the spices, in the pantry. A few sips of that and she would be able to face the rest of the day.

It wouldn't dispel the anger that coursed through her. But it would make the anger easier to take, and that was good enough for now.

Chapter Thirty-six

Mo Kanouse had piled stacks of *Tombstone Epitaph*s all over the office, grumbling the entire time. Tuck sat at his desk with about thirty of them, paging through them one by one. He didn't know what he was looking for, exactly, but he figured he would know it if he saw it.

Maier claimed the murderer they had killed was only a man. Tuck didn't know what he was, but men didn't have skin that could have been torn from the deepest shadows or the darkest part of the night sky. Men couldn't squeeze through a space between two boards barely large enough for a cat. Men didn't melt when you wrapped them in a blanket and draped them over a horse's back.

And men didn't have three-inch claws like the ones in Tuck's desk drawer.

He hadn't slept at all during the night. The words on the page swam before his eyes, but he blinked and rubbed them and tried to focus. Most of the articles were about fights or shootings in saloons, mining news, and rampant gossip and speculation. There seemed to be a particular interest in an ongoing conflict between the Earp faction and outlaws known as the Cowboys, a group that included folks like the Clantons, the McLaurys, Curly Bill Brocious, Frank Leslie, and Johnny Ringo. Tuck had heard of them; they had reputations as hard men, quick with a gun or their fists. They were Confederate sympathizers and Democrats, so Sheriff Behan was on their side despite what the *Epitaph* described as repeated violations of local law.

But the Earps didn't come off much better in its pages. They were northerners, Republicans, and therefore—like Tuck—not always welcome in this area. And although they *were* the law—Virgil Earp was Tombstone's town marshal, his brother Morgan an undersheriff—from the sound of things, they abused their authority so egregiously they might as well have been outlaws, too.

Still, Tuck pored over the pages, occasionally shoving a stack of papers off his desk onto the floor and bringing up another. He found reporting of some strange incidents, but they didn't match up with what he had encountered, and most sounded far-fetched. One group of men had been hunting in the Mule Mountains when they shot a dragon, or so they said. Eleven feet long, it had sky-blue scales and translucent wings and six legs. Unfortunately, although they had successfully brought it back to Tombstone, it had disappeared from one man's barn before they'd had a chance to show it to anyone else. The *Epitaph* hinted that there might have been a significant amount of liquor consumed on that "hunting" trip.

Another man reported seeing something rise up out of a pond created on his property by a monsoon storm, two summers earlier. He said it had a long neck—at least twenty or thirty feet long, he claimed—and a small, rounded head, and when it saw him it smiled and spat water at him. But when the pond dried up again, it was nowhere to be found.

And a woman told a tale of a bizarre creature, multi-legged like a spider, but nearly as big as a Conestoga wagon, that had appeared one hot afternoon when she was watching a dust devil spin across the valley. It was, she said, the creature that had created the dust devil. It had been whirling like a dervish, pausing at her place just long enough to snatch up a goat with its many limbs, and by the time it was out of sight, the goat had been half-eaten.

Those and similar stories were one of the *Epitaph*'s specialties, it appeared. Anyone who had anything out of the ordinary to report went to them, and the paper printed the tale in all its breathless glory.

Tuck was willing to admit that there were things in the world he didn't understand. The dark man he had fought, and whatever had left those claws behind, fell into that category. He closed the newspaper he was reading and dropped it onto the nearest pile, then slowly rose from his seat and stretched, going up onto his toes and arching his back. He was beat, and every muscle he had ached. Some he hadn't even been aware that he had ached. He put his hands against the hollow of his back and twisted this way and that, trying to limber it up.

As he did, he watched out the window. Morning sunlight washed the street and blazed off the windows on the other side, almost blinding in its yellow fury. Between him and those windows, Sadie Cuttrell walked, straight up the middle of the street. Her fists were clenched at her sides, her jaw tight, her gaze fixed on the way directly before her. She walked with rapid, deliberate strides. Tuck wouldn't want to be whoever it was she was on her way to see, because she had the air of someone ready to commit violence.

He was turning back toward the newspapers, ready to take up the next stack, when another motion outside caught his attention. A dark wagon rolled past, black as a hearse, drawn by a pair of magnificent black horses. Tuck didn't even have to look up to know that Jasper Montclair was driving it. The first time he had seen it, he'd assumed it belonged to Chalmers. But the undertaker's rig wasn't as impressive, or as somber.

Montclair sat rigidly upright. The reins were loose in his hands, but the animals knew what he wanted. If he didn't slow, he'd run right over Sadie Cuttrell. Remembering how their last encounter had gone, Tuck stepped out of his office, ready to intervene if necessary.

It wasn't. Mrs. Cuttrell heard the wagon behind her, and spun around to meet it. Montclair brought it to an easy halt, and she walked up to him. Tuck couldn't hear their conversation, but it appeared civil, and the rage that had seemed to be driving her was no longer in evidence. She rested a hand easily on the bench, and her face had softened. She even smiled briefly. Tuck could only see part of Montclair's back, but his posture had relaxed as well. They might have been two old friends catching up on the news.

Then Montclair surprised Tuck, and Sadie took the surprise a step further. He reached out a hand, and she took it and used it to hoist herself up onto the wagon. She lowered herself to the bench, sitting with her thigh pressed against Montclair's.

The street was uncrowded by its usual standards, but there were more people out than the night before, when fear had ruled the darkness. Tuck observed the other townsfolk, and on every face, he read shock. If Montclair and Sadie had any kind of relationship at all, these people hadn't been aware of it. Montclair and Sadie seemed to ignore the wide-eyed gazes of their neighbors. Montclair gave the reins a jerk, and those big horses started up the street again, drawing Montclair and his passenger toward the end of town.

With that many witnessing their departure, it wouldn't be long until Colonel Cuttrell heard about it. Tuck wondered what might happen then. Anybody's guess, he supposed. He didn't know the colonel, and didn't care to speculate on his reaction. What would happen would happen. With luck, it would happen at Montclair's ranch or on the fort; out of his jurisdiction, either way.

Tuck returned to his desk and his newspapers, slightly refreshed by the few moments outside. He thumbed through the papers, glossing over the parts that didn't interest him. But in the fourth paper he studied after getting back to it, he found an item, buried on the sixth page. Not trusting his own tired senses, he read it over four times. It was only a few paragraphs long.

It described some killings at a ranch between Tombstone and Carmichael. An eleven-year-old boy had survived, because he had been playing in the barn instead of inside the house like the rest of the family. He reported having seen a "shadow" leaving the house and riding away on a similarly midnight-black horse. He insisted that what he had seen was no man, because it had no features but was just a black form with blazing yellow eyes. His mother, father, and two sisters had been ripped to pieces, the paper reported, as if by a pack of wolves.

The newspaper was from seven months earlier. Was it possible that Daisie's killer had been in the area then?

Of course it was, he decided. When one was dealing with the seemingly impossible, it was foolish to put artificial limitations on it. Daisie's murderer had not been human, and describing him as a shadow made as much sense as anything. And there had been another one killing people in the alleyway behind Senora Soto's, just last night. And maybe one in his own jail, while he slept nearby, as if drugged. He couldn't try to impose any kind of normal standards on these things, whatever they were.

The writer of the *Epitaph* piece expressed a degree of disbelief at the boy's story, and ended it with a thinly veiled suggestion that the boy himself had likely been the killer. Tuck didn't believe that. He was heartened by the boy's description, which so closely matched his own experience. He dug into the other papers with renewed vigor, and before long had come across five additional articles describing similar events—killings in which the bodies had been torn apart, or at which mysterious yellow-eyed, ink-black beings had been observed, or both.

In one from a little more than a year earlier, the reporter had tried to track the creature that had been seen near the murder scene. He had followed its trail into the fringe of the Huachuca Mountains, he wrote, before he'd lost it. His writing was flamboyant and at times hard to follow, but the implication that Tuck read was that the man had not so much been unable to follow the trail as he had been chased away from it, once he'd reached the mountains.

There were still stacks of newspapers around the office. Tuck could page through each one, but he was satisfied. Six tales of savage killings, all with hints of the same sorts of creatures Tuck had seen. Seen, and killed. Someone else had managed to wound one, cutting off some of its claws.

They weren't human, and he didn't believe they were animal, either. He wasn't sure what that left. Hellspawn of some kind? That didn't seem far from the truth.

He lay the last newspaper down on a pile, and sat back in his chair. If he hadn't seen the thing—hadn't fought with it, felt it in his own hands, smelled it, then watched as it melted away to nothing—he wouldn't believe any of it. Not for an instant.

But he had. Now he didn't know what to make of it. But he had no problem believing. Whatever they were, wherever they had come from, he believed.

He was still at his desk, reflecting on his findings, when Mo Kanouse came into the office. "You read those already, boss?" he asked with a dismissive scowl.

"Enough, Mo. Thanks for fetching them."

"Not like I had anything else to do. Or mebbe I did, after all."

"You work for me, remember? You do what I tell you to."

Kanouse furiously scratched his left armpit. "Yeah, so I hear."

"Listen, Mo. I was reading about some killings in the area, over the past year. Usually more than one person murdered. The victims were always torn into shreds. Sometimes a killer was seen, and if he was, he was always described as having skin as black as a raven feather and burning yellow eyes. You remember hearing about any of those?"

"Boss, the *Epitaph* ain't exactly the most reliable source of information. The folks who write that usually have rotgut poisonin', or they're just plumb crazy."

"That might be, but those stories match what I saw when Hank Turville and I fought Daisie's murderer. That was no human being. Neither was what killed people behind Soto's last night."

"You been sippin' the rotgut, too?"

"I'm just asking if you remember anything about those killings."

"And I'm tellin' you if you keep talkin' that way, folks are gonna think you're a lunatic. Like I already do."

Tuck had had enough. He had never liked Kanouse, but Turville had kept him on, which made Tuck think the deputy must have had some good qualities he just wasn't seeing. But Kanouse had been scornful, rude, and antagonistic ever since Tuck had taken the job. The only thing he'd done that was remotely helpful was pick up some newspapers, and Tuck figured with a little training, a monkey could do that.

"Hand me that badge," he said. He pushed himself to his feet and extended his right hand.

Kanouse looked at him as if he'd completely lost his mind. Tuck supposed there was a slender possibility that he had—that everything he believed about the dark creatures was the result of his own insanity.

But he didn't think so.

"Why?" Kanouse asked.

"Because you're obviously not interested in being my deputy. Maybe you worked well with Hank, but I've had all the guff from you I care to take. Hand it over."

Kanouse puffed out his chest and thrust his chin toward Tuck, as if prepared to fight for it. But then, perhaps realizing how foolish that would be, he reached to his chest and unpinned it. Instead of handing it to Tuck, he tossed it to the desk. It bounced once and skidded, dropping to the floor. Tuck left it there.

"That gun yours, or the department's? Don't lie, because if it belongs to us there'll be paper on it."

The deputy—*former* deputy—glared at him, but then lowered his eyes and pulled the weapon from its holster. "Don't throw that," Tuck warned.

Kanouse held it by the butt and set it gently on the desk. "How's that?" he asked. He obviously didn't care what the answer was. Tuck reached for it and slid it closer to his side.

"Now the key to the office."

Kanouse swore, but dug into his pocket. He came out with a key, which he flipped at the desk. It bounced once, then hit the floor. "Anythin' else? My gold tooth?"

"You can keep that," Tuck said. "Now get out of here. I don't want to see you here again unless it's in chains."

"Don't worry, Bringloe. I got no interest in keepin' company with you."

"That's two of us. Get gone."

Kanouse paused in the doorway. "Men who think like you don't live long around here," he said.

"Is that a threat, Mo?"

"Take it however you like, rummy." Kanouse showed Tuck his back and stepped into the street.

After his former deputy left, Tuck settled back into his office chair. Instead of opening another newspaper, he put the new hat Missy had given him carefully on a stack of them and patted down his hair. Then he folded his hands on his chest, leaned back, and closed his eyes.

He wasn't there long before the door opened again. Tuck opened his eyes, half-expecting to see Kanouse back for more, perhaps with another gun in his hand.

Instead, it was the girl known as Little Wing, and the Apache scout who always seemed to be trailing around after her. Kuruk, Tuck remembered. He lowered his hands to the desktop and sat up straight. "Morning, Miss," he said.

"Good morning, Marshal," Little Wing replied.

"Have a seat, if you can find one that's not buried in newspapers."

"A lot of words," she said, her gaze wandering about the cluttered office. "Is there wisdom in them?"

"A lot of nonsense in these, I think." Tuck got up and cleared off a chair for her, then one for Kuruk. The Apache thanked him and sat. "If there's much wisdom, it's hidden pretty well."

"Isn't that always the way?" Little Wing asked.

"I reckon it is."

She fluttered a hand toward the southwest. "The wisdom this

world contains amounts to a few pebbles in those mountains. A few leaves in the deepest forest. Hard to find, harder to recognize."

"Don't you want to sit, Miss? Little Wing?" he asked.

She eyed the chair as if she had never seen one before. Kuruk gestured toward it, palm up. Finally, she nodded her head once and lowered herself onto it. "Thank you," she said.

Kuruk edged forward in his seat, until he was perched right on the edge. "Little Wing wanted to talk to you," he explained. "She said it was important. So here we are."

"Talk about what?"

Little Wing looked at the scout and took a deep breath. Her hands moved constantly, and her gaze rarely settled in any one place for more than an instant. Still, she seemed more solid, somehow, than when Tuck had first met her. It was almost as if part of her had been missing, and she'd been as insubstantial as steam. The more time she spent in town, the more substance she took on. He no longer felt like he could see through her, if the light was just right.

"About me," she said. Even her words carried more weight than they had. Once they had seemed like they would float away on the lightest of breezes, and they'd made no sense to Tuck. "Who I am."

"Who are you?" Tuck asked. "Little Wing isn't your name?"

"It is the name Kuruk gave me," she said. "It does what a name needs to do. If someone speaks it, I answer. If someone wants to talk about me, they know what name to use."

"But your original name—"

"I do not remember that. Little Wing works. I like it."

"Then what do you mean, who you are?"

She touched her breast, but then her hand flitted away again, as they both did. "Who I am. What I am, where I came from. Why I am here."

"And you want to tell me? Why me?"

"Because you matter."

Tuck felt his cheeks start to warm. "Matter how?"

"In what is to come," she said. "You are part of it. Central to it."

She was veering into confusing territory again, saying things he couldn't parse. "What's to come? What is that?"

"I cannot say."

"You don't know, or you can't say?"

"I . . . cannot say."

"Well, what can you tell me?"

She glanced over at Kuruk, and got an almost imperceptible nod. "There was a Catholic order called the Sisters of Charity. The sisters helped run a field hospital at Cemetery Ridge."

"Cemetery Ridge."

"I believe so, yes."

"And what's that got to do with you?"

"I was . . ." She paused, and then closed her mouth. The pause went on for a minute.

"Go on," Tuck urged.

"I . . . I do not remember much after that. Until the mule train."

The jump surprised Tuck, but the whole story, such as it was, didn't hang together in any coherent way. "The one where the army found you?"

"Yes."

"You remember what happened?"

Those always-moving hands stopped at her throat, and she looked as if she might cry. "I do not care to. But I do."

"Can you tell me?"

"It was . . . horrible. We were almost ready to make camp. The sun was low and our shadows were long before us. I remember being hungry, and thinking about biscuits and beans. And then . . . then they came out of the hills. Dozens of them."

Tuck looked at Kuruk, but the scout just gave him a blank stare. "Who did?" Tuck asked. "Came out of the hills?"

"Not-men," she said.

Tuck's blood chilled. "If they weren't men, what were they?"

"Shards of night. They came and they . . . and they—"

"You don't have to say it," Tuck said. "I've heard as much as I need to."

"It was bad," Kuruk said. "Real bad. I was there when we found them. Found *her*."

"And you survived? You were the only one, right?"

"She was."

"I . . . I do not know how. They were . . . they were tearing, rending. Everybody. Everything, even the animals. I . . . I fell asleep. Unconscious. When I awoke, Kuruk was over me."

"And that's all you remember?"

"Yes."

"How did you come to be with the train?"

"I do not remember."

Something about the quickness with which she'd answered caught Tuck's notice. "Don't remember, or don't want to say?"

"I . . . I was walking."

"Where?"

"I do not know. In the desert."

"Where were you before that?"

Sweat filmed her brow, and she was clutching her left hand with her right, holding it so tight her fingers were white. "I do not remember."

Her story didn't make any more sense than the things she usually said. He supposed she could have been so injured, or frightened, that any memories of what came before had been lost. Her mind seemed less able to hold thoughts in than most people's, as if it were a net and her thoughts and memories liquid. "Then what?"

"I was thirsty. Lost. I heard animals, voices. I found them, spoke with them, and they took me in. I walked with them, or rode in a wagon, until the . . . the attack."

Tuck opened his desk drawer and brought out the bandanna with the claws wrapped inside it. "I don't want to upset you, Miss. But I wonder if you could look at these and tell me if they came from the—what'd you call them? Not-men?"

She sucked in a deep, stuttering breath, then swallowed hard. "I will try."

He set it on the desktop and unrolled the cloth. The claws were as black and shiny as obsidian.

Little Wing gave a frightened yelp and jerked back in her chair. Tuck quickly covered the claws again.

"Y-yes," she said. She was quaking with fear, pressed against the chair's rungs, as far from the desk as she could get without standing up. From the looks of her, her legs wouldn't hold her anyway. "Please, put them away!"

He took them off the desk and shoved them back into the drawer. "I'm sorry. I had to know."

"Th-they are," she said. He had seen soldiers under fire who weren't as frightened as she was. "I . . . I wish I could tell you more, about that day. I do remember the not-men, and their claws. They were terrible. But I cannot . . . there is more, but I cannot recall it."

Tuck waved his hand at her. "It's all right, Miss. Don't try. It's not that important."

"I believe that it is. Very important."

"Not right this second. It appears things are coming back to you a little at a time. That'll work. Let it come, and if you think of something else you think I should know, I'll be here."

"Yes," she said. She looked relieved, as if he had given her license to not force memories to come that she wasn't ready to face. "Yes, I will. You will need to know everything, before it is over."

"Before what's over?" he asked. As soon as the words were out of his mouth, he regretted them. He had just given her leave not to think about whatever was troubling her, and then demanded to know more.

Her mouth opened and closed a few times. She met his gaze and held it. "I cannot say, exactly. Not that I do not want to. I almost know, but not quite. The image will not become clear for me. I can almost see it, but as if through a smoky haze. All I know is that it is getting worse, fast."

"What is?"

"That is what I cannot tell you yet."

"I don't understand what you're saying, Miss. Are you telling me you see things that haven't happened yet?"

She smiled for the first time since entering the office. "So it appears."

Tuck wasn't about to ask for more clarification. "When you can see it, let me know."

"I will. And I will do what I can to help. I pray that it will be enough."

She rose and walked out the door without another word. Kuruk stood, and started to follow, but he stopped just inside the doorway.

"Cemetery Ridge," he said. "Do you know what that is?"

Tuck had known it the moment she'd said it. "It's Gettysburg."

"She said something about it before. She was incoherent. Delirious. But I thought she said Cemetery Ridge, and something about a devil's deck, and something about mead. I asked around, and finally an old soldier told me it sounded like somebody talking about the battle at Gettysburg. Devil's Den. Meade was a Union general. And Pickett's Charge was against the Union line at Cemetery Ridge. Casualties were—"

"I know how they were."

"Were you there?"

"No. But you didn't fight in the war without hearing about it."

"Anyway, this old fella said they were there. The Sisters of Charity. A Catholic order, like she said, helping tend to the wounded."

"But what does that have to do with her? She wasn't there. That was 1863. Eighteen years ago. She might be eighteen, but no more than."

"Who can say, Marshal? This world is a much stranger place than most people ever know. I wouldn't want to be the one to say what's possible and what isn't. Would you?"

Chapter Thirty-seven

Reconsidering his initial reaction, Tuck went to the fort to see Colonel Cuttrell. What the man's wife did was no business of Tuck's, and she had seemingly climbed onto Montclair's wagon of her own free will. But maybe that impression had been mistaken. There were all kinds of pressures one person could use against another, and physical force was only one of them. Some of the others were worse, because they could break down a person's spirit, and that was a wound that healed more slowly than the kind caused by violence.

Cuttrell would probably hear about it from others, maybe from several. But Tuck had been a witness, and however ill-suited he felt for the job, he was an officer of the law. The encounter had taken place in his town. He bore a responsibility to make sure Sadie Cuttrell was safe, and that she had gone with Montclair willingly.

A dark-haired, muscular lieutenant named McKenna was Cuttrell's aide-de-camp. Tuck told him what he wanted, and after about five minutes, McKenna ushered him into the colonel's office. It was a big space with a map-covered table on one end, surrounded by chairs, and a desk at the other, with a bookcase beside it. The walls were bare, but a couple of braided rugs covered some of the floorboards. Cuttrell sat at the desk with a big ledger book before him. When the men entered, he set his pen down on a blotter next to the book and capped his inkwell. He didn't stand. "Welcome, Marshal," he said. "It isn't often we see the law from town on our fort. Something I can do for you?"

Cuttrell was a lean man, his face weathered by hard duty. His golden hair was tinged with silver. It curled off his ears and around his collar. His chin sported a neat, graying beard, and his eyes were brown and small. His most prominent feature was a thin nose that jutted forward as if it carried a grudge and wanted everyone to know it. His ears were small, almost without lobes, but they stood away from his head like half-open doors.

Tuck crossed the office and extended his hand. At that prompting, Cuttrell rose briefly from his seat, gave Tuck's hand a single, perfunctory shake, then sat again. Tuck remained standing. "I'm here about your wife," he said.

McKenna's boot scraped the floor, as if he'd been caught off-guard by Tuck's statement. That made Tuck curious, but the lieutenant was behind him, by the door, and Tuck wanted to watch the colonel's reaction.

As it happened, Cuttrell barely reacted at all. He scanned the ledger book, wet his thumb, and turned the page. "Sadie? What about her?"

"I saw her get into a wagon with Jasper Montclair. They left town together. I thought you should know."

At that, Cuttrell looked up at Tuck, regarding him as one might a busker with a traveling medicine show. "You're confused. She barely knows the man. I'm not sure she does at all, for that matter. *I* barely know him."

"I'm sorry, Colonel, but I'm not. I have made her acquaintance, and his." He gave a brief account of the heated conversation he had interrupted before.

"Jimmy?" Cuttrell said. "You often accompany her into town. Have you seen any such encounters?"

McKenna cleared his throat. "No, sir, I have not."

"To your knowledge, is my wife familiar with Mr. Montclair?"

"No, sir."

"Where is she now?"

"I'm afraid I don't know, sir. As you're aware, I've been on duty, here with you all morning."

"Yes, quite." Cuttrell returned his attention to Tuck. "I'm not casting doubt on your powers of observation, Marshal Bringloe. I'm merely saying that you must have been mistaken. Perhaps the sun was in your eyes."

Tuck remembered the glare from the windows across the street. "It may have been, Colonel."

"As I thought. Jimmy, show the Marshal to the front gate, and then locate Mrs. Cuttrell."

"The front gate, sir?"

Cuttrell uncapped the inkwell, dipped his pen, and looked down at the ledger book. "The marshal has no jurisdiction on this post, and therefore no reason to be here. Ever again, Marshal Bringloe. I make myself clear, do I not?"

That was an extreme reaction—civilians went into the fort all the time, and troopers visited the town. He had done something to anger Cuttrell. He just wasn't sure quite what it had been. "Thanks for your time, Colonel," Tuck said. Cuttrell didn't answer.

As he followed McKenna out, he reflected on the brief conversation. He had learned two things from it. First, there was trouble between Cuttrell and his wife, and McKenna might figure into that trouble. And second, he knew what he had seen, and so did the colonel. For reasons of his own, Cuttrell wanted to be the one to deal with it. She was his wife, so Tuck couldn't object.

He guessed there was a third thing he'd learned: Cuttrell considered Fort Huachuca his own personal fiefdom, and he didn't want anybody around who might remotely threaten his authority. During his hard-drinking days, Tuck had been thrown out of plenty of places. He knew when he was unwelcome, and Cuttrell had made it very clear that he wasn't wanted on the fort.

He would make every effort to oblige the man.

Jasper Montclair's ranch house was like no place Sadie had ever seen.

On the way in, she thought she had seen strange things. At one point, she was certain she'd seen a big mesquite with impossibly long thorns, its branches moving of their own accord, picking apart a coyote that had somehow been caught up in it. Closer to the house, at the front gate and in the yard, there had been bones, stacks of them. In one spot a pile of skulls—human ones, she believed—formed a small pyramid. All of it was a little frightening, or would have been without the lingering effects of the laudanum. And something else, something about the way Jasper talked. His voice was soothing, and even when she couldn't understand his words, the tone of it put her at ease. Now that she was inside, everything she had seen out there was already fading in her memory, like something she might have witnessed as a child.

The house, though. That she could see and touch, though even here, her vision seemed somehow cloudy around the edges. Jasper abandoned her for a few minutes when they first arrived. Left on her own, she fairly floated from room to room, her feet seeming to barely touch the floor. That, too, was the laudanum at work, at least in part. Part of it was the air inside the house, scented with something sharp but not unpleasant. Part of it was everything else, the weight of everything arrayed around her. Every inch of the place seemed to contain *something*.

In the front room had been more books than she had seen in the rest of her life put together. Books were everywhere, stuffed onto shelves, stacked hip-deep on the floor, spilling off tables. They were bound in leather of various hues, and although she had never been a good reader and her vision was more than a little blurred at the moment, many appeared to be written in languages other than English. She flipped through the pages of one that looked like some kind of a science thing, a handwritten journal rather than a printed book. She couldn't even make out the title, which she thought was in Latin, though she could read the name Dr. Darius Hellstromme written underneath it in a cramped, unsteady hand. Three other books, massively thick ones, rested on their own stands, open to the air. She saw other names she didn't recognize on two of those: Mina Devlin, Herbert Whately, and the third had no name at all.

"What are those ones?" she had asked.

Jasper smiled. "Those? My grimoires. The volumes I live by."

She hadn't known what he'd meant by that. The unfamiliar word had no resonance for her, but she didn't ask. Instead, her attention was snagged by the skeleton of a small animal, perched atop an ungainly stack of books. "Won't it fall?" she asked. "What is it?"

"It's a tiger," he said. "A baby; they grow much larger than that."

"I've never seen one."

"Most people haven't. And no, it won't fall; it holds up the books."

"From on top?"

"Don't question, my dear. Just accept."

Something about his voice. She *did* accept.

That was when he excused himself, and she drifted from that room into the next. It was illuminated by candles on iron stands. They were bigger around than her thighs, and greasy smoke rose from the flames.

In this one, there were more skeletons, dozens of them. Some might have been from bears or apes, some full-grown tigers or other big cats. She saw birds and what must have been rodents, rats, or mice. The skeletons appeared to all be intact, at least as far as she could tell. Some were protected by glass domes, others sat on tables or racks, and some just stood there, as tall as she was.

Besides the skeletons, books were scattered about in this room, though not nearly as many as before. Hanging on the walls, in heavy frames, were photographs of people. Looking closer, Sadie saw that every photograph was of somebody dead. Some showed children in caskets, looking as if they might awaken from a refreshing nap at any moment. In one of those, so many flowers surrounded the casket that it might have been a jungle scene, and the dead boy was hard to find. Others were of adults, often sitting up in chairs, a few with their eyes open

and others with coins over them. Three of the images were of bare-chested or naked men with bullet holes pocking their flesh, including one in which a wound of some kind had split open the man's cheek, showing bone underneath the ravaged flesh.

In most of the frames, Sadie found, there was something else besides the photograph. One held a dried flower, its petals fallen, its stem looking brittle and dead. Several contained hair of various colors, tied with ribbons or braided into shapes, or just loose at the bottom of the frame. The one of the man with the ruined face held what appeared to be chips of bone.

Ordinarily, being here with these bizarre objects would terrify her. But the laudanum and the aroma and Jasper's presence—although it had been several minutes now since she had seen him—together served to comfort her.

"Jasper?" she called, having remembered who brought her here. "Jasper, where are you?"

He appeared in the doorway a moment later. Something was different about his face, but she couldn't put her finger on just what. Had he had those red streaks on it before? Three of them cut across his forehead, one ran down the center of his nose, and three marked each cheek, running from his nose back toward his jaw.

"I'm here, my queen," he said. "I'm getting ready."

"Ready for what?"

"You needn't worry about that. I'll take care of everything."

"I—" Sadie started to disagree. No man ever took care of everything, though they all said they would. But before the words were out of her mouth, they slipped from her mind.

"Yes, my queen?"

"I . . . I don't know. Nothing." She looked at him. Those marks on his face. She meant to ask him something about those, but couldn't remember what. "Nothing," she said again. "Nothing at all."

Chapter Thirty-eight

Cale thought his lungs would split right down the middle.

He had run until he could run no longer, then had sat under the uneven shade of a spindly ocotillo until he thought he could go on. This time, he couldn't run for as long, but he found that if he alternated walking and running he could keep moving, even if that progress was slower than running full out would have been.

Still, he was beginning to think he would never reach town.

Clouds were starting to form to the southeast, but there was no certainty that they would reach the mountains, and even if they did, they might be too sparse to cool the baking heat of day. Rain might or might not come, and too much rain could make travel harder than none at all.

So when he saw a horse-drawn wagon in the distance, heading toward him, he broke into a sprint, waving his hands above his head and shouting to make sure he was seen.

The wagon's driver turned out to be the banker, Mr. Harrell. Cale knew Mr. Tibbetts was angry with the man, because he had refused a loan, then sold the note he already held to Montclair. But Cale had no choice. He would be lucky to ever make it to Carmichael on foot, and Harrell had a wagon and horses. Cale explained what had happened at the J Cross T, and the banker seemed sympathetic.

"I'll give you a ride, son," he said. "Into town, if that's where you want to go. But first, I'll want to see the ranch for myself. Make sure the Tibbettses are safe."

Cale nearly refused the offer. Mr. Tibbetts was probably unhappy with him for running off. Even if he explained why he had left, that might not help. With the rest of the hands dead and the animals slaughtered, Tibbetts might have needed him at the ranch. All Cale had been able to think of was letting the townsfolk know, in case they could raise a posse or the army. Something. He hadn't yet accomplished that, and he didn't want to face Mr. Tibbetts, who would see him and think he had just been scared, running to save his own life.

In the end, Cale agreed to go with Harrell. He would explain when they reached the ranch. Mr. Tibbetts would believe him. He had never lied to the man before. On the way, Harrell barely spoke a word.

When they arrived, Cale found out why.

Mr. and Mrs. Tibbetts heard the wagon coming, and came out of the house. When they saw Harrell and Cale, Mrs. Tibbetts broke down weeping. Mr. Tibbetts left her by the house and walked up to meet the buckboard. His face was impassive, hard to read. "Wilson," he said when the horses came to a halt. "Cale."

"Mr. Tibbetts," Cale said rapidly. "I tried to make it to town. I figured people needed to know what happened. But I couldn't make it. I was running and running, and finally, I saw—"

"It's all right, Cale. We'll handle things here, like we always do."

"But, Mr. Tibbetts, without the boys, I thought—"

The rancher interrupted him again. "I said, we'll handle it. Thanks for bringin' him back, Wilson."

"I was headed here anyway," Harrell said. Cale stared in stunned surprise—the banker had not mentioned that on the way. Cale climbed down from the wagon and went to stand with his employers.

"What for?" Tibbetts asked.

"Why don't we go inside, Jed?"

"Let's stay right here."

"Jed—"

"I said here, sir. I'm not about to invite you into my house. It is still my house, isn't it?"

Harrell pulled up the leather case he'd had down by his feet. "That's what I'm here about, in fact."

"I figgered."

"I'd like you to sign some papers. To make the transfer official."

"You mean to give Montclair my land."

"It isn't yours any longer, Jed. He owns it, by rights."

"There's nothing right about it, Wilson Harrell!" Mrs. Tibbetts shouted. She had dropped her hands from her face, bunched them into fists, and advanced toward the wagon as if she intended to deliver a whipping. "Nothing right at all!"

"Mrs. Tibbetts, the law is the law."

"The law is what men make it to be," she argued. "It's not as if the good Lord caused it to be that way. Where is it written in the sky, on the wind, in indelible letters on the sides of mountains? It is only what men who want to be able to take from other men have decided to make it, in order to make the taking easier."

Harrell chuckled, a sound so unnatural that it might have been a rattlesnake singing "Come, Come, Ye Saints." "Now, Mrs. Tibbetts, I didn't write the laws. I'm a banker, not a politician. All I'm doing is what the law requires of me."

"You could have fought for us," she said. "You know my husband is as honest a man as was ever born. You know we're good for our obligations. We always have been."

"In the past, yes. This time, I'm sorry to say, I could not be certain of that. From what young Mr. Ceniceros tells me, I have to say that sadly, it looks like I made the right decision. Mr. Montclair thought he was acquiring a going concern, if a troubled one. But now it appears that all he owns is a disaster."

"Give me the papers," Tibbetts said, his voice tight. Cale could tell he was furious, by the way he held his hands, and the vein that popped out on the side of his head when he was mad. It looked as if it might burst.

"Jed, no," Mrs. Tibbetts said. "Don't sign those."

"I have to, Edith. He's right. The law says we got to give the place up."

Tears brimmed from her eyes again, rolling unimpeded down her cheeks and thumping softly into the earth at her feet. Harrell fished around in his case, and came up with some papers.

"I'll sign those," Tibbetts said. "But first I want to show you somethin'."

"What?"

"Get down off that wagon and come with me," the rancher said. Harrell looked like he wanted to decline, but Mr. Tibbetts's tone didn't offer room for argument. Harrell climbed down. Cale started to follow Mr. Tibbetts and Harrell, but Mrs. Tibbetts caught his shoulder and held him back. She held on to him the whole time the men were gone, her grip like iron, as if he were the only thing mooring her to the world.

When the men returned, Harrell was pale and wiping his mouth. Vomit flecked his black frock coat. "We're gettin' out of here," Mr. Tibbetts said.

"What do you mean, Jed?" his wife asked.

"I mean, get anything you need together."

"What, right now?"

"We're trespassin'. Wilson's got a wagon and horses to pull it. We've got wagons, but no draft animals. Fetch whatever things you need. You too, Cale."

Cale thought about what little he owned outright. A couple of shirts, a change of jeans. A few other small odds and ends. All of it was inside that bunkhouse, along with Mrs. Tibbetts's book. Except for his saddle, which was in the tack room at the end of the barn. "I won't need but a minute."

Mr. Tibbetts eyed him suspiciously, then nodded once. "What about you, Edith? Better get your necessaries packed up. Cale can help if you want. Wilson, how long we got?"

Harrell looked at the sky. "An hour, no more."

"You heard the man," Tibbetts said.

"I'm sorry I ever got mixed—" He stopped, midsentence, cleared his throat and spat on the ground.

"Sorry, Mr. Harrell?" Tibbetts said. "What was that?"

"Nothing, Jed. I'm sorry it all came out this way, that's all."

Cale didn't know what the banker had intended to say, but he was certain his last word had been "mixed." The way he saw it, the only word that could have followed was "up." Harrell was mixed up in something that he regretted. At least, he did now that he'd seen the results, since presumably Mr. Tibbetts had shown him the corral and the bunkhouse.

"Come on, Cale," Mrs. Tibbetts said. "Help me out, won't you?"

"'Course, Mrs. Tibbetts," Cale said. He hoped she would stop crying while they worked inside, though he doubted it. Her tears were calling to his, about to fetch them from him despite everything he was doing to hold them back.

One hour, to get everything from the house she would ever need. Then they would get into Harrell's wagon and ride into town, toward an uncertain future. And every hope and dream and wish that the Tibbettses had ever known—and most of Cale's, too—would be left behind them.

Cale was young. He felt the disappointment like a crushing weight, but at the same time, he knew other adventures awaited him, once he was past this. But for the rancher and his wife, this had been everything. Their life.

How did anyone come back from losing that?

Chapter Thirty-nine

I ran into Mo Kanouse earlier," Alf Maier said. He was in Mayor Chaffee's office, joined this time by the mayor and Colonel Cuttrell. Wilson Harrell wasn't back from the J Cross T, and Jasper Montclair hadn't been invited to this emergency meeting of the town council. "Bringloe fired him."

"On what grounds?" Chaffee asked.

"In Kanouse's words, if I remember correctly," Maier replied, "on the grounds that Marshal Bringloe is a 'useless, self-righteous, pitiful bag of drunken dog shit.' Or something to that effect. There might have been a few more curse words mixed in."

Cuttrell barked a laugh. "He's right on that score."

"You don't like him, either?" Chaffee asked him.

"I only just met him today," Cuttrell said. "I invited him to get off my fort and never come back."

"It is as I told you," Maier said. "He is dangerous to our plans. What Kanouse told me makes that all the more plain."

The mayor was on his feet, leaning back against his desk, while the other two sat in visitor's chairs. At Maier's statement, Chaffee scratched his ribs and angled his head toward the grocer. "What'd he tell you?"

"After he left, that girl went to see him. The one from the mule train."

"The one who's going to be a laundress?" Cuttrell offered.

"I suppose, yes. Her. And that Indian scout who goes around with her."

"Kuruk."

"If you say so. Kanouse told me that he stayed close by, so he could listen in."

"I don't like Bringloe," the colonel said. "But that Kanouse is a lout."

"That may be," Maier answered. "But he told me that Little Wing warned Bringloe of something coming. Something bad. She told him that she would help as much as she could."

"What can she possibly know?" Chaffee demanded.

"Who can say? The fact that she seems to know anything at all disturbs me."

"The girl is mad as a wet hen," Cuttrell said. "Nothing she says makes a lick of sense. I only hope she's capable of washing uniforms and blankets."

"According to Kanouse, she sounded like she made sense. Like she really did know something."

"Kanouse is an idiot," Cuttrell said. "Worrying about anything he says is a fool's game."

"Just the same," Maier said, "he was our man. Hank Turville was our man—"

"Until he let a bunch of whores shame him into chasing someone he should have left well enough alone," Cuttrell interrupted.

"Yes, until that," Maier agreed. "I went along to try to keep him out of trouble. I failed, and I am sorry for that. My point is that Tucker Bringloe is not our man, and he never will be."

"Alf thinks we should fire him," Chaffee told Cuttrell.

"Wilson Harrell agrees."

"Where is Harrell now?"

"He is arranging the transfer of the deed of the J Cross T to Jasper Montclair."

"And that's the last piece Montclair is waiting for?"

"So he says. He is already the biggest landowner and most successful rancher in the area, and he has been very generous with all of us. Now he will be the biggest in the entire Arizona territory, and I expect that his generosity will only grow with his wealth and influence."

"So nothing can stand in his way now," Cuttrell said. "Why are you worried about Bringloe?"

"I do not like surprises," Maier said. "At my store, I stock my shelves carefully. I try to carry the goods people will want, but not so much of anything that it spoils before it can be bought. I try to run all my affairs that way. The unpredictable worries me. Bringloe is unpredictable. We cannot know what he might do. We should fire him—at the very least—and appoint Kanouse in his place."

"Kanouse is an idiot!" Cuttrell said again. This time he emphasized his statement by punching his left palm with his right fist.

"He is *our* idiot," Maier countered. "That is the difference."

Cuttrell rubbed his temples vigorously, as if suddenly aware of a pain there. "Fine," he said after a minute's pause. "Throw Bringloe down a well, for all I care. I don't like Kanouse either, but if it'll make you two stop yammering, I'm for it."

Walking back to the fort, Cuttrell's head was pounding. He had just agreed, with the other men who ran the town, to further consolidate Jasper Montclair's power in the region. He had no clue what Montclair planned to do with that power, though the other men seemed to have some idea. All he knew was that, as Maier had pointed out, in the past he had been generous indeed.

Now, though, Montclair had taken his wife away. As with everything else about the rancher, the reason was a mystery. Cuttrell wanted to mount up and ride out to Montclair's place and put a bullet in the man's head. He liked the wealth Montclair threw his way, more than doubling his officer's salary. And he liked the power he and the others wielded over the town, in part because they could judiciously spread Montclair's money around and buy whatever favors they needed.

He hadn't been much of a husband. But Sadie wasn't much of a wife, either, between the laudanum she believed was a secret and the man or men who she slept with. Their identities, at least, were unknown to him, even if their existence wasn't. Perhaps Montclair was one of them, after all.

His first thought, when Bringloe had told him that she'd left in Montclair's wagon, had been to muster the troops and attack the Broken M in force. There would be a certain raw satisfaction in bringing down the wealthiest man in the area, simply because he was that. And because, as long as he shared his wealth with Cuttrell, the colonel was under his thumb. He was bought and paid for, and there might never be a better opportunity to break free.

Upon further reflection, though, he came to realize that he didn't want to break free if it meant giving up the largesse he had been enjoying. Although he had gone into the meeting not sure of where he stood, by its end he had agreed that every effort should be made to protect Montclair's plans, whatever they were. They would put a man who Cuttrell wouldn't trust to walk his dog, if he'd had one, in charge of enforcing the town's laws. They would increase their wealth and their standing in the community, and if the community grew, their power would grow with it.

It was a hell of a bargain to make. But they had all agreed, and they'd made it.

When he reached the fort, he sent a runner to find Ezra Hannigan. Then he sat in his office, alone, his head in his hands, until the captain knocked on his door. "You sent for me, sir?"

Cuttrell raised his head slowly. "Dismiss the men," he said, his voice hoarse and gravelly.

"I'm sorry, Colonel?"

Cuttrell cleared his throat and said it again, louder.

"Dismiss them? How many?"

"All of them."

"Sir?"

Cuttrell roared his answer. "I said all of them!"

"I don't understand."

"You are not required to, Captain. You are only required to follow orders."

"Yes, sir." Hannigan snapped off a salute and spun on his heel.

Cuttrell knew it was an extreme measure. It might affect his standing with the men, and if it got back to Richmond, it might cost him his career.

But if he had troopers at his disposal, he would be tempted to use them. Already he was second-guessing his decision. Perhaps he should have made the other call, let love for his wife overrule his love for money and position and power.

He had not, however, made that choice, and it was too late to change course now. Sending away his men was the safest thing he could do. With them gone, he couldn't change his mind, and if he did he couldn't do anything about it.

When you had abandoned your wife and sold out every principle you had once held dear, making sure you couldn't take action against your own failure was, he believed, the best thing you could do.

Tuck had taken the map off the wall and spread it on his desk. With a pen, he marked the locations of the incidents he had read about in the *Epitaph*, as well as he could estimate considering the newspaper wasn't always as precise as it might have been. He added the place where they'd fought Daisie's killer, and the approximate location of the mule train slaughter.

When he was finished, he pressed it flat with his palms and looked at it from arm's length.

The marks made a half-circle. At the center of it was Jasper Montclair's ranch, and behind that, the uneven fringe of the Huachuca Mountains.

He wasn't sure yet what that meant. But he was convinced that it meant something.

And he intended to find out what.

Chapter Forty

Carmichael's only hotel was the Grand, which was far too ambitious a name for the place the sign hung on. The lobby was small and crowded, the ceiling low, and it smelled like a chamber pot and a spittoon had been combined and then poured behind the walls. The rooms were not much better. Wilson Harrell dropped the Tibbettses and Cale there with the few bags they had packed at the house. The boy had ridden the whole way with one arm wrapped around his saddle, as if it were the last friend he had. Maybe it was. Once they were inside, Harrell turned the wagon around and headed out of town again. He had allowed them too much time to pack, and had underestimated how long it would take to get back into town from their place.

His day wouldn't be finished for hours yet. His task wouldn't be done until he had delivered the deed to Jasper Montclair. That meant heading back out into the high desert valley where the ranches sprawled. He hoped the rain would hold off, because a storm could mire his wagon for hours. And Montclair had made very clear his insistence that he needed the deed today, as early as he could get it.

The route to Montclair's spread was a familiar one he had driven many times, though the last time had been several months ago. The ground along the way was hard-packed and rutted from wagon travel, except where passing herds of cattle had roughed up the road and obliterated all else, or flash floods had washed the path away. Harrell was heartened by the fact that the clouds were holding off. Lightning splintered on the southern horizon, but that was well into Old Mexico.

He knew when he reached the outer edge of the Broken M. Montclair didn't fence his land, but at the property's boundary he had built stone markers that flanked the roadway on either side. The banker had seen them dozens of times, but had never before noticed how much the round stones resembled human skulls, dulled and dirtied by time. He twisted around in the seat for a better look, but the horses had already carried him far enough past that even in the afternoon sunlight, he couldn't get a clear view.

Beyond that point, the road continued the way Harrell was accustomed to. It cut between two low hills and then dipped to slice across a rocky wash. On the other side a steep grade rose up through a cholla forest containing hundreds of the short, many-armed cacti. They looked fuzzy from a distance, and sunlight glowed through their apparently soft thorns, but nobody petted one more than once. After that, the way leveled out and made a wide, sweeping curve toward the southwest and the particularly deep, shadowed canyon that sliced into the Huachucas behind Montclair's house. The road would bend and curve many times before the ranch headquarters, but Harrell always felt, when he reached that point, that he was almost there. The journey was largely flat from that juncture, the mountains growing nearer, and it was a particularly lovely stretch of country. Harrell felt almost at peace, for the first time that day. He would deliver the deed to Montclair and be done with the whole business.

He eyed the cholla with suspicion. Fist-sized, thorny balls of it had a habit of seemingly leaping out onto the legs of passersby, and a horse's hoof could kick a wayward one into the footwell of a wagon. But when he passed through the densest stand of it and into the open country, mentally ready for the landscape to open up into that heavenly view, he was surprised to find that the road hooked off to the east.

"No!" he said aloud, surprised that his memory could prove so faulty. "No, this isn't . . ."

He let the sentence trail off. There was no one there to address it to but the horses, and they didn't care what he had to say. They followed the road without comment.

Harrell thought that perhaps he'd been momentarily confused. He had let his mind wander, and he wasn't precisely where he had thought. He would spot something familiar in the next couple of minutes, reorient himself.

Instead, the road circled around toward the north—the direction he had come from. He *knew* that wasn't right. Sweat began to gather under his arms, tickling his ribs. Had he somehow turned onto the wrong road? That must have been it. He half stood in the wagon, scanning for any landmark he recognized, until its rocking motion nearly pitched him out.

Sitting quickly, he slowed the horses while he assessed the situation. He might well be lost if he kept going on this path. He needed to backtrack, follow the road to wherever he had made the mistake.

Convincing the horses of that took some doing. On the narrow road, there wasn't room to make a forward turn. The brush, mostly thorny mesquite in this area, with low beaver-tail cactus packing the space around it, was too dense. Harrell got down out of the wagon and half walked, half pushed the animals into backing up, then coming forward a little, then back again. Each time they went backward, the wagon threatened to capsize. As he worked them, the sun kept lowering toward the west, and he was beginning to fear that he would still be out here after dark, trying to find his way along a road that had suddenly become unfamiliar.

Finally, he had the horses turned around, headed the way they had come. He climbed back into the seat and encouraged them onward. Around the long curve, down through the cholla forest and the wash, between the hills—sometime before that, there had to be another spur, the one he had missed.

But when he rounded the curve, he found, instead, a narrow,

rutted track that led straight in a southerly direction. The plants on either side were even more menacing here; reaching into the roadway with thorn-covered arms.

Harrell stopped again. This wasn't possible. He had just come this way. Only it hadn't been the same. Not twenty minutes had passed. He stood again, turned this way and that. Nothing looked familiar, except the changeless mountains he couldn't seem to reach.

He sat on the bench, gathered the reins in his trembling hands, and tried to remember how to pray.

Cale had no money for his own hotel room, but the Tibbettses, ever generous, had said that he could sleep in theirs for as long as he needed. He appreciated the gesture, and he would have to accept their offer or sleep in the streets. But he didn't want to be a burden; he would find work as soon as he could and get out of their hair. In the meantime, he wanted to let them have the room to themselves as much as possible. They were grieving, as surely as anyone who'd had a death in the family. They needed their privacy.

He spent some time on Main, wandering up one side and down the other, peering into shop windows at things he would never own. Townsfolk passed him by, some saying hello or touching their hats, others ignoring him.

Finally, he had seen all he could stand of that street. He stepped off the boardwalk near Senora Soto's and walked down Maiden Lane, toward the south. He knew Senora Soto's was a brothel, and there were three more in the other direction on Maiden Lane, north of Main Street. He had no interest in seeing those women or hearing the things they would call out.

Over by the Methodist church, he stopped again. On the slope below the church was a cemetery, most of the graves marked with wooden crosses or slabs. He wondered how so many people could have died already; the town wasn't that old, after all. There was a Catholic church on the other end of town with its own graveyard, and the fort had one, too.

In the last few days, Cale had seen more death than in the rest of his life all together. He had thought about it more, too. What it meant. What it was like. He didn't know if the churches were right, and he could expect an eternity in torment and flames, or—unlikely, he knew—to be sitting on clouds, strumming a harp and grooming feathered wings.

Most of the people he had known well, his fellow hands from the J Cross T, were dead. He hadn't wondered, until now, what would become of them. Would someone haul them into town to bury in one of the graveyards? Who would have the unpleasant duty of cleaning out that bunkhouse? Probably Montclair's boys, he guessed. If it were left to him, he would set a torch to the thing and burn it down, bodies and all. No force on earth could make him go in there.

"There you are," a gentle voice called from behind him. Cale turned to see Little Wing coming toward him, her hands held out at waist level. Her smile made her face seem luminous. "I was looking for you."

"For me?"

"Yes, Cale." He took a couple of steps toward her, and when she was within reach, his hands rose almost as if by their own accord to clasp hers. She squeezed tight. "I wanted to see you. I know about what happened at the ranch."

"You heard already?" he asked. "How?"

She released one hand, and holding the other, led him away from the church and down behind the buildings on the far side of the alley. Cale noticed that the Apache scout was never far away, but he waited politely out of earshot. "I know," she said. He noted her unusual phrasing, and chose not to pursue the question.

"I am sorry," she went on. "I know those men were your friends."

"Some of them," Cale said.

"You knew them. You worked with them. It is hard to see those you know die."

An image of the bunkhouse interior, seen through the open door, flashed through his mind. "It surely is."

"I wish it had not happened."

"So do I."

"There will be more dying," she said. Cale looked at her. She was staring at the ground as they walked, pointedly not looking his way. Her profile was lovely; her nose had the slightest upward tilt at the end, her chin was strong, her lips full and elegantly shaped.

"What do you mean?"

"More," she said.

"You won't . . ."

"I cannot say who. Only that the dying is not over."

This time, he couldn't help himself. "How do you know these things?"

"I cannot—"

"You cannot say! There's a lot you can't say, isn't there?"

"I am sorry, Cale."

He suddenly felt ashamed for having snapped at her. She was just being nice, and she was the prettiest girl he had ever known, and he had just about bitten off her nose. "No, Little Wing, I'm sorry. I don't understand who you are, or what. I don't mean to be rude or impatient."

"You hold no fault in the matter," she answered. "I would tell you more if I could. Some I do not remember, and some is not meant for anyone to know."

"You surely are a confusing girl," Cale said. "I've never known anyone like you."

"I am not sure there has ever *been* anyone like me, Cale."

He was willing to grant that she was correct on that score, and was about to say so when she stomped in a rain puddle, splashing his legs with slick, runny mud. She had done it deliberately, angling her leg in to direct the splash toward him. She shot him a mischievous grin.

"What'd you do that for?" he asked.

"Because I could."

"How'd you like it if I did it to you?"

"You would have to catch me first." With that, she spun away from him and took off at a sprint, laughing.

Cale hesitated, still surprised by her sudden attack. Then her laughter and the way her body moved as she ran dug hooks into him, and he gave chase.

Little Wing ran away from town and into open desert. Afternoon sun picked out individual leaves and thorns, bathing them in a golden glow that made the landscape sparkle. Cale had seen the effect many times. Usually he just saw it as a nuisance, because it meant the sun was on its way down to where it would be in his eyes. Today, though, he was so enraptured by its beauty that he lost track of Little Wing.

A peal of laughter revealed her hurtling alongside an arroyo, dropping into it when she had to avoid a thorny bush growing too near the edge, then popping out again on the other side. He raced toward her, cutting a diagonal path, sometimes leaping over low brush. Once a thorny branch caught his leg and he tumbled over, catching himself on hands and knees. Palms stinging, he lifted his head and saw Little Wing standing nearby, wearing an expression of concern. When he laughed and vaulted up, she darted away again.

Finally, he outpaced her as they climbed a rock-strewn slope. She seemed to be getting winded, although when he grabbed her arm and pulled up beside her, she broke into laughter again, bending over, hands on her thighs, in sheer merriment. Her cheeks were slightly reddened, but Cale was panting from exertion and she was breathing normally.

"You caught me fair and square," she said when she could speak again. "What will you do with me?"

He hadn't been anticipating such a question. Standing so near to her, what he wanted more than anything was to kiss her. But she would slap him back down the hill for that, and rightly so. "Reckon I'd like to get to know you better," he said. It seemed a reasonable intermediate step.

"I said I would tell you what I could."

"Then tell."

Little Wing gave his hand a squeeze, then released it. She hugged herself, as if simply thinking about her own past was terrifying. He was a little sorry he had asked, but if it meant she would open up, not too sorry.

She started back down the hill, in the direction of town. Now Cale saw that the Apache scout had followed along, keeping them in sight. "I had been born in Virginia," she told him after a while. "I had grown up like any little girl, I suppose. My family had had little, but I had played with my doll. I had had tea parties in my room."

"Why do you say it like that?" Cale asked. "You had had tea parties?"

"I am merely trying to be accurate," Little Wing said. "That is what you want, isn't it?"

"I don't understand."

"Let me go on," she said. "I will try to describe it the way you would like."

"I don't care how you say it, Little Wing. I just want to know."

The late afternoon was hot and sticky, but Little Wing didn't appear to be perspiring at all. "As a girl, I was without faith," she continued. She spoke more slowly now, as if making an effort to consider not just what she said, but what phrasing she used. "That changed one day, when I had a revelation."

"What kind of revelation?"

"The kind that comes about when you suddenly realize that the world is a gloriously complicated place, yet everything in it makes sense. Trees house insects, birds eat insects from the trees and use their branches for their homes, we use birds for food and companionship, and we enjoy the shade the trees offer and the wood they provide. Rivers feed the trees and the birds and us. All is connected. Take away one part of it and the whole collapses. From this, I had de—I mean, I deduced that only a wise and powerful God could have made the world in just this way. Without words, with just a growing warmth in my heart, God told me that I was right, and showed me the path I must take."

"What path was that?" Cale asked. When his parents had been alive, the family had attended mass regularly. Since becoming a cowboy, he'd had precious little opportunity, although sometimes on Sundays a few of the hands said prayers together and talked about the Good Book.

"A path that led me to dedicate myself to the Sisters of Charity."

"What's that?"

"Do you ever run out of questions?"

"I just want to know about you," Cale said, feeling sheepish. "I don't mean to pry."

"I am not angry, Cale. Asking questions shows intelligence. Asking about other people shows unselfishness." Unsure how to take that, he didn't answer, and she went on with her tale. "The Sisters of Charity are an order dedicated to serving the Lord through acts of charity in this life. We fed the hungry, cared for the sick, looked after widows and orphans. We ran field hospitals during the war, tending to the wounded from both sides. I was blessed. At . . . at one such battle . . ."

Cale looked at Little Wing. Her face had taken on a sickly pallor, and she was biting hard on her lower lip. She looked afraid of something. Cale turned this way and that, looking for any threat. He didn't see whatever it was that scared her, then realized it must have been a memory, something to do with the story she was telling. "It's all right," he said softly. "I'm here, Little Wing. You're safe."

"No!" she said sharply. "There is no safety here, Cale. None at all."

"Why not? What's like to hurt us here?"

"I cannot . . . I cannot see it. I cannot say it."

"You don't have to," Cale said, mostly just to be talking.

"I was telling you about . . . the time. The time I . . ." She hesitated. She had her fists clenched so tight he was worried she would cut her palms with her nails.

"Yeah?"

"The battle was bad. The worst in the war."

"The whole war?"

"The whole thing. So many people died there."

The war had been a long one, with many brutal battles. Battlefields across the country were soaked in blood; when Cale imagined what they must be like, he pictured himself walking across that scorched, tortured ground, each footstep bringing to the surface a wet, scarlet imprint.

But the one they talked about, the bloodiest of all, was Gettysburg.

He'd heard stories about it—many too outlandish to be believed—since he was a little boy.

That would mean she'd have been a little girl, though. Surely a small child couldn't help at a field hospital.

"I thought Gettysburg was the worst one," he said.

At the mention of the name, Little Wing blanched. She rocked back on her heels, and Cale caught her arm in case she fainted. "Yes," she said. Her voice sounded far away, and her eyes were fixed on some distant point that Cale couldn't see.

"Little Wing," he said. She gave no sign that she heard, so he said it louder, and sharper, and accompanied it with a shaking of her shoulder. "Little Wing!"

She continued as if her spell hadn't happened. "Yes, Gettysburg was the worst. The dead littered the fields like leaves in autumn. Everywhere the smells of blood and powder enveloped me. I tried to only breathe through my mouth, but then I could taste it, and that was worse. And the wounded! I helped a man whose arm was gone, severed just below the shoulder. He wore his own blood like a second shirt. He died. There was a man whose chin was missing—beneath his mouth, nothing but a ragged, bloody mess, like a shred torn hastily from a bolt of cloth. He died, too. One who lived lost both his leg and his privates. He survived, although I often thought he would rather not have."

"But how could you—?" Cale began.

"Blessed," she said. She had said earlier that she was blessed. He assumed she meant blessed to be able to work alongside the Sisters of Charity, but he didn't know for sure.

"Everywhere I looked, they were dying. Some went quickly, quietly. Others wailed and cursed the heavens. The wounded were even worse; crying out for help, screeching with pain. Weeping like lost children. We tried to help. My clothes were stiff with the blood of the wounded, my arms coated in it, red past the elbows. Mostly, they came to us, but sometimes we had to go to them, those who could not walk and no one would carry. I was tending to one of those that I . . . that I . . ."

"What?" Cale asked.

Little Wing offered a brief smile, sincere for all that it was short and quickly vanished. "You would not understand. Would not believe."

"Little Wing, I don't think you would lie to me."

"And I would not. Nonetheless, you could not trust my words."

"How can you know, lest you try?"

"Let me just say that strange things happened. I thought I was—" She drew back the hair over her right temple, and Cale saw a long scar there. It had long since healed over, but he could hardly imagine that such a wound could be survived.

"How much have you heard?" she asked. "About what happened there?"

"Just bunkhouse talk. I'm sure most of it's made-up nonsense."

"Perhaps. I do not know which stories you were told. But some might be true."

Cale tried to catalog in his mind the tales he'd heard. Most, as he had indicated, had been told in the bunkhouse or around campfires, late at night, by cowboys trying to scare each other. He had always believed the stories about the savagery on display there, the nearly constant raining of lead down upon the soldiers on both sides, the wounded men stabbed with swords or bayonets, souvenirs taken in the form of ears or noses or fingers. Those tales were horrible, but possible. Probable, even, in the midst of that carnage.

But one hand, whose older brother had reportedly been in the battle, had told other stories. The battle, he said, had been furious

and deadly to uncounted soldiers. But as the fields were beginning to quiet, when the two sides had retreated to their own positions to regroup and treat their wounded, there had come what
the cowboy said his brother could only describe as a wave, a tidal
surge, not of water but of something else. "Evil," the cowboy had
said. "I can still see Clem tellin' me about it. He was sittin' on his
bed, and I was standin' in the doorway. Clem had lost his arm
from the elbow down, and I was still tryin' t'figger out how he'd
get by. But when he tole me this, he was as serious as all get-out.
He weren't jokin' or funnin' me. He was scairt, still, though it
had been four or five months since the battle. I was just a sprout,
and Clem, he stopped what he was sayin', and said, 'I shouldn't
orter tell you this, on account of you're too little and will have
nightmares over it.' I tole him he already started to, and now he
had to finish or I'd tell Pa, who'd whup him good."

Somehow, that detail had always made it all seem more real to
Cale. Not that he was inclined to believe the story. But he believed
that the cowboy did, and probably his brother Clem had, too.

The cowboy leaned in and told the rest of the story in a rush,
as if he couldn't wait to get it out, to be shut of it. The wave of
evil, his brother had said, washed over the fields, flooding the
valleys and climbing the rolling hills, covering everything and
everybody, living and dead. He couldn't see it, but he could sense
it, somehow, not quite tasting it or smelling it, but something in
between.

And when it was past, he saw the dead rise.

At that, a couple of the other hands had broken out in laughter and disparaging remarks. The cowboy had sat and waited, his
expression somber, and when they quieted again, he continued.
The first dead man he saw get up was a Confederate lieutenant
who had taken a minié ball in the throat. He had fallen, then
tried to get up again, making it as far as his knees before the
Union soldier who had shot him rammed a bayonet through his
skull. Clem had, he swore, seen brain matter come out the other
side of his head, on the bayonet's tip. The lieutenant went down
again, as dead as anyone Clem had ever seen.

But after that wave went by—Clem said it made him feel dirty, even though he had not bathed in weeks—the dead lieutenant stood up. His skull was destroyed, his throat had been mostly torn away, and a mongrel dog had been chewing on his left hand. But he rose and started walking, listing a little to his left but otherwise almost normally. A soldier who knew him ran to his side, believing him only badly wounded and offering to show him to a field hospital.

"And this lieutenant," the cowboy said, "he grabbed the soldier by the face. Drove his fingers right through the man's flesh and pulled him close and tugged the skin away, then bit into it like it was fine calf and he a starving man."

Well, that was when Cale had stopped believing. The cowboy claimed that other dead men got up and attacked those nearest them, which in most cases meant those from their own side. He said the dead killed more folks at Gettysburg than the battle had. Cale had doubted the veracity of that.

But he hadn't forgotten it, either. He still remembered almost every word the cowboy had said, though he couldn't even recall the man's name.

Little Wing was looking at him—looking through him, almost—as if she knew every thought he had. "Yes," she said. "That."

"When the dead rose?"

"I was . . . I was innocent. Pure. I served God, as a Sister. I tried to care for the sick and the wounded. And when I . . ." She let the sentence trail off, and touched the scarred place on her temple, hidden again by long hair. "A different power touched me that day. Not evil, but good."

"You don't mean to say that you was dead, and came back."

"I have told you too much, already."

"But . . . tell me that much. Is that what you mean? Did the dead really rise that day?"

"So it is said."

"And . . ." He almost couldn't bear to ask the question, but he couldn't stop himself. "And you? Did you . . . rise, too? Were you . . . ?"

She touched her scar again, and held his gaze with her deep brown eyes. Her lips curled into an almost-smile, and dimples carved her cheeks. "There are things that can be known, Cale. And others that cannot. Some, I can speak of, others I am forbidden to mention."

"Forbidden by who?"

She ignored that question and tilted her head in the direction of Fort Huachuca. "If it were allowed, I could tell you about the way that fort will change; the things that will come to pass there, the weapons and machines of various sorts that will be used against enemies you can't even imagine. I could tell you about an ancestor of Kuruk's, so long ago that Kuruk has never heard his name, who very near this spot encountered three rattlesnakes twined around one another. When Kuruk's ancestor stepped into the circle they made, the snakes separated and wrapped themselves around his ankles. None bit him, and when he left, they were once again twining around one another's tails. While they were on his legs, though, they told him secrets, and it is those secrets I cannot speak."

"Are you saying you can see what's gonna happen? And what happened long ago?"

"I am saying only that the mysteries of this world are greater than you can imagine, Cale. In number and in majesty, and in some cases, in depravity. I am saying that you are part of those mysteries, now—that you have a role to play."

"Me?" Cale asked. "I never done anything special."

"Perhaps," Little Wing replied. "Perhaps not. But your time will come. This much, I can say for certain."

"I don't . . . I ain't no kind of hero or nothing. I'm just a cowboy. I know horses and cattle, and that's about it. You're smart, not me. I don't know much of anything."

She took his hands and held them tight. "Cale, there is so much I do not know. But I know this: life is struggle after struggle after struggle. Any time it looks easy, beware, because that simply means you cannot see the next threat. But then you feel the warmth of a loved one's smile, or you experience faith or the unfailing joy of service to a cause bigger than yourself, or you see something like this." Using his hands, she turned him toward the landscape they had just run in. The sun had dropped another degree or two in the sky, and its light was snagged on more surfaces than ever; every leaf, every branch, every thorn or stone or tuft of grass seemed to catch it and throw it back, so that the whole expanse appeared to have been littered with flakes of gold. "You see something so beautiful that it takes your breath away, and you remember what your purpose on this earth is: to live, to feel, to experience all that life has to offer, the dark as well as the light. Only by seeing darkness do we appreciate the light when it comes."

Cale stared at the scene before him. As unexpectedly moved by it as he had been at first, it was even more lovely now. Breathtaking, as Little Wing had said. It was nothing he hadn't seen thousands of times, but he saw it with fresh eyes, with new appreciation. And having done so, he didn't think he would ever not see it again.

"Life is struggle after struggle," Little Wing continued. "But life is rich and full and wondrous and touched with magic and grace and joy and love and beauty, and those things make the struggle worthwhile. More than. And life is tinged with mystery, as you will soon find out. You are up to it, Cale. This I know. I do not know as much as you think I do, but I know that."

Cale didn't understand how she could, but there was no doubting the certainty in her voice and in her words. She believed it.

He dearly hoped she was right.

Chapter Forty-one

Watching Jasper Montclair, a mixture of terror and lust burned in Sadie's chest and loins. He was naked, as she was, and covered in designs she had made there, following his directions, with blood from a pot he kept inside his house. He had made similar designs on her, painting her with his fingers. His chest was deep, his shoulders broad, and for a man so lean he was surprisingly muscular. He had built a fire that blazed, throwing its yellow-red glow on his body, gleaming off the blood patterns, which still glistened as wetly as if she had just now drawn them. She ran a finger over one on her own breast, which looked as fresh, but it came away clean.

The sky was filling with clouds, pregnant with rain. To the south, lightning lit them from within, and the sound of thunder reached her ears, carried on gusty winds that fanned the fire and brought its sharp scent and the softer smells of distant downpours. The afternoon was hot, but when the rain came that would change.

She still wasn't sure what she was doing here, but Jasper had told her that her part was critical, and her reward would be great. For reasons she could not understand, she took him at his word and didn't ask questions.

On the ride over, in his buckboard, he had talked almost without stopping to breathe. Sadie caught a little of what he said, and understood less of it. "Look at that landscape," she remembered him saying, indicating with a sweep of his arm what he meant. The mountains were behind them, and they were de-scending into the shallow bowl of the valley. "All of it belongs to me now. To *us*. Do you like it, Sadie?"

She had muttered something in reply. She couldn't remem-ber what. There was so much she couldn't recall, blank spaces in her mind. The land looked strange to her, not what she would have expected to see. But somehow, with Jasper beside her, it looked right.

Jasper pointed to a jumble of rocks cascading down a slope toward a wash. The way they were arranged suggested a corpse, with one arm reaching toward a head that had been separated from the rest. Patches of weeds added to the impression, and a yucca stalk jutted out from between some of the bigger stones, suggesting that it had impaled the figure. "It's called 'terrorform-ing,'" he said. "Fear—the fear from the people in the town, people at the fort, travelers passing through, even the Apache—transforms the land. To some extent, I can control it. After to-night, that control will be much greater. Almost without limits."

"Why?" she had asked. "What happens tonight?"

He had gazed up at the sky. "The Thunder Moon rises," he said. "That's what they call July's full moon, the first one after the monsoon rains wash the earth. I have been waiting for this Thunder Moon for a very long time. And for one more thing."

"What is that?"

"The J Cross T. Tibbetts owned something I needed. Now it's mine, and there is nothing in my way. Our way."

"I don't understand."

"You will," he had promised. "Soon enough, you will under-stand everything, Sadie. You'll stand with me and your eyes will be opened to the glories that await us. Power, Sadie. Power you could never have imagined, derived from knowledge like no one on Earth has ever possessed. That's what you'll taste tonight, and then forever after. Power that most never even glimpse, but that you will hold in your hands, like a hammer or a shovel or any other tool. Are you excited by that?"

She hadn't been, not really. She had been numb, since the

moment he had touched her hand in town, before she even climbed into his wagon. If she hadn't been, she was certain she would have been frightened and excited and probably much more. As it was, she had taken in the information passively.

That had been more than an hour ago. Since then, helping him build the fire and scratch out, with branches, a star-shaped pattern in the earth around it, the numbness had begun to wear off. She had become at the same time more interested and more scared, not sure what her purpose here was, not sure that he was what he claimed to be. But even though the numbness was leaving her, and her own feelings starting to return, she still found that she trusted Jasper, believed his every utterance as if she had seen the truth of it with her own eyes.

Those utterances had been increasingly bizarre; she understood that, even if she couldn't bring herself to doubt their veracity. "I am, Sadie, a magician," he had told her. "I have spent many years—and a considerable part of the fortune that my father's business interests provided me—studying what people sometimes call the Dark Arts. I have seen things, learned things, done things that would curdle your blood if I described them to you. Even in your current, compliant state. I have bought, stolen, and otherwise acquired rare books that promised knowledge and understanding of things most men never even dream of. You saw some in my house. The journal of a madman named Darius Hellstromme took thousands of dollars and three murders to get my hands on, but it provided a scientific basis for much that I was learning. My grimoires, ancient texts bound in human flesh, contain the secrets of others who studied those arts long before me. Certain artifacts and tools have taken considerable outlays of treasure to acquire. It is not, may I say, a pursuit to which any but the wealthy can devote themselves with any success. The wealthy or sometimes, if they're lucky, the exceedingly ruthless. If they're both, so much the better."

There had been something about his grin, and the glimmer in his eyes, that she might have taken for madness if not for the things she had already seen and the unquestioning faith with which she listened. "It is this course of study that has brought me here," he continued. "Here, to this seemingly forsaken piece of ground. That has brought me to you, dear Sadie. Because here I have what I need—now, as of today, I have what I need—to take the next step. A step that will put me above those I learned from, more powerful and more feared and more accomplished in the arts. With you by my side, I will surpass every teacher, every past master. I will be the great deliverer, bringing forbidden knowledge into this world for the first time. And from this point forward, everyone who speaks of the great magicians will have to begin with the name of Jasper Montclair."

She recalled his words as she watched him. Behind them, outside the pattern they had inscribed on the earth, shadowy figures moved in a perverse sort of dance. Her gaze would not rest on any of them, as if some aspect of their being resisted being seen by human eyes. From them, she got a sense of darkness, of power, of danger. Her excitement grew, filling the emptiness. She didn't know why she was taking on his ambition as if it was her own. A day before, she would have told him to leave her alone, might have told Del to direct his troopers to arrest Montclair, or to shoot him on sight.

But on this day, he had stopped his wagon and spoken a few words and touched her hand, and from that moment, she had been his. Willingly and without reservation.

Soon, she believed, she would understand why.

Wilson Harrell wanted nothing more than to wheel his horses around and race back to Carmichael, never to set foot on Montclair's ranch again. But the land itself seemed determined to prevent his escape. The wagon path kept changing, sometimes right in front of him, as he watched. He was being herded somewhere. He couldn't know where, or why, but it was entirely beyond his control to affect. If he tried to leave the path, mesquite or cactus sprang up to block his way with impenetrable walls of thorns. The horses had long since given up responding to his commands and instead followed the course set before them. And whenever he tried to leave the wagon, fissures opened up in the ground, belching steam that would have scalded the flesh from him and assailing his nostrils with a sulfurous stench.

Eventually, he had just settled back in the seat. If he was being taken someplace, he would just wait and learn his destination. As clouds thickened in the sky, hiding the sun, he began to worry that he would be rained on after all. But whatever intelligence was behind his plight probably had worse ideas in store than that, so being soaked was only a minor concern.

After a while, he saw the smoke of a fire in the near distance, and determined that his path would take him right to it. He checked the revolver he carried whenever he left the safety of town, making sure it was loaded, and then folded his arms and let the horses carry him along.

When the path dropped down off a rise, through a sandy wash, and into a wide depression, the sight before him made his blood cold.

Jasper Montclair stood on the far side of a blazing fire, half obscured by billowing smoke, naked as a newborn. Arcane symbols were painted on his body—every part of his body, Harrell noticed. Sadie Cuttrell was nearby, also naked and similarly painted. The colonel would have a stroke if he saw his wife here, looking like that. Montclair was holding his arms out in front of him, almost into the fire, perfectly parallel to the ground. He chanted something, but Harrell couldn't make out any of the words, or even the language. Sadie clutched her hands to her full breasts like an excited schoolgirl. In a loose circle around them stood dark forms, vaguely human in appearance, but as Harrell drew closer he saw that they were not entirely so after all. Their limbs were too long and thin and their heads shaped wrong, as if they'd been squeezed at chin and cheeks and the excess had swelled the rest. He could barely make them out through the smoke. He believed they too were naked, but couldn't tell for sure. He couldn't distinguish much detail; they were like

shadows, or silhouettes; but for their glowing yellow eyes, they were only black marks against the sunless sky.

Then Montclair saw him approaching. He changed his stance, threw his arms toward the sky, and shouted at the heavens. As if in response, lightning darted to the ground, accompanied by a deafening crack of thunder. Harrell thought sure the bolt had struck Montclair, and when the flash had gone from his eyes and he was able to see, the rancher's charred corpse would be on the ground before him.

Ears ringing, Harrell rubbed his eyes. Instead of a corpse, he saw Montclair, still standing in the same place. His arms were at his sides, but if anything he seemed bigger than he had before the lightning. More substantial, somehow, as if it had lent him strength. The banker didn't know what sort of scene he had happened upon, but he didn't like it. Not a bit.

"Mr. Montclair," he said. His voice caught in his throat, and the words were barely audible. He spoke again, louder. "I have the deed for you. But I must object to the manner in which I was brought here, and further, I object to . . . to *whatever* in creation is taking place here."

"Let us have it," Montclair said. He held out his hand, as if to accept the deed, but didn't move from where he was. Harrell was going to have to get off the wagon and carry it to him. He didn't want to do that. He didn't want to go near Montclair or Mrs. Cuttrell, didn't want to get close to those inhuman things standing around them. He wanted to hurry back to Carmichael and go into his house and bolt the doors and climb into his bed, and maybe when he woke in the morning, all this would be forgotten, like a dream too insignificant to recall.

But he doubted the horses would obey any commands from him, and even if they did, the landscape itself would block him. Somehow—he didn't know how, and didn't want to know— Montclair had engineered all this.

"Come on, man!" Montclair demanded. "I haven't time for foolishness."

Harrell shifted, picked up his case from the footwell. The

pistol in his coat pocket poked him in the side, and he thought about just how useless that would likely be. He tugged it free, bent over again, and laid it where the case had been. As he shifted in his seat, to exit the wagon, he realized just where he had wound up.

Where the fire was, there had been a fence. Off to each side, the fence posts yet stood, barbed wire curling around them. But it had been cut and pulled away from the area where the fire was, and he suspected those posts might have been first to burn.

Seeing the fence, he knew that this had been the line between Tibbetts's land and Montclair's. Tibbetts had fenced in his pastures when Montclair started buying up every acre in sight. Montclair hadn't even waited to have the deed in hand.

"Wilson!"

Montclair's patience was waning. Harrell didn't want to find out what might happen when he lost it altogether. He slipped down from the wagon and tugged the deed from his case. His legs didn't want to work. He feared they would fold on the spot, and then Montclair would send one of those stilted silhouettes to take the paper from him. But he made himself press forward, legs threatening to buckle at any moment. Montclair stood, arm out, hand making grasping motions.

Finally, Harrell got close enough to hold the deed out and thrust it into that hand. Montclair closed his fingers over it and snatched it from him. He glanced at it, briefly, then tossed it into the fire. It ignited before it had a chance to come to rest.

"Montclair!" Harrell said. "That is a legal document! That is what confirms your ownership of the J Cross T."

"I am aware of that, Wilson."

"Then why . . . ?"

"The laws of men have power," Montclair said. "That power is not insignificant. But it is power that will no longer bind me, after tonight. I needed to have the deed, needed to have that legal affirmation of ownership. But having received it, I need it no longer. After this night, power rests with me."

"I . . . don't understand."

"Nor need you," Montclair said. "Sadie."

She walked to his side. Her gaze didn't leave his face. Harrell felt ashamed of the fact that he took in the sway of her heavy breasts, the switching of her hips, the dark patch between her thighs. Even in the midst of the strangest, most terrifying moments of his life, he couldn't help himself. When she reached him, Montclair stroked her cheeks, a lover's touch. He bent over and lifted something from near his feet. When the firelight caught it, Harrell realized it was a knife. Montclair tangled his fingers in Sadie's hair, and pulled her head back, exposing her throat. The motion made her arch her back. Harrell tried not to look at her breasts, but failed.

Montclair kissed her once, a glancing brush of lips against cheek, and drove the knife deep into her chest. He made some swift motions, pushing the blade this way and that, and before she fell, he had carved an opening in her. Blood gushed from her in a torrent, washing down her front and pattering onto the dirt. He lowered her to the ground, then thrust his fist into the space he had made. When he brought it out again, it held her still-beating heart.

Chapter Forty-two

Jasper Montclair lifted Sadie Cuttrell's heart toward the sky. As he did, thunder crashed even louder than before and lightning forked the ground, knocking Harrell off his feet. Struggling to rise, he realized that all the hair on his body was standing up, and he could barely see for the lingering effects on his eyes.

At first, he attributed the incredible tableau to his impacted vision. Perhaps he had hit his head on a rock when he fell. But the longer it went on, the less convincing such an argument was.

Lightning had blackened the heart that Montclair still held. He stared at a spot on the ground, just past the fire, on what had been Tibbetts's land only that morning.

And that spot, a grassy patch about a dozen feet across, was moving. *Changing.* First, Harrell noticed grass twitching, responding not to the wind but to some other force. Then it seemed to grow taller. It took more than a minute to understand that the grass wasn't actually growing, but that the earth itself was rising beneath it. That became more evident the higher it thrust. Dirt and rocks cascaded down the sides as it pushed up two inches, four, then still more. Soil-caked roots showed at the exposed edge, reaching into empty air. As if gathering its strength, the upward motion paused briefly, but before the grass and weeds atop it had stopped trembling, the earth gave a last mighty heave. When it stopped this time, the surface was almost waist-high on Harrell, tall grass on top adding another eighteen inches or more.

Harrell had not managed to stand yet, and during that display, had not bothered to try. He doubted that his legs would support him. What he saw should have been impossible, and that certainty compounded the horror of Sadie's gruesome murder. He had left his pistol in the buckboard, a decision he now regretted. The only question was whether he would turn it on Montclair or himself.

He was about to try to stand when the upthrust mound started to change yet more. Dirt and grass around its edges fell away, a miniature landslide dropping back to the level at which they had started. As the soil releasing itself got closer to the center, it fell faster, in big chunks. At last, that slowed, too, until the mound was almost a cone, like a miniature volcano that came to a rounded point at its exact center. A few last dribbles of dirt and small stones dropped away, revealing something that had been hidden until now.

Harrell's weight had been on his hands and one leg, but he collapsed again when he saw it. Darkness closed in at the edges of his vision, so he lowered his head and tried to breathe. What had he done? What was he a part of?

Whatever it was, he wondered if it was too late to get out, and decided that it almost certainly was.

Montclair stood, transfixed, in this moment of triumph. Then he set Sadie Cuttrell's lightning-charred heart in the dirt and stepped forward. He scooped up the ghastly treasure revealed by the earth. For the first time, he held the relic he had sought for so long, the skull of the ancient shaman, Thunder Moon. He turned it in his hands, admiring the yellow and black discoloration that almost seemed to suggest some sort of writing. The back of it had been caved in, leaving a dark hole nearly as large as Montclair's palm.

"Do you see it, Harrell?" he asked. "Do you see what you have delivered to me, by bringing me the deed to the J Cross T? Your part in this will not be forgotten, I assure you."

"What . . . what is that . . . that thing?" Harrell asked.

"You have, no doubt, heard of the Spaniard named Francisco Vásquez de Coronado," Montclair said.

"Certainly."

"In 1540, he led an expedition up from Mexico, in search of the fabled but nonexistent cities of gold—the Seven Cities of Cibola. They crossed into what would become the Arizona territory, and the United States, a few miles south of this spot.

"Before they arrived, an Apache shaman, a holy man, had visions of European encroachment, and what it would mean. He met the Coronado expedition's leaders right here, on this precise spot, and tried to persuade them to turn back. When they refused, he implored the Indians traveling with them—there were about three hundred Spaniards, accompanied by almost eight hundred Indians—to rebel against the whites and slaughter them, else their ancestral homelands would be forever lost.

"To quiet him, Coronado ordered him slain. One of the Spaniards fitted a bolt into his crossbow, which they called a *ballesta*, and dropped Thunder Moon with one shot."

"They killed him? Just for that?"

"People are often killed for far less, Mr. Harrell. A few coins, a woman's favor, a card game. However dear you might believe life is, the truth is that it's cheap. Easily given and more easily taken away, as Thunder Moon's story shows. Although he was important to the local people, to the Europeans he was worth less than a mule. In death, however, he achieved a significance he'd never had in life.

"Thunder Moon was the first native killed by whites on that expedition, and quite possibly the first anywhere within the boundaries of what would become our country. He was left on this spot, where he fell, as none of the expedition's members, Spanish or Indian, dared touch him. Neither did his own people. Presumably after the expedition passed, wolves or coyotes scattered his bones, but his skull remained here, where it has been ever since." Montclair held the skull so that its empty sockets faced the mountains. "It stayed here, within sight of the

Huachuca Mountains—the Thunder Mountains. Resting. Storing power. Waiting for this day and the coming night: the night of the Thunder Moon. And for the one man who could bring him once more into the light."

"I . . . I don't understand," Harrell managed. "How did you know about it?"

Montclair chuckled drily. "That's none of your concern, banker." Still holding the skull in his right hand, with his left he made an almost casual motion with his fingers, as if shooing a fly. Harrell gave a brief groan, his eyes shut, and he dropped to the damp earth, unconscious. Montclair had better things to do than answer more of the man's feeble questions.

The truth was, Montclair had the story from one of the expedition's members, who had kept a journal of the trip so detailed that it was confiscated by a priest and hidden away in the Vatican for centuries.

After the event known as the Reckoning—to those who knew it at all—about which Montclair believed himself as well informed as any living man, a possessed priest stole the journal and sold it at a most exclusive auction. Montclair had been spending a considerable portion of his father's wealth studying matters of the arcane, so he was invited to that auction, and there he purchased it.

After studying the volume, he had come to the Arizona territory. He'd started acquiring land so that he could own everything between the mountains and Thunder Moon's resting place. To make that spot reveal itself, he'd had to alter the landscape itself, using fear to terrorform it so it would, in time, shed its disguise. Once he was certain it was on J Cross T land, driving Tibbetts off had become an urgent necessity. Fortunately, to help spread the fear that would power the terrorforming, and to encourage Tibbetts to sell, he had the help of the abominations who had guarded Thunder Moon's skull until the coming of the right man.

That man was Jasper Montclair, and the power Thunder Moon

would grant him, under the rising of the full moon that bore his name, would be spectacular.

Fat drops of rain splashing against his face brought Harrell around. He stirred, blinked, opened his eyes. Time had elapsed, but he couldn't tell how much. For an instant he hoped that he had been dreaming, but that hope vanished when he smelled the fire and heard Montclair's voice, softly intoning some sort of spell or prayer. Harrell groaned and sat up, though his head swam with the effort. Montclair raised the skull in his left hand and the charred heart in his right, holding both over his head. His quiet incantation became words shouted toward the clouds, from which rain spat with increasing fury. Lightning flared yet again, its white heat burning into Harrell's eyes. Still, before he was blinded, he thought for sure he saw the lightning strike the skull, then the heart, then the still form of Sadie Cuttrell.

Harrell pawed at his eyes with his fists, shook his head. When his vision cleared, he wished it hadn't. Sadie was crouched, with the fingers of her left hand touching the ground. Her right went to the open wreckage of her chest, feeling the edges of the wound and venturing into the gulf there. The light had gone from her eyes, but otherwise she was alive, or ambulatory, at any rate. She rose to a standing position and held out a hand to Montclair, who gave her back her heart.

Of all he had seen that afternoon, that was the worst. Still sitting on the ground, he wet himself. He bit his lip to keep from crying out, because he was terrified of calling attention to himself. He had seen—*was* seeing—things that no human, he was sure, had ever witnessed. *Should* ever witness.

Then, it got worse.

Sadie looked at her blackened heart, held it close to her nose as if inhaling its aroma, then lowered it an inch and took a bite, as she might from an apple. She chewed, swallowed, and smiled at Montclair. Those dark, dead eyes exhibited no mirth.

As the rain fell harder, a downpour in the making, she carried the grisly prize to those shadowy onlookers. She held it just beneath their yellow eyes, and each one, in its turn, bit into the heart. Finally, she carried the last morsel to Montclair, who swallowed it whole.

Harrell cried out in mortal terror.

"I see you've joined us again, Wilson," Montclair said, his neck craning in the banker's direction. "I wasn't at all certain."

"I've l-l-lost my mind," Harrell sputtered. "Th-that's the only possibility! You . . . she, she fed those . . . those . . ."

"I call them my *abominations*," Montclair said, as calmly as if they were discussing the weather on a sunny spring morning. "For lack of a better word."

"They're not human!"

"Of course not. They're getting closer, though, or some are. When I first arrived they were far from it. They lurked around Thunder Moon's skull, or hid deep in the mountains when no one threatened the relic's hiding place. Had you seen them, you'd never have thought they were remotely human. As I began to transform the land—to terrorform it, in the vernacular—they were also transformed. They took on more human characteristics, and perhaps more significantly, the ability to mimic humanity, at least for a few hours at a time. A few days, for some."

The words Montclair spoke were in English, but they made no sense to Harrell. "But—they *ate* her heart. *You* ate it!"

"That is one area where they're still not even close to human. Their appetites, in fact, grow ever less human, the more human they become in outward appearance. Less *recognizably* human, I should say, for no matter what can be eaten, somewhere on this world there is someone who will eat it. The same holds true for every other manner of human expression."

Harrell found the strength, somewhere, to regain his feet. He backed away from Montclair and the dead yet upright Sadie Cuttrell and Montclair's abominations, until he bumped up against one of his horses. Surprisingly, they had remained in place through all that had occurred. Harrell wasn't sure how long it had taken; it felt like hours, but the pale, hidden disc of the sun didn't seem to have moved much at all.

Shaking, Harrell started to climb into the wagon, then changed his mind. If the horses hadn't budged, they probably wouldn't respond to his commands now, and there was no room to turn the wagon around anyway. Instead, he went past the wagon, then broke into a run, back down the trail he had followed to get here.

He had barely taken a dozen steps when the path ended at a wall of agave plants, their sword-pointed, sharp-bladed leaves bunched close together, tall stalks jutting skyward. Looking back, he saw some of the abominations breaking from the pack and coming toward him. In desperation, he waded into the agave thicket, trying to ignore the pain and push through. The leaves sliced his legs, stabbed him. His clothing in ribbons, he kept going, but he was too slow. The plants slowed him down, and he saw that beyond these, a ring of mesquite waited. Escape, if possible, would be hard-fought and painful.

He didn't have long to worry. The abominations shoved through the agave leaves as if they weren't there. For one brief moment, Harrell saw a way out—he was almost through the agave, and there was a single gap in the mesquite, barely big enough, he thought, for him to squeeze through.

But as he finally broke free of the bladelike leaves, one of the abominations caught him by the shoulder and sliced into it. Then the others joined in, and Harrell had just an instant, before he lost consciousness for the last time, to realize that they were tearing him to shreds.

Montclair watched his abominations return. He caught the scent of Harrell's sweat and flesh and blood on them, and he smiled. "Well done," he said. "But our day is far from over, and I have another task for you."

The abominations stood in a clump, awaiting instructions. "There is one in town, a Blessed one." He jerked a thumb toward

Sadie. "I can still smell her on my queen. Some of you, breathe in her stink, and find her. Every minute she lives, she is a threat to us."

Sadie stood still, expressionless, as abominations encircled her, catching the scent of the one Montclair had described. When they had it, they dashed off, into the storm.

With a satisfied grin, Montclair watched them go.

Chapter Forty-three

Tuck stood in his office, looking out the window as rain drenched the street. The road had become a muddy bog, pocked by the barrage. Thunder boomed in the distance, and though he couldn't see the lightning flashes from here, he could see when it illuminated the cloud-dark sky. It was the kind of storm that filled the washes and sent flash floods hurtling across the desert with enough force to sweep away people and livestock and even wagons. There had been folks outside earlier, but once the cloudburst hit, they had disappeared.

Even as he thought that, a door at the hotel opened. Through the screen of water, Tuck saw a man emerge. He'd seen the man around town a few times, but didn't know his name. He had a weathered, craggy face under a hat that looked like it had survived dozens of cattle drives. He wore no coat, just a shirt that the rain quickly plastered to his lean frame, jeans, and boots. On his hip he wore a holstered six-shooter, and he was fingering the grip as if he meant to pull it.

Tuck eyed the street, up and down, as well as he could from behind the window. Seeing no one else about, he returned to his desk, put on the hat Missy had given him, snagged a duster that Hank Turville had probably left behind, and slipped into it. Then he hurried through the door, once again looking both ways at a town that might as well have been abandoned, except for that one lone figure walking across the soupy road. Tuck hurried up the boardwalk toward him. At first, he thought the man was only crossing the street, but then instead of stepping up under the covered walkway, he kept going, past the buildings.

What was he up to? Meeting someone for a gunfight? Laying for somebody he expected to pass by? Tuck was more than curious.

"Hey! Mister!" he called out.

The man stopped and eyeballed Tuck. "It's not against the law for a man to walk in the rain, is it, Marshal?"

"Not a bit," Tuck said. He was still closing the distance between them, walking fast while trying to make it look unhurried. "Why don't you come up under some cover and let's have us a chat?"

"I got other things to do," the man said.

"Buy you some hot coffee."

"No time."

"I'm Tucker Bringloe. I've seen you around a time or three."

"Jed Tibbetts," the man said.

"You look like you have something on your mind, Mr. Tibbetts. Why not step out of that rain for a minute?"

"Just as soon not. Suits my spirits."

"Somebody done you harm?"

"Might could say that."

"Of what nature?"

Tibbetts stood there in the rain, more soaked by the instant. He sucked in his cheeks, chewed on one for a moment, thinking it over. "Wilson Harrell sold my loan to Jasper Montclair. Montclair foreclosed. This mornin' I owned a ranch and livestock. Now I don't."

"I am sorry, sir," Tuck said. Somehow, he wasn't surprised that Montclair and Harrell were involved. Those two seemed to have their hands in everything that happened around Carmichael.

"Sometimes life's like that, I reckon."

"I have to ask, Mr. Tibbetts. I understand why you'd be upset. You planning to use that iron?"

Tibbetts forced a laugh. "What, on them?"

"I'd understand the urge."

"You don't have to worry about that, Marshal. I'm no killer."

"A gun in the hands of a scared or angry man has turned plenty of folks into killers who didn't start out that way."

"I'm sorrowful," Tibbetts said. "Was angry, but that's passed. Now it's just sorrow."

"I believe you, Mr. Tibbetts."

"If it's all the same to you, I got things to do."

"I'm sorry for what happened, sir. You take care, now. Drop by and chat if you've a mind to."

"Might just," Tibbetts said. He turned away and continued, down the block and behind the buildings.

Tuck was almost back to his office when the hotel door banged open again. A woman burst out. Like Tibbetts, she wasn't dressed for the storm. She hitched up her skirts and ran into the street, ignoring the mud that splashed all over her. She was plain-faced, worn raw by the elements, and her mouth hung open in confusion or concern. There was as much silver as brown in her hair, if not a little more.

Tuck swore softly and hurried back to the edge of the boardwalk. "Ma'am? Anything I can do?"

"I'm looking for my husband," she said.

"What's his name?"

"Jed. Jed Tibbetts."

"Why, he was right here, ma'am. Right about where you're standing, not two minutes ago."

She swiveled her head around. "Where did he go?"

Tuck nodded toward the alley that ran behind the street. "Back there. Said he had something to—"

"You're a fool, Marshal," she snapped. "Jed! Jed Tibbetts!"

She had only taken two steps in that direction, mud sucking at her feet, when they heard the gunshot.

Tuck came off the boardwalk, into the mud. "Ma'am, you stay here. I'll check."

She slapped him, a stinging blow that wounded him on more levels than he cared to examine. They both ran through the bog, Tuck outpacing her to the corner.

When he reached it, he tried to hold her back. "You should really let me do this," he said, his face still burning from her palm. "You don't want to see this."

"I've been married to him for thirty-three years," she said, writhing out of his grip. "I've seen him in every state there is. I can see this."

"It's bad."

"Of course it is."

She broke free and went around him. When she saw her husband, she gave a yip of sadness tinged with terror.

He lay on his side in the mud, partly up against the back of a building. His finger was still inside the trigger guard. On the wall above him was a bloody spray with chunks of bone and brain mixed in it.

She raced to his side and dropped to her knees in the mud. Tuck grabbed her again, trying to pull her away. "Mrs. Tibbetts, please, let me—"

A new voice rang out, one that he recognized. "Stand away from there, Bringloe!" Mo Kanouse called.

"Mo, this isn't the time," Tuck replied. He glanced back over his shoulder and saw Kanouse bearing down on him, holding a shotgun Tuck recognized as the double-barreled sawed-off from the rack by his desk. Behind him, drenched despite a derby hat and a heavy black coat, stood Mayor Chaffee. Alf Maier brought up the rear, rain dancing off his shiny scalp and spotting his glasses.

"That ain't your call to make," Kanouse said. "Seein' as how you ain't the marshal no more."

Tuck released Mrs. Tibbetts, who was trying to scoop her husband out of the mud as if that was the only thing sapping the life from him. "What are you talking about?"

"He's right," Chaffee said. "Mr. Bringloe, the town council has discussed it, and our determination is that you're not the right man for this job after all. You'll be paid for two weeks' work, which is more than you've done. I think that's a generous offer. Please, hand your badge and gun to Marshal Kanouse."

"You're letting this blowhard be marshal?" Tuck asked. "You must hate this town more than I thought."

"Hobble your lip, Bringloe," Kanouse said. He kept the scattergun leveled at Tuck's midriff with his right hand, and held out his left, palm up. "Let's have that star. And the six-gun."

Although he had only taken the job because Turville had insisted upon it, Tuck found that he hated to give it up. Especially to Kanouse. Didn't the fact that Tuck had fired him tell the town council something about his character?

But that was a foolish question, since the mayor and another councilmember were backing his play. He wondered if he could draw down on Kanouse, clear leather before the man squeezed the trigger. That idea vanished as quickly as it had come—he was no fast-draw artist. He hated guns, and hadn't worn one for years, until Turville had conscripted him onto that posse. He'd be as likely to shoot himself in the foot. And at this range, Kanouse would blow him all over the wall and both Tibbettses.

He yanked the badge from his vest, then gingerly drew the pistol using his thumb and one finger. Kanouse twitched his hand again, and Tuck gave him what he wanted. "Now beat it," Kanouse said. "Before I run you in as a vagrant."

Tuck walked slowly through the clinging muck to the corner. There he stopped for a moment and eyed Kanouse, talking to Mrs. Tibbetts's back as she grasped the husband Tuck had failed to save.

He went on, then, around the corner and out of sight. Halting again before the boardwalk, he considered his situation. He had a few dollars in his pocket, and more on the way, though he didn't know when. The new clothes he was wearing—sodden, now—were the only things he owned. He couldn't go back into what had so briefly been his office, and he had no other home.

He was, all things considered, right back to where he had been before he had seen Daisie's murderer on the stairs.

It was not, he thought, much of an accomplishment.

PART THREE
Thunder Moon

Chapter Forty-four

What does a drunkard do, Tuck asked himself, when he has a little money and no prospects?

Answer: he drinks.

At least Senora Soto's was dry on the inside. And so was he.

He could practically feel that liquid fire splashing down his gullet. An hour before, he'd have kicked the mud off his boots before he went in. But an hour ago he'd had a job, a purpose, some degree of dignity. Like his rise to captain, though, that had been a mistake, a coincidence of timing combined with his capability to kill when necessary. His mother's legacy had returned in full force. He didn't amount to anything; never had and never would. If death was his only offering to the world, then maybe what Tibbetts had done was an example he should think about following.

First things first, though.

Senora Soto looked up from her card game when he walked in. Three men sat around her at the table. "What brings you here, Marshal?"

"I'm not marshal anymore," Tuck said. "I'm just a man who needs a drink."

"You're not? Since when?"

He peeled off his hat, dumping rainwater on the floor. "About five minutes back."

"I won't ask what happened," she said. "This town."

"Quite a place," he agreed. He went to the bar, where one of the upstairs girls, a slender blonde named Sally Jo, was filling in for Jack. "Whiskey," he said. "Don't be stingy."

She poured the drink. Tuck put some coins on the bar and downed it. Liquid fire. He hadn't known how much he'd missed it until he had it again. "Another."

"Hard day?" she asked as she poured.

"Aren't they all?"

"Some're worse than others."

"This is one of those, then." He held the glass in his hand for a few seconds, swishing the amber liquid around. His life had contained few pleasures, and most of those fleeting, costly, or both. This one wouldn't fail him. The color, the flavor, the warmth already spreading from his gut—he loved them as he had never loved anything or anyone. Drink fought back the chill from the rain and the memory of his mother's disapproval of everything and everyone. Especially him. "Just like your father," she had complained. "I was a fool to ever let him make you."

"Guess that makes us both fools," he muttered.

"Sorry?" someone said from behind his shoulder.

"Nothing." Tuck held the glass to his lips, sipped from it. He would savor this one, make it last awhile. Then the next few he would put away fast.

"What are you doing here, Tuck?"

"Go away, Missy."

Her hand came down on his arm. Her grip was unyielding. "I mean it, Tuck. Why?"

"I—oh, hell, Missy. Don't tell me you never take a drink."

"I do, time to time. But you stopped. And you were . . . you're a better man when you're not."

"I reckon you'll have to get used to a worse man, then. Or don't." He shook her hand off and finished the glass. Never mind savoring. He slammed it down on the bar. "Another."

Sally Jo caught Missy's eye. Missy shrugged, and Sally Jo poured.

He took a couple of sips, leaning against the bar, enjoying

the taste and thinking that Sally Jo was getting more attractive by the minute. Then Missy took a position next to him, so close he could feel her heat. "I wish you'd talk to me," she said. "Tell me what's bothering you."

"Where would I start?" he asked.

"Start with what happened, maybe."

He drained the glass. "What happened? You tell me. I was perfectly happy being miserable. Then Daisie got killed and Turville roped me into his damn posse and then who knows what? And don't get me started on Montclair—"

"What about Montclair?"

Tuck eyed her. She was pretty, all right. When she'd been younger, probably beautiful. The years had marked her, in the way that time did. Little scars here and there on her face, faint lines at the corners of her mouth and eyes that would grow deeper and more pronounced. Her green eyes were clear and animated by what he suspected was a fierce intelligence.

"I'm not sure," he said after a while. "All the killings in these parts. Everything. He's in the middle of it all, I think."

"But what does that mean? What would he have to gain?"

"I don't know. Thought for a while I'd find out, but I reckon there's no point in it, now."

"I never took you for a quitter, Tuck."

"When you met me, I had already quit. Turns out that was the right thing, after all." She was staring at him now, hands on her hips and a look on her face like she was a schoolmarm and he a misbehaving student. "What?" he asked. "I guess you want your hat back."

Her expression changed, and he could see that the question had stung. No, more than that—it had pierced her heart, as surely as a knife or an arrow might. Tears welled in her eyes. Her lower lip quivered as she started to say something, but then she changed her mind, spun around and walked away from him. He watched her go up the stairs and out of sight.

He was sorry he'd hurt her. But it was for the best. There could be no passengers on the trip he was about to take, no spectators.

It was a one-man voyage, and one-way, too. Straight from here to the bottom.

He bade Sally Jo bring another glass, and he had just raised it to his lips when he heard a commotion outside—a high-pitched scream, followed by angry shouts. Tuck put the glass down and took a step toward the door, then stopped himself.

Whatever was going on out there wasn't any of his concern. Not anymore. Only one thing was, and he had left that behind on the bar. He went back to his spot and swallowed the rest of it. "Keep 'em coming," he said.

The barkeep obliged. While she was pouring the next one, though, some of the men playing cards with Senora Soto went to the window and looked out. "Looks like somethin' to do with that Apache scout," one said. "The one's always follerin' that white girl around."

"Little Wing?" Tuck asked. "Kuruk?"

"Never knowed their names," the man replied. "White girl they found with the slaughtered mule train."

Little Wing. For a few long seconds, Tuck was torn. His next drink was on the bar in front of him, and he wanted it as much as he had ever wanted anything in his life.

But Little Wing and Kuruk had been decent to him, when not many were. They had trusted him. He wouldn't say they'd be-friended him, but they were as close to friends as he had in this place.

He left the drink where it was, left his coins on the bar. He would come back once he'd found out what was going on. Wincing as the rain pummeled him, he stepped back into the storm.

Kuruk was at the corner, squatting down and tending to a young cowboy who had a gash across his forehead and blood running down his face. The rain carried it away as fast as it flowed, but there appeared to be plenty more behind it.

"What happened, Kuruk?" Tuck asked.

"Cale and Little Wing were spending time together," the Apache said. "Most of the afternoon. I think they're sweet on each other."

"It ain't that," the cowboy said.

Tuck saw that he was not much more than a boy, seventeen or eighteen at the oldest. "I've seen you before," he said. "You work for that rancher? Tibbetts?"

"Did," Cale said. "Not no more. Ranch is gone."

Did was right. It didn't sound as if the boy knew about Tibbetts yet.

"Anyhow," Kuruk went on, ignoring the interruption, "I gave them a little privacy when it looked like maybe they wanted to kiss or something. I had been keeping them in sight, but I let them go around the corner for a few minutes so they could be alone."

"Then what?" Tuck asked.

"Then someone jumped us," Cale said. "Like they was waiting back there the whole time. They knocked me down. Little Wing tried to fight them off. I got up and tried to help. But they was too strong, and they rode away with her."

"What'd they look like?"

"I hardly saw 'em. Just guys. Wearing black, riding black horses. They rode south."

"Where did this happen? Right here?"

Cale waved his hand toward the alley running behind the north side of the street. "Back there. Right around the corner."

"Be right back," Tuck said. He hurried to the corner Cale had indicated. He didn't think it was possible to get more soaked, but his clothes were getting heavier by the second, his boots ever more caked with mud.

At the corner, he breathed in. The downpour had diluted it, but some of the familiar stink still lingered. Those pitch-black creatures he had encountered before had taken Little Wing. Why, he couldn't know.

When he returned to the others, Cale was on his feet. His head was still bleeding a little, but Kuruk had packed some mud over the wound. Tuck put a hand on Cale's shoulder. "Listen, son, I don't know if you've heard about Jed Tibbetts."

"What about him?"

Tuck remembered Tibbetts's body, the wall behind it splattered from the close-range gunshot. He couldn't think of a gentle way to say it, and he was more interested in going after the things that had grabbed Little Wing than in sparing the boy's feelings. "He's dead," Tuck said. "Shot himself. His wife and I heard the shot, but we were too late to stop him."

Cale's eyes widened, then filled with tears. His mouth opened, his jaw dropped, his cheeks sank in. "No. He'd never do that."

"I'm sorry, Cale. I saw him, right after."

Cale swallowed hard. "He . . . he couldn't."

"He did."

The boy's chest hitched, his shoulders bucked, and then the sobs came on strong. He put his hands over his face, as if ashamed of his tears. Kuruk stood with him, holding his shoulders and glaring at Tuck.

"He had to know."

"There's better ways to say it."

"A man's dead. Little Wing's been taken. I thought those were more important than sparing his feelings."

"They are," Kuruk said.

"Then we ought to do something about Little Wing."

He heard boots approaching, but didn't look to see whose until he heard Kanouse's voice. "Anything wrong here?"

"This boy was attacked, Mo. Somebody grabbed his friend."

"If a crime's been committed, Bringloe, you ain't the man should be dealin' with it."

"Aren't you the marshal?" Kuruk asked Tuck.

"Not anymore. He is."

Kuruk shot Kanouse a scowl. "Him?" He spat into the mud.

"Now listen," Kanouse said. Then he dropped it and turned his attention to Cale. "Boy, if you'd like to make a report, come by my office in the morning."

"The morning?" Tuck repeated. He could barely contain his rage. "The girl's missing *now*."

"I got other things to do, Bringloe. And if it's the girl goes around with this Indian, she don't even live in town. She's the army's problem."

Tuck looked at Kanouse's ugly face, his thick lips formed into a smirk, his tiny eyes lacking the slightest glimmer of intelligence. The man had his shoulders back and his gut forward and his legs wide, and he exuded a confidence Tuck had never felt in his life.

Tuck's mouth worked, but nothing came out. He wanted to say something—a lot of things—but he didn't know how, or what, or even why.

Instead, he took a fast half step forward and struck out with his right fist, leaning into the punch, putting his shoulder behind it. His fist slammed into Kanouse's left cheek, and Tuck felt something give behind it. Kanouse's head snapped to the right. His hat flew off and he started to sway backward. He tried to catch himself, pinwheeling his arms, but in the soft mud he couldn't keep his balance. He fell back, as inexorably as a tree cut off at the base, and landed on his back, arms out, spread-eagled in the muck.

Tuck stood there, his fist already starting to ache from the contact. But Kanouse would hurt a lot more, and he was glad for that.

The new marshal sat up in the mud. He shook some from his hands and carefully touched his face. Blood was running from his open mouth, and he spat something into his palm. Two teeth. Tuck had been kind of hoping he'd broken the man's jaw, but he'd take it.

"That weren't a smart thing to do, Bringloe. Keep in mind who's the law here. I won't haul you in for that, even though I could do. You already stink of liquor. I were you, I'd keep a close watch on my back."

Again, there were things Tuck could have said, but he thought the punch had done a pretty good job of speaking for him. Kuruk and Cale were still standing there. Cale was no longer sobbing, though his eyes and nose were red from his tears. "Come on," Tuck said. "He's not going to be any help."

Kuruk looked at the former deputy, still sitting up in the mud and feeling his cheek with his tongue. "Not now, anyhow."

"He was right about one thing," Tuck said. "The army. Think we can bring them in?"

"The army?" Kuruk chuckled. "What army? Colonel Cuttrell sent everybody away."

"Everybody?"

"Pretty near. We could maybe find a few troopers around, but the fort's empty."

"Why?"

"Beats me. I'm just a scout, and Apache to boot. You think they tell me anything?"

"What are you thinkin', Mr. Bringloe?" Cale asked. "Do you know who took her?"

"I have an idea," Tuck said. He had been thinking about it since talking to Missy earlier, and he was embarrassed that it had taken him so long to put the pieces together. He hadn't had a lot of pieces to begin with, and nothing definite. But he had a series of little ones, and combined with some hunches, he thought they added up to something.

The incidents he had found described in the *Epitaph* had centered around Montclair's ranch. The route that Daisie's killer had been taking would have led him back to the same vicinity, if the posse hadn't caught up to him. The night he had slept so soundly at his desk, one of Montclair's men had delivered flowers to the office—it was those, he was sure, not drugged coffee, that had put him under. Montclair had taken over the Tibbetts ranch, and he had done it the same day that Cale had been attacked in town. Montclair had taken Sadie Cuttrell from town—apparently of her own volition, but Tuck couldn't help feeling it was more complicated than that—and Little Wing had been taken from town.

He didn't explain all that. He simply said, "Jasper Montclair."

To his surprise, Kuruk nodded. "He's no good, that one."

"You know?"

"Some things a man can tell."

"If Montclair's got her," Cale said, "that's where I'm going."

"Not so fast, son," Tuck countered. "We need a plan of some

kind. If I'm right, Montclair's got some very dangerous allies. I don't even know how to describe them, except to say they're vicious, not human, and extremely hard to kill."

"A plan? Ride in and shoot everyone until I get her back. That's my plan."

"You own a horse? Or a gun?"

Cale hesitated. "I can get those."

"You mean steal them? So you can not only have Montclair and his thugs gunning for you, but the law, too?"

"I mean, I'll do whatever it takes to get her back. If you two won't help, then I'll go by myself."

"Simmer down, Cale," Kuruk said. "Nobody is saying we won't back you. Just that riding in there on our own might not be the way to do it."

"If you have a better idea—"

"I might," Kuruk interrupted. "I just might. If Jimmy Mc-Kenna is still around. Or Clinton Delahunt . . ."

"Who?" Cale asked.

"Don't worry about it," Kuruk said. "Just come with me."

Chapter Forty-five

In its emptiness, the fort seemed huge and oppressively silent.

Given his reception the last time Tuck had visited, the lack of troopers ready to hurl him through the gates was a pleasant surprise. He remembered what Kuruk had said about Cuttrell dismissing everyone, but he hadn't quite been prepared for the reality of it.

He wondered, too, if the colonel's act had anything to do with the disappearance of his wife.

A few troopers remained in evidence, presumably because they had nowhere else to go. Tuck didn't see any in full uniform, or doing anything that could remotely be described as military. One soldier in striped pants and no shirt was turning circles in the rain, his arms outspread, palms up and mouth open, as if he'd been dying of thirst and it was the first water he had seen in months. Another was ushering a goat out of a building. Tuck hoped it wasn't a barracks, but he couldn't tell for sure.

He looked toward Cuttrell's office and saw the colonel through a window, shaking clenched fists at the ceiling. Tuck couldn't tell if there was anyone else there or not.

Kuruk led them past that and some other buildings, around a corner, and between a set of low, blocky structures set close together on what would have been a narrow, dusty alley any other time of the year. Now it was a running river, inches deep.

Beyond the buildings were the fort's stables. The musky smell of wet horses filled the air.

Nearing those, Tuck heard the banging of a hammer or some other implement on steel. It was a steady, rhythmic sound, just irregular enough not to be mechanized. As they grew closer to the farthest building on the stretch, wading through the deluge, the banging got louder. That building had a wide opening at the far end. The scents of wood smoke leaking from the chimney into the storm and the tang of metal on metal mingled with the animal musk.

"Where are you taking us, Kuruk?" Tuck asked as they neared it. "You fitting us for suits of armor?"

"You said Montclair has inhuman allies," the scout replied. "That don't surprise me. I never did like that fella. But I think we need something more than the three of us and some stolen guns and horses to fight them."

"So we're going to a blacksmith's shop?"

"That's right. Like most whites I've known, you'd learn more if you could close your mouth and open your eyes."

Tuck did. When they reached the doorway of the shop, his eyes opened even wider.

McKenna, the lieutenant who had banished Tuck earlier, was there, along with three Buffalo Soldiers, all working on . . . on what, he couldn't say. Something that looked vaguely like a steam-powered wagon. It had four wheels, at any rate. But those wheels were enormous, the rear ones almost as tall as Tuck, and the front ones about five feet in diameter. The wagon itself was bigger than any Tuck had ever seen, with a deep bed with walls that appeared to be inches thick. Set a couple of feet in from the front was a steel-and-glass compartment jutting up above the bed, with what looked like a Gatling gun barrel emerging from an opening. Another, similar configuration sat near the other end. The bed itself was clad in some kind of dull, gray metal, and it had various apparatuses affixed to it for which he had no names, much less comprehension.

A furnace blazed in a corner of the shop, making the place

swelteringly hot. Standing just inside the doorway, Tuck thought his clothes were already drying.

"Kuruk," McKenna said. "This is supposed to be a secret. You brought *him*?"

"Bringloe is a good man," Kuruk said. "I trust him."

"I heard he was a drunk."

"He is," Kuruk said. "Smells it, anyhow. But still, he's got steel in his spirit."

"Colonel Cuttrell told me to never let him back in the fort."

"All the more reason to trust him, seems like."

"You could be right."

"Is this thing ready?" Kuruk asked.

"It look ready to you?" one of the Buffalo Soldiers countered. "We're makin' progress, but we ain't there yet."

"We might need it," Kuruk said.

"What do you mean? Need it for what? And who is 'we'?"

Kuruk indicated Tuck and Cale and himself. "Us. To save Little Wing."

"Little Wing?" the soldier asked. Concern was evident in his change of tone, and the sudden gravity of his expression. He was heavily muscled, shirtless, his torso gleaming from sweat in the heat of the furnace. "What happened?"

"Somebody took her. Hit Cale in the head and snatched her right out of town."

"Who?"

"The real question might be 'what?'" Tuck said. "I don't know what you've built here, but I have an idea what we've got to go up against. It's not going to be easy. It's going to be dangerous as all hell. People are going to die, most likely. If this is something that could help, then—"

"You hear what the man said, boys?" the soldier asked. "*Dangerous*. Maybe we *are* ready."

"You think?" another one of the Buffalo Soldiers asked.

"We could keep workin' on it. We could work on it forever. But we can't really test it out unless we got somethin' that's right to test it on. We been workin' for months and months, without knowin' that we'd ever find the right use for it. Just wanted to know we had it, could bring it out if need be. Well, maybe now it's need be."

"I expect you're right, Sarge," the third one said. "Let's find out what it can really do!"

Kuruk introduced Tuck and Cale to the soldiers. Sergeant Clinton Delahunt, the highest ranking of the Buffalo Soldiers at the fort, was, McKenna said, the mad genius who had conceived what he called the "battlewagon." The other troopers, Willie Johnson and Riley Taylor, were skilled in blacksmithing and the other crafts necessary to put the whole thing together.

Once those introductions had been made, Delahunt showed off his invention. The battlewagon had, he said, started out as a standard-issue army chuck wagon. Delahunt had stripped out the parts he didn't want, and had a wagon maker in Tucson build a new bed with the chuck wagon's dimensions but with the thickness, depth, and solidity of an ore wagon. Delahunt replaced the gears, axles, and brake with massive steel ones of his own manufacture. The wheels were iron, with double spokes. Delahunt had waterproofed the bed and otherwise toughened it up at every conceivable failure point, because he would be adding a lot of weight to it. Then he had clad the exterior in two layers of steel and bolted iron fittings over every joint. He'd attached huge lanterns facing off in almost every direction. Wherever they had used wood, it looked like highly polished oak, pine, even some red Manzanita from the nearby mountains. The brass gleamed, the steel was burnished until it shone, and every bit of glass was highly polished.

With that as a base, he had started to build onto it. First he'd added the steam engine, dead center, to power the rest of it. Brass coils snaked from there to the various devices mounted around the wagon, and a couple of brass tubes served as chimneys. The steam engine also turned the wheels, he said, eliminating the need for horses. On either side of the engine were tall steel boxes holding ghost rock, to keep the fire fed.

"Now we get to the best parts," Delahunt continued. He gestured toward one of the twin, raised compartments, which he called cupolas. Each was outfitted with one of the guns that made Tuck think of Gatling guns. Delahunt gave the barrel of one a shove, and the cupola spun around in a smooth, easy circle. "These here are mounted on swivels that allow them to be turned in any direction," he said. He opened a door and showed them a seat on the inside, with controls for the gun, and small windows, some of which were actually magnifying lenses, for sighting over long distances. "Each one only needs one operator, to aim it and feed in the ammunition belts," Delahunt said. "The guns are automatically cranked, twice as fast as a man could hand-crank it. Air-cooled. The man inside can swivel the cupola three hundred and sixty degrees."

"Impressive," Tuck said.

"Best part is, they fire explosive rounds. Not much bigger than a .44-40 cartridge, and we've adapted magazines to hold three hundred rounds each. Six barrels, six magazines, six hundred rounds a minute. The operator can reload any one while any other's in use." Delahunt moved toward the wagon's center, and indicated a contraption that seemed to be mostly pulleys and gears and foot-long steel poles. Delahunt fingered what looked like a sling, made of some sort of steel netting, at one end. "This here's a catapult," he said. He tapped a steel box beside it. "It'll throw these black powder-and-ghost-rock bombs for a hundred feet. More, if the wind's right."

"Do you use a lot of ghost rock?" Cale asked. His eyes were full of excitement and wonder, like a child at Christmastime.

"Every bit we can get our hands on," Delahunt said. "That mule train's supply helps a lot. Used a little in the outer layer of armor, to help repel bullets. On the wheels." He tapped a steel tube jutting from the wagon's front end, a little more than an inch in diameter. "More in this."

"What is it?" Tuck asked.

"I call it a fire-spitter," Delahunt said. "We need to, we can divert some of the fire from the steam engine through this. The ghost rock magnifies the effect. It'll shoot a burst of fire fifteen or twenty feet."

"For how long?"

"Not too long," Delahunt admitted. "We divert the fire for long, the water stops boiling. No hot water, no steam. No steam, no power."

"I've never seen a steam wagon like this one, Sergeant. I was a military officer once, a long time ago. Seems like a different life. But something like this—well, it would have made an enormous difference. Changed the course of the war, I think."

"That's what we had in mind, Mr. Bringloe," Delahunt said. "War is awful, any old way you look at it. With this thing, I was hoping to make it a little less awful for my side, and a little more so for the other, no matter who the enemy is."

"Who or *what*," Tuck said.

"You said not human. I got no problem with that. This world is a strange place, Mr. Bringloe. Stranger than most of us allow. Way I see it, only way to deny that is to live with your eyes closed."

"Could be you've seen more than me, then. But mine are starting to open, and I reckon I won't be able to shut them again now."

"It's hard to go back," Kuruk said. "Anytime, anyhow. Once you get somewhere, what's behind you isn't what you thought it was."

"Is that some old Apache saying?" Tuck asked.

Kuruk laughed. "Naw. Something I read in a book once. I don't remember who wrote it, though. Some white man who's dead."

Taylor rapped on the brass chimney. "Steam's goin'," he said. "She's ready to roll."

"We waiting for anything else?" Delahunt asked.

"Can we get some horses? And guns?"

"Mister, this is an army fort, and it's mostly empty. Troopers we don't have many of. Horses and guns, we got."

Chapter Forty-six

The battlewagon, Tuck thought, was a monstrosity. A steaming, spitting, roaring monstrosity.

And it might be just what they needed.

Once the steam was going, Johnson, youngest and smallest of the Buffalo Soldiers, climbed into the front cupola. There, Delahunt explained, he had the controls to select the thing's direction, to make it go forward or back, and to brake it. The young soldier left the door open for the moment.

Tuck, Kuruk, Cale, and the other soldiers were mounted on cavalry horses. They had army rifles in scabbards and pistols on gun belts. The rain had slackened, and the wagon's iron wheels cut deep grooves in the mud but weren't slowed by it. On the way out of the fort, they had to pass Colonel Cuttrell's place again, and as they did, he came out the front door. He wore a gray officer's coat over his uniform, his boots were polished, and his hat was perched at a jaunty but militarily acceptable angle.

His face was another story. It was the face of a man in mourning, or suffering soul-deep hardship of some kind. He looked stricken. His flesh had an unhealthy pallor, setting off the gray bags under his eyes. The lines around eyes and mouth were more pronounced than Tuck remembered them, as if years, not just hours, had passed since their last meeting.

Cuttrell stared at the battlewagon in blank incomprehension. "Mr. McKenna," he said, almost shouting to be heard over the thing's racket. "What in the hell is that contraption?"

McKenna waved, and inside the cupola, Johnson applied the brakes. With a hiss of steam, the wagon slowed, quieting as it did.

"Sir," McKenna said. "This is a special project I've been working on with Sergeant Delahunt and some of his men."

"We call it a battlewagon, sir," Delahunt added.

"Is there a battle on of which I am unaware?" He looked at Tuck and Cale as if noticing them for the first time. "You? I thought I told you not to come back here. And aren't you the beef boy?"

"*Was,* sir. You switched the contract to Mr. Montclair."

A cloud seemed to pass over Cuttrell's face at the mention of the name. "Him. Yes."

"That's where we're headed, sir. We think Montclair has taken the girl. Little Wing."

"The crazy laundre—" He spotted Kuruk with the party, and caught himself. "Yes, of course. And Montclair has her? Jasper Montclair? Whatever for?"

"I can't really say, sir," McKenna replied.

"So you're going there? To get her back?"

"Yes, sir."

"And you're taking this thing with you. This battlewagon."

"That's correct, sir."

Cuttrell whipped off his hat and ran his fingers through his hair. "To Montclair's."

"That's right, sir."

Tuck knew what the colonel was thinking about. His wife, going off with Montclair. He had denied it, but it was the truth. By this point, Cuttrell had to know.

"I'll join you."

"Sir?"

"I'm going with you. To Montclair's ranch."

"Sir, we don't know what we'll be dealing with. Bringloe says it's dangerous, that we'll be up against some sort of, I don't know, supernatural forces, or something. Inhuman. And we don't know how well the battlewagon will work."

"If you're trying to dissuade me, Lieutenant, you're going about it all wrong."

"It's just that—"

"Damn it, man, Montclair has Sadie! She's a mess, I know. She's a laudanum addict, she's probably unfaithful, she's temperamental, rude, and dismissive. Nothing but trouble, really. But she's my wife, and I want her back."

"Yes, sir." McKenna's tone had changed, and his gaze shifted away from the colonel and landed somewhere on the ground between them. Tuck wasn't entirely sure what to make of that. But it wasn't his concern. If they rescued Sadie Cuttrell, that was fine and dandy. But his interest was Little Wing. And he wanted to know, once and for all, what those night-black creatures were, and what connection they had to Jasper Montclair.

The safety of Carmichael was no longer his professional concern. But he felt a certain responsibility just the same. Not because he was being paid, but because he was a human being. And human beings, he was convinced, had a responsibility to other humans. He had not known that for a long time. Most of his life, really. Between the horrible example of his mother, his time as a drunkard, even his time in the Union Army, to some extent—he had enlisted with high ideals, but had become nothing but a paid, uniformed killer of men—that lesson had been lost. But recently, it had been taught to him, by Hank Turville's trust and kindness, by that of Missy Haynes, by Little Wing and Kuruk. Even, in a way, by his failure to recognize the desperation of Jed Tibbetts in time to help him.

He had tried to live a life on his own, disconnected from others. That hadn't worked out so well. Drink had cut the bonds that linked him to the world, but even in drunkenness he had depended on others to pay him for work done or to give him money when he begged for it. Riding with the posse, he had remembered his army days and earlier times, when he had been part of something bigger than himself. And he had, once again, accepted that as the natural state of man. Like it or not, he was part of a community, part of a nation, and with the benefits of that came certain duties. Those included a responsibility to step in if he could, to protect those who couldn't defend themselves, to ease suffering where possible, to try to give aid and comfort to those in need.

So he found himself on a borrowed CSA horse—a lovely, powerful chestnut mare—with a slotted cavalry saddle, armed with borrowed CSA weapons, riding in the company of men he barely knew: Kuruk, McKenna, Cuttrell, Cale, Delahunt, Taylor, and Johnson. They had a shared goal, a mission of as yet uncertain focus.

And they had a clanging, spewing, self-propelled battlewagon that was as terrifying as it was fascinating.

He hoped it would be enough.

Mo Kanouse stood on the corner near Maier's store, watching the town come back to life as the rain let up. It would most likely return; the sky was thick with clouds, layer upon layer, with only small patches of sky showing through. More rain by sunset, he reckoned, and then off and on through the night.

Mostly, he was letting the town watch him. Every now and then someone would mention the star on his coat, and he would explain that he was the new marshal, that Bringloe had simply not been up to the job. He had his arms folded over his chest, with the scattergun in his right hand. He wanted people to know that he was the law, and that he wouldn't be trifled with.

The other reason he wanted to be seen was that the town was full of soldiers from the fort, dismissed, at least for the moment, by the colonel. That had never happened before. Some of the troopers were already in the saloons and brothels, and Kanouse expected a raucous night. If the soldiers saw that he was the marshal, they might be easier to corral when they got out of hand.

As he stood there, a commotion up the street drew his attention toward the fort. A small procession had emerged from the main gate. It was turning onto the southbound road, rather than cutting through town, but it was attracting notice because, in addition to men on horses, it included a noisy, horseless, steel-clad steam wagon that appeared, from this distance, to be full of junk. A few of the troopers ran over to see what was going on. The army's business wasn't his, so Kanouse stayed put. A few minutes later, the soldiers came back, chattering among themselves. "What was that thing?" Kanouse asked.

"Some kind of war wagon," one of the men said. He was a young private with an open face. When he spoke, Kanouse saw that he was missing at least half his bottom teeth. "They wouldn't say much. Looked like a strange deal to me."

"They say where they're headed?"

"Colonel said somethin' 'bout gettin' his wife back. That's all I heard."

"Thanks," Kanouse said. He twitched his head toward the saloon the trooper's friends had already entered. "You're fallin' behind."

The trooper nodded and trailed his companions inside. As soon as the young man was out of sight, Kanouse hurried to Mayor Chaffee's office. He told the mayor what he'd seen, and what the trooper had said.

Chaffee's brow knitted when he heard the news. "Montclair's got Sadie Cuttrell," he said. "I didn't like the idea, but how do you say no to that man?"

"Do you think they're headin' to Montclair's spread?"

"How would I know?" Chaffee said. "You're the one who saw them leave."

"Bringloe was with them. And that Apache scout. I don't like the whole thing."

"I don't either, Mo. You better let Montclair know what's going on."

"Me?"

"You're on the payroll now. Time you started earning your keep."

Chaffee turned his attention to some papers on his desk. Kanouse didn't appreciate being made to feel like an errand boy. But Chaffee was right—he was taking their money, so his place was to do as he was told. He left the office without saying goodbye and went to fetch his horse. All he had to do was get to Montclair's before they did, and give him the word. Montclair would have to handle it from there.

Chapter Forty-seven

Cloud cover had turned day into dusk. The sun was behind there, somewhere, no doubt sinking toward the Huachuca Mountains. The battlewagon couldn't keep pace with horses at a full gallop, but it maintained a steady clip, rolling over uneven trails and rocks and through swiftly running washes without difficulty.

As they neared the Broken M, the sky turned darker still. The air cooled, too, as if the ranch harbored its own secret winter.

When they crossed the ranch's farthest-flung boundary, things got worse.

The road became clogged with low, spindly mesquites, almost invisible in the gloom, but hardy and thorny enough to snarl and slice up the horses' legs. After a few minutes of that, the mounted men pulled back and let the wagon go first. Its steel-clad wheels pushed through the tangle, flattening the plants as they went.

Shortly beyond that, the road was choked off altogether by a mass of larger mesquites, packed close together—closer than Tuck had ever seen them. "This is not natural," Kuruk said, giving voice to Tuck's concerns.

"Not hardly," McKenna agreed.

"Let Johnson handle it," Delahunt said. He banged on the cupola. "Willie, you know what to do."

Johnson's reply was swift and eager. "Yes, sir!"

The wagon stopped. Delahunt dismounted and fed more ghost rock into the furnace. Thumping noises came from within, followed by a whooshing sound. Moments later, a jet of flame issued from the front tube, what Delahunt had called the fire-spitter. It went for about twenty seconds before giving one last, more powerful burst, then tapering off.

When it was done, the mesquite blockade was still crackling. Blue and yellow flames flickered along some of the branches, but most were too soaked to burn for long. Still, they glowed and smoked, and when the wagon started rolling again, it crashed through easily. The horses followed, anxious but willing to be urged through.

Tuck couldn't tell if the obstacles were meant to test them or to stop them altogether. He had already given up worrying about what was impossible, and accepted that the world he had thought existed for so long wasn't the true world, after all. He had seen too much, experienced too much, that would have been beyond the bounds of belief even a few weeks earlier. Now, he just accepted what his senses told him as the truth, or as close to it as any man could hope for. When their ever-narrower path took them into a thicket of yuccas, and the yucca stalks dropped from their bases and, upon hitting the ground, became six- and seven-foot-long rattlesnakes, he didn't doubt, just unsheathed his rifle and started shooting. The smell of spent powder and the dull, bitter stink of dead rattler filled the air, and Tuck's unquestioning acceptance of the preternatural scene surprised him more than the tableau itself.

They continued to follow what was left of the trail. As they approached a wide arroyo, a thick, brown river roared into it, quickly overflowing its banks and carrying chunks of wood and whole trees along with it.

"What do you think?" Tuck asked McKenna.

"If we're going to Montclair's, we have to cross it," the lieutenant said.

Tuck looked at the fast-moving flood. The arroyo was four or five feet deep and maybe twelve to fifteen wide, he figured, though that estimate had been made from the crest of the hill and not up close. Horses could ford rivers, or swim them, so he didn't think they would have a problem, but he wasn't so sure about the wagon. Heavy as it was, it could be mired in the sandy bottom. And if it tipped over, he didn't know how they would ever right it again.

"I'm game," he said. "Sergeant Delahunt, can your wagon make it through that?"

Delahunt gave the flash flood only a brief glance. "Not a problem." He went to Johnson's cupola and spoke a few words. Johnson adjusted something inside, and with a metallic clank, the battlewagon's wheels seemed to fall apart. Then Tuck realized that they were, in fact, unfurling small, pennant-shaped segments. As the segments reached their limits, they extended out and away, acting as spikes. Each one hit the ground and dug in, helping push the wagon forward. The wagon surged ahead, down the bank and into the stream.

As it splashed in, water shoved against it, then ran under and around. The other men urged their mounts forward. Tuck's mare hesitated at the edge, drawing back her head and whinnying, but at Tuck's insistence she went in anyway.

The water was ice-cold, far colder than a flash flood from a summer's rain should be. The chill Tuck had felt in the air hadn't dissipated, and he was already cold from riding in wet clothes. The horses objected when they felt the water. Delahunt's tried to wheel around, and it took all the man's strength to keep the animal heading in the right direction.

Midstream, Johnson called out a panicked "Sarge!" Tuck looked his way and saw the battlewagon shift sideways. Just a little, at first, then more.

"Keep her steady, Willie!" Delahunt replied. He looked like he wanted to help, but he had his own struggle to contend with.

Anyway, there wasn't much a man on a horse could do to haul a wagon that probably weighed a ton or more. Tuck watched in alarm as the rear of the wagon skewed yet more to the side. Through a window he could see Johnson at the controls, frantically turning dials and pulling levers. The wagon came to a dead stop in the water, and Tuck thought it was hopeless. He was starting to maneuver his horse over to it, so Johnson could climb on, when the engine chugged and a puff of smoke belched from the chimney and the thing started to roll again.

Tuck reached the far bank and his mare scrambled out, no doubt happy to be free of the icy current. The other riders climbed it, too. The battlewagon still fought the current, but it was coming inexorably nearer to the bank, and the back end was starting to shift back into a better alignment with the front. When it hit the bank and those spiked wheels emerged from the water, digging into dry land, Johnson let out a victorious whoop.

That did not, however, mean the way ahead was clear. Cuttrell had been to Montclair's place on numerous occasions, and he tried to keep them on the proper course, using the unchanging profile of the Huachucas as a guideline. But he complained that the road was no longer the one he knew. Like Tuck, he and the rest had all stopped denying the evidence of their own senses. What had been reality elsewhere—just on the other side of Montclair's property—was not that here, and expressing disbelief was too much trouble.

For a time, the road was free of obstacles, and Cuttrell started to relax. "We're getting close," he said. "Another thirty minutes, no more."

"Good," Delahunt said. "I'm gettin' tired of this trip. I know Willie'd be glad to stretch out his legs."

"Nearly there," the colonel replied. He gigged his horse to a faster pace.

But before they had covered much more distance, the landscape changed again. The road had cut through the softly undulating grasslands, but coming down off a low hill, it dropped at a precipitous angle that almost sent the battlewagon careening down. At the bottom, it sliced between two rocky outcroppings. "This is new," Cuttrell announced. "I have no idea what we'll encounter in here."

"Let's find out," Delahunt said. "Long as it's wide enough for the wagon."

They slowed to a walk and entered the space, Cuttrell and

McKenna in the lead, Delahunt behind. Then the wagon went in. Cale, Kuruk, Taylor, and Tuck brought up the rear. The farther they went, the higher the walls became, until they were deep inside a winding, sheer-walled canyon. The light was thin, and in the gloom they couldn't see the tops of the walls. Johnson did something inside his cupola, illuminating the lamps all around the battlewagon and casting a warm, yellow glow on the walls and the path ahead.

Still, the walls went higher. "There are no canyons like this in these parts," McKenna said. "Not even in the Huachucas."

"There's one now," Cuttrell responded. He grazed the fingers of his right hand against the wall. "It might not have been here long, but it's here."

"Did you hear something?" Cale asked suddenly.

"I can't hear anything over all the noise that damn wagon makes," Tuck said. "What kind of something?"

"Behind us," Cale said. "Like a grinding noise."

"We being followed?" Taylor asked.

"Nothing would surprise me anymore," Tuck said. "Hold up for a minute!" he called to the riders in front. "We're going to check something."

"Don't dawdle," Cuttrell said. "We're not far off now, but it'll be full dark before too long."

"We won't." Tuck, Taylor, and Cale turned their mounts. Kuruk stayed with the wagon. As they rounded the first bend and were out of the wagon's glow, Tuck heard the grinding noise. More than that, he felt it, bone-deep: a low, loud rumble. Around the second bend, Tuck had to stop, blink, rub his eyes.

"Do you . . ."

Cale was swiveling in his saddle, looking every which way. "We just came through here!"

"Can't argue with that," Tuck said. "I remember it that way, too."

But "through" was no longer an option.

The trail stopped up against a cliff wall, like the ones on either side. This way had become a dead end, with no way out without scaling a sheer vertical face. "Leastways it's behind us," Taylor said.

"We got to make sure it's not in front, too," Tuck pointed out. "Come on."

He whipped the mare around and pushed her as fast as she could go in the tight canyon. Taylor kept pace with him, step for step. They drew even with the battlewagon and the other men, and Tuck reined his mount in. "Canyon's closed up that way!" he shouted. "We'll make sure it's clear ahead! Hurry it up, just in case!" Then he urged the mare on again and took off at a gallop, chasing after Taylor.

He had rounded three sharp curves when he caught up to the other man. Taylor brought his horse around and pointed up-canyon. "The walls are closin' in up ahead!" he said. "You can't hardly see it—they're not goin' fast. But they're goin', jus' the same."

Tuck brought his animal to a halt and eyed the canyon walls. Sure enough, even through the gloom, he could see that the slight wedge of visible sky ahead was being blocked, minute by minute. "They'd better get that wagon through here in a hurry," he said.

"I'll let 'em know," Taylor offered. He brought his mount around again and started back toward the others.

As he did, Tuck noticed something strange about the canyon floor. Something wrong. Precious little light filtered down from the dusk sky, but he was able to make out shadows and rock faces that reflected the scant illumination. But in the center of the canyon, right where Taylor was headed, he saw a deep shadow, oval-shaped and bigger than a man on a horse.

Looking up, he saw nothing that could have cast such a shadow. "Taylor!" he cried.

Too late. Taylor screamed as he started to plummet into nothingness. He released the reins and his arms shot up, as if maybe somebody could grab one and hold on. But Tuck was too far off. All he could do was stand and watch.

Taylor's screams seemed to go on for a long, long time.

Chapter Forty-eight

Kanouse had been to Montclair's place once, a couple of years back. The rancher had thrown a barn dance for some of the people supporting his effort to take over the vast swath of ranchland between the river and the mountains. It had been the strangest, most uncomfortable dance Kanouse ever attended. All the basic elements were there: drink and music and dancing and conversation around the edges. But it had felt a little like they were all there to bow down before the king. That's how Montclair had carried himself, anyway, as if his family name and money made him not just richer than everyone else, but better. He was wealthy, he was educated, he owned land and controlled politicians, and he used words Kanouse couldn't begin to understand.

By the end of the night, Kanouse had hated him. Resented his high-and-mighty attitude. He would have been happy to put a bullet in Montclair's brain. But the people there with him, Marshal Turville and the mayor and the rest, were people Kanouse respected—people who had higher stations in life than he did, but still treated him like a human being. They looked up to Montclair. They didn't seem to mind the way he peered down his nose at them, the way he tried to pretend his Eastern airs didn't exist and he was just another rancher. He didn't think they were blind, so he figured they must have overlooked those things for good reason. And if they could, he could.

In the end, he didn't shoot Montclair. But for a few days after that, he felt bad about himself. Unclean, somehow. He drank a lot and spent some time with whores, and after a while he started feeling better again. But he had never liked Montclair, and after that he had liked him even less.

On this occasion, though, he felt a surprising fondness for the man. For one thing, his own station in life had improved. He was marshal now, not Hank and not that worthless Bringloe. Montclair would still look down on him, but Kanouse could tell himself it didn't matter. I'm the marshal, he thought. In Carmichael, what I say counts. When Bringloe had fired him, he had thought his hand was all played out, and he would wind up the way Bringloe had been—a drunk, living in the streets, a joke or an eyesore to the rest of the townsfolk. But he had been wrong. He was too much of a man to fall into a trap like that. The world had plans for him. Big ones.

Yesterday, maybe he had been on the verge of collapse. Now, overnight, he had prospects. He had power. He had respect.

And he meant to keep them.

He followed a seldom-used trail, too rough and rocky for that strange wagon to travel, but that would put him well ahead of Bringloe and the others. Riding onto Broken M property, now that he too was a man of distinction, was a different experience than before. He felt a comforting coolness, as if Montclair was exempt from the ravaging heat of the Arizona summer. The hard-packed road, neat and well maintained, by all appearances, seemed to unspool before him like a welcoming presence, inviting him into the ranch's interior.

He was almost to the ranch headquarters—he had spotted it a couple of times, nestled there against the foot of the mountains, when topping one rise or another—when he thought he saw Montclair himself.

Only what he thought he saw, he couldn't have seen. He drew back on the reins a little, slowing his palomino, trying to give himself time to think. Through a gap between a pair of low hills, he had seen Montclair's face. But that face had looked as large as if the man were standing right next to him, though clearly he was still some distance away.

"Easy, Mo," he said aloud. "You been thinking about him and your mind got ahead of you, is all."

Almost convinced, he rode on through the gap. Beyond it, in a small patch of earth and gravel, almost perfectly round and nearly devoid of plant life, Montclair waited. He had his hands behind his back, and he offered Kanouse a broad smile. "Welcome, Marshal," he said.

His voice boomed from him, loud as thunder. It seemed to echo off the mountains behind him. Kanouse fought the urge to cover his ears with his hand, in case Montclair spoke again.

"Hey, Mr. Montclair," he said.

"To what do I owe the pleasure?" Montclair asked.

A chill raised the hairs on Kanouse's neck. The Montclair standing before him hadn't moved, not a muscle. His mouth had not opened. Yet Kanouse had heard his voice. Not as painfully loud this time, but coming from behind him. He twisted in the saddle. On that side of the cleared patch stood Montclair, hands at his sides.

Kanouse jerked his head back around. Montclair stood before him. Montclair stood behind him. Then he saw another one, off to his right. It was only then that he realized that none of the Montclairs were altogether substantial. Kanouse could see the desert through each of them, dim and indistinct, but unmistakably.

"I . . . I don't . . ." he said, unsure of how to answer Montclair's question. Or whether he should. The confidence he had felt, just minutes before, was shaken by the scene before him.

"Out with it, man," Montclair said. This one was off to his left. When Kanouse turned his head that way, he saw three more. Each held a different pose and facial expression, though they were all dressed identically, in white shirts under vests, striped pants, boots, and a dark hat. "You came for a reason, did you not?"

"Yeah, but . . ." Kanouse managed. His hands were trembling, the reins he held flicking against the horse's neck. The palomino was uneasy, too.

Then Montclair's voice boomed again, louder than the last time. At the same instant that Kanouse heard it, he saw Montclair's face in front of him. Just his face. It was at least the size of the shack Kanouse lived in, and it floated about ten feet off the ground. "Speak!" it said.

The force of the word had an almost physical presence. Kanouse shrank from it, nearly blown out of his saddle. "I . . . the mayor wanted me to let you know," he said, the words spilling out quickly in hopes of forestalling any more such sonic explosions. "That colonel from the fort, Cuttrell, he's headed this way. He's got some other soldiers with him, and Bringloe, and some sort of fancy wagon that don't need horses to pull it."

The giant Montclair face broke into a manic grin, and started to laugh. All the other Montclairs did the same. The laughter surrounded him, terrible in its volume and its omnipresence. Kanouse knew if he sat here much longer, he would start to cry, wet his pants, or both. He tried to steel himself, and tightened his grip on the reins.

When Montclair spoke again, the voice came from all the Montclairs at once. They all looked exactly the same now, their stance casual but their common face tense and angry. "Do you think I'm unaware of that? I know who's on my land. The land itself knows, and will deal with them as I bid it to. What you encounter is not what they find, and what meets them is not what anyone else would see. This earth defends its master."

Kanouse didn't know how to answer that, or if he should even try. He had come to deliver a message. He had delivered it—if not to Montclair himself, to something, some nightmare vision, that resembled Montclair. He had done what he'd set out to do, and he didn't plan to wear out his welcome.

"That's it, Mr. Montclair," he said. "I just wanted to let you know. I'll be on my way."

Before the various Montclair images responded, he jabbed his spurs into the palomino's sides. The horse bolted. Kanouse hung on as the animal charged through the nearest Montclair. He didn't feel any resistance, but passed through the figure as easily as through the air. He wound up on the wrong side of the clearing, and didn't intend to go back through, so he urged the horse off the trail and cross-country. He skirted around past the cleared area—at a glance, Kanouse didn't see any Montclairs still there, but he didn't intend to investigate further—and found his way back to the main road.

Once there, he gigged the horse again, and kept it going at a hard gallop, back toward town.

He needed a drink, he told himself. Maybe two. Maybe a dozen. Maybe a fight, instead of or in addition to. Whatever it took to convince himself that he hadn't seen what he thought he had. Whatever it took to forget it.

If he ever could.

Tuck dropped from the horse and ran to the edge of what seemed to be the endless pit into which Taylor had fallen. The blackness was infinite, and reminded him of the color—no, the absolute absence of it—of the strange creatures he believed served Montclair in some way. He couldn't see so much as an inch of the side; the pit had no more visible substance than a shadow. But if he put his hand in, it touched empty air, slightly warmer than that outside.

Kneeling, the fingers of his hands wrapped over the pit's edge as he listened to the horrible, fading but still audible screams of man and horse from deep within, he realized that the pit was moving away from him. He released it, backed up a few steps, and watched as it shrank. Soon, it was not much larger than the span of both his hands, and then it was gone altogether. He went back to his knees and felt for it, but the ground was solid. It was as if the pit had never existed at all.

By then, the rest of his party had rounded the last bend. The battlewagon's lights washed over him, showing him that the canyon floor remained solid. Or seemingly so. It had first appeared out of nowhere, without warning. To hope that another one wouldn't do the same seemed like a dangerous idea.

"Hurry up!" he called. "Canyon's closing in ahead of us. And keep those lights pointed toward the ground. If you see something like a shadow, a big one with no obvious source, don't go near it."

"Where's Taylor?" Delahunt asked. "He scouting up ahead?"

"He's—" Tuck hesitated. He didn't know how to answer. As far as he knew, Taylor was still falling into the earth, victim of a trap that couldn't exist, but did. "He's gone."

"Gone?" Delahunt echoed.

"Don't ask. Let's just get that wagon through here. I don't think there's much canyon left, but I'd hate to be stuck in here when the walls come together."

Delahunt eyed him with naked suspicion. Tuck couldn't blame him. He and Taylor had been alone, and now Taylor was gone. The only argument in his favor was the fact that the world had turned strange and decidedly antagonistic since they'd crossed onto Broken M land. "I'll explain later," he said. "Let's go."

McKenna waved the group onward. Cuttrell outranked him in the army, but on this journey, they had all started looking to the lieutenant for leadership. Johnson pushed the wagon as fast as he could. The lights dimmed slightly, which Tuck figured meant he was devoting more of the steam's energy to turning the wheels and less to other uses. He wasn't sure how any of it worked, but that seemed a reasonable guess.

Soon, the canyon's end was before them, with open country visible on the other side. Tuck was behind the wagon, along with Kuruk and Cale. The rest cleared the narrowing space, but as the wagon tried to squeeze through, the rocky walls came so close together that it scraped on both sides, shooting out sparks where metal rasped against rock. Tuck wondered what would happen if the wagon made it through. Would the walls slam together, crushing the last three riders?

As the wagon's front burst free of the canyon's brutal embrace, the walls closed more tightly on the back end. The armored sides groaned. Lights were crushed and torn from their moorings, and the end caved slightly. But then, with a final shriek of steel on stone, it broke away.

"Ride!" Tuck screamed. He didn't wait around to see if Kuruk and Cale obeyed, but put his heels to his mount and flew toward the wan light on the far side. When he had cleared the gap, he wheeled around in time to see Cale bolt through. Kuruk came last. The scout's muscular paint was more than a match for the roan Cale rode, but Tuck figured the scout had let the boy go first to make sure he got out. Kuruk inched through at the last possible moment, and Tuck wouldn't have been surprised if some hairs from his paint's tail were trapped between the walls when they finally came together.

Johnson climbed out of his cupola, dripping with sweat. While Tuck tried to explain to Delahunt what had happened to Taylor, Johnson and McKenna examined the damage to the battlewagon. The two hindmost lights were gone, and some of the armor plating had been scraped off. But the wheels appeared straight, and when Johnson got back in and tested his controls, all the systems seemed to function normally. Having determined that, they continued on their path.

As if the canyon were the last obstacle they had to brave, beyond it the road seemed to revert to what it should have been all along: a frequently traveled but muddy thoroughfare that sliced through the fields of native grasses where cattle grazed and horses huddled together, heads down, looking miserable in the rain. Where the grasslands blended with high desert scrub, the mesquites and creosote bush and beavertail and cholla behaved. The yuccas and agaves stabbed at the lowering clouds but didn't detach from their bases and attack. The ground stayed whole and solid beneath their feet, and the trail toward Montclair's ranch headquarters didn't deviate from its usual course.

Chapter Forty-nine

At one point, Johnson stopped the wagon and climbed out, complaining that his limbs were painfully cramped. "I know how to work it," McKenna offered. "I'll take a shift inside. You can use my horse."

"Thanks, Lieutenant," Johnson said. "I'll spell you again in a bit."

While they were making the switch, Cale ambled over to where Tuck and Cuttrell stood, watching the men move around the wagon with grace born of familiarity. "Mr. Bringloe," Cale said. "Is it always like this?"

"Is what, Cale?"

"The world. Seems like those who already got, get more. Folks like Mr. and Mrs. Tibbetts, honest people who work hard but don't have much, get stepped on every which way, till finally they can't take no more steppin'. But somebody like Montclair, he's already got more money than Croesus, and everything he does makes him more. I don't think he cares who gets hurt, long as he gets what he wants. It don't hardly seem fair."

"If it's fair you're looking for, son, you were born into the wrong world," Tuck said.

"You're right about Montclair," Cuttrell added. "I'm ashamed to say that I helped him amass some of his holdings, consolidate his wealth and power. Now he's got the mayor and council dancing like puppets on strings. The army, too, until now. But no longer. However this ends up tonight, the CSA is out of the Broken M business."

Tuck must have been wearing a surprised expression, because Cuttrell gave him a smile. "What? A man can change his mind. Even a starchy, washed-up old soldier. Changing my mind on this might be one of the best things I've ever done."

Kuruk interrupted the conversation. "Rider coming," he said. He pointed toward the south, and Tuck saw the rider, still some distance off. He was hunched over his horse, which in a drier season would have been raising a thick cloud of dust. Instead, it was kicking up a spray of mud clots, but despite the poor road conditions, it was making good time. Soon enough, man and horse were hurtling toward them. Tuck was moving to the side of the road, as were the others, to let the rider pass, when he realized it was Kanouse.

"Pull your irons, boys," he warned, jerking his borrowed pistol from its holster. "That man's likely teamed up with Montclair, and he doesn't mean us well."

The other men did the same, except Johnson. But his cupola swiveled a little to the right, adjusting as Kanouse drew nearer to keep him in its sights.

Kanouse surprised Tuck, though. He barely seemed to notice the procession until he was right on top of it. When he lifted his gaze from the road and saw several mounted men and a strange wagon twenty yards ahead, his expression turned to one of terror. He started, and yanked back on the reins, and his right hand dropped to his rifle scabbard. He tugged out that sawed-off, which was the only part that Tuck was expecting.

When Kanouse noticed figures in the road, his first thought was that they were more of those Montclair mirages. He kept his head down and jabbed his spurs against the horse's flanks. The animal was already running all-out, but Kanouse didn't want it to let up.

Then he glanced up again and saw that crazy wagon he'd spotted in town. That prompted him to look again. This wasn't

Montclair, and probably no mirage. He tugged back on the reins and slowed the confused horse. Remembering who had been with the wagon in town, he took another look at the men standing around it.

Bringloe. Colonel Cuttrell, and some others he recognized as soldiers from the fort. Some kid he didn't know. And that Apache who was always with the white girl.

They all had guns in their hands, and something that looked like a Gatling gun was pointed at him from the wagon.

Kanouse came to a stop and yanked his scattergun. Montclair had filled him with doubt, made him question everything he knew about himself and the world he lived in. Would the man he had thought he was have turned tail and run from pictures in the air, with no physical substance? How could they hurt him? He had showed Montclair a side of himself he had long tried to bury: the fearful side. Once, a man had told him he was a moral and physical coward, because he had refused to intercede in a fight between a husband and wife down at the Palladium. The husband broke her nose and blackened her eye, but they had left together, seemingly at peace. Kanouse had caught up with the other man, the one who had called him a coward, on his way home from the saloon. He'd gutted the man with a Bowie knife and left him to die in the dirt, then gone home and slept like a baby.

He had lost that knife in a card game. It was too bad; he'd always liked the heft of it.

Now he had acted like the coward that man had said he was. Only Montclair had witnessed it—if, in fact, he could see with the eyes of those mirages. But Kanouse knew, to the depths of his soul, that he had been terrified, and that he had run away at the first opportunity. If that wasn't cowardice, what was it?

Here, he had a chance to redeem himself. He faced six men with guns in their fists. A coward wouldn't wade right into that, would he? For a moment—less than, just the briefest instant— he thought about showing his hands, talking to the men. They didn't have any reason to shoot him, after all. If he did that, though, and they let him pass, then he would return to town only to have to live with the absolute certainty of his cowardice. He couldn't ask for anyone's respect if he didn't believe he deserved it.

Instead, he yanked his scattergun. He would show what he was made of, or go down trying.

"Kanouse!" Tuck called. "Don't be a fool!"

Kanouse swung the gun toward him. His hand was tight on it. White-knuckled and trembling. He was scared, or had been recently. That could explain the way he'd been riding, like something bad was hot on his trail.

"You got six guns pointed at you," McKenna said. "You can't win this."

It was as if McKenna's words had cut a tether holding Kanouse fast to the earth. He gigged his horse and bolted toward them. As he charged, he tugged on one trigger, then the other. Both barrels spat fire. He broke the weapon open, reloaded, and fired again, and McKenna fell. Somebody opened fire—Tuck thought it was Delahunt and Cuttrell—but Kanouse was riding fast, shifting this way and that, and their rounds went wide. Johnson probably hesitated to fire the Gatling because Tuck and the others were between Kanouse and the wagon.

Tuck leveled his pistol at the man. Kanouse was bringing the sawed-off around toward him, but time seemed to slow down as he did. Tuck saw his arm swinging the gun, his finger tightening on the front trigger, his eyes narrowing as if anticipating the sound and impact of the shot, his mouth going slack. All of it happened at the same instant, but to Tuck's eyes, each was a separate moment, distinct from the rest.

He hadn't killed a man—a real man—since the war. He had spilled as much blood as he could stomach. Even during the war, every time he'd had to take a life, he had seen his father's face and heard his mother's voice. He'd been good at killing, and that talent sickened him.

But Kanouse left him no choice. McKenna was already down, and Tuck was next. He didn't want to kill. But he didn't want to die, either.

He squeezed the trigger, twice, in rapid succession. The gun bucked in his hand and he almost thought his eye could follow the path of each bullet as it hurtled toward its target. The first hit Kanouse in the chest, and the man made a surprised noise. The second caught him in the throat. Kanouse's head snapped back and he tumbled off the horse.

As soon as he hit the damp earth, everything sped up again. Kanouse bounced a little, but the mud sucked him back down. His right hand twitched a few times. The shotgun landed near him, bounced, and wound up entangled in a nearby mesquite. Tuck spun around toward McKenna. Delahunt already knelt beside him.

"He's all right!" Delahunt announced. He stood up, helping McKenna to his feet. The lieutenant's left sleeve was ragged, and there was blood running down his arm. He looked pale, but he tossed off a grin.

"I took some buckshot," he said. "Hurts, but I'll live."

"The marshal won't," Kuruk said. He had rushed to Kanouse's side. Kanouse's fingers clawed at the ground, but they slowed even as Tuck watched. Kuruk snatched the star from his chest. "He don't deserve that title, anyhow. Or the badge."

He carried it over to Tuck. Behind him, Kanouse's chest fell once, then stopped, and his hands went still. Kuruk handed the badge up to Tuck, still mounted. Tuck took it. There were drops of blood on it, glistening in unexpected moonlight.

Tuck looked over to see a full moon rising in the east, below the clouds, just emerging from behind the Mule Mountains. It was orange and enormous, looking like it could swallow the mountains and be hungry for more.

"Thunder Moon," Kuruk said. "First moon of the monsoon."

"I'm not the marshal anymore," Tuck said, still holding the badge in his hand.

"Should be," Kuruk said. "You're better than him, anyhow."

Tuck shoved the star into a pocket. He didn't want the thing. But he didn't want to leave it out here, sinking into the mud with Kanouse's corpse. When he got back to town, he would deliver it to the mayor.

If he got back to town.

He had a feeling the night's trouble was just beginning.

Chapter Fifty

Soto's was as busy as Missy had ever seen it. Sometimes rainy evenings brought people in, and other times it kept them away. Tonight the rain had been on and off, but it seemed like everybody who came into the place stayed. The tables were full, the bar was packed, and the girls were busy, Missy included. She was taking a break, for the moment, though Senora Soto glared at her when she ignored a trooper who was holding cash money in his hand and waving her down.

Most of the people in the place were soldiers, she noticed. It wasn't unusual to see troopers from the fort in the place, even filling a table or two. But never this many, not all at once. She did a quick count, and came up with fifty-three men who she was certain were with the army. There were a handful more she thought might have been, but she couldn't say for sure.

Who she didn't see was Tuck. She thought about their conversation earlier, the way he had treated her, and a wave of sorrow washed over her. She had seen him when he was a drunk. Sober, he was an entirely different man. A better man. One she wanted to know.

Sally Jo had told her that after she'd gone upstairs, a couple of hours earlier, there had been a disturbance of some sort outside, and he had left, abandoning an untouched but paid-for glass of whiskey. Nobody seemed to know the exact nature of the commotion, although there were rumors that it had to do with Little

Wing. Nobody had seen Tuck since, or Little Wing, or the Apache scout.

She liked Little Wing, and she liked Tuck. Maybe it was nothing; maybe he had gone to one of the town's other saloons, or had enough to drink and was sleeping it off in a rain-drenched alley somewhere. But she didn't think so. She thought there was a steel core to the man that wouldn't let him slide back as far as he had before. He might think he would—he probably thought it would be easy. But she had known a lot of men, good, bad, and indifferent. She believed Tuck was one of those who, having seen what he could be, would in the end settle for nothing less.

If he, Little Wing, and the Apache were all missing, after some sort of trouble, it wasn't because he had gone back to drinking. If he'd wanted to do that, he'd have come back inside where there was a glass waiting.

No, it wasn't that. A cold finger of worry traced her spine. Something had happened, and it wasn't good. According to Tuck, the killings of Daisie, and Calhoun, and the men behind Soto's, and maybe others, were all connected.

She could look for them, but she didn't know where to even begin. Then she remembered what Tuck had told her earlier, about Montclair—that he was "in the middle of it." She had an uneasy feeling that the commotion, and the fact that Tuck had never come back for his drink, might be connected, too.

He had come to Carmichael and sobered up and tried to do something to help the town when it was most in need. Now he might be in trouble, and somebody had to stand up for him.

She doubted that she could do anything about it, though. Not by herself, anyway. Even Tuck had seemed disturbed by whatever was up, and he had demonstrated a certain fluency with trouble. But there were plenty of men in the saloon tonight who were more conversant than she with the kind of thing that might set Tuck to worrying. And though she didn't have much to offer them in return, she could talk to the other girls, and maybe threaten to hold back on what she knew the men wanted.

She fixed one with a steady gaze, a sergeant she had been

with before, a man with graying hair and an enormous jaw. He worked it constantly, which made him look as if he had a half a muskrat in his mouth and was chewing on it slowly. As she crossed the room toward him, his smile brightened. He put his hand on her behind when she reached him, and kept it there until she lowered herself onto his lap. "It's good to see you, Missy," he said. "But I ain't got the price of a ride."

"It's not money I'm after," she said.

"That don't sound like the Missy I know."

"Well, it's so. Today I don't need money, Frank. But I might have need of some soldiers. You think you could rustle me up some?"

Frank barked out a laugh. "Joint's full of 'em," he said. "How many you want?"

"I don't know yet," she said. "A few, to start, to help me look around some. After that, maybe all of them'd be a good idea."

Montclair stood in the doorway, still naked and painted in blood, watching the clouds roiling overhead and the Thunder Moon rising to meet them, when the abominations rode into the yard. These looked nearly human on horseback, in their dark hats and long dusters. One horse carried two of them, with the girl sandwiched between. When she saw Montclair, she struggled, trying to break the hold the abominations had on her. But they were strong, which was part of why Montclair liked them. They had been here for centuries, guarding Thunder Moon's resting place, so in effect he had inherited them. They did his bidding; they had, after all, been waiting for one to come along who knew the right words to speak, the rituals to perform, to transfer their loyalty from the long-dead shaman to him. Waiting for the one who had come to claim Thunder Moon's sleeping power.

The arcane knowledge he had amassed, thanks to his father's money—and perhaps thanks to the way his father had made that money—had brought him to this place, at this time. The Thunder Moon was on the rise, Sadie was already his, and soon this other one, the girl so powerful her essence stung his breath and lungs, like a sudden inhalation on a frigid day, would also be his.

And power unmatched in the history of the world would flow to him. Through him, once-forbidden knowledge would be unleashed into the world.

He had told Sadie that he would be a king and she a queen, but the truth was, with only her by his side, he would never amount to more than a duke in the mystical realms. With this other one, in whom power ran like the waters of a flash flood, he could indeed be a king.

The abominations holding her handed her down to others already standing on the ground. The ones who had gone into town were some of those that had taken on human form on a nearly permanent basis. They were not fully human and never would be, but they had adopted that shape, could speak intelligibly and function in human society to some extent. Those were the ones Montclair used as ranch hands, and for any interactions with other people. The rest were essentially shadows given substance, beings that had taken on vaguely human shape without necessarily replicating any of what made people what they were. They were good for spreading terror, but not much else.

Still, the value of that couldn't be overstated. Look at all it had brought him.

As some of these dragged Little Wing, kicking and writhing, to Montclair, they made raspy, chittering noises he had never been able to interpret. They stopped a few feet from the door, one holding each arm and another one behind her. She glared at Montclair.

"You're angry," he said. He could see that on her face, but there was something else there, too. It took him a moment to isolate it. Pride? Defiance? Something along those lines.

"Your not-men stole me," she said. "They hurt my friend. Let me go."

"I can't do that."

"I know you."

"You might have seen me in town."

"No. I *know* you. For what you are."

He couldn't help smiling at that. "And what do you imagine that I am?"

"Evil," she said.

"Perhaps."

"Not *perhaps*. *Evil*. You will kill and burn and destroy to have what you want."

"Yes," Montclair said. "That is true. Does that make me evil?"

"What makes you evil is what you would do *and* what you want."

He reached forward and squeezed her cheeks with the strong fingers of his left hand. She tried to squirm away, but the abominations held her fast. She tried to snap at him, but he only squeezed harder. He waved the abominations away. Now that he had touched her, she was bound to him. "What I want? You know what I want?"

"You want power. Power to bend still others to your will. Everyone you see, everything you touch, you want to command."

"I want only what is due me," he said. "What I've earned through my own effort and toil."

"No one needs that much power. No one but—"

He squeezed her cheeks harder, cutting off the word. "Do *not* speak that name here. Since you know so much, girl, do you know what your role here is?"

She held his gaze with her eyes. Defiant, yes, she was that. Proud. Unafraid. Unbowed.

Her lack of fear infuriated him.

"According to you?" she asked. "I am to be a sacrifice."

"Yes," Montclair said. "You are to be consumed by my followers. Your power will nurture them, imparting to them yet more abilities for them to use at my bidding."

"My power? Used at your bidding? Are you certain?"

"The power comes from you, yes. But I will be the one giving them the gift. Their indebtedness and their loyalty will redound to me."

She tried to break his mystical grip. She concentrated, almost shutting her eyes, letting her lips part. He could feel the energy rush off her in waves. It nearly worked. He had to redouble his own concentration. If she hadn't been on his own land, at his house, with his minions around them, and him so recently fed on Sadie's heart, she might have done it.

She was *strong*. Stronger than he had realized. It would not do to underestimate her.

She was bound, by ropes that could not be seen and were tougher than any made by man's hands. But he was suddenly afraid that wouldn't be enough. He raised his right hand and made a beckoning gesture. Abominations surged forward. He nodded his head toward the girl, giving an unspoken command. They swarmed her, lifting her off her feet and hoisting her onto their shoulders. She tried to fight, but her limbs were no longer hers to control.

She didn't scream, though she could have. Montclair wasn't preventing that. He admired her courage.

Pity it would do her no good in the end.

He looked into the house. "Sadie? It's time to go, my dear."

Sadie knew so much more in death than she had in life.

She understood so much. Jasper Montclair had eaten of her, and in so doing, had made her part of him. She remembered her own short, unhappy life—child, young woman, prostitute, wife. But she remembered his life, too, even parts that he had forgotten.

She followed him out the door. His abominations were carrying that girl, Little Wing, into the mountains. As they went, they were chittering but also calling, making sounds almost like birds, like the strange, throaty, reverberating chuckles of quail, but much louder, interspersed with low, undulating whoops. Montclair followed them. She followed him.

Other abominations—dozens, a hundred, more—flooded from the hillsides. She'd had no idea there were so many, until he had eaten her heart, and then shared it with some of them.

When that happened, she had been immersed in an emotion somewhere between love and acceptance. It was nothing she had ever felt, but it was warm and good, so much better than even the best moments on laudanum. It was as if by giving up her own heart, she had been taken into theirs. Montclair's, and whatever the abominations had that passed for hearts.

On the way, following Jasper into the hills, she poked around in his memories. On a day he had been watching her, in town, he had seen a boy in the street, and that boy had reminded him of another one, from his childhood. He had recalled that the boy had been kicked by a mule, and he had died right before his eyes.

What he didn't remember—or if he did, he hid it from himself—was how that had come about.

The boy had been a playmate of young Jasper's, once in a while, but he had not come from the same social class. Even then, the Montclairs were rich. The boy's father had been a tradesman, someone who came to the Montclair estate once in a while to work in the gardens. Sometimes, he brought his son, who was Jasper's age. Usually the boy worked alongside his father, but on one occasion, the boy had been ill, and the father—humiliated by the necessity of asking—had begged for him to be allowed to rest while the man did his job.

Jasper's mother had agreed. But when Jasper had happened upon the boy, sitting in the shade instead of working, he had insisted that the boy play with him. The boy hadn't wanted to play—he had been weak from illness, overheated, sweating. Jasper was the young master, though, so the boy had relented, and played until he felt dizzy and feverish. Then he had pushed Jasper, hard. Jasper fell and struck his head on a flagstone, opening a gash on his cheek and damaging his right eye—the eye that remained damaged even now.

Jasper's maid had taken him inside and washed the cut, then bandaged it, while they waited for a doctor to arrive. As she held him, rocking him gently to soothe his nerves, she had promised that the boy would get what was coming to him. "Nobody hurts my little man," she had said, over and over.

What Jasper had not understood until later in life was that his maid had dabbled in the dark arts herself. He had never known, in those days, why she sometimes tied knots in pieces of string and put them in what seemed to him to be odd places, or buried things in the garden, or lit candles and made patterns with the hot wax. There were other signs, things he couldn't interpret and only remembered as dreams, if that.

But he knew now what had been going on then. She had been practicing witchcraft, or something like it. And when she promised her young charge that the boy would get his, she had meant it. The coach that knocked him into a building's corner and opened his skull was proof of that.

At that age, Jasper Montclair had not understood any of it, though he had begun to within a few years. That understanding had led to a lifelong passion for the arcane. His father's fortune had ensured that he could study with the best, acquire the texts that would advance his knowledge, and practice any ritual, however perverse or flatly illegal, without fear of punishment.

That pursuit had led them to this place, this time. Here, under the light of the Thunder Moon, with a light breeze stirring the oaks, the earthy smell of damp soil blending with the harsh but somehow sweet stink of the abominations, with their ululating calls echoing back and forth, and the love she felt for them and Montclair, and they for her. She didn't need her heart to love, as it turned out. Or to be loved.

Whatever she needed for that, she had.

She had never been so happy, and it occurred to her, in an offhand way, that there was something odd about the fact that true happiness had eluded her until after she had lost her heart.

Chapter Fifty-one

Another downpour hit between the place where they left Kanouse's body and Montclair's ranch headquarters. It drenched them and moved on fast, leaving behind fresh, thick mud and a lightning-torn sky and thunder that echoed from the canyons that carved the Huachuca Mountains into a series of jagged peaks and deep clefts.

By the time they neared the headquarters, the clouds were breaking and the big moon was shining through, paling toward white as it climbed. A barbed wire fence surrounded the place. Tall pillars flanked the gate, with a beam suspended between them that had BROKEN M painted on it. Atop each pillar, as if judging all who entered, was the skull of a longhorn steer.

Tuck was staring up at them when Cale spoke. "Uhhh, Mr. Bringloe? Kuruk?"

"Yes, boy?" Kuruk said.

Cale didn't answer. He was pointing at something on one of the wooden fence posts, just down from the gate. It looked like a flap of leather, nailed to the post. "Oh," Kuruk said. Tuck edged his mare over for a closer look.

He needed a few moments to understand what he was seeing. It was a piece of . . . something, tacked at the top and hanging loose beneath. There were two holes, about five inches down from the top. Below them was a protuberance, then another, larger hole, and a few more inches below that to the bottom.

When it became clear, he shuddered. "It's a face."

"That's what I thought," Cale said. "I seen one before. Is it . . . ?"

"It's human."

"I think I'm gonna be sick."

"Save it," Kuruk advised. "There's worse to come."

"Worse?" Cale asked.

"Worse."

The scout had already passed through the gate. Tuck didn't want to know what he had seen that made him say that, but he had to find out. No point in coming all this way if they didn't finish what they'd started. "Come on, Cale," he said. "We'll meet it together, whatever it is."

"Thanks, Mr. Bringloe," Cale said. He didn't sound at all cheered by the idea.

The stench that had been present but subdued since they had entered Montclair's land, cut by the rain and the plant life, was much stronger here, and the chill was more pronounced. Tuck shivered and swept his gaze across the area inside the fence. He saw perhaps a dozen buildings, including a solid looking adobe ranch house, a good-sized barn, a couple of bunkhouses, a tack house, and others with less immediately apparent uses. Scattered around those were mesquites and yuccas, and the ranch house was nestled among live oaks that had spilled out of the mountains the ranch shouldered up against.

At first glance, it looked like any other thriving ranch. But the moonlight was too bright to allow him to ignore the rest of the scene.

Piles of bones gleamed in the silvery light, each about five feet tall and topped with a layer of human skulls, vacant-eyed and grinning. Hanging by ropes from the branches of the oaks were arms and legs, hands and feet, in various stages of decomposition. Jutting from the ground in spots, as if they had rooted there along with the trees and brush, were poles, ten feet tall and sturdy enough to hold the corpses impaled on them. Lines stretched from the house to some of the trees, the poles, even to stakes driven into the ground as if around a tent, and tied

to those lines were more body parts: faces and scalps, long peelings of flesh as if from torsos or backs, and more.

Tuck's mother, he thought, would have felt right at home.

Cale leaned off the side of his horse and retched. Tuck stayed close until he was done. He felt for the boy. He was sickened, too, at the inhuman cruelty before them. Whatever else Montclair was, he was a monster of the first order.

Tuck worried all the more for Little Wing, and even Sadie.

The buildings seemed empty. The front door of the house was wide open, and moths clouded the doorway, drawn by the glow of lamps from within. Delahunt and Johnson dismounted and took a quick look inside. When they returned, they were ashen. "Just like out here," Delahunt reported. "Only worse. Ain't nobody inside, though."

"Let's keep going, then," Tuck said. The ground between the house and barn was heavily trodden. Lots of people had passed through, and recently. He followed the trail. Cuttrell came behind him, then Kuruk and Cale. Delahunt and Johnson flanked the wagon as it trundled along after them.

Between the house and the mountains, things were even stranger. There were dozens of small, rough-hewn structures back there, little more than lean-tos constructed from branches, yucca stalks, and skins. Those, Tuck realized with a grimace, were both animal and human. Bones were scattered everywhere, not neatly stacked like the ones in front. This place was an abattoir, and had been for a long time. He kept riding, though his horse stepped lightly, snorting often, obviously disturbed by the surroundings.

The small structures continued, seventy or eighty or more, leading away from the house and up into the foothills. From the reeking miasma around them, Tuck was sure these were the dwelling places of those creatures Little Wing had called "not-men." There must have been more than he could have imagined.

But where were they? And where were Montclair and Little Wing and Sadie Cuttrell? The trail led up, through a fringe of oaks and into a deep, shadowy canyon. It was narrower here, choked with trees and huge rocks. He wasn't sure the battle-wagon could negotiate it much farther. Water coursed through streambeds and creeks that had sat bone-dry for most of the year. The scents of mountain air and rich vegetation would have been invigorating, but for the remnant stink of the not-men.

"I don't like this," Kuruk said.

"You and me both."

"We celebrate the Mountain Spirits," Kuruk continued. "The *Gah'e* are dancers who represent them in our ceremonies. The Chiricahua, I'm talking about, my people. The Mountain Spirits keep us safe from enemies and disease. But when they're angered, they're very dangerous. I don't know if Montclair is using the Mountain Spirits, but if he is, and has somehow twisted them into spirits that murder and mutilate, then . . ." He let the sentence trail off, then swallowed and picked it up again. "Anyhow, there's gonna be trouble ahead. Bad trouble."

"You don't have to come, Kuruk," Tuck said. "We're all volunteers, here."

"Little Wing is up there," Kuruk said. "I'm going."

"Fair enough," Tuck said. His words were swallowed by a deafening peal of thunder. Lightning threw the canyon ahead into stark contrast, trees and boulders catching the brilliant flare against the shadowed walls. On the tail of the thunder, he heard something that sounded like a voice, speaking words in a language he didn't know. It boomed from deep in the canyon's upper reaches, and when the thunder faded, he still heard it. Although the lightning was gone, lights still flashed in the distance, rolling through the treetops like tumbleweed across a flat plain.

"What the hell's that?" Johnson asked.

"It's a voice," Cuttrell replied. "It's *Montclair's* voice."

"It's so loud," Cale said.

"This is no good," Kuruk said. "He's messing with things he don't understand."

"Or he does understand 'em," Delahunt said. "Might could be worse that way."

"Can't argue with that," Tuck said. "But we're here. Let's find out what's going on."

While they were stopped, the hatch on the wagon's cupola opened and McKenna climbed out. He was dripping with sweat, as soaked as if he had been out in the rain. "I don't know how you did that for so long, Willie," he said. "It's killin' me."

"Take five, Lieutenant," Cuttrell said. "There's no point in us killing ourselves before we engage the enemy."

McKenna stepped down from the wagon and stretched. He was standing beside it, arms reaching toward the sky, when Cuttrell gave a cry of alarm. A leafy branch of an oak tree had stretched out and encircled his neck. By the time Tuck saw what was happening, the colonel was being lifted out of his saddle and McKenna was rushing toward him. The lieutenant sprang off a boulder and into the air, grabbing the branch with both hands. His weight pulled it down, and it released Cuttrell. McKenna let go with his right hand and drew a big knife. He hacked at the branch, which writhed in his grip like a kraken's tentacle. It fought back, whipping him around, but McKenna kept stabbing and slashing. Cuttrell drew a pistol, as did Tuck, but neither man dared to shoot with the thing swinging McKenna this way and that.

Finally, in what Tuck guessed must have been its death throes, the branch lashed out three times. On the last, McKenna lost his grip—or it let go of him—and went flying. The branch slumped beside the trunk like a relaxed arm, but McKenna slammed into a rock. Johnson reached him first, then Kuruk.

When Johnson turned back to the others, his cheeks glistened with tears. "He's gone," the soldier said. "Lieutenant's gone."

"Yup," Kuruk agreed. "Hit his head pretty good."

"Get him on the wagon," Tuck suggested. "I'm not leaving him. Who knows if this place will look the same next time we come through."

"You mean *if* we come through," Delahunt said. "*Trees* are attacking us, now. What else'll get after us?"

"There's no telling," Tuck said. "But I have a hunch it'll only get worse from here. Anybody want to turn back?"

"Y'all need me," Johnson said. "Sergeant and I are the only ones know how to operate the battlewagon."

The thunderous voice and strange lights had continued from the higher reaches, though Tuck had hardly noticed them while McKenna battled the animated branch. He worried about those, but even without them, he worried about being trapped here in the dark, surrounded by not-men and who could say what else? They were here, though, and he meant to see it through.

He pointed toward the lights. "That's where we're headed," he said. "No telling what the trail might be like from here."

"There must be a way," Johnson said as he climbed into the cupola. "You find it, and I'll follow it." He slammed the hatch and worked the controls, and the wagon lurched forward.

As Cuttrell swung up into the saddle again, an eagle swooped low, just past his head. He yanked his pistol and tried to lead it, but it flew in a zigzag pattern, gaining and losing elevation while staying close by. Just enough moonlight struck its wings to keep it visible.

"Don't shoot!" Kuruk shouted. "That's Little Wing!"

"It's a damn bird," Cuttrell said. "Or worse."

"No, it's her! She wants us to follow!"

"Bringloe?" Cuttrell asked.

What makes me an expert? Tuck almost said. Instead, he shrugged. "Kuruk's usually right about these things, seems like."

Cuttrell gave in. The eagle circled around until they were all in motion again, and then it struck off along a route none of them had noticed. This way offered an easier path for the wagon, which clanked and sputtered and whistled its way up into the canyon. It was noisy, but the racket from above was enough to nearly drown it out. At least, Tuck thought, anyone in the vicinity of whatever was making that noise—the voice that boomed like cannon fire, and another sound, sibilant and sinister at the same time—would be unlikely to hear them coming.

If they were headed toward what he was starting to be afraid they were, a single battlewagon might not be enough. A dozen would be better, but he wouldn't be entirely comfortable unless he had fifty or more on his side.

Chapter Fifty-two

Some of you," Montclair thundered, "have already eaten of my queen. My Sadie." He made a sweeping gesture toward her, standing naked behind him on a dais formed from the bones of the dead. Thunder Moon's skull rested on an altar of bone and skin. Before him were gathered more than a hundred of his abominations. Many of them blended together, black against black, almost invisible in the shadows except when his witch fire roiled overhead. Those of a more human cast were easier to distinguish. At the mention of Sadie's name, the abominations chittered and hissed or shouted their appreciation. "From her, you gained the strength to capture this one and bring her to me." This time he used the long-bladed dagger in his left hand to indicate Little Wing, who still wore the loose blouse and long skirt she'd had when they had delivered her.

"When you feast upon *her* heart," he went on, "you will become more powerful still. Stronger, fleeter of foot, more cunning, more deft in every way." And more easily controlled than ever, he thought but did not add. "You will fulfill your promise to Thunder Moon, and your promise to me, who has earned his mantle by dint of blood and fire, terror and death. You have been allowed to feed to your hearts' content, to prey upon any beast or being you happened upon, human or otherwise. Once you have consumed the heart of one so gifted, your needs will change, as will your abilities and your mission. No longer will you be confined to these mountains and their environs. No

more will the resting place of Thunder Moon's skull bind you to it. Instead, you will be at liberty to roam, to plunder and pillage, to rend and tear and destroy whatever comes into view."

And they would want to, because he would so will it. His goal was for them to fan out, to Tombstone and Tucson and beyond, to every town, large and small, to every ranch and village and camp they could find. In all those places, they would indulge their deepest hungers, which were terrible indeed.

In this way, they would—at his behest and to his benefit— spread terror and death across the land. The blood of thousands would be spilled onto the earth, and in turn, the earth would transform in the manner of his choosing.

Finding the skull of Thunder Moon, claiming the power stored within it over the centuries, was only one step. It was a building block for his greater goal—to terrorform the land into a bridge that spanned the mystical distance between the world of humans and the supernatural plane called the Hunting Grounds. From there, he would bring knowledge into the world, and with it true, raw power, the kind never before known by man.

And he would be its vessel. He would carry it into this world, and when he did, he would remake all he saw.

The abominations looked on. If they'd had faces, expressions, they would have been expectant, but he could tell from the silence and the way they leaned toward him that they were waiting. He had tested their patience long enough. He spoke seven more words in the old tongue, and turned to Little Wing, standing behind him. The clouds had parted and the full light of the Thunder Moon shone upon her. He brushed her cheek with his right hand—she flinched, only slightly thanks to the spell that held her still—and then he raised the dagger high in his left and spoke one more word of power and drove it into her breast.

For a moment, nothing happened.

No spurt of blood. No look of shock, of pain. She wouldn't be able to fall, but he expected that her knees would buckle. They didn't. He tugged the blade free. It came out as clean as it had gone in.

She looked at him and smiled. Had he missed her heart, somehow? He drove it in again, through the fabric of her blouse, through flesh and fat and muscle, felt it glance off bone.

Nothing.

But then he noticed that the handle was warming. No, getting *hot,* and in less time than it took to reach that conclusion, it was too scorching to hold. He yanked it from her and dropped it in the same motion, and in the sudden quiet it was loud against the bone dais on which he stood.

The abominations stared. Horror gripped him for a moment, as he feared that this failure would break his hold on them and they would storm the dais, tearing him apart as they had done to so many others over the centuries.

And yet, in the instant before panic overtook him, he caught the scent of something, beneath that of his abominations and the aroma of the one called Little Wing, so rich with potential. He looked to his left, where a rocky ridge overlooked the natural amphitheater in which the creatures had gathered, and he pointed toward those he knew had to be there.

"Intruders!" he cried. He lifted Thunder Moon's skull and shook it before returning it to the altar. "Defilers of Thunder Moon's memory! Enemies of us all! Start there, my abominations! Feast on them, so we can continue what we came here to do!"

Almost as one, the abominations turned and started to attack.

The stench was almost overwhelming, and the cold flowing from the canyon penetrated clothing and flesh alike. There were so many of the not-men, and they were packed into a clear, bowl-shaped space at the bottom of a canyon. Some looked human, or nearly so. Those wore black clothing and hats and were armed with pistols, rifles, or both. The rest were the sort of featureless, vaguely human-shaped black figures Tuck had seen before. They faced Montclair and Sadie, both naked, and Little Wing, the three of them standing on a stage made of bones. He and the others had stopped behind an outcropping of boulders big enough to hide them and the wagon, elevated slightly above the clearing, and watched the proceedings from there. Tuck hadn't known what to expect, and the scene they had found was beyond anything that had ever haunted his worst nightmares.

When that knife had gone into Little Wing's heart, Cale had cried out so loudly that Tuck was sure Montclair would hear him. Kuruk had remained silent, but his hand had gripped Tuck's shoulder almost hard enough to draw blood.

Then Montclair was pointing at their hiding place and shouting, and the mass of not-men flooded toward them.

"Bring that wagon around quick!" Delahunt ordered. He jumped into the second cupola while Johnson responded to the command, and the battlewagon chugged into a position beside the rocks from which the Gatling guns had clear lines of fire.

Tuck, Cale, Kuruk, and Cuttrell kept their sheltered positions and opened fire with their rifles, though Tuck doubted they would be effective against those creatures. Their horses, picketed behind them, stomped and whinnied their discomfort. Tuck didn't blame them a bit.

The Gatling guns both opened fire at once. The automatic crank made the ratcheting sound regular and mechanical. The barrels emptied and rotated and the rounds plowed into the thick of the advancing horde, each one exploding upon impact. The effect was immediate. Not-men were blown apart, shards of black scattering everywhere, like raven feathers in a tornado.

Tuck derived no pleasure from the sight. Even as their comrades—if that word could apply to such inhuman creatures—fell, others advanced. He reloaded his rifle, rested it back on the rock he'd been using to steady it, and continued firing. Most of the not-men were unarmed, though he'd seen enough examples of the damage they could do without guns to let that cloud his view. Others fired rifles and pistols toward the rocks. Stone chips flew up from a close one, stinging Tuck's face. The bitter smoke of rifles and Gatling guns filled his nose and mouth, which was a marked improvement over the stink of what Montclair had called his abominations.

To Tuck's right, Kuruk lay atop a flat rock, firing down into the oncoming mob. Cale was on his other side, shooting and ducking, shooting and ducking. His shots were wild, and his cheeks were wet with tears.

On Cale's left, Colonel Cuttrell fired through a gap between two boulders that served as a natural battlement. He matched Tuck, shot for shot. Picking a target was no challenge; in that sea of black, every shot hit something. Whether those rounds did any damage was another question, but at least they were shooting, and the barrage seemed to hold the not-men back for the moment.

Then Tuck noticed that the colonel had stopped firing. He was staring down through the gap, the rifle forgotten in his gloved hands. "Colonel?" Tuck said. "You all right?"

"Sadie," Cuttrell said. "She's hurt!"

Tuck had noticed her, there on the dais behind Montclair. But his attention had been on Montclair and Little Wing. He was embarrassed by Sadie's nudity, and had looked away from her. He risked another glance and saw what Cuttrell must have noticed: what looked like a massive, open gash between her breasts.

"She's upright," he said. "She doesn't act injured."

"You can see it from here, man!" Cuttrell countered. "I've got to get her out of there."

He took a moment to reload his rifle. "Colonel," Tuck said, "you can't go down there. There're too many of those things. You'll never make it."

"She's the whole reason I came, Bringloe. I've made mistakes. I've mistreated her terribly. But I need her. Without her, what am I?"

You're a man on your own account, Tuck wanted to say. Were before you met her and will be again. But how did you tell a man he was too late to save his wife, or that the effort wasn't worth making? He took one more look. She was standing, all right, but stiffly, not moving. Her gaze appeared to be resting on some indeterminate point before and slightly above her, not on the abominations or Montclair or Little Wing. She seemed unconnected to anything around her. Her flesh was ghostly pale.

He was convinced that she was already beyond help. He didn't know how that could be, but when it came to Montclair—to anything that happened around Carmichael—he had stopped asking that question. "Cuttrell," he said. "She's already dead. Look at her!"

"Mr. Bringloe, I apologize for the way I treated you, in my office," Cuttrell said. "I hope you'll forgive my rudeness." Without waiting for a response, he started around the rocks and down into the valley.

Tuck tried to lay down covering fire for him, but without knowing if his rounds did any damage to the not-men, he couldn't gauge its effectiveness. He raced to the wagon and pounded on Delahunt's cupola. "Cover Cuttrell!" he shouted when the sergeant opened the door. "He's going in there!"

"He's a lunatic!" Delahunt said.

"I know! Just try to keep him alive!"

"Got it!" Delahunt returned to his task, and started aiming his explosive rounds at anyone threatening Cuttrell. His marksmanship was uncanny, Tuck realized; each round was finding its mark. Johnson's too. Tuck used the catapult to hurl some bombs into the crowd ahead of Cuttrell, then hustled back toward his rifle position. He paused beside Cale for a moment. "Hit what you can," he said. "All we're doing is slowing 'em down anyway. It's those Gatling guns that'll win the day."

Cale grunted something in response. The young man was badly shaken, and Tuck couldn't blame him. Punching cows did nothing to prepare someone for combat against vicious, inhuman beasts. Cale had never seen war, and the kind confronting him now was nasty and brutal.

Tuck took up his spot again, and resumed firing at the advancing horde.

Chapter Fifty-three

Little Wing couldn't move, but that didn't mean she couldn't help.

She didn't believe the skull Montclair clutched was the sole source of his magic. He was too practiced, too proficient, and she could tell by the way he held it that the skull was new and unfamiliar to him. It was more of an engine, powering his existing abilities to new heights.

He was too powerful for her to block, if that was even a capability she had. She was still learning about herself and her own gifts, day by day. There were, however, some things she did know.

One of those was that she could share her gift, in a manner of speaking. Whatever power was in her wasn't truly hers. It belonged to no one, but it could, on occasion, be borrowed. And what could be borrowed could be loaned. The men who were under attack—men who she could tell even from here included Kuruk and Cale and Bringloe—had gifts of their own. Not like hers, but they had their own abilities, talents, and skills. And while she could not grant them the power to do what she was able to, she could enhance their individual abilities. She reached inside herself, found the force humming at her center, gathered it and beamed it out toward the men on the hill and the colonel, who had left his companions behind and was riding into the thick of it.

When it touched them, she felt it, like sinking into warm water. She had to smile, despite the brutality that took place around her. Good couldn't outweigh evil—if it did, there would be no evil left in the world. But good made a difference, just the same, and she believed that what she had done was good. No matter what else happened, she could hold fast to that.

Cuttrell urged his charger down into the mass of the enemy force, the men and the vaguely manlike figures trying to swarm him. He wore twin Colts, and he gripped the reins with his left hand and fired with his right. He used his ammunition judiciously, only shooting when one was close enough to be a threat, or when he saw one of the more human ones aiming a weapon at him. He wasn't sure how much impact his bullets had; the creatures seemed able to absorb them, exhibiting little damage. The men in the battlewagon were helping, carving a path for him with their explosive rounds.

As he emptied the last round from his second pistol and considered whether to try to reload under these conditions, an odd sensation passed through him. It was almost as if he had passed through a membrane of some kind, warm and slightly sticky. A kind of peace enveloped him, a sense that he had all the time in the world. He pulled the hammer back to a half cock, opened the loading gate, slipped bullets from the loops on his gun belt and inserted them into the cylinder, filling every chamber. His fingers were sure, his touch with the reins he held in the same hand as the Colt deft. Within moments, the gun was reloaded. He raised it, cocked, and aimed, squeezing the trigger while keeping the horse moving toward his goal with minute adjustments of his weight and the pressure of his legs. He had never in his life felt like such a skilled horseman, or gunman, for that matter.

Every shot he fired found its mark. He could almost follow the trajectory with his eyes, though he was certain that was impossible.

Where before, he hadn't been sure his bullets had any effect, now he watched the featureless things drop before his assault.

He looked ahead and saw Sadie standing on the dais of bones. She had spotted him, and she stared, open-mouthed. Was that a trace of a smile on her lips? He wasn't sure.

She moved to the stand on which Montclair had placed the skull he had held up earlier. With stiff motions, as if she'd been sleeping for too long, or confined, she lifted the horrible thing.

Cuttrell's gun was empty again, and despite his best efforts and the work of the men in the battlewagon, the enemy horde was closing in around him. Rather than reload again, he hurled the weapon at the nearest one and drew his saber. As the creatures swarmed him, he slashed down, slicing through boneless torsos and limbs. Some fell away, but others seemed to mend themselves, their flesh—or whatever it was—closing up right after his blade passed through. Others, he stabbed, with similarly mixed results.

Just the same, he made steady progress toward his goal. He would, he was certain, reach Sadie. He would sweep her off the dais and into his arms, then turn his horse around and retreat back up the hill. Sadie was the reason he had come—if the others wanted to engage Montclair after he had her, that was up to them.

She still held the skull, and had lifted it above her head, her arms fully extended. Thunder rolled overhead and lightning tore the sky. As Cuttrell watched, she turned the skull so that those dark, empty eye sockets were pointed directly at him. He didn't understand what she was doing. Surely that wasn't an expression of loving kindness, but what was it?

Then lightning shredded the night again. A bolt lanced toward Sadie. Cuttrell had an instant to fear that he had lost her, but she remained standing, skull held toward the heavens.

He barely had time for gratitude before lightning blasted out from both of its empty eye sockets. He saw it coming in the same strange way he had seemed able to see bullets rocket toward their targets. Every hair on his body stood on end, and his flesh felt like there were ants crawling about beneath it. Then the lightning reached him, and heat and hair and ants and Sadie were all forgotten.

Chapter Fifty-four

Tuck closed his eyes against the blinding brilliance of the twin lightning bolts. When he opened them again, Cuttrell and his mount had fallen to the ground. Smoke rose from their corpses, and the colonel wasn't recognizably himself anymore, or—in his curled-up, blackened state—very distinguishable from the not-men swarming over him.

Looking away, Tuck swore softly. Their tiny force was being winnowed away, bit by bit, and they were no closer to reaching Little Wing. Kuruk was right about Sadie—she was on Montclair's side in this. And probably dead, besides.

He had experienced a strange moment of absolute peace and clarity, after which his eyesight seemed to have improved, along with his aim and his command of his weapons. Watching the others, he was sure they had felt the same thing. Even Cale was firing with calm purpose.

"I'm going for Little Wing," Kuruk said.

"I'll go, too!" Cale cried.

"No, boy," Kuruk said. "Stay with Mr. Bringloe. I'll get her."

"You saw what happened to Cuttrell," Tuck argued. "Wait till we've killed more of them!"

"She can help us."

"I think she already is."

"More, then. Anyhow. I'm going."

"Kuruk . . ." Tuck began. But the scout was already slipping down off the rock he had been shooting from. He reloaded his rifle and his pistol, checked the knife in its beaded sheath on his belt, and started down the hill without looking back.

Tuck didn't like it, but Kuruk was his own man. He was pleased that Cale seemed willing to obey the scout; he squatted on the ground and reloaded his rifle. "Barrel's hot," he said.

"They'll do that. Don't touch it any more than you have to."

"Reckon I'm getting used to it, though. I'm shooting better."

"We all are," Tuck said. "Little Wing's doing, I think."

"What *is* she?"

"I don't know, Cale. She's something special, but I don't know what."

"Will Kuruk be all right?"

"I hope so. We'll have to do what we can to keep him safe." He went back to the catapult and once again loosed bombs into the crowd. The wagon offered cover, but bullets from those of the not-men who were human enough to use firearms were coming closer.

"Cover Kuruk!" Tuck shouted, loading another bomb into the sling.

Delahunt flung open the hatch and leaned out. "What'd you say?"

"Kuruk's headed—"

He stopped mid-sentence when a bullet caught Delahunt under the cheek, tore into his head and blew out the other side, misting the battlewagon with blood.

In the other cupola, Johnson was still blasting away with what seemed like a never-ending supply of explosive rounds.

"Damn it!" Tuck said. Delahunt, McKenna, and Johnson were the only ones with any training or practice with the battlewagon. But the wagon was the one weapon they had that was effective against Montclair's abominations. "Keep shooting, Cale!" he called. "Try to hold 'em back as long as you can."

"What are you gonna do?" Cale asked.

Tuck climbed onto the wagon. Delahunt lay half inside the cupola. Blood and brains coated the near side of the steam engine. Tuck had to muscle the big man out of the hatchway, and although

Delahunt deserved respect, there was no time for it. He rolled the corpse off the side of the wagon and let it fall into the mud.

More bullets thudded into the wagon's bed, stopped by the thick wood and ghost steel. The not-men had the range and they were getting too close. Tuck crawled into the cupola and slammed the hatch.

He had seen the controls inside the cupolas, back at the fort. He had thought it would be impossible to learn without several lessons. But as soon as he put his hands on the levers and knobs, he knew what was what and how to use everything. He peered out through the nearest window and it seemed to magnify the view. It somehow brightened the scene, too, making it look more like dusk than full dark. The first wave of not-men was almost on them. He squeezed a control lever, and a long jet of flame shot out from the fire-spitter.

Not-men burst into flames as if they were made of lamp oil. The rest fell back. Tuck shot another burst at them, to hold them away.

This was an incredible weapon, he thought. Delahunt was a genius. A mad, dead genius. He squeezed another lever and felt the thrum of the Gatling gun vibrating through him as it fired its rounds. The magnifying window showed him the not-men blowing apart as they struck.

But watching the scene through that window, he saw four not-men rush Kuruk. The scout fired two shots with his rifle, then turned it around and swung it like a club, smashing the butt into the nearest abomination. The thing grabbed the rifle, so Kuruk let it go and whipped his knife from the sheath. He stabbed the closest one several times, and it dropped away, only to be replaced by more. Kuruk killed another one, but there were too many. One came from behind and shoved an arm deep into Kuruk's back. They swarmed around Kuruk, too close for Tuck to risk firing. One explosive round would kill Kuruk along with the not-men.

But if he didn't act, they would kill the scout anyway.

Shoot or not? The choice ripped him apart, as surely as that blade-sharp arm sliced through Kuruk's flesh. Either way, Kuruk was dead. If he didn't shoot, though, the creatures that killed him would live to kill others.

Tuck hated killing. Sometimes, however, he had no choice.

He squeezed the trigger and watched as explosive rounds darted toward the abominations, then blew them apart into fiery, black chunks.

And Kuruk, too. Through eyes suddenly full of tears, Tuck saw the blast shred Kuruk's face, open his chest, rip an arm off just below the shoulder, and hurl it ten feet away.

It was down to him, Cale, and Johnson, against nearly a hundred abominations, darkly sinister creatures that would overrun their position in minutes.

Little Wing was still a prisoner, Montclair still in charge.

This adventure had been a gigantic mistake, start to finish. He had convinced good men to join him on a fool's errand, and those men had died. The only question remaining was whether he could get Johnson and Cale out of there before they fell, too, or would they all die together.

He eased off the trigger and opened the hatch again. With the fire-spitter, he believed he could hold off the abominations long enough to give the others a head start. Maybe they'd survive the night, even if he wouldn't.

But once his head was outside the cupola, he heard something unexpected: the steady rumble of approaching riders; the creak of leather and the jingle of steel. Somebody was coming up the hill behind them, and it didn't sound like more of Montclair's not-men. Tuck eased back into the cupola and swung it around, ready to open up on whoever showed himself.

A few moments later, the first riders came into view. They were CSA troopers, wearing partial uniforms or full. Tuck lowered the weapon and climbed out. "What are you men doing here?" he asked. "We've got serious trouble down below."

"That's why we came," the man in front said. He wore the single star of a major on his collar. "Figgered you might could use a hand."

"But . . ." Tuck began.

"Close your mouth, Tucker," a woman's voice said, "unless you're *trying* to catch flies."

He thought the voice was familiar, but it wasn't until Missy Haynes rode out from behind the major and a few other soldiers that he was certain. "Missy? What is all this?"

"Some of us noticed you weren't around. You and a few others. We happened to know where there were plenty of troopers with nothing better to do—well, nothing better that wouldn't cost them."

"So you tracked us up here?" Tuck asked.

"T'weren't hard," the major said. "That wagon leaves a mighty clear trail."

"How many men do you have?"

"Hunnert n' fifty," the major replied. "Give or take."

"And about thirty-five women," Missy added. "Not just from Senora Soto's. We got girls from every house in town."

"Armed?"

"Believe it."

"I don't quite know what to say."

"Just tell us who to shoot," the major suggested. "We'll do the rest."

Tuck briefly explained the situation. "Better hurry, though," he said as he finished. "They're coming fast. We've been holding them off with fire and that Gatling, but it won't work forever."

"Bugler," the major said. "Sound the charge."

Within seconds, a bugle call turned the quiet rumble of their advance into a roar of hooves and voices and gunfire. The reinforcements crested the hill at a gallop, then rode into the enemy's midst. Tuck watched them go—soldiers and soiled doves alike, all brandishing weapons—shaking his head slowly as he did.

Chapter Fifty-five

Tuck stopped one of the troopers and had him take over inside the battlewagon. A few seconds of instruction was plenty; the young soldier took to it as if he'd been born there. Jumping down from the wagon, Tuck saw Cale still at his position by the rocks. "Take a break, son," he said. "Let the troopers do their jobs." He glanced down and saw that the soldiers had already engaged the abominations and were making progress. "They've got it well in hand, looks like."

"But . . . look!" Cale said. "At that altar or whatever it is, that bone thing!"

Tuck looked. The dais was empty; even the old skull was gone. Montclair, Sadie, and Little Wing were nowhere to be seen. "Where'd they go?" Tuck asked.

"I'm not sure. I was watching those things coming up toward us, then the soldiers riding to meet them. When I looked back, I saw some of them critters grab hold of Little Wing and hoist her up over their shoulders. Mr. Montclair, he took the skeleton head and they all went back into them shadows, Mrs. Cuttrell, too. I can't see 'em no more, and I don't know where they're going."

"Let's see if we can't head them off," Tuck said. "They might not be moving too fast, carrying the women like that. Especially if Little Wing can slow them down some."

"But we don't know which way—"

"We'll get between them and the ranch. If we don't see them that way, we hurry the other and try to catch up."

"I don't . . ."

Tuck had about lost patience with the boy. "Look, you want to find her, or don't you?"

"Yeah, but—"

"Then quit wasting time. Let's go."

Tuck started off without waiting to see if Cale would follow. After a few seconds, he heard the crunch of the young man's feet and the huff of his breath. At the base of the hill the eagle had led them up, another path had forked off on a lower course. Tuck was sure that one led to the clearing Montclair had used; the muddy trail had been thoroughly churned by the passage of many feet. If Montclair was heading back to his ranch headquarters or any place beyond that, he would take that route, like as not. From the fork, it was farther to the clearing than to the place among the boulders the eagle had shown them, so if they hurried they could still get ahead of Montclair and his captives.

Of course, if Montclair went deeper into the mountains, in any direction, he would be harder to find. He didn't know what Montclair had in mind, although from what Tuck had seen it didn't look like Little Wing would survive whatever it was. That meant time was a factor, in addition to location. They had to catch up with Montclair, and fast.

The worry had barely passed through Tuck's mind when the screech of an eagle sounded overhead, followed by the furious flapping of wings. He looked up and saw the same eagle that had guided them before. "It's her!" Cale shouted.

"I believe you're right," Tuck said. "Follow her!"

The eagle led them away from the path they had taken on the way up. For a few minutes, Tuck wondered if they had made a mistake; this way was thickly overgrown and barely passable. But then it widened into a game trail that appeared to cut a more direct path toward the ranch. This way would have been far too narrow and steep for the wagon, but a couple of people on foot could negotiate it.

"Is this the way Montclair's going, Little Wing?" Tuck shouted at the eagle. The bird gave a short screech in seeming reply and continued to lead the way out of the mountains.

Soon, they passed between the rough dwellings of the not-men, with the ranch headquarters visible beyond, silver-edged in the moonlight. All was quiet. If Montclair was coming, he wasn't here yet.

"Let's take up ambush positions," Tuck said. "We don't know for sure as they're coming, but if they are we want to be ready." He pointed out a likely spot for Cale in a pool of shade beneath a stout-trunked oak, then found one for himself under one of the not-men's lean-tos, and settled in to wait.

The wait wasn't long. Ten minutes, maybe fifteen, Tuck judged. It seemed longer, though, on account of the stench of the not-men that lingered in the shelter. Every few minutes he stuck his head out of it to suck in some fresher air. Then he heard voices, raised in anger. Sadie's came first, and he recognized it despite a certain flatness in her tone. "I don't know why we have to drag her around," she was saying. "She's just in the way."

"We need her," Montclair countered.

"Why? You have me. You have Thunder Moon. You have the abominations—what's left of them, anyway, after you let them get slaughtered."

The voices grew louder as the speakers neared, and soon Tuck heard the sounds of their footsteps. Montclair said, "She's too powerful to simply ignore, Sadie. Yes, I am powerful—more so, perhaps, than any man who's ever lived. With you and Thunder Moon by my side, I am even more so. But with her . . . if I can harness her power, yoke it to my own, I will truly be unstoppable. That is what you want, after all, isn't it? An all-powerful companion? To be queen to my king?"

"Yes, of course, but—what's that?"

"What?" Montclair asked.

"You don't smell it? Humans. Close by."

"Yes, perhaps. But—"

Tuck had heard enough. If they didn't act, they would lose the slender advantage of surprise.

He lunged from the lean-to with a shout and brought his rifle up, firing three times at Montclair. The range wasn't quite point-blank, but it was near enough, and Tuck's aim was true. The rounds slammed into the naked man, slid off him, and dropped to the ground. Montclair didn't bat an eye.

At the same time, Cale broke from cover and opened fire on the three not-men surrounding the one carrying Little Wing. Two rushed toward Cale, who levered and fired as fast as he could.

This wasn't working. Those things would rip Cale to pieces, then turn on Tuck. He'd hoped that if he could put Montclair down, his minions would give up the fight. He hadn't counted on Montclair being able to withstand close-up rifle fire. He levered another round into the chamber, fired, levered.

Empty.

Tuck hurled the rifle at Montclair, who just batted it away. Tuck had killed one of the abominations with a knife before, though Turville had wounded it first. He didn't know if he could kill three, but he had to try. Darting to where Cale was about to be overrun, he wished Little Wing could do something to help. As he ran, he drew his knife. He barreled into the abominations without slowing, knocking the first one back into his fellows. Although the stink and the cold nearly overwhelmed him, he slashed and stabbed at anything he could reach.

One of the creatures sliced Tuck's right side with a dagger-edged hand. Tuck bit back a cry and tried to ignore the pain. He kept fighting; he could tell his blade was cutting through something, though he didn't know what. He fought furiously, savagely, grunting with exertion as he stabbed again and again, barely cognizant of the fact that Cale had joined in.

Then Montclair's voice boomed. "Leave them, my abomina-tions," he ordered. "You have done well, but I will finish this in my own fashion."

The not-men obeyed immediately, releasing Tuck and Cale

and backing away. Tuck noted with grim satisfaction that one still lay on the ground, its limbs scraping at the earth as if it were trying to honor its master's wishes, even as whatever life it possessed slipped away.

Tuck wanted to say something to Montclair, but he didn't know what. "You won't get away with this" came to mind, but that was a lie, since to all appearances he already had. He wanted to remind Montclair that he was human, too, or had been. He wanted to tell Montclair that all the power in the world wasn't worth the lives he'd taken, the misery he'd sown. But the words wouldn't come, and in the end, he kept his mouth shut.

As did Montclair. The man didn't bother with a speech or even a threat. He started to raise the skull. In the same moment, the eagle swept down from the sky and attacked Little Wing.

No, that was wrong. It landed on her, but it was tearing at the ropes that bound her, using beak and claws. In just an instant, she was free.

Quickly, Montclair raised the skull higher. Lightning flashed overhead and thunder rocked the earth. Sadie and one of the abominations grabbed at Little Wing, but she dodged them and made straight for Montclair. He was speaking his incantatory phrases, and above him, the sky was alive with electricity.

The eagle arrowed straight into his hands, and the skull tumbled from his grasp.

Chapter Fifty-six

Little Wing lunged for it.

Her feet left the ground and she soared for several feet, eluding the reach of another abomination. She caught the shaman's skull in her outstretched left hand, and as she dropped back toward earth, she brought it to her, closing her right hand over it and tucking it against her chest. She landed shoulder first, rolled, then sprang to her feet, yards away from the astonished Montclair.

"Young lady," he said, holding out his hand as if she would simply give it back. "You have no idea what you've got there."

"I think I do," Little Wing replied. "It is the skull of the shaman Thunder Moon, murdered by men from the Coronado expedition in 1540."

"How . . ." Montclair began.

"You are not the only person who knows about arcane subjects, Mr. Montclair. Or who can pick up impressions from ancient artifacts."

"Its power is enormous. Give it back before you hurt someone."

"I know about its power," Little Wing countered. "I can feel it." She lifted the thing even with her face and held it there, eyeball to empty socket. "He really does not like you, Mr. Montclair."

"Nonsense!" Montclair snapped. He closed the distance to her with a few rapid strides, but when he grabbed at the skull, Little

Wing pirouetted effortlessly away from him. He snatched again, catching only air as she put several more feet between them.

Before he could make another try, she lifted the skull above her head, her arms rigid, elbows locked. At once, lightning blazed across the night sky and thunder crashed. The full moon—the Thunder Moon—shouldered out from behind a mass of dark clouds.

"No!" Montclair cried. "Don't be a fool!"

Holding the skull aloft, Little Wing shouted a single word toward the heavens. In immediate response, a bolt of lightning linked skull and sky. The skull seemed to suck it in, as if inhaling it. It glowed in her hands, red hot, then white. Tuck feared for her life. If nothing else, she would lose both hands.

Little Wing held on to the thing, lowering it until it was once again at her eye level. When she halted its descent, blue fire crackled around its outer surface for a moment. Then lightning erupted from its eye sockets, nose, and mouth. Instead of turning that lightning on someone else, though, Little Wing directed it at herself. Blinding white fire connected her eyes, nose, and mouth to the skull's. Overhead, thunder roared, and all around them lightning jabbed at the earth.

At first, Tuck was certain that what happened next was an illusion, caused perhaps by the blistering brightness before him. He blinked, rubbed his eyes, but he still saw the same thing. Little Wing not only accepted the lightning raging from Thunder Moon's skull, she was, it appeared, thriving. While he watched, open-mouthed, she grew in size. Her proportions didn't change, but she became taller and heavier, as if she were taking in energy from the skull and turning it into mass.

As if that realization had broken a spell that kept everybody rooted, Montclair and Sadie both rushed toward Little Wing. Tuck saw their objective—to wrest the skull from Little Wing before whatever strange ritual was taking place had finished. "Cale!" he shouted, nodding toward Sadie.

Cale tossed him a nod back, to show he understood, and

charged into Sadie Cuttrell, blocking her before she could reach Little Wing. At the same instant, Tuck went for Montclair. He caught the man's shoulders and tried to yank him backward, but Montclair just kept walking, dragging Tuck with him.

Tuck let go and tried a different tack, shoving his leg between Montclair's. Instead of tripping, Montclair kicked it away. Tuck felt like a tree had fallen on it.

Still Montclair trudged toward Little Wing. Tuck grabbed his arm, used that to build momentum to swing around in front of him, and drove his fist into Montclair's jaw.

Montclair flinched, but not much. Tuck punched him again, this time in the gut. Montclair swept his arm in a roundhouse circle that sent Tuck sprawling. Tuck scrambled to his feet again and rushed the man, head down. He plowed into Montclair's back, threw his arms out, and tried to run right through him. Montclair was treating him with the disdain he would a bothersome gnat, and Tuck didn't like it.

This assault staggered Montclair. Just a little, but it gave Tuck hope. He tried to swipe one of Montclair's legs out from under him while punching him, hard, three times, in the solar plexus. Montclair bit his lip and hunched forward.

Tuck planted his feet and tried to hold Montclair back. The man was preternaturally strong and he tried to muscle through, but Tuck held his ground. He kicked at Montclair's knee three times, four, and took pleasure in Montclair's wince when the leg buckled. Tuck threw another couple of punches to the man's jaw. His hand already ached, and he wouldn't be surprised later to find that he had broken some bones in it.

Still, he had gotten to Montclair. The big man tried to shove him roughly from the path, but though Tuck's boots scrabbled and slipped in the mud, he held on. His side, where he'd been slashed, was in agony, bleeding through his shirt. His hands felt like an entire cavalry regiment had galloped over them.

Where at first Montclair's expression had been dismissive, his attention focused on Little Wing, now his face was a mask of rage. He was far stronger than Tuck, and he could have continued swatting at him like a fly, but Tuck had penetrated his resolve. Montclair lowered his shoulders and charged, his arms looping beneath Tuck's and enveloping him in a crushing bear hug. Both men went down in the mud, Tuck on the bottom.

Montclair rose off him, but just for an instant. Then he straddled Tuck, holding him down with his left hand on Tuck's right shoulder. With his right fist, he began pummeling Tuck's face, breaking past the defensive arm Tuck tried to raise. The pain in his side didn't make that any easier. Tuck felt teeth loosen, and worried that one more solid shot would smash his jaw. He had to do something.

Instead of blocking with his left, he threw it out flat and pawed at the earth, hoping to find a big rock or something else he could use as a weapon. His quest, though, seemed in vain. The soft ground offered up nothing hard enough to do real damage. He was trying to brace for the next punishing blow when his fingers touched on something solid. Drawing it into his hand, he grasped it tight—a broken mesquite branch, about as big around as both his thumbs together. Montclair was drawing his fist back, so Tuck, disregarding the half-inch thorns driving into his hand, swung his arm up and jammed the stick as hard as he could into Montclair's right eye.

Montclair screamed in pain, but the blow that had already started to fall continued, and when it slammed into his forehead, Tuck lost consciousness.

Cale was tired of trying to kill Sadie again.

She didn't want to die. He emptied his rifle into her, then his revolver. She didn't quite shrug off the bullets—he saw her jerk when they landed, so she could feel them—but they didn't stop her, either. She didn't bleed. She just kept walking toward Little Wing, who still drank in the energy flowing from that old skull.

So Cale changed his tack. If he couldn't kill her, maybe he could cripple her, and that would be just as good. He gripped his rifle by the barrel and swung it as hard as he could at the backs of her knees. She staggered a little, so he shifted his position and slammed it into her kneecaps. That set her back a couple of steps. He did it again and again. Her pallid flesh tore, showing blood-less muscle beneath, and bone under that. He did it again and again, until finally her right knee separated altogether and that leg flopped uselessly when she tried to move it.

At that, she finally fell over.

He had thought that would be the end of it, but she persisted, trying to drag herself through the mud toward Little Wing.

Cale took his rifle, its stock now splintered, and started in on her arms.

Tuck came around in moments. Montclair's weight was off his chest, but when his vision cleared he saw that the man had once more started toward Little Wing. Reluctantly, every inch of him protesting, Tuck hauled himself upright and caught up to Mont-clair. He drove his boot, hard, into the back of Montclair's calf. Montclair spun around to face him, a look of the purest hatred Tuck had ever seen on his face. That right eye was white-gray jelly laced with blood, oozing from the socket.

"This is about you and me," Tuck said. "We need to finish this. Leave the girl out of it."

"I have no interest in the girl," Montclair said.

"The skull, then?"

Montclair didn't answer. Instead, he took two unsteady steps toward Tuck and swung a fist that drove into Tuck's chest like a sledgehammer. Tuck staggered back, arms pinwheeling, then tripped over one of the small lean-tos and went back down in the mud.

When he rose again, Montclair was closer to Little Wing. Tuck charged, caught Montclair's arm, dragged him back a half step. Montclair swatted him with the back of his hand, and Tuck was down once more.

He got back up. Every time he did, he caught up to Montclair and bought Little Wing another second or two. Every time, Montclair dealt him a punishing blow and sent him reeling. Every time, Tuck rose and tried again.

The last time, he could barely stand. One more shot like that, maybe two, he feared, would be his last. His head was so scrambled he could barely think, could only react. Montclair wanted Little Wing. Little Wing needed time—why, Tuck couldn't say, but she did—so he needed to keep Montclair away from her.

Montclair was almost there, and Tuck's legs wouldn't obey him. He zigzagged this way and that, more unsteady even than the times he'd been too drunk to walk.

Those times, though, he hadn't had a mission. His goal had never been any more profound than sobering up enough to earn a few coins to buy more liquor. Now it was. He floundered his way to Montclair and threw his arms over the man's shoulders, trying to pull him back through sheer weight.

Montclair stopped, shrugged him off. He was hurt, too, Tuck noted with satisfaction. Not as bad, not so nearly fatally, but hurt just the same.

After a few seconds, he realized that Montclair hadn't started forward again, and he wondered why. When he looked, he saw Little Wing standing before them. In her hands was the skull. But Tuck could tell the mystical force had been leached out of it. Before, even when it hadn't been a conduit for lightning, there had been something about it, an invisible energy crackling from it. Now it was a hunk of old bone, nothing more.

And Montclair knew it.

"You are too late, Mr. Montclair," Little Wing said. "What Thunder Moon had, he has given to me. I swallowed it in and drowned it, like a bucket of water does a match."

"You . . . you couldn't have . . ."

"I could," she said. "I did."

"But . . ."

Tuck had an idea that Montclair's incredible strength had been connected, somehow, to that old skull. Even the man's voice was sounding weaker by the second. Tuck twined his fists together and swung them like a club into Montclair's temple. Montclair gave a sound that fell midway between a squeal and a whimper, and sank to the mud.

Coda

Montclair was dead. Tuck looked around with bleary eyes and spotted Cale, squatting beside the form of Sadie Cuttrell, ghostly pale in the moon glow. "Is she . . . ?"

"She's dead," Cale reported. "Finally. She wouldn't die until that skull stopped spitting fire at Little Wing."

"What about the not-men?" Tuck asked, suddenly aware that they were no longer in view. "Why didn't they fight us?"

Little Wing let the skull slip from her fingers. It hit a rock and cracked open, falling in crumbled chunks to the earth. She wore a strange smile, but when she spoke, her voice was weak. "He . . . commanded them to . . . leave you alone. He never gave . . . another order, so . . ."

"So they left us alone," Tuck finished. "And now that he's dead and the skull is dust, they've got no reason to stay. They'll go back into the mountains, or maybe just disappear. Long as they leave me and mine alone, I don't rightly care."

"You . . ." Little Wing began. Without another word, she tumbled forward, landing on her face in the mud.

"Little Wing!" Cale cried. He dashed to her side and crouched beside her, scooping her into his arms. With his fingers, he scraped mud away from her nose and mouth, then tried to wipe it off her forehead and cheeks, smearing it in the process. "Little Wing, are you . . . what happened?"

"Too . . . too much," she managed, her voice barely a whisper.

"Too much?"

"Too much power from that skull, I figure," Tuck said. "Even she couldn't hold up to all that."

Tears streamed down Cale's face, cutting tracks through the caked-on dirt. "I don't understand," he said. "I don't understand any of this. You're getting lighter as I hold you. Who are you, Little Wing? *What* are you?"

"What am I?" she asked. "Hope."

"That don't make no sense, Little Wing."

"Shh. Listen . . . I haven't long. You asked the right question, so let me answer. Hope, and faith. Grace, and charity, and love. Dreams, and courage, and promises kept." She raised a trembling hand to Cale's chest. "I am you, Cale. And I am Tucker. I am everyone else on this Earth who does the right thing, or tries to, however hard it might be. That is what I am, Cale. That is all I am. And though I have to leave you now, whenever you do the right thing, or try to, you will know me again. You will feel my touch, the warmth of my breath on your neck. You will touch my cheek, and you will see me smile, and you will know that I am there with you. Beside you. Always."

By that last, her voice had gotten so weak Tuck could barely hear it over the beating of his own heart. He heard noises in the distance, coming closer, and for a bad moment he was afraid it was the abominations. Then he realized there were voices, which meant more likely it was the troopers and the women.

When he looked back at Cale and Little Wing, what he saw astonished him, though by this point he had thought he was beyond astonishment. "Cale," he said.

The boy was weeping, eyes shut and head down, holding the still form of Little Wing in his arms. At the sound of his name, he looked up.

"Look at her."

Cale looked, and his jaw dropped open. In his arms, Little Wing's form was dissolving into a floating conflagration of tiny, brilliant lights, like sparks from a campfire at the end of a hard day on the range, or flecks of gold drifting in dark water and catching the glow from a lantern. They drifted up, past Cale, past the tops of the trees, and up and up and up until they were lost in the night sky, mingling with the constellations in the cloudless darkness overhead.

Then she was gone, really gone, the last of the sparks wafted away, and Tuck helped Cale to his feet and put his arms around the young man in an awkward embrace. "You did good," he said. "None of us would have made it without you."

"But . . . Little Wing . . ."

"I know," Tuck said, releasing him. "You heard her, though. She's always here."

"I just don't understand," Cale said.

"Don't need to. Understanding isn't the only thing, Cale. Sometimes it's not even the main thing. Just believe her. That's what she'd want. Just believe."

They stood that way for a few minutes more, and then the soldiers and the ladies filtered down through the trees, accompanied by the clanking, hissing contraption that was the battlewagon. Missy Haynes found Tuck and clasped his hands in both of hers, and kissed his sore, bloodied lips, and in spite of the pain, he kissed her back.

And like that, on foot, battered and weary and clutching Missy's hand with every bit of strength he could manage, Tuck headed back toward the town that had given him purpose and something like a new life. He was surrounded by troopers who laughed and swore and spat, and by women who did much the same, some of it more fluently, and by a heartbroken young man who would nonetheless heal, and by memories that would never leave him so long as he lived. In the west, the Thunder Moon sank behind the mountains, but just before it went their moon shadows stretched out far across the desert, toward the east. Toward the direction that would bring tomorrow, and all the tomorrows after that.

Always.

Tuck laughed, and Missy squeezed his hand and looked at him. But he couldn't explain the impulse, or the unfamiliar sensation rising in him that he identified, after a few long moments, as peace.

He didn't even try.

Instead, he put his right hand in his pocket, fingered the piece of glass there, and wondered how she felt about the color blue.

About the Author

JEFFREY J. MARIOTTE is the award-winning author of more than fifty novels, including thrillers *Empty Rooms* and *The Devil's Bait*, supernatural thrillers *Season of the Wolf, Missing White Girl, River Runs Red,* and *Cold Black Hearts,* horror epic *The Slab,* the Dark Vengeance teen horror quartet, and others. With partner (and wife) Marsheila Rockwell, he wrote the science fiction/horror thriller *7 SYKOS* and has published numerous shorter works. He also writes comic books, including the long-running horror/Western comic book series Desperadoes and original graphic novels *Zombie Cop* and *Fade to Black.* He has worked in virtually every aspect of the book business and is currently the editor in chief of Visionary Comics.

http://jeffmariotte.com,
http://www.facebook.com/JeffreyJMariotte,
and @JeffMariotte on Twitter.